I0773554

# An Ocean of Stars

# AN OCEAN OF STARS

## BECCA MIONIS

SIMPLIFY
media

This book is a work of fiction. Any references to real people, events, establishments, organizations, or locales are used fictitiously. All other names, characters, events, and places are products of the author's imagination, and any resemblance to actual events, places, or persons, living or dead, is entirely coincidental.

Copyright © 2023 by Becca Mionis

All rights reserved. No part of this publication may be reproduced, stored or transmitted in any form or by any means, electronic, mechanical, photocopying, recording, scanning, or otherwise without written permission from the publisher. It is illegal to copy this book, post it to a website, or distribute it by any other means without permission.

First paperback edition January 2023

Cover design by Rena Violet

Interior illustrations by Gabby Fisher

ISBN 979-8-9854688-3-0 (paperback)

ISBN 979-8-9854688-4-7 (ebook)

Published by Simplify Media

www.simplify-media.com

*To everyone who, at any point in my adolescent life, was asked to read or forced to listen to any version of Foxx, in any capacity—it may be barely recognizable from the original, but at least I can say that my 10+ years of beating that dead horse were not (totally) in vain.*

*And I have you all to thank for it, a little or a lot.*

"The sea is everything. It covers seven-tenths of the terrestrial globe. Its breath is pure and healthy. It is an immense desert, where man is never lonely, for he feels life stirring on all sides. The sea is the only embodiment of a supernatural and wonderful existence. It is nothing but love and emotion; it is the 'Living Infinite.'"

-Captain Nemo, *20,000 Leagues Under the Sea* by Jules Verne

# Current

# My Qualifications Include an Abundance of Charm

"Xanorra Nepier, the council will see you now."

I looked up from the *Deep Space Quarterly* magazine I'd been pretending to read, stunned to finally hear my name after two hours in the waiting room of Aster Hall. Stretched to the limits of my sanity by the looped elevator music and dull news recaps, I'd concluded that if there were such a thing as purgatory, it might look a bit like bureaucracy.

I stood and straightened out my dolphin-gray jumpsuit, the uniform of a Space Technical Academy graduate. My dad, who had accompanied me for moral support, patted my back and said, "Go get 'em, X."

I grimaced and gave him a lame thumbs-up as the pixie-like receptionist led me down the hall to the council chambers.

I'd been inside our seat of government before; every

kid on board the colony ship *Aster* got to tour Aster Hall in primary school as did, I assume, every kid aboard the *Selene* and the *Cosmo* as well. Education was pretty standardized across the three colonies, after all.

But there was a stark difference between shuffling single file through the chambers as a bright-eyed ten-year-old and sauntering up to the stand alone as a nerve-wracked eighteen-year-old.

I'd like to go back to the field trip option where we got to eat old-timey astronaut ice cream, please.

Five council members presided over my case, seated behind an elevated podium. Each represented one of five habitable Earth continents: North America, South America, Europe, Africa, and Asia. (Australia, for whatever reason, had opted out.) Colony ships were a melting pot, to say the least.

The chief counselor was a Russian man with impressive sideburns named Viktor Krominov, who sat front and center to speak to me on behalf of the council. "Appeal number oh-two-seven-three, constituent six-four-one-five-seven. Xanorra Jade Nepier, recent graduate of the STA. Congratulations, by the way."

"Thank you, sir," I said. My voice echoed in the circular chamber, heightening my self-awareness.

"You are here to appeal for a work assignment, correct?" Krominov asked.

"Yes, sir."

He checked the brief. "Aboard the newly minted *USE George Washington*, no less!" This he said as if it were the first time he'd read it. Then again, it probably was. They saw a lot of cases in a day. "I cannot imagine why."

His surprise was well-warranted. The *USE George Washington* wasn't just any deep space research vessel; it would be the first ship sent on a long-term mission through the only known wormhole in the galaxy: the Current. Seated right at the edge of our solar system, it had gone undetected by satellites until just a few decades ago. It was the most monumental discovery of our generation.

The *Aster*'s primary scientific objective was to explore it, and ever since the announcement of the *Washington*'s maiden voyage, everyone and their mother had clambered for a seat at the table.

A table, that, mind you, only sat about thirty-five, in a colony of about 2,400. You do the math.

"Yes, sir," I said. "I know you've probably gotten hundreds of applications just like mine, but I'm here today to plead my case."

Krominov gestured to me. "By all means." If I didn't know any better, I'd say he looked amused, as if daring me to persuade them.

Well, that sparked my resolve if nothing else. This was it. All that time spent rehearsing my speech in my head while dying of boredom in the lobby was about to pay off. "As the council is surely aware, my sister is Quinette Nepier, the astrophysics prodigy."

The council nodded in recognition. Of course they'd heard of my younger sister. Most of the *Aster*'s administrators had.

"She's been drafted to serve aboard the *George Washington* as part of their Advanced Space Training Internship Program." (Or ASTIP for short—they sure loved their acronyms here in the Space Exploration Alliance. SEA for short.) "My father has accepted a post as head engine technician. And my mother has applied for and been granted a role as overseer of the ASTIP curriculum. My field of advanced study is General Education, like my mother. Had she stayed here on the *Aster*, I would have interned under her."

That didn't sound as strong out loud as it did in my head. Sure, the SEA preferred to keep families together when they could, especially when the mission in question was projected to last eight years. However, not every crew member aboard the *Washington* would have their entire family with them.

I had to convince them that I could be an asset on my own merits if given the chance. Maybe not indispensable like my sister, but useful.

"Have you received other offers of employment since graduating?" Krominov asked plainly.

"Three total, sir." I rattled off my prospects—one as a third-grade student teacher, another for fifth grade, and another as a ninth-grade teacher's assistant. (Hard pass on that one—there was no way I'd teach kids who were practically my age.)

"And how would serving aboard the *George Washington* be an improvement over these prospects?"

Questions like these were just standard procedure. Or so I told myself—my real fear was that my transcript was so helplessly mediocre compared to everyone else assigned to the mission, including the interns, that granting my appeal was out of the question.

I took a deep breath and answered the question with

a question. "How many general educators can put an eight-year deep space planet-scouting mission through a wormhole on their resume? I believe the best way to learn is through experience, and that a teacher who has experienced life in deep space will add more value to her students' lives. The newly graduated generation of spacers—my generation—will already be teaching plenty of subjects that they have no hands-on experience with. Earth science. History. Pre-Space Age technology. I might as well gain as much knowledge as I can about the things I can experience first-hand."

I could tell by the looks on the council members' faces that I'd made a good case. They liked to hear how eager the next generation was to advance the SEA's glorious mission to find and terraform habitable planets. Even if I wouldn't personally be drilling any holes—leave that sort of ground-breaking to the actual planetary engineers—someone had to teach their kids reading, writing, and arithmetic.

Krominov spoke in low tones to the other council members while I stood as still as possible, trying to ignore the sweat beading on my forehead.

Finally, he faced me again. "Your logic is sound. We will grant your appeal, provided you are willing to take any open assignment, including but not limited to menial labor."

Part of me wondered if I'd heard wrong. "Really? You're serious? Oh my God, of course! I'll scrub toilets if I have to!" I remembered myself and cleared my throat. "I mean, yes, sir, I am more than willing, sir."

Krominov gave me half a smile. He had a daughter

around my age—I knew her from classes—so he was at least a little understanding. "I will inform the commanding officers of the *Washington* of your assignment and see that you get your debriefing packet promptly. Case dismissed." He tapped a button on the stand and a soft gong signaled the end of my hearing.

I thanked them, nearly skipping out of the chamber and into the lobby, where my dad stood with a question in his hazel eyes. I had hoped to prank him by faking disappointment, but I couldn't contain my emotions and he read me instantly.

"They said yes?" he guessed.

"They said yes!" I exclaimed, giving him a hug. I recapped the conversation as we exited Aster Hall into the courtyard, a mock-downtown square where all the administrative offices on the ship were located. The fake sky curving overhead told us that it was still mid-afternoon. Today's weather was a pastel blue sky with wispy, white clouds moving at a leisurely pace. The perfect sky for my perfect mood.

"I'm gonna go tell Mom," I said to Dad. "I'll meet you in engines."

"Be quick. If you're late your boss will dock your pay," he said.

"Ha, ha, so funny," I said, wrinkling my nose.

He was my boss.

The *George Washington*'s launch was slotted for two weeks from the day of my hearing. The days could not pass quickly enough. When I wasn't working, I was going through the briefing packet; there were a lot of pre-mission instructional videos to sift through but I was determined to watch them all.

Despite Krominov's warning that I could be scrubbing toilets, I'd actually ended up assigned to the engine operator room, i.e., working for my dad like I did aboard the *Aster*. Shocker.

My dad's job was to sit in the operator booth and monitor all the computer code generated by the engine's internal mechanics—and try to catch problems when, if not before, they happened. My job was to double-check his work. Sometimes, we went out on the floor to run inspections, but mostly, we stayed in the engineer's watchtower, also called the "bird's nest."

The *Aster* was a huge ship, so it required an extensive team of computer scientists and engineers to keep everything running like clockwork. The operator who usually sat closest to us was named Rodney Alcott, and he was often shadowed by his son, Sebastian.

Seb was my age and super cute—not that the teenage dating pool on a colony ship was anything to write home about, but he truly was a good-looking kid. Half African American, half Polish, he had flawless copper skin and hazel-green eyes. He was gangly, all limbs and hands, but he was so graceful you hardly noticed.

My sister, Quin, worked with us in the bird's nest sometimes too, but not as often since she had more rigorous studies—studies that had only gotten more intense since her recruitment. Her primary focus was a thesis on faster-than-light (aka, FTL) travel—a technology that was still decades away from realization. This mission would serve as a prime opportunity to continue her research and was one of the main reasons she'd been drafted.

After all, the SEA was very interested in the prospect of FTL travel.

On our last full day aboard the *Aster*, Quin spent most of it with us in engines. She was a comfort zone person, so I suspected she wanted to savor one last taste of normalcy before everything changed. I didn't blame her.

"Are you packed yet?" I asked her.

"I packed this morning," she said. "Are you?"

She knew perfectly well that I wasn't. "I pack better under pressure."

"Uh-huh. Sure."

Seb had been pretending not to listen, but anybody with eyes would've noticed him glancing over at us, or more precisely, at Quin. Word around the colony was he had a thing for her, which I suspected as well. I approved of Seb, and I think Quin liked him too, but she was about as interested in dating as I was in astrophysics. Fortunately, I knew for a fact that Seb and his father would be on the *Washington*, too.

Looks like they would have plenty of time to figure out where they stood.

Both in an effort to include him and to call him out, I said, "Hi, Sebastian."

He swiveled toward us in his chair and waved as if we were across the room and not right next to each other. "Hi, Xan. Hi, Quin."

"Excited for the launch tomorrow?" I asked.

"You bet," he said, flashing his butter-melting smile. "It's gonna be mathematical. I can't wait. What about you?"

"I don't think I'll be able to sleep tonight," I said.

"Yeah, because you'll be too busy packing," Quin joked.

"If it helps, I haven't packed yet either," said Seb. "You're more prepared than we are, Q."

Quin chuckled awkwardly and avoided eye contact, her usual routine when interacting with him. "Not really, I just hate doing things last minute."

"You get that from your mother," said Dad, swiveling in his chair to face us. "Speaking of being prepared, have you both been taking your electrolytes like I asked you?"

"Yes, Dad," we said flatly.

"Good," he said. "I cannot stress enough the importance of being properly hydrated before going through the Current. All of the mission reports from the test crews said that the side effects weren't as drastic when they took electrolytes."

"Yes, Dad, you've told us twenty times," I said, but he was right. The Current was not to be taken lightly, even if the test crews had gone through and come back without complications.

"That goes for you too, Alcott," said Dad, eyeing Seb. "Though I'm sure Rodney's been on you about it already."

"Yes, sir, he won't give me a moment's peace," said Seb with a wide smile.

Rodney, overhearing, scowled lightly and cuffed his son on the arm. "I'll show you a moment's peace. Eight years on a ship the size of a tin can, compared to the luxury you're used to. You better start kissing up now."

"God, this is why they say to never work for your parents," Seb said with an exaggerated eye roll.

"Correction, son: this is why they say never to let your kids work for *you*."

# 2

# You Are Now Free to Roam About the Galaxy

Suffice it to say, I didn't sleep very well that night, but then again, I didn't expect to. As Quin in her infinite wisdom predicted, I spent most of the night packing instead.

And reassuring myself, with partial success, that I had been granted access to this mission on the basis of merit—not just because my entire support system was going.

Early in the morning, I ate breakfast with my family, went through the final health screening required of all spacers before they left the *Aster*, and arrived at the vast docking bay terminal, where the *Washington* sat patiently while engineers milled around it with their final pre-launch checklists.

The *Washington* was a pretty standard deep space explorer—sleek, oblong, and reminiscent of a very large submarine. Since it was new, it was as shiny as they come, moon dust gray with "USE GEORGE WASHINGTON" displayed in clean, white lettering along the side, followed by the SEA symbol: a geometric rendition of a colony ship inside a circle with a space shuttle shooting through the center.

We got in line for boarding and before we knew it, we'd passed through the final checkpoint and onto the ship. I'd toured one deep space vessel before, the *Scheherazade*, when it had docked at the *Aster* for repairs several years back. Although the interior of that one had been clean and cutting edge, the *Washington* was on a whole other level of pristine. It had that "new ship smell," which was to say, not yet filled with spacer farts.

Hopefully, the ventilation system was as advanced as everything else seemed to be.

We were then directed to our living quarters on the top level of the ship. As a family, we had a suite, small and compact yet comfortable—about a third the size of our apartment on the *Aster*. Quin and I were bunked together, as per usual, and there was a package for each of us with uniforms, schedules, and mission debriefs.

"Wow, this is, like... the real deal," I said, totally geeking out. Even now, part of me still couldn't believe I'd been granted permission to come. I just hoped I could live up to the honor.

"These pants are something else, though," said Quin, holding up her mobile gravity suit, otherwise known as a Mobi.

They were essentially a pair of overalls with a vacuum system built in, designed to simulate ground-reaction forces and offset those pesky long-term effects of microgravity living. Everyone knew that, but what most people didn't know was that they made everyone's lower body look like elephant legs.

Well, at least we would all be equal in that regard. From the least to the greatest, no one was immune to the unflattering effects of the Mobi suits.

"At least you won't have to worry about anyone staring at your butt," I offered. "Or vice versa."

"Yeah, I don't think these have a butt to speak of," she said, turning them front to back.

A soft bong sounded over the intercom, followed by a calm voice: "Ladies and gentlemen, this is Commander Rodrigo Peralta speaking. Welcome to the maiden voyage of the *USE George Washington*. At this time, please prepare for launch."

We quickly donned our Mobis—officially transforming ourselves into fabulous truck-legged people—and made our way to the observation deck above the bridge along with the rest of the crew, as was the protocol for deep space launches. Historical significance of this particular mission aside, a launch wasn't a particularly dramatic event—just open the airlock and go.

However, seeing the *Aster* from the outside in all its donut-shaped glory and watching it grow smaller was a big deal for those of us who'd never left the colony before, let alone on a mission to a wormhole.

Seb saw us approaching on deck and waved for us to join him. There were half a dozen other teenagers on this mission, and one would think we'd all clump together. Not so. In reality, cliques were practically second-nature. It wasn't hostility that caused the divide, but rather that we liked to feel as if we had a private circle in an environment where everyone knew everything about everybody.

The cliques would most likely shift around, merge, divide, and eventually disperse throughout the course of the mission. For Quin's sake as well as my own, I hoped we didn't lose Seb too soon. There were a couple of particularly gorgeous girls amongst our peers, and if any of them made Seb their target, my baby face and Quin's frizzy hair didn't stand a chance.

Although, I shouldn't sell us too short. I wasn't half bad when I bothered to try and Quin was very pretty in my totally unbiased opinion, with a heart-shaped face, full lips, and dancer's build. People often told us we looked alike but I honestly didn't see it; she had tawny brown hair and green eyes, I had auburn red hair and brown eyes. She was lean, I was lush. She had sparse freckles, I had a galaxy of them.

I guess we were similar in the face if you squinted.

A hushed silence fell over the congregation when another bong sounded over the intercom. Of course, since we all stood on the balcony above the bridge, we could see Commander Peralta speaking into the mic. "Ladies and gentlemen, at this time, please activate your Mobi suits. Bridge crew, prepare for launch."

A moment later, the airlock doors opened and we moved from the familiar, white-and-metallic walls of the docking bay to the infinite, inky blackness of space. The crew cheered, but the spectacle wasn't over yet: those of us who didn't have essential ship operative duties were required to stay where we were until we'd passed through the Current.

"What do you think it's actually gonna feel like?" Seb asked. "I always pictured that stomach-flipping feeling you get on a flight simulator."

"I heard it feels like g-force in reverse," said Quin solemnly. "Pulling instead of pushing."

"Well, as long as the pulling doesn't mean I'm pulled apart into atoms, I'm good," I said.

"Why are we speculating?" Quin said, her voice edging on anxiety. "It's going to feel like what it feels like."

"It's all right, Q-Dog," said Seb, placing his hands on Quin's shoulders as if to massage them. I watched, wide-eyed, as she visibly stiffened. "Everything will be interstellar."

I thought my sister would implode before Seb finally removed his hands from her shoulders and nondescriptly shoved them into his pockets. We spent the next hour and a half making small talk with him, my mom, (the dads were on engine duty,) and the surrounding crewmembers. We even paid our respects to the other interns at Seb's behest. Social butterfly. He's worse than me.

From the wall of viewing windows, we could see the Current as we approached it. By all counts, it looked like a black hole. But it wasn't—and thank goodness for that, because if you went traipsing into a thing with so much gravity even light can't escape, you wouldn't be coming back. The Current was its own space anomaly, though part of why it had avoided detection for so long was because scientists had assumed it was a black hole. After they sent a probe out, however, they started to pick up on strange, non-singularity-type behavior. Then someone had the idea to send a probe through it, and the rest was history.

Another bong from the intercom. "Ladies and gentlemen, we will be entering the Current in t-minus twenty-five minutes. At this time, please activate the gravity lock on your Mobi suits and prepare for entry."

The next twenty-five minutes ticked by with all the urgency of a planet forming, but we felt it before we truly saw it—a pull, just like Quin had surmised, and a sort of lightness, like floating in zero-g, even though we were all anchored to the floor.

And then it was as if we were standing still while the entire universe moved around us—which was, in a sense, what was happening. My stomach did, in fact, do that flippy thing Seb had talked about and my head spun like a top, but since I'm an adrenaline junkie, I didn't mind.

Others, however, weren't so inclined.

We'd been prepared for the side effects and told that everyone reacts to the Current a little differently. Some just get an adrenaline rush, others get nauseous, some throw up, and some even faint. To my surprise, Seb fell into the upchuck category. I rubbed his back while Quin held onto me for dear life. My mom had her arms around us both. Other families did the same.

Sounds terrifying, doesn't it? But it was still infinitely better than getting crushed into a two-dimensional object or ripped apart into atoms. Nausea and lightheadedness were a small price to pay for shattering the paradigm.

The electrolytes really did help, though. Who would've thought?

In less than five minutes, it was over. A significant lurch pitched us all forward, signaling that the *Washington* had emerged on the other side of the wormhole... and the galaxy. A distant star that was not our sun stood out in the speckled expanse, and while there were no planets in our current line of sight, that's exactly what we were here to find.

"We did it," said Seb triumphantly.

Another bong. "Ladies and gentlemen, welcome to the edge of the Zion system, approximately two hundred and ten lightyears from our solar system. You may now report to your posts and begin your start-of-mission checklists. If you've experienced any unpleasant side effects from the Current and they do not wear off within the hour, please report to the infirmary."

"Ohp, that's my cue to go to work," said Seb, chipper despite the fact that he'd been dry-heaving moments ago. "I'll see y'all in class. Tomorrow morning?"

"Be there or be triangular," I said.

Once he'd left, Quin hit me upside the arm. "'Be there or be triangular?' Really?"

I leaned in with a mischievous grin and said, "He put his hands on your shoulders! Actual physical contact. Are you okay after that? Are you running a fever?"

"Very funny," Quin sneered. "How about we just forget it ever happened?"

"Whatever you say, Q-Dog," I said, clapping her on the shoulders dramatically.

She responded by hitting me in the arm again, this time hard enough to sting.

This was going to be a very long, very entertaining eight years.

# 3

# It's Totally a Space Squid.

The first two weeks on board the *Washington* passed in no time at all. We had class in the morning for six days a week on an alternating schedule; the odd-numbered days were devoted to what I can only describe as "standard cosmonaut stuff" while the even-numbered days functioned as a glorified study hall where we could pursue our own SEA-sanctioned interests.

Quin spent that time devoting herself to her FTL thesis. Seb studied medicine, his chosen career path. The rest of the interns followed suit. Meanwhile, I studied pedagogy like a true, boring nerd.

And yes, I got made fun of for it. It was mostly in good humor, though when the other teens asked me why I'd been assigned to the mission, my explanation came out sheepish and utterly unconvincing. Why was I here? Because I'd said, "pretty please."

These were the only times when I truly felt like a fish

out of water. After all, everyone got to apprentice in their field of study except for me. And while I did, surprisingly, enjoy working in the bird's nest, it wasn't exactly what I wanted to do with the rest of my life. If anything, it was a backup in case teaching didn't pan out. (I.e., the SEA ever pulled the trigger and replaced all educators with robots. And yes, that was a real concern.)

After lunch each day, we reported to our assigned stations, where we spent the remainder of the afternoon until dinner. Rinse and repeat for six days with one day of rest. The routine came naturally to me and I was satisfied by how quickly time moved—not because I wanted it to end, but rather because I wanted the experience that came with years on board. Call me ambitious, I guess.

But my ambition was peanuts compared to Quin's. Since day one, she'd spent every spare moment she had in the lab or in the classroom, running equations, tracking space objects, and going full-on mad scientist. I'd seen her like this before—plenty of times—so I could generally tell when her laser focus started to transition into unhealthy levels of obsession.

To her credit, two weeks is a pretty long time for her to go before showing signs. When she didn't show up for dinner in the mess hall three nights in a row, that was our cue to intervene. Dad sent me to track her down with a tray of food, so I went to the classroom first and, when she wasn't there, moved on to the lab. Sure enough, there she was, looking into a telescope and scribbling furiously into her tablet.

"Q," I said. "Earth to Quin."

"That's an ironic turn of phrase even for you," she mumbled without looking up.

"Har, har." I came around to her left side and waved the tray in front of her. "You need to eat. You're hyper-fixating."

"I ate breakfast," she said.

"And it's dinner now."

Now she looked up from the lens. "What time is it?"

"Eighteen hundred."

She rubbed her eyes. "Ah, farts."

"What are you working on that's got you so tied up?" I asked, shoving the tray into her hands.

"Well, I *was* working on my latest FTL equation, but then something else distracted me, and I've been stuck on it ever since."

"What would that be?"

After a brief pause, she answered, "There's a space object moving out there, but it's not emitting any of the normal wavelengths. I thought it might be an asteroid, but it doesn't make sense if it is. And it's coming toward us, at an angle. I know it sounds crazy, but I think it might be a spaceship."

"What?"

"Look." She moved aside so I could use the telescope. Sure enough, there was something, but it was teeny-tiny, and it didn't look like any space object I'd ever seen. Except, perhaps, a spaceship.

"Um, that's weird," I said. "Are there supposed to be any other ships out here?"

"No," said Quin. "We're the only ones in this sector

of space, according to the SEA. Don't worry, I already checked it against all the radars and ship logs."

"So then... it's..."

"An unidentified space object, yes. But I want to be completely sure before I bring it up to the commander."

"You mean no one else has seen this yet?"

She shook her head. "No one else is looking for it. Even I stumbled across it by accident." Now she looked up at me. "What do I do? Is it even worth investigating?"

"Are you kidding me, Quin? Of course it is. This could be... well, I don't even want to say what it could be, but it's big. We need to speak with Commander Peralta right now."

In most cases, that would be easier said than done, but thankfully, he was still at dinner, so after informing our parents that Quin had found something of ship-wide significance, Dad escorted us to the commander's table at the front of the mess hall.

Stalwart and military without any of the callousness, Commander Peralta had a reputation for being approachable, which was very good news for us. He smiled as we came near and said, "Nepiers. What can I do for you?"

"Quinette here has something she needs to tell you," said Dad. "She says it's of ship-wide significance."

Peralta raised a dark eyebrow. "Should we speak somewhere private?"

"No, sir," said Quin. "That won't be necessary. I just, um..." She leaned forward and spoke in a low tone. "I was in the lab, using the telescope, and I happened to see... something abnormal. A space object traveling at high speeds. I ran a spectrograph and it doesn't match any of the expected frequencies of a star, a comet, an asteroid, anything. It actually... looks like it might be a ship, sir. Whose, I don't know, but you should probably see it for yourself."

A lesser commander might have laughed it off and declared that she'd made an amateur mistake, but Peralta treated everyone on board equally—after all, just because we were students didn't make us any less part of the crew, officially instated or not. So, of course he took her seriously and asked her to lead him to the lab immediately.

While she did that, Dad and I returned to our seats and I filled him and Mom in on what Quin had found. The other dozen or so crewmembers in the room were understandably curious, having witnessed how quickly our commander had left the room with Quin after just a short conversation. Lieutenant Commander Mei Xiao stood up and told everyone to go about their evenings, which was commanding officer speak for "stop being gossipy little bitches, you'll know when you need to know."

Not that it stopped us from talking about it for the rest of the night. We just did so elsewhere.

When Quin returned to our room about an hour after she'd left with Peralta, all she had to say was that he'd probably hold a ship-wide meeting in the morning. Apparently, he needed to discuss this with his officers before he made a formal announcement.

Well, there was nothing left to do but wait, then. And sleep. But neither Quin nor I seemed inclined toward the latter. I kept pestering her about where she thought the ship had come from, knowing full well how much she detested baseless speculation.

"Humor me for a second," I said, leaning over the edge of the top bunk. "What if it's, you know…"

"Please don't say aliens," she said.

"I was going to say space pirates," I said. "But aliens are probably more likely."

"Exactly. Besides, *if* space pirates existed, why would they be all the way out here? There's nothing to pillage."

"Maybe they raid space rocks for valuable minerals," I suggested.

"And maybe we're completely wrong about it being a spaceship, and it's just a weird rock or a… satellite probe, or something."

"But whose satellite probe?" I asked. "Not the SEA's, you don't think?"

"People have been launching things into space for a long time. It could be old."

"And it made its way all the way out here without the Current? Unlikely. They would've had to know about the wormhole before we did."

"Who's to say someone *didn't* discover it before we did?" she posited. "Why don't you sleep on it, X?"

"Like either of us are getting any sleep tonight. You could've just made the next discovery of the century."

"Or I could've just wasted our commander's precious time and my credibility is about to plummet into the abyss."

"See, this is what I love about you, Q. You're just a glass-half-full kind of girl."

Well, there was definitely something out there. And it definitely wasn't a rock.

Commander Peralta did, in fact, call a ship-wide meeting the following morning. Every crewmember reported to the observation deck to hear the verdict, which is something you generally didn't want to do unless it was important.

From his station on the bridge, Peralta said, "As some of you may already know, an unidentified space object was discovered by one of our scientists at fourteen-oh-five yesterday. It appears to be on a perpendicular course, moving quickly toward us. Any threat of collision could easily be averted with a few navigational adjustments. However," he paused, "this particular object is unlike anything we've ever seen. It is not a meteor, nor a satellite, nor a piece of space debris. By all counts, it appears to be a spaceship. But there are no records of the SEA sending a ship in front of us, nor do our observations ascertain it to be of a make or model that the SEA has used, past or present."

He motioned behind him to the viewscreen. Usually, on the bridge, these were simply windows that allowed the crew to see where they were going, but they could also be used to project data and images (or watch funny videos, which I'm sure happened from time to time). We all watched as an enhanced satellite image of the ship appeared on the glass; it was still too far away to make out the details, but you could at least see its shape.

And boy, was it weird.

It didn't look like any spaceship I'd ever seen. It had a sleek, egg-shaped body with dorsal-like fins on the top and bottom, which wouldn't be so abnormal if not for the long tail of softly glowing, tentacle-like appendages trailing behind it. If anything, it looked like a sea creature.

A space squid, perhaps?

"What in God's universe is that?" a crewmember near me said as the rest of us murmured similar sentiments.

"Has anybody seen anything like this before?" the commander asked us.

No one had anything to say. We were all equally flummoxed by the squid.

"As you know, the SEA keeps a public record of every ship that has ever been registered and approved for space flight, even private shuttles," Peralta continued. "This ship does not match anything in the database from the last fifty years. It is unmarked, unregistered, and unknown. By process of elimination, that leaves two explanations for what this object is, however unlikely they may seem: a fabled rogue ship... or something not human-made."

Another ripple of murmurs moved through the crew, some nervous, others excited. In layman's terms, it was either pirates or aliens.

I gave Quin an "I told you so" nudge and she rolled her eyes.

"As explorers and scientists of the SEA, it is well within our mission protocol to investigate this unknown space object and determine its source of origin. However, in the interest of full transparency, I will warn you that there are considerable risks should we pursue it. The ship may be hostile, though the chances of an unknown vessel of any origin attacking another in deep space are marginal at best.

"With that said, I now leave the decision to investigate up to a majority vote. In the event of a tie, I will act as a tie-breaker. All in favor of continuing on course toward the unknown vessel, raise your right hand."

Mine shot up without a second thought. So did over half of everyone else's. We were a curious bunch, I suppose. Surprisingly, however, Quin kept her hand down. I looked at her in shock.

"Don't peer-pressure me," she said as the commander asked for the "nays." Then she raised her hand. As expected, she was in the minority.

"At least you made your vote count," I joked. She rolled her eyes again.

"It's settled, then," said the commander. "We will investigate the unknown vessel. This is now an official ship-wide assignment. Everyone, please report to your stations. According to navigation, we will come within close communication range of the ship in approximately six hours. I will broadcast the exchange over the ship's intercom system."

Quin and I hustled toward our posts, meeting up with Dad in the hallway.

"Well, this is something," he said, sounding more apprehensive than anything. I wondered if he'd voted against it; I couldn't see him or Mom from where we'd been standing. "You girls know what to do in the worst-case scenario, right?"

"Get to the nearest escape pod," we recited.

But come on, like it was really going to come to that. What kind of a moron would shoot at an SEA deep space vessel just because we'd dropped by to say hello?

Even aliens and/or space pirates had to have some degree of tact.

# 4

# Captain's Log, Year 17, Day 230, 0214 Atlantean Time

An unprecedented event compels me to record an impromptu log entry so that I may properly chronicle the procedure to follow.

As a reminder for posterity, the mission thus far has been next to seamless. Aside from a few minor mishaps, many of them external in nature, everything up to this point—including the recent pass through the wormhole—has gone according to plan. Textbook, one might say.

But naturally, there is always the chance that an unaccounted-for variable might come into play. Such is the case with recent events.

Nevertheless, I, Captain Omen of the independent deep space ferry *Atlantis*, am fully prepared for any and all possible scenarios, including the one I now face: another ship, no doubt an exploration vessel commissioned by the Space Exploration Alliance, has appeared on my radar.

Based on the fact that they appear to be approaching the *Atlantis* at a constant rate, I can safely conjecture that they have spotted me as well, which leaves only one due course of action: I must eliminate them. If I do not, the mission could be in grave jeopardy. I cannot stop, I cannot alter course, and I certainly cannot make contact.

If they try to hail me, which is likely, I will decline, for I know the risks of such an interaction: if I speak with them, they may try to coerce me into compliance, and while I am astute enough not to be swayed by mere curiosity, I am also prudent enough not to submit myself to the temptation.

[Pause]

For the purposes of transparency, I will confess that, having had zero interaction with another living, conscious soul for the entirety of my seventeen years, mere curiosity is, indeed, a cause for concern.

But I must not give it any more thought than is necessary to act. I have been trained and prepared for this day just as I have been trained and prepared for every other aspect of this mission. No human life is more sacred to me than the ones I currently carry onboard. And no manner of fleeting curiosity will override my sense of duty.

There is only one due course of action. Following this log, I will charge the solar guns and await interception. I will be swift and efficient, which will be an act of mercy. It is not my intention for anyone to suffer.

Nor is it my intention for anyone to survive.

# 5

# I Really Should've Paid More Attention in Ship Ops 101

The six hours until contact crawled by, serving as a painful reminder of just how relative time could be. Dad and I attempted to remedy the problem by working, as did everyone else. And just like everyone else, we got antsy.

When Dad suggested we run a quick inspection, I happily obliged. But then we got stuck talking to one of the engineers, speculating about the mysterious ship. When the fateful hour finally arrived, we were still on the floor and froze in place as the intercom sounded its gentle tone.

The commander said, "Crewmen and women of the *George Washington*, we are about to establish first contact with the unidentified space object. Please stand by."

Dad, the engineer, and I exchanged looks of wary

excitement. "Here goes nothing," the engineer said, his impressive mustache rising in a smile.

"This is Commander Rodrigo Peralta of the SEA deep space vessel, *USE George Washington*. If you understand this transmission, please acknowledge and state your name and place of origin. This is a courtesy call." He repeated himself, as per standard protocol, and ended with, "You are not in any kind of danger. We are simply requesting more information about the unregistered vessel this far out in open space."

The entire ship held its collective breath as we waited for a response. None came. No crackle of static, no strange, alien language. Just radio silence.

Commander Peralta began to repeat his message in full for a second time, but halfway through, he stopped abruptly and shouted in a panicked voice, "All hands to stations! Defensive! Defensive!"

Then, something made impact with the ship so forcefully that we actually shifted at an angle. We would've toppled over if not for the railing we grabbed onto.

"Holy *shit*," I said. "They're attacking!"

My dad whipped around, his hazel eyes stained with a level of panic I'd never seen in him before. "Xanorra, back to the bird's nest, now!"

I turned and ran just as another blast knocked us to our knees. An alarm blared somewhere near the turbines. What the hell kind of ship was this?

As we scrambled to our feet, Dad pulling me up with him, another hit shook the entire ship like an earthquake. We covered our heads as we dropped to the ground. When the tremors finally settled, we got up again and sprinted, but before we could make it to the shaft that led up to the bird's nest, the catwalk above came loose from its welding and half-floated, half-crashed toward us, propelled by the ship's momentum.

We dove to either side—myself to the left, Dad to the right. The catwalk lodged itself between us, blocking me from the shaft while leaving him with full access. Dad tried to move the catwalk, but it wouldn't budge.

"Xan, can you climb over that?" he asked.

"Maybe. Let me try."

As I looked for a way over or under, the intercom began to blare in an automated voice: "Emergency evacuation protocol activated. All crewmembers, please follow the illuminated path to the nearest escape shuttle or escape pod."

Emergency evacuation? This could not be happening! This wasn't supposed to happen! We weren't even a month into our eight-year mission! And now we had to leave all because this space squid didn't want to talk things out like a grown-up?

Screw that!

I tried to climb over the catwalk back to Dad, but the railing was too narrow and the space above it too cramped. Then, there was another hit to the engines, and a devastatingly loud, siren-like alarm drowned out everything else. The one sound that no spacer wanted to hear.

A hull breach.

"Xanorra, get to an escape pod," Dad said urgently. "Quickly! Go! Remember your training!"

I turned and sprinted away from the catwalk, following the blue, pulsing arrows toward the nearest pod; in the engine room, individual escape capsules sat like barnacles along the hull, ready to transport one or at most two people in the case of an emergency.

I guess they figured that it was more efficient for the engineers, who wouldn't have time to evacuate to the upper levels and get to the roomier escape shuttles. The pods were then designed to seek out and attach themselves to the shuttles en route, enlarging the amount of livable space on board while simultaneously keeping more people alive.

I dropped down a small notch between the wall and the floor into the nearest empty pod and waited a moment to see if anyone else was coming, my heartbeat pounding as adrenaline coursed through my veins like molten lava. When it looked like everyone had already found a pod or doubled up with another engineer, I sealed the door and swiveled the chair around to face the viewscreen, trying to keep my breathing as even as possible.

From there, I flipped the switch that turned the pod on and then activated autopilot mode. It could be piloted manually, but I shouldn't need to unless there was a problem. Plus, I definitely did not remember that unit from Ship Ops 101. They make you take it your freshman year as if that's the year you'll need it, and the professor was so painfully boring I couldn't have absorbed the material if I'd tried.

As I sped away from the *Washington*, something exploded behind me—something big, possibly the engines—and the resulting thrust propelled me way faster than the pod was designed to go. The autopilot went on the fritz as it tried to course-correct, but it couldn't take the extra speed.

Well, shit. Perhaps I should've paid more attention in Ship Ops 101.

I switched the pod to manual and attempted to slow it down the only way I knew how: by pulling back on the yoke as hard as I possibly could.

I realized too late that may have been a bad idea, because the explosion had definitely jettisoned high-velocity space debris away from the ship, and a piece of it definitely hit me in the back of my pod, causing it to lurch forward. I went flying and whacked my head against the glass window.

And then I definitely blacked out.

# 6

# Fifty Ways to Die in Space...
# Actually, More Like One

When I came to, my head hurt like a bitch and the data readings on the dashboard hurt even worse. The viewscreen was cracked and the escape pod had suffered major damage to its thrusters thanks to whatever the hell had just hit me.

How long had I been out?

I couldn't remember what time it had been when I'd gotten into the pod, much less what time it had been when I'd passed out. I was moving forward, likely still propelled by the force of the explosion. But as I turned the small vessel in a 360 to observe my surroundings, all I could really see was wreckage. The once-glorious *George Washington* was now a disemboweled mass of metal, glass, and machinery floating in the void. To my immense relief, I didn't see any people-shaped objects among the ruins.

I didn't exactly see any escape shuttle-shaped objects either.

*Oh my God. Did they leave me behind?*

*How long was I out?*

I tried to switch the pod back to autopilot and locate the nearest shuttle, but the system was shot and the console kept telling me there weren't any vessels in range. I tried to open a broadcast channel so I could transmit an SOS message, but it said I only had a broadcast radius of thirteen miles.

Which was basically the outer space equivalent of shouting across a room.

My breathing grew rapid. Was I all alone out here? Oh my God, I was all alone out here, wasn't I? In a broken transport pod meant to support two humans for no more than a day in the best of circumstances.

And was I wheezing because I was having a panic attack or was I wheezing because I lacked oxygen? Or both? The thought just made me hyperventilate more, which definitely was not going to help me figure out what to do next.

I forced myself to take deep, even breaths. *Get your head on straight, Xan. Think. Are you really alone?*

Technically, no.

The vessel responsible for this heinous act of douchebaggery sat menacingly in my field of vision, retreating gradually into the distance like an eldritch abomination off in search of its next unfortunate victim.

I seemed to be moving along with it, either propelled by my own momentum or caught in the wake of its magnetic field. Well, that was both incredibly annoying and incredibly convenient, because it meant I was close enough to attempt to make contact.

What choice did I have? If they wouldn't help me, I was going to die. That much was as obvious as it was terrifying.

I opened my broadcast signal as wide as it would go and said, "This is Ensign Xanorra Nepier of what was *formerly* the *USE George Washington*. Come in, unidentified vessel. Over."

I repeated that three more times and was about to give up when the console said, "Unknown receiver detected."

"Then why aren't they saying anything?" I lamented, holding down the transmitting button again. "My escape pod is damaged and I have no recourse. I surrender. I repeat, my escape pod is damaged and I surrender. I'm kind of stuck tailing you anyway, so..."

The readout flashed red, alerting me that the oxygen levels were low. Dammit. There was probably a leak in the oxygen tank, not to mention a freaking *crack* in the viewscreen. Even a pinprick-sized hole would be enough to drain the air. I was going to die way faster than I'd anticipated. Great.

"Update: I have a leak in my oxygen tank. Oxygen levels are depleting. If there's anyone there... if you're going to accept my surrender, I'd do it soon. We can negotiate terms once I'm on board. Please..." I paused. Was I really going to beg for my life? But I couldn't just end it on "please," so I added: "If you can hear me, if you're human... if you have even an *ounce* of humanity in you, please have mercy."

I'd like to think that's what got to them. I saw the ship

pivot just slightly and a small compartment near the airlock open. The towline.

"Oh my God," I said aloud. "They're actually coming for me."

I braced myself for the towline and was surprised when I didn't feel an uncomfortable lurch, just a steady pull. Huh. A towline system that smooth could only be state-of-the-art, which was counterintuitive to the ship's novel appearance.

A sea creature was an interesting choice, that was for certain. Points for creativity I suppose. But *why*, though? What did it *mean*?

While I pondered the logistics (and the irony) of marine aquatic ship architecture, I also focused on taking shallow breaths to conserve oxygen. My head screamed and my heart rate was through the roof, which might've been incidental if I didn't notice the tips of my fingers turning blue. Hypoxemia. That was the last cognizant thought I had before my brain started to cloud over.

I vaguely registered that I'd stopped and that a door had opened—the ship's airlock, probably? The inky blackness of space and my own fading vision became washed out by a blinding, white light.

*Am I supposed to go toward it?*

Despite my hazy misgivings, my subconscious kicked into gear and piloted the damaged escape pod toward it anyway. The door behind me closed, sealing off the dark from the light, but there was still a complete and utter lack of air in the small space. I couldn't think. I could barely feel. Points of light crowded my vision.

And then, a breathy, pneumatic sound sealed the exit

and started pumping fresh oxygen into the airlock. With my final brain cell, I hit the button that opened the top hatch of the pod and let the air pour in. I gasped on the first breath and then gulped it in with reckless gusto as if someone had jumpstarted me. My senses returned. The cloud slowly lifted.

The door to the docking bay began to open. I quickly unbuckled my harness and prepared to disembark so I could face my attacker-turned-rescuer with dignity.

Unfortunately, I was not prepared for the zero gravity and nearly floated away before I grabbed the railing of the external ladder and eased myself down, mumbling expletives. Looks like the space pants were shot, too. Of course they were. So long, elephant legs.

I looked up to see a lone figure approaching me, shadowed at first by the strange, low light of the docking bay but soon illuminated by the brighter lights of the airlock chamber. I gripped onto the ladder like a bashful child, forsaking any semblance of grace or poise for the shock of coming face-to-face not with a hardened marauder or a many-limbed alien, but with a boy my age.

And perhaps I was still oxygen-deprived, but my first thought was that he was an *attractive* boy my age.

He was lean with strong shoulders and held himself tall—in fact, it was instantly noticeable how perfect his posture was. His dark, wavy hair hung just below his thick eyebrows and even darker eyes. From the look of his facial features and olive skin, I supposed he was of Middle Eastern or Mediterranean descent.

And he wasn't floating. Somehow—and my brain was

still a bit too French-fried at the moment to consider why—he could walk in normal gravity while I was stuck bobbing around like a helium balloon.

"Hi, there," I said lamely.

He stopped a few feet in front of me, his eyes so intense I couldn't look away, and raised his arm to my eye level. My hazy awareness instantly sharpened when I realized what was in his hand: a gun.

Suddenly, he wasn't so attractive.

"You're not actually going to shoot me, are you?" I said, my fear manifesting as righteous anger.

He seemed shocked that I would question his homicidal intentions as he lowered the gun.

My heartbeat pounding in my aching head, I said, "If you were just gonna kill me anyway, why bother saving me at all? Why not just let me suffocate? It's inconsiderate, is what it is. It's downright uncivilized."

"Uncivilized?" he said, apparently offended. It sounded like he had a British accent. Must've hit a nerve.

"Gone-dammit, I can't even believe this," I went on. "If you're not gonna kill me, just take me to the commander of this god-forsaken sea cucumber, please. I'd like to speak to someone who *isn't* going to point a gun at me."

He didn't respond. Instead, with a look of incredulity, he holstered the weapon and produced a syringe from the breast pocket of his dark blue jumpsuit.

I instantly regretted my adrenaline-fueled rant as he approached me. "What are you doing? What is that? Get away from me."

"It is a sedative," he said flatly, and then he stuck it in

my arm so fast I hardly had time to process it before my consciousness began to slip away.

"What an asshole thing to do," I slurred, and then everything went black.

# 7

# Quin's Journal #1

I'm not really big on journaling (that was more Xan's thing), but I feel like if I don't write down what happened, I won't be able to process it in a healthy way. I've never been super good with emotions and my default is to repress the things I don't want to feel, but this is too much for even me to handle. And I have to be able to handle it or I'm probably going to lose my freaking mind.

Okay. Let's start with the facts. I'm good at that.

On February 25th, 2159 Universal Time, the *USE George Washington* was attacked and obliterated by an unidentified space object—some kind of pirate ship, we think, though no one really knows for sure. Everyone was able to evacuate to escape shuttles or pods in time, and even though Xan was separated from Dad in the engine room, he knows she made it to an escape pod unharmed.

Meanwhile, Dad, Mom, and I made it to one of the two shuttles on the main deck, along with half the crew. Everyone was accounted for except the five engineers (Xan included) who had to use the individual escape pods. We expected them to converge with the shuttles within an hour or two because the pods weren't designed for long-term use.

I was worried, but no more than I should've been, because Xan was okay, and she'd either meet up with us or with the other shuttle. We just had to be patient.

Seb had somehow ended up next to me in the seats that lined the sides of the passenger bay, and naturally, he wanted to know why Xan wasn't with us. So I told him what Dad had told me. In the process, I may have expressed my concerns.

"Damn, that sucks," Seb said. "But I'm sure she'll be fine. She's tough. And she knows what to do."

"Yeah. You're right."

Then, to my surprise, he added, "Are *you* okay?"

I gave a half-hearted nod.

"I can't believe this," he continued. "This isn't a thing that happens. Attacked in open space? What kind of a psychopath does something like that? What was there to gain, anyway? If they were after resources, they just destroyed them all. It's gotta be blind malice. Right?"

I closed my eyes and nodded. I wanted to respond—I always wanted to respond to him—but my mind tended to go completely blank when I was around him. And this situation was not helping at all.

"Hey, it's gonna be okay," Seb said and put a hand on my arm. I was overstimulated as it was, but his touch did me in. I shuddered involuntarily and jerked away from him in embarrassment. It wasn't repulsion, but it certainly could've been interpreted that way. He dropped his hand and said, "I'm sorry."

I shook my head, unable to communicate. Now wasn't the time or place to worry if I'd hurt his feelings, but I already felt guilty about it. What if he never talked to me again?

While I was preoccupied with all these incredibly trivial thoughts, the escape shuttle continued to zip away from the wreckage. Once we were at a safe distance, Commander Peralta's voice sounded over the intercom.

"Reporting in from the *Virginia*." That was the other shuttle. Ours was the *Pennsylvania*. You think maybe Americans had built them? "We're now free from any imminent danger, and our radars show that the unidentified vessel is moving away from us. I've already sent a distress signal to the SEA. It will take a few hours to receive their reply through the Current. In the meantime, our objective is to rendezvous with all five of the escape pods that left the engine room. So far, I've heard from four of them, but there could still be interference from the explosion."

My heart went through the roof. Four out of the five?

The commander kept talking, trying to put everyone's nerves at ease, but the ringing in my ears blocked him out. Something he said made everyone laugh, but I was lightyears away from being in on the joke.

Within the next couple of hours, we were updated every time an escape pod reached a shuttle. Two found the *Virginia* while two found us. The fifth one was still unaccounted for, and now my parents and I were really starting to worry. Neither of the pods that had met up with the *Pennsylvania* contained Xan.

"That means she's on the *Virginia*," said Mom optimistically. "We'll ask Xiao to reach out when she comes around."

We asked. The lieutenant commander went to the cockpit to talk to the other shuttle. She returned a moment later with a grave expression on her face. "Casper, Lindsay, Quin, I think we should speak in private," she said.

That was the last thing you wanted to hear at a time like this.

"Just say it," said Dad, his voice unrecognizably somber.

Quietly, Xiao said, "She's unaccounted for."

Mom burst into tears. Dad was stoic. I was numb.

"That doesn't mean she isn't still out there," Xiao added. "We will leave no stone unturned. I will talk to the commander immediately and ask to do a sweep of the wreckage. It would be easy for the radar to detect a damaged pod or a biometric signal at a closer distance. Her communications or navigation could've been knocked out by the explosion. For all we know, she's simply flying blind on manual."

Dad nodded, taking Mom's and my hands in his. "That would be... We would appreciate that. Thank you, Lieutenant Commander."

Everyone in the shuttle looked at us with concern and sympathy. They all felt our pain, even if their families were safe beside them or on the *Virginia*. It was a risk we all shared in space and no one took it lightly. Nobody said anything to us but that was their way of helping: silence and prayer. What else could they do?

I glanced at Seb once and saw that he looked helpless. Xan was his friend, too. Sometimes I thought they would make a great couple, even if she insisted he had a crush on me. What did he see in me, anyway? I didn't even know how to talk to him. Xan was the social one. Xan was the reason I had any friends at all.

What would I do without her?

The next few hours were painfully slow as the *Pennsylvania* doubled back on the wreckage and scanned everything within sight. We were invited to come into the cockpit and watch through the viewscreen in real-time, which of course we did.

The mysterious squid ship was long gone, and there was no sign of anyone, living or otherwise. With each second that ticked by, I grew more and more nervous and I could sense that my parents did, too.

*She has to be here. She has to be.*

"There! What's that?" Mom exclaimed, pointing to a white, spherical capsule floating apart from the rest of the debris.

My heart nearly shot out of my mouth. "That's an escape pod," I said. "That has to be her."

"Archer, zero in on that pod," said Xiao to the navigator. "Scan for biometrics. See if there's a transmission signal open—"

The view of the pod became magnified onscreen, spinning slowly in space. I held my breath as the front of it rotated toward us, trying to prepare myself for anything...

"What?" Dad exclaimed.

"No," said Mom.

It was empty. Completely empty.

"Is this some kind of sick joke?" said Dad. "Where is she? She has to be there!"

"Our scans aren't coming up with anything organic within the blast radius," Xiao said slowly. "I'm sorry, but she's simply... gone."

Mom burst into tears and buried her face into Dad's shoulder. Dad and I were silent, equally incapable of accepting what our eyes saw.

She was gone. Not even a body to bring home. Those guns, those solar canons... a direct hit would be enough to obliterate a human being. Melt them from the inside out. But it wasn't fair. It couldn't be true.

"I wish we could do more," Xiao continued, "but we can't afford to linger much longer. We have to rendezvous with the others. I'm so, so sorry."

Dad nodded, one arm wrapped around Mom and the other across my shoulders. "I understand. Thank you so much for all that you've done."

He escorted us out of the cockpit and back into our seats, ignoring the horrified looks of the other crew members as they put two and two together. My eyes trailed across the floor to where Seb was, in the seat next to mine, but when I looked up, I saw that he had stood. So had his father, Rodney.

Seb made a fist and pressed it to the center of his chest. His father followed suit. One by one, the other crewmembers on the shuttle stood and saluted us in the same way—it was an old spacer gesture of solidarity, so I'd heard, but I'd never seen anyone do it before.

They stayed that way until we returned to our seats.

"Thank you," Dad said hoarsely, still holding onto Mom. "Thank you all."

I dared to look over at Seb and saw that his eyes were glossed over with tears. He gave me a weak smile but said nothing, and I couldn't help but think that he was too beautiful for something as ugly as crying.

I wished I knew what to say to comfort him. I wished I knew what to do to help. I wanted to fix it, but I didn't know how.

The only sorts of problems I knew how to solve were on paper, and there was no equation for something like this.

# 8

# This is Fine. I'm Fine.

When I woke, I found myself strapped to a hospital bed in an unfamiliar room. A soft, lulling beep came from somewhere behind me and pale, blue lights glowed up above. I tried to speak but my tongue felt heavy and numbed. I tried to lift my head but that felt heavy, too.

Then a figure came into view: a woman, very pretty, with flawless bronze skin and closely-shorn hair. It took me a full minute of waking up to realize she was an android—she was too perfect, her movements too fluid. Even then, I wasn't completely certain of it until my vision sharpened and I saw the familiar designation of a medidroid on her dark blue coveralls, a triangle with a caduceus inside it. Next to that was a spiral symbol that looked like the golden ratio, but I had no idea what that could mean.

"Hello," she said. "My name is Phala, the resident medical android on board this vessel." She had a pleasant voice, very nuanced, with an ambiguously British accent. This was some high-caliber stuff. "What is your name?"

"Xanorra," I said, too bewildered to be cautious.

"Hello, Xanorra. I have treated you for hypoxemia and a mild concussion. I ran all the typical diagnostics and your vitals appear to be perfectly stable. I have also sterilized and bandaged the cut on your forehead, which was only a minor injury. The rapid healing spray I applied to it should mean it completely scabs within twenty-four hours. Is there anything else I can help you with today?"

"Yeah," I said, feeling some clarity return to me. "You can tell me where the hell I am."

"You are in my infirmary. It is state-of-the-art."

"Yeah, great, but where is your infirmary? What ship is this? Where is your commander? Okay, actually, scratch all those previous questions. I'd like to speak to your commander, please."

I swore I saw her twitch before she said, "I am sure he will introduce himself soon. He is a very busy man. But until then, you are under my care."

"I'm perfectly well," I said. "You don't need to babysit me anymore."

"I am afraid my orders are not to let you leave this room."

Fantastic. "Or this bed, apparently. Do I have to be tied down?"

"To keep you from floating away, yes."

"That boy," I said, my recent memories returning to me. "The one who shot me with a tranquilizer, the little asshole. He could walk in zero-g. Who was he? How did he do that?"

"You have just experienced a lot of trauma, Xanorra. You are overwhelmed and your adrenaline levels are still high. I recommend that you hold your questions and allow yourself time to process all this new information."

"Oh, fantastic, you're programmed with neuro/psych, too. My lucky day." Usually, standard medidroids didn't come with neurological and psychological processors. There were separate androids for that or just good old humans. This *was* an advanced machine.

"I am the sole physician on this vessel," she said. "I am equipped to handle every aspect of human health, both physical and mental. If you ever need someone to talk to, I am here."

I didn't like how she said that. It implied the passing of time, and lots of it. The escape pod... it was damaged, but maybe not beyond repair. I couldn't be stuck here indefinitely, could I? "Um, thank you."

"I'm going to unstrap your upper body so you may sit up," she said and undid the top two restraints. The buoyancy lifted my torso upward like Dracula rising from his coffin.

Phala turned, retrieving a bundle and a pair of chunky boots from one of the countertops. "The captain requests that you change into this suit," she said. "I think it will answer your question about the zero gravity."

I took the bundle in my hands and let it unfurl. It was the same midnight blue as Phala's with the same silver embroidery of the spiral symbol.

*No, wait. It's that seashell... what's it called again? A nautilus.*

"Is this a mobile gravity suit?" I asked, even though it felt much too lightweight.

"No," she said. "It is a regular uniform threaded with steel. Your boots are also made with steel."

I paused, putting the pieces of the puzzle together. "Electromagnetism."

"Correct."

I gaped. "This ship... achieves artificial gravity through electromagnets?"

"Correct."

"So, everything has to have metal in it or it floats."

"Correct again."

"Huh." I scoffed. "That can't be cheap."

"I do not know the exact figure, but you are correct to assume that it took a significant amount of resources."

Like hell it did. Who were these people? What, exactly, had I stumbled into?

I continued to wonder as I untethered myself and worked on getting my SEA uniform off and the weird gravity suit on in zero-g—Phala helped, God bless her little robotic heart.

Actually, all things considered, I liked her. Her programming must be spot-on because she had all the desirable characteristics of a caretaker. It was probably the lowest margin of the uncanny valley I'd ever experienced with an android.

Which was as off-putting as it was impressive.

Once the suit was on, I immediately felt the familiar tug of ground-reaction forces, but it wasn't until I put the shoes on that I felt fully situated in one-g, or at least, something incredibly close to it.

"Whoa," I said.

"You may experience some lightheadedness as your blood and bodily fluids redistribute," said Phala. "But that should go away within the hour."

Mm, yummy. "Fits like a glove. Must be enough people living aboard this ship that someone happens to be my size, huh?"

She gave me a patronizing smile as she said, "I took your measurements while you were unconscious. It was tailor-made specifically for you."

"And that's not creepy at all."

"Why don't you have something to eat and drink? I'm sure you are famished."

I was, but my appetite was also addled with nerves as the gravity of the situation began to dawn on me, no pun intended. I needed answers, and I needed them *now.*

"I'd like to speak to the captain now, if you don't mind," I said simply. "Surely, he can spare a moment for an unsolicited visitor?"

Phala sighed, almost human-like. "He has politely requested that you oblige him for a while longer."

So he had manners. Space pirates didn't have manners, did they? Maybe, maybe not. After all, I'd never actually met one. They technically weren't supposed to exist.

"All right," I said. "Okay. I'll *oblige* him."

Phala smiled pleasantly as she gave me a water pouch and a meal that might've been high-protein oatmeal. It wasn't half bad, actually, though maybe I was just hungry.

I thought I wouldn't be able to sleep, but once the adrenaline wore off it left me with nothing but exhaustion. When I finally woke, it felt like I'd been in a deep, primordial slumber.

It also took me a few anxiety-filled moments to remember where I was and what I was doing there. But once I did, and I realized I was alone, I quickly got out of bed and tested the door to the infirmary. Not surprisingly, it was locked from the outside, assumedly so I wouldn't attempt a futile escape. Okay, they knew they had me trapped, so why be jerks about it?

"You are not permitted to open that door," said a calm voice from behind me.

I spun around to face Phala, who had entered from a narrow entrance on the other side of the room.

"I was just admiring the craftsmanship," I lied, stroking the doorframe. "This is a very unique ship, after all. I couldn't help but notice the sea life motif. Is there a reason for it?"

Phala smiled in a way that told me I was about to get a very unsatisfying answer. "Humans have always been as fascinated with the ocean as they are with space. It is only natural that the imagery would overlap."

Yep. Vague and unsatisfying.

"Would you like some lunch?" she said, retrieving a covered tray from the counter.

My stomach growled in response. The pre-nap oatmeal had not cut it, apparently. "Sure."

I sat on my temporary bed and ate while Phala busied herself by sanitizing everything I'd touched. Knowing she'd been ordered to keep an eye on me but assuming she had nothing to do in the meantime, I got the sense she was literally trying to "act natural." It was kind of amusing.

"So, what's the plan?" I asked as casually as possible. "Does the captain intend to keep me confined to this room forever with nothing but a robot for company? Is that his idea of saving my life?"

Phala smiled, calm and saccharine. "I can provide you with mental stimulation if you are feeling restless. We have books and videos on nearly every academic subject you can think of. What interests you?"

I paused. Finally, a nugget of information. "Why academic?"

"To increase knowledge," she said matter-of-factly. "A useful pastime while unoccupied in space."

"You sound like my mother," I drawled.

"I am programmed with maternal characteristics. Any resemblance I may bear to your biological mother will be purely coincidental."

I tried again. "Why maternal?"

"Maternal characteristics are the most well-received in a caretaker. I was designed to be the most optimal medical android in existence."

"Designed by whom?" I asked carefully.

She smiled. "I admire that you are curious, but I'm afraid that there are many questions I am barred from answering. I'm sure you understand."

I sighed and paced the room instead, observing the medical equipment stored neatly in cases behind clean, plexiglass cabinets. I should also mention that it was a small room, as in, I could cross it in four paces. On the long side.

What a cozy little prison cell.

I passed by the door in the back that Phala had entered from and asked, "May I see what's in here?"

"Of course," she said, opening it remotely.

Inside, it was nothing too interesting. A closet-sized room, barely big enough for one person, with a charging station in the wall. Phala's quarters. Androids really didn't need too much.

"So luxurious compared to mine," I said.

Phala smiled as if she understood the joke. Maybe she did; some androids could learn sarcasm given adequate exposure. I guess it would depend on how plucky the human crewmembers were.

Speaking of which, now that I'd exhausted the length and breadth of my imprisonment, the wheels in my head began to turn. If they really intended to keep me isolated like this, they were in for a hell of a time.

"You said something about entertainment?" I said to Phala.

"Not entertainment. Stimulation. And yes, I did. If you give me a moment, I can retrieve a tablet for your personal use."

I tried to remain as unaffected as possible. Was she actually going to leave the room? "That would be great, thank you."

She nodded and approached the infirmary's exit. There was no keypad or physical lock; the door must be able to detect those who had clearance because it opened as soon as she neared it and locked again as soon as she was gone.

I crouched to the right of the door and waited for her to return. I would only have one shot at this, and it would probably end badly, but at least I would have made my point.

A moment later, the door opened. Phala entered. In the second between when she walked in and when the door should've closed, I ducked out and sprinted down the corridor.

# 9

# Enter Captain Omen

I expected to encounter crewmembers, for an alarm to be raised, something—but all was quiet as I veered left and found myself in what had to be the docking bay, based on the round, silver ship on the right that looked like a giant nautilus shell.

Apparently, the infirmary was not far off from where I'd begun. I wasn't planning on trying to escape (yet), just get ahold of someone with a beating heart, but this was as good a method as any.

Now that I wasn't panicked or sedated, I could actually observe the interior of the ship, which immediately struck me as unique—at least as unique as the exterior. On most ships, you're used to seeing a lot of white, gray, and metallics, especially in a docking bay. But here, the walls and floors were mostly a palette of blues, illuminated by blue strips of light that reminded me of bioluminescence.

For God's sake, someone really loved the ocean.

But then I noticed something else. My damaged escape pod should've been here, too. Unless they'd left it in the airlock, which would be unusual. Just to be sure, I approached the airlock doors and peered inside the long port window. The escape pod wasn't in there either. It was gone.

"They *jettisoned* my pod?" I exclaimed. "No! They can't do that!"

Technically, they could, but even if it couldn't have supported me in space, it still made my heart ache to think that my sole connection to my family and crew—my only chance of getting home, however meager—was now floating aimlessly in the vacuum.

And that's when it truly hit me: I *was* stuck here.

Was I happy to be alive? Indescribably. But was I devastated by what it had cost? Undeniably.

I sunk to the floor, my back against the airlock doors, my breath coming out in short gasps as if I lacked oxygen again. Now was not the time to panic, but my body betrayed me. For the first time in my life, I was alone. No parents, no teachers, no support system.

No Quin to keep my feet on the ground.

But I did have God and my wits, which would be enough if it didn't feel like someone had shaken my brain like an aerosol can.

I told myself I had to keep my composure. That the spacers who had come before me would not have been able to do the things they'd done without incredible strength of character. We'd had to study it. We'd had to learn the techniques.

I just wasn't sure I'd ever had to apply them.

Thus, in spite of telling myself to be a brave cosmonaut and suck it up, I didn't. I cried like a baby, and my tears floated in the zero-g like dew drops.

I sat there for a long time in the dim light, crying, trying to stop crying, and expecting someone—a crewmember, the captain, anybody—to come and throw me back into their infirmary-turned-brig before I could summon the willpower to continue on.

Just as I finally calmed down a little, I heard footsteps at the far end of the docking bay, which stirred my heartbeat into a frenzy all over again. I forced myself to take slow, deep breaths as I pulled myself to my feet and braced myself for whoever was coming for me.

My preparations were in vain. It was Phala.

"We thought it would be best if we gave you some time to process," she said in that calm, uncannily comforting tone of hers.

"We?"

"The captain and I."

"How kind of him," I said with a mocking edge. "Or maybe he's too much of a coward to face what he's done?"

"You will meet the captain when he is ready."

"And when will that be? Never?"

"Please, come back to the infirmary with me," she said, dodging the question. "You need to rest. I'm sure you are still more exhausted than you realize."

I was, but spite compelled me to deny it. "I'm not moving until I speak to a human being," I said. It was a bold move, but I told myself I was well within my rights. A sort of "parlay" situation.

Phala looked irritated, her brow creased in concentration, her head tilted slightly to the side. Then I realized what was happening: she was communicating with him. Was the captain watching me right now? Eesh.

Her face relaxed again and she said, "He says no. Not until you are in a better state of mind."

"How do you expect me to be in a better state of mind when I'm being treated like a prisoner?" I asked her, but more precisely, him. "I understand that I asked to be here, but you complied. The least you can do is let me negotiate with you!"

Phala said, "Xanorra, I had hoped not to have to resort to this, but if you will not come quietly, I will be forced to employ the use of sedatives. For your safety."

"Like hell you will," I warned.

She reached toward me, but I ducked out of the way and sprinted past her out of the docking bay. No sooner did I throw a glance over my shoulder than I collided directly with a wall.

Not a wall. A person. The same steely-eyed, gun-wielding a-hole from before.

He caught me by the arms and froze, startled. I was equally startled, I'll admit. We stared at each other for what seemed like a full minute.

"You are supposed to be on the bridge," said Phala from behind me. Calm but reprimanding. Like a mother.

The boy released me and looked over my shoulder at the android. "Phala, you may return to the infirmary," he said in an even tone.

After what seemed like a longer pause than necessary, Phala said, "Of course," and disappeared through the door to her right.

"Finally, a person," I said, brushing myself off. "I'm guessing he's finally come to his senses and agreed to speak with me after all?"

He stepped back and stared at me, arms crossed, like I was a particularly irritating math problem.

"Hello? Are you deaf? I asked to be taken to the man in charge," I said.

"Fascinating," he said.

"What?"

"It is fascinating," he said louder. "Your utter lack of rationality."

I scoffed. My ire had returned. "Listen, kid, I'm not here to play mind games, kapeesh? Do I have to spell it out for you? I want to speak to the captain. Now."

"You are speaking to him," he said. "Disrespectfully, I might add."

I blinked. "What?"

"My name is Captain Omen. I am the commander of this vessel."

"Captain? But you're so..."

"Young?" His eyes had a question in them. "So I am."

I scoffed again. "You were toying with me!"

"You made an assumption based on your limited understanding of the facts. I gather you were expecting someone else."

"Yeah, someone *taller*," I said.

He stared at me, dead-eyed. He actually was taller than

me, but he couldn't be much older. Seriously, though? Captain?

I changed tactics. "Whose ship is this? Where are you from?"

He continued to stare blankly at me, like a computer processing data. "You have not told me your name," he finally said.

"Yes, I did. In my transmission."

"But this is a formal introduction, is it not? Would it not be a breach of etiquette not to reciprocate, even if I technically know your name already?"

"Breach in…?" Was this kid some kind of highly advanced android, or was he really that pretentious? I sighed. "My name is Xanorra Nepier. Most people call me Xan."

"Seeing as we are hardly acquaintances, may I call you Miss Nepier?"

I scoffed. "Hardly acquaintances? That's generous! You destroyed my ship! My parents—my *entire* family—was on that ship! They probably think I'm dead!"

"Parents," he repeated as if he didn't understand the word.

"Yeah. Parents. Where are yours?"

"You assume yours survived."

"I sure as hell hope—" I stared at him in horror as I processed his words. "Don't tell me you gunned down the escape shuttles. As God as my witness, if you killed them—"

"I was not aware of any escape shuttles," he said. "I only had ample time to target the ship."

"Oh, yeah, great. So if you'd had more than ample time, they would be dead."

"The protocol is infallible," he said, almost to himself.

"Protocol? What protocol?"

He looked at me with sharp urgency as he said, "You told no one of my location. You had no contact with any of the shuttles. Correct?"

"I don't understand."

He got in my face, so close it startled me. "Does anyone know how to find me?"

"No," I said, taking a step backward. "No, and I doubt anyone will try, now that you've demonstrated just how well you treat your neighbors."

He paced wall to wall in the narrow corridor, a dark expression on his face.

This was so weird. How was I supposed to handle this? Was he even sane? Was he even human? As confidently as I could muster, I said, "Why did you attack us, exactly? If I may ask. It's not like we were a threat to you. We just wanted to talk."

"Irrelevant," he said. "It was an act of self-defense."

"Self-defense?" I exclaimed. "It was a *research vessel*. We crossed paths by *accident*."

"Also irrelevant. I had no choice but to follow the protocol. Rest assured it was not personal."

"Like hell it wasn't," I scowled. "It was heartless."

"Heartless?" He said it as if he couldn't fathom the idea.

"You're a pirate ship, aren't you?" I said. When he didn't answer, I scowled. "I guess they really do exist after all. Who'd you steal all this fancy tech from, huh?" I plucked at the gravity suit in disdain.

"I stole nothing," he snapped, clearly irritated. "This ship was built by my family, and to my family it belongs."

"Then what is its purpose?" I asked.

His jaw twitched. "I am afraid that is not any of your business. I have already said too much."

I laughed at the absurdity of it all. "Then I think it is in your best interest as well as mine, *Captain*, to get me off your ship as soon as humanly possible."

"I am afraid that is not an option, either."

I swallowed a fresh surge of panic, but it made it up to my eyes before I could stop it. I refused to cry in front of this weirdo, but my tear ducts insisted on preparing themselves anyway.

"Then what?" I said. "You're gonna keep me in that tiny room with that android mom forever? Do you have any idea what that *does* to a person? Have you ever been in solitary confinement? I mean, isn't being on a house-sized spaceship in the middle of nowhere confining enough?"

His expression took on a far-off look, and though it was difficult to read, I could swear I'd made him uncomfortable by turning it around on him. Or maybe it was the watery eyes. Either way, good. He deserved to be uncomfortable.

"It was a temporary solution," he finally said.

"All right," I said, lifting my chin. "Would you care to elaborate on the permanent solution, then?"

He stared through me as if he were processing data again. I hadn't completely ruled out the android possibility yet, but, despite his formal vernacular and general rigidness, there was still a human authenticity to him that you just can't replicate artificially.

"Very well," he said. "Let us discuss this somewhere more appropriate. Follow me, if you would please."

# 10

# No One Told Me This Would Be an Interview

In spite of myself, I was relieved. And intrigued. The captain and I were finally going to talk, and I was finally going to see other parts of the ship!

He led me to the opposite end of the hall, where a ladder led up to a small landing with two doors: one in front of us, the other behind. He opened the latter and we stepped inside a room that was, by all counts, a lounge.

However, this lounge was unlike anything I'd ever seen on the *Aster* or the *Washington*, mixing elements of old-world style and craftsmanship with modern, geometric design. The ornate rug, the mahogany furnishings, the antique astronomical equipment dotting the room, and most of all, the glass display cases of preserved marine life from Earth lining one wall all looked like they belonged in a museum, not a ship. Overhead, a crystal chandelier glittered with pristine beauty. The ceiling had been painted to look like an astronomical map, midnight blue with golden stars. I assumed it was of our solar system but my senses were too overloaded with colors and textures to really scrutinize it.

"Wow," I breathed.

Captain Omen motioned for me to sit on the dark gray, faux-leather couch. I obliged him. He took a seat on the matching chair to the right and watched me intently, as if I were a fascinating zoo animal.

Seriously, had he ever seen a girl before?

"So..." I avoided eye contact. "This is a nice room. Do you entertain much?"

"I never entertain," he said.

"The crew has their own mess hall, then?"

He continued to stare at me, impassive. "There is no crew on this ship. No real crew, at any rate."

I threw my head back in an exaggerated display of utter shock. "I'm sorry, *what?*"

He laced his fingers together like a professor in a teen drama and sighed. "Miss Nepier," he said. "If you are going to react with this degree of skepticism to everything I tell you about this ship, then let me be the first to warn you that the nature of my crew is the least of it all."

Now I was nervous. My mind raced to solve the riddle. It didn't take long. "Robots," I said. "Your crew, they're all robots. Aren't they?"

He leaned forward. "You are very smart."

"Not really, I'm just good at puzzles. Are you... the only human on this ship?"

He paused. "Let us just say yes."

I wasn't sure I liked that wording very much, but for the sake of moving the conversation along, I asked, "How long have you been here?"

He paused again, glancing upward, and said, "By this ship's reckoning, seventeen years, two-hundred thirty-one days, and approximately…" He checked the metal band around his wrist, evidently some kind of smartwatch. "Eighteen hours."

I didn't know whether to be impressed or deeply disturbed. "And how old are you?"

"Seventeen."

It was just as I feared. "You've been on this ship… for your entire life? Alone?"

"Not alone," he said. "Just without a human presence."

*No freaking way.* So he'd been raised by robots. Theoretically, it was possible. Advanced AI could imitate most human behavior, and there were plenty of medidroids like Phala who took care of patients. But artificial intelligence and artificial consciousness were two different things, and the latter definitely didn't exist.

He'd never experienced real, human connection. No wonder he looked at me like I was an alien.

"Then this must be a very big day for you," I finally said.

For half a second, he deigned to look amused before that blank look of mild impatience returned. "Social etiquette dictates that I reciprocate with a parallel question. How old are *you*?"

"Eighteen," I said. Then I grinned. "Which makes me your superior."

"Age does not surpass rank," he said, and I could tell I'd irritated him. Boy, oh boy, he was going to be a bucket of fun, wasn't he? "Where are you from?"

"The colony ship *Aster*," I replied. "I just graduated from the academy and was assigned—well, got permission to be assigned—to the *USE George Washington*. The first long-term mission through the Current. It was supposed to last eight years, but... the rest is history." I gave him a meaningful glare that he promptly ignored.

"What did you do on the ship?" he asked. "What is your area of expertise?"

"Oh." I suddenly felt self-conscious. "I'm technically an engine operator's assistant. But that's just my day job. Or 'hand job,' as the kids say. Jokingly, of course." I anticipated a smug reaction, but he remained so unfazed I had to wonder if he even knew what a hand job was, strictly speaking. "Engineering is my dad's trade. But my area of study is General Education. My mom's a teacher. I'm training to be one, too."

"A teacher," he said. "Interesting choice. Are there not androids who serve that function in your society?"

I was used to reactions like that, but coming from someone so utterly far removed, it stung even more. I summoned my composure and said, "They can, but the SEA values human connection, especially in early education. No edudroid can care about its students, no matter how advanced its programming."

What I didn't say, and didn't want to admit, was that the Educators of Space Guild had to fight tooth and nail to keep their jobs by reiterating this exact argument to the SEA about once every five years. My mom actively lobbied for educators' rights and I expected that one day I would, too.

Captain's face displayed no comprehension, which didn't surprise me since he'd been raised and taught by androids. But it was definitely irritating to think that he might see me as obsolete on multiple levels.

"How much do you know about astrotech engineering?" he asked.

"Enough," I shot back, bordering on defensive in case he tried to undermine my utility there, too.

"Then your knowledge must spark some curiosity as to how this ship works."

"Oh, extremely," I said. "I'd be curious even if I didn't know squat about engineering."

His eyes brightened, implying that he had to be at least a little excited by the prospect of showing off his ship to another human being. Especially one who knew stuff about ship maintenance, however basic.

He sat back and scrutinized me with scientific intensity but said nothing else. Thirty seconds passed. Then a minute. I'd almost forgotten the original purpose of this meeting: to discuss what to do with me. Awkward staring aside, we'd somehow lapsed into an actual conversation.

Then why did it feel like I was under evaluation? Was this some kind of test? Had I passed? Did I *want* to pass?

"You know, it's rude to stare," I said.

He flinched as if he hadn't realized what he'd been doing. "Is it?"

I blinked. I'd thought he was Mr. Etiquette with the formal introductions, but now he didn't even know a basic social norm? Or was he just messing with me? This guy was impossible to read, and I considered myself very good at reading people.

"Generally speaking," I said. "When you're not talking to them."

I thought maybe he'd get that social cue, but he continued to look on at me for ten more seconds before finally sitting forward and saying, "This situation we have found ourselves in is very precarious. I have spent a fair amount of time meditating on it and would have spent a fair amount more, but I suppose your restlessness cannot be helped."

I scoffed but held my tongue.

"Nevertheless, in the interest of scientific curiosity, I think it is only fair that I show you, rather than tell you, what manner of ship you now find yourself aboard."

I blinked, still processing how anyone my age could sound so pretentious and yet own it so well. I guess when it was all you knew, it came as naturally in speech as slang and colloquialisms did to a peasant like me.

The accent also helped.

"Does this ship of yours have a name, Captain?" I asked glibly.

"Of course," he said. "Consider yourself nothing more than a passenger of the *Atlantis*."

# 11

# In Which I Get the Grand Tour of the Atlantis

Captain Omen moved to leave the lounge through a door on the opposite side of the room. I went to follow him, but halfway there, I stopped. Maybe it was the knowledge that we were the only humans on the ship or maybe it was the strange way he had approached this conversation, as if I were interviewing for a job.

Maybe it was the fact that despite his elevated speech and mannerisms, he was still the bastard who'd destroyed the *George Washington.*

Or maybe it was the fact that without even giving us a chance to discuss it, he'd implied that I was stuck here whether I liked it or not.

In any case, I said, "Wait."

He turned, obviously surprised. "Yes?"

I took a deep breath. "Before we go any further, I need you to make me a spacer's oath."

"A spacer's oath?" He actually looked confused. Good. I'd caught him off-guard.

I huffed. "That you won't harm me, or vice versa, so long as I'm on your ship."

He tilted his head slightly. "You think I mean you harm?"

"Well, you did kind of try to shoot me earlier!" I exclaimed.

He opened his mouth as if to defend himself, then pressed his lips in a hard line, brows furrowed. "Say we make an oath. How do you know I won't go back on my word? Is there a legal document we have to sign, or something of that nature?"

"Have you really never—?" I backtracked. The question answered itself. "It's the honor code. Our word is our bond. I mean, in space, there's so few of us... and when it comes down to it, all we have is trust. It's just a thing we do. To protect ourselves. And each other." I held my hand out to him.

He hesitated for a second, as if I might shock him. Then he took my hand in his, the first step of a handshake. I suppose I shouldn't have been surprised that his was warm and unmistakably human, but I still had to bite back a snide remark before I said, "I'll go first since I know the words. What's your first name?"

"Captain," he said.

"No, not your rank. Your birth name."

"My birth name is Captain," he said without a hint of irony.

"Your name is Captain, and you're a... captain," I said. "Subtle."

"Is there a problem?"

The problem was that I wanted to slap his mother, if he had one. "Nope. No problem. Okay, fine. I, Xanorra Nepier, hereby swear never to harm or allow harm to befall you, *Captain* Omen, so long as I am on your ship. May God hold me to this oath. Now you repeat it, but with your name, obviously."

Again, there was a second-long pause before he said, "I, Captain Omen, hereby swear never to harm or allow harm to befall you, Xanorra Nepier, so long as you are on my ship. May God hold me to this oath."

"Now we shake." I pumped his arm and released. His fell limp at his side as if I'd sucked the life from it. Did he already regret this? Too late now, because what's done was done.

"That is it?" he said, his sharp eyes scrutinizing me.

"That's it," I said.

"Follow me, then," he said, leaving the lounge through the back door. This time, I did follow. And even if there was no guarantee that he would honor a pact made with a total stranger, it still made me feel better. Because if he really hadn't wanted to make me any promises, then he wouldn't have shaken my hand.

There were two doors in the back of the lounge. He showed me the one on the right first; it was a gym, and a nice one at that. From what I could see, there was a treadmill, a weight machine, a punching bag, a rower, and a stair-climber.

"Physical fitness is paramount to maintaining optimal health, even on a ship with artificial gravity," Captain pontificated, as if that were something every spacer hadn't had drilled into them from the time they could walk. "You are welcome to use this room as much as you would like."

"Fantastic," I said.

Next, we went into the other room, which looked like a small dining hall. There was an open counter directly to the left, on the other side of which was a standard ship kitchen and a server bot who greeted us as we walked in. But other than that, the room was empty. No furniture. Nothing to indicate that meals were eaten here at all.

"Spacious," I remarked.

"You will receive your meals here, from Lambda," said Captain, motioning to the abstractly humanoid-looking bot. "He is one of two internal maintenance droids, but he stays primarily on this level."

"A pleasure to meet you," I said to the robot.

"The pleasure is all mine," he answered in a smooth voice.

Turning to Captain, I asked, "What's the food situation like?"

"Food... situation?"

I sighed. "What do you eat? How is it prepared?"

"Mostly reconstituted rations, but I also have a greenhouse in the cargo bay supplementing fresh produce."

"And double the people to feed won't throw things off?" Surely, I was a liability in that respect.

"I have done the math," he said evenly. "Neither of us needs to worry about going hungry."

"Well, isn't that a relief." So he could afford to keep me here. Great. I wanted to ask more questions about this so-called math, but instead, I said, "I take it most of the cargo bay is dedicated to food storage."

"Indeed. But this ship still carries less mass than any spacefaring vessel in the known galaxy, which also makes it the fastest with respect to its size. The addition of your mass is not likely to have a noticeable impact on its continued acceleration."

"What a compliment," I said, and the contented look he gave me told me that he definitely didn't understand sarcasm. "That's why you had to jettison my escape pod, huh? Extra mass."

"Yes," he said. "It was damaged beyond repair anyhow."

"Sure it was," I said, but while part of me did believe him, I would've liked to have seen it for myself first, just to be sure.

He turned to exit back the way we'd come, but I spotted a door on the opposite side of the room and asked, "What's in there?"

He turned slowly and said, "Storage."

"I thought the first level was storage."

"Can there not be storage on multiple levels?"

Now I was suspicious. "There can, but it seems a little odd."

His expression darkened as he said, "I hope you understand that some areas of the ship are off-limits. That room is one of them. That is all I will say about it."

A chill went up my spine, but I let it go for now as I followed him back through the lounge to the foyer, where he stopped in front of the door on the other side of the ladder.

"Now," he said, holding my gaze, "would you like to see how this ship runs?"

My breath caught in my throat. We were very close together, and for the first time, I could smell him—a sharp, citrusy scent that reminded me of a freshly-sanitized floor. He smelled like a thing, not a person.

Absently, I wondered how I smelled after all the sweat and adrenaline. Not good, I surmised.

"Absolutely," I replied, trying to exhale as little breath as possible.

He opened the door and we stepped inside the semi-circle-shaped bridge. Wide viewscreens offered a clear view of the Zion system and the depthless void surrounding it. In the center of the bridge was the helm, and beyond that, running the length of the windows, was the control center.

And at each of the five stations where you'd normally find a person, there was a robot crewmember.

Of course, they were all roughly shaped like people, but they also had the mechanical functionality typically found in task bots. The only true android stood at the helm, dressed in a uniform that matched the style of the captain's. His back was to us, but I could tell just by looking at his stature that he was highly advanced like Phala.

"Wow," I said. "So you weren't kidding."

"I never kid," said Captain as he joined me. I didn't doubt it. "Most of them are simple task bots. The four on controls are called Delta, Gamma, Epsilon, and Zeta, respectively. They are intelligent, but not very good company. Only two of my crew members have AI drivers."

"Phala," I inferred. "And him?" I pointed to the android at the helm.

"Yes. That is my first mate, Beta."

"Ah. And that makes you Alpha, then, I presume?"

"Correct."

"A wonder your parents didn't name you that instead," I muttered under my breath.

If Captain heard me, he pretended otherwise. "I would like to introduce you, if you don't mind." There was actual emotion in his voice, something akin to pride.

*Don't tell me this is like his robot dad.* But what could I do? I nodded and allowed him to lead me across the deck to the podium. Though it was poetically called the helm, it wasn't a spoked wheel like the seafaring ships of old. Rather, it was a curved dais with several readout screens—usually live data feeds from the control center along with its own navigation, radar, and specs. The captain could also use the helm to take manual control of the ship if needed, but it was a rare occurrence.

"Beta," said the captain. "I would like you to meet our guest, Miss Xanorra Nepier. Miss Nepier, my first mate, Lieutenant Beta."

Beta locked the screens and turned to face us. Like Phala, he had no hair and was uncannily handsome, with Middle Eastern features that were not unlike Captain's. Had the designers done that on purpose, I wondered, to emulate his real parents? The thought made my stomach turn.

"Ah, yes," Beta said, his voice as smooth as Phala's.

And as British, naturally. "Welcome aboard the *Atlantis*. I think you will find the accommodations quite satisfactory."

"Yes, it's the most interesting ship I've ever had the pleasure of boarding," I said, hoping this AI wasn't advanced enough to detect irony.

"We are very proud of our captain," said the first mate. "His performance record is exemplary."

"I do have one question, if you don't mind me asking." I glanced at Captain Omen. "If the AI is advanced enough to pilot the ship, then why do you need a human at all? Why not unmanned, or robot only?"

Beta's eyes flicked over to Captain, silently prompting him to answer the question. Almost as if it were some kind of test.

"An AI can only do what it was programmed to do," Captain replied. "Even critical thinking is limited by the capacity of the driver. But a human can think beyond the expected. They can process unaccounted-for variables and problem-solve accordingly. In simple essence, it is the principle that has always governed manned versus unmanned travel: no computer can replace human intuition."

I nodded in satisfaction, a wave of relief washing over me. At least he knew he was different from an android on a fundamental level. His weird formalities must be simple imitative behavior, the result of growing up around humanoid machines and learning language and mannerisms from them.

"Touché," I said.

"I spend the majority of my time here on the bridge,"

said Captain with an air of importance. "It is my primary role and requires a substantial amount of focus."

"I gathered that much," I said.

"In fact, you are unlikely to see much of me at all."

"What a shame. I was already growing used to your superior sense of humor."

He gave me a befuddled look and then furrowed his brow. "I have not employed the use of humor."

"I was being sarcastic, Captain."

"Ah." He nodded as if I'd just classified an artifact. "I see."

*No, I don't think you do*, I thought, amused in spite of myself.

The next stop on our tour was the first level, where my journey had begun. All of the rooms down here were storage compartments save for the infirmary and the docking bay, but there were two other areas in particular Captain wanted to show me.

The first appeared to be a nondescript cargo hold packed to the gills with numbered cases, but there was a narrow path that ran down the center, which we followed to the back of the room. There, a single device had been mounted to the floor and ceiling. It looked like an x-ray machine mixed with a metal detector.

I stared at it in bewilderment. "Wow, neat. What is it?"

"What you are looking at is a highly advanced 3D printer," said Captain. "It is called Iota."

"Ohhh. I see it now."

"It can make practically anything you need: clothes, tools, furniture. Basically, anything homogenous. It can simulate different materials, too, if you want something with more or less tensile strength. The amount of material is fixed, though, so when you are done with an item, or you want to make something else but do not have enough material, you must recycle it back into the machine."

"That's ingenious," I said. "Do you use it often?"

"When I need it," he said. "More so when I was younger. But you are welcome to use it whenever you want, hence my showing it to you."

"Can I make something now?"

"Well..." He faltered. "I suppose so. If you would like. There are presets or you can design something from scratch. Iota is very intuitive. You can search for practically any keyword and she should be able to find what you are looking for."

I approached the small input screen that jutted out at chest level from the machine's frame, but I faltered when I realized I couldn't read it. "Um, I think this is in Arabic."

"Oh, my mistake." Captain tapped a command into his smartwatch and the writing on the screen instantly switched to English. "I'll make sure the rest of the interface is Galactic Standard as well."

"Did you grow up speaking both?" I asked. His English was so flawless I'd assumed it was his native language, which I'd chalked up to a lucky break. Just imagine what might've happened if we hadn't been able to communicate.

"I speak five languages," he said haughtily. "English,

Arabic, Greek, Latin, and French. Though yes, I was raised with the first two primarily."

"I got an A-minus in Mandarin," I offered.

He looked less than impressed.

I turned my attention back to Iota, racking my brain for something to make. I wanted to think of something that would baffle him, but my mind churned up blanks. I decided to go with something practical instead and inputted a hair tie. Since it was small, it took no time to make. I picked it up from the platform and presented it to him like a proud child.

"Interesting choice," he said.

"Well, I doubted it was the sort of thing you had lying around," I said as I tested the elasticity. Felt like a hair tie to me. I gathered my tangled, shoulder-length hair into a low ponytail and tied it back. "And mine broke, so *voila*. I hate zero-g hair."

Contrary to popular belief, it does not make you feel like a mermaid. There was a reason why short hair was the fashion on deep space ships, for men and women both. Quin and I were just too stubborn to cut ours before the mission.

That's when I realized: Captain's hair wasn't floating around. And his wasn't short, either. I knew for a fact that hair wasn't made of steel, so I was instantly stupefied.

"Wait, why isn't your hair all floaty?" I asked, resisting the urge to reach up and tousle it.

"Ionized hair products," he said. "I will get you some."

"Amazing," I said. "Magnetic hair."

"It is not magnetic," he said, perturbed. "It is more akin to static than anything."

"So if I touch it, would it shock me?"

"What do you think?"

I took that as an invitation, but as soon as I moved my hand toward him, he stepped back in alarm. I snapped my hand back, embarrassed.

I'd forgotten who I'd been talking to.

He cleared his throat and said, "Would you like to see the greenhouse?"

The answer was yes. Anything to escape that awkward ordeal. Thankfully, it was just across the hall in a separate storage room. All four walls, including the doorway, were covered in an insulating tarp, and the long, bright heat lamps hung suspended from the ceiling, casting the room in a warm, sunny yellow. But the dominant color by far was green—lush, fresh, growing green.

The produce grew in raised vacuum beds with thermometers and hygrometers placed at regular intervals. I recognized tomatoes, lettuce, onions, peas, potatoes, and rice, if you could believe it. There must've been herbs somewhere too because I could smell parsley and dill. There wasn't much room for trees, but a small one grew in a pot in the far-right corner.

"This is amazing," I said.

"Thank you," he said, to my surprise. "I was provided adequate instructions with which to construct it, but I confess I may have made a few modifications."

I walked down the middle of the rows toward the back. "What kind of tree is this?" I asked as I approached it.

"It is a fig tree," he replied.

"It looks incredible."

"It took me years just to get it to grow," he said. "It should finally reach maturity this year."

I carefully touched one of the small, green fruits clinging to the branch. "So you did all this yourself, then."

"What do you mean?"

"I mean, you take care of the greenhouse, not an automated system?"

"Yes," he said hesitantly. "I suppose a bot could do it, but..."

"You enjoy it," I finished.

"I wouldn't go that far. I just prefer to do things manually."

"Uh-huh. Human intuition, right?"

"Precisely."

I didn't buy it, not for one minute. Was he embarrassed that he liked to garden or something? I didn't see anything wrong with that. In fact, it was pretty neat.

"Would you like to see the engines now?" he asked, changing the subject.

I snapped back to the present and smiled. "Of course. Lead the way, Captain."

[12]

# And They Were Roommates!

I'll spare you the gory details of the engine room—just kidding, it's too fascinating not to explain. To a nerd like me, at least.

The hatch that led to the engine room was in the docking bay. As we passed through, I asked about the seashell ship. It hadn't occurred to me before, but perhaps it could make a good escape vessel.

"That is the *Nautilus*, a simple transport cruiser," said Captain. As if reading my mind, he added, "It is not made for long-term travel. In fact, it has less life-supporting capabilities than an escape pod, I'm afraid."

"Well, isn't that convenient."

He locked eyes with me and said, "If you are thinking of trying to leave in it, I would advise against it. You will be dead within a week."

I froze, at a loss. I supposed he could be bluffing, but he

didn't seem like the type. "Thanks for the tip. I'll take it into consideration."

"The oath we made explicitly stated that I would not allow harm to befall you while you are *on* my ship. If you leave the ship, I am no longer under oath to protect you."

Now I was dumbstruck. "Yes, that is technically true."

His dark eyes bore into mine. "If you leave the ship, I have to follow protocol."

A chill went up my spine as I caught his implication. Despite the intensity in his expression, I couldn't tell if it was a threat or a warning. Or both. "No seashell ship if I value my life. Got it."

The engine room itself was skinny and long, running almost the entire length of the underside of the ship but barely wider than the infirmary. There were no overhead catwalks, no ladders or platforms, just a narrow path that ran down either side with one or two places where you could step over the reactors. Two engineering bots, boxy and computer-like, roamed up and down the paths, one on each side.

Their names? Eta and Theta. Adorable.

To quote Captain verbatim, apparently, the secret was in the length. (And yes, it took every ounce of self-control I had not to laugh at that, because he said it with a straight face.) Internally, the engine wasn't unlike the nuclear engine of any other high-speed, deep space vessel, just a hundred times more efficient.

Basically, it pressurized the fuel as it pushed it from the front of the ship to the back, so by the time it reached the exhaust, it was more powerful than *four* deep space engines.

But it took time to build that pressure, Captain said. Apparently, the *Atlantis* was not quite so zippy when it first launched. (And yes, my attempts to get him to extrapolate on that were in vain.) But thanks to the very real magic of acceleration, it had reached speeds that the SEA could only dream of.

Which meant that it would've been easy for him to fly right by us instead of taking time out of his busy schedule to shoot at us. A very comforting notion.

But that wasn't all. Those tentacle-like fins in the back of the ship, flying like the tail of a comet? They were electromagnetic absorption panels. Like solar panels but for radiation. I'd heard of this sort of technology on a small scale, or on probes, but never on a whole-ass ship.

It was impressive. No, it was groundbreaking.

Why hadn't anyone heard of this?

Oh, right. Because dead men tell no tales.

It did make one wonder how many ships Captain had encountered in his lifetime. I tried to imagine a seven-year-old or even a twelve-year-old going *Ender's Game* on an SEA ship and felt queasy. Then again, if something like this had happened in the past, everyone would've heard about it.

No, I had every reason to believe that the encounter with the *George Washington* was the first time Captain had ever crossed paths with another ship.

Which left just one more question.

"How did you know about the Current?" I asked as we made our way back to the upper level.

He stopped at the ladder and turned. "The wormhole?"

"Yeah. We call it the Current. We haven't known about

it that long. I told you the *Washington* was the first ship to be sent through it on a long-term mission. But you were already here. How is that possible?"

He paused, that robotic brain of his practically whirring with the effort of formulating a response. "I am not at liberty to discuss it," he said.

Aggravatingly blunt. I was detecting a pattern with this one. "Of course. The protocol, right?"

"Precisely," he said and climbed the ladder.

Back in the lounge, the Captain motioned to a door catty-cornered to the left of the entrance. "Your quarters," he said.

"My quarters?" I approached the door. "You have a guest room?"

"Of course not," he said. "It was my room previously. But I do not use it these days, so I believe it would better serve your needs than mine."

His room? I guess that would make sense. There wouldn't be a need for more than one bedroom on a ship with one person. But I had to wonder if he was lying about not using the room to be polite. If so, it was an unexpectedly nice gesture.

I entered the triangular room, not knowing what to expect. It was small but comfortable and contained a single bed next to a shuttered porthole window, a nightstand, and a lamp. Simple, sterile, and practical. Now I believed that he hardly used it; no human being would keep their room this clean and lifeless.

"Through that door is the shower and lavatory," he said, pointing to a narrow entrance on the left side of the back wall. "Unfortunately, there is only one restroom on this ship, for obvious reasons. But there is a door that separates the lavatory from the shower, and a second door to the lavatory on the bridge side. I suggest that we lock both doors when in use, that way we do not—we prevent—"

"Walking in on the other taking a shit," I said without thinking. "Got it."

He looked confused at first, but then his brain connected the contextual dots and he suddenly looked mortified. "Right. *That.*"

Prim and proper, this one. "Sorry. Walking in on the other *relieving themselves.*"

Deadpan, he asked, "Is vulgarity a common attribute of space colonists?"

"Um, let me think about that for a moment: yes. But I'll try to tone it down if it offends you."

"I just don't see the utility in it."

I rolled my eyes. "Speaking of utility, when do you normally shower?"

Now he looked alarmed. "What?"

"*When do you normally shower?*" I repeated slowly. "Morning or evening? Or are you one of those psychos who showers in the mid-afternoon?"

"I do not see why that is important," he said, flushed. Oh my God, I'd embarrassed him. It was kind of adorable.

"Look, I can see that this is your first time having a roommate. Being in close quarters with someone means you get to know their routine inside and out, *including* bathroom breaks. But it helps prevent awkward situations if we can coordinate. That way, we can respect the other's privacy."

"Right. Of course," he said, recovering. "I shower very early in the morning. You will likely be asleep and should never hear me come or go."

"Great. Was that so hard?"

"Will the room suffice?" he said, dodging the question.

"It's perfect," I said. "Thank you."

He nodded brusquely. "This is where I leave you, then."

"Wait a second," I said. "I might need a change of underclothes at some point. And a toothbrush. And a hairbrush." Gosh, I'd never had to build my everyday essentials from scratch before. Oh crap, what would happen when my period started? That would be a fun conversation.

Maybe I ought to talk to Phala about that instead.

"Right, of course," he said. "I shall send a service bot with a parcel shortly."

It dawned on me then just how real this was. Just how stuck I was. "Thank you. Ehm... is there, like, a dinner time?"

"Eat whenever you are hungry," he said as if that should be obvious. "You will receive three meals a day at your discretion."

"When do you eat?" I asked out of curiosity.

"*When I am hungry*," he said like I was an imbecile who didn't know how eating worked.

"Okay, jeez." I put my hands up. "Great. See you around, then."

He left without ceremony, and in spite of my hunger, I stayed in the room for a while to process everything that had just happened. I had so little information, and at the same time, more than I knew what to do with. Where was his family? Why was he traveling alone? Where was he going? And most of all, what sort of mission could possibly be so important that he needed to blow up an SEA ship to protect it?

There was a bigger picture here, I just knew it. A scarier picture with a lot of unknowns. But for the moment, I took the opportunity to shower and clear my head. Showering was the only thing you still had to do in zero-g here, and the familiarity was oddly comforting. Still, I made it quick.

Then I made my way to the dining hall.

# 13

# I Really Hate the Number 32 Now for No Particular Reason

Of course, the dining hall was empty except for Lambda, who stood behind the kitchen counter and greeted me when I entered. Unlike the very practical, humanoid designs of the bridge crew, Lambda was sleek and minimalist, a smooth, round head atop a long, inverted triangle of a body.

"Good evening," he said in an even, pleasant voice. "May I interest you in something to drink?"

"And something to eat," I said, making my way to the counter. There wasn't even a stool to sit on; I just stood there as Lambda turned around to retrieve my meal from the dispenser and prepare it. In no time, he handed me a water pouch and a tray of what appeared to be falafel on rice with a side of fresh, steamed sweet potatoes. "Thank you."

"You are very welcome," he replied and proceeded to

stand there in idle mode, his LED eyes following my movements. Now I could see where Captain got the creepy staring from.

I glanced around the room until my eyes landed on the door Captain had claimed was storage. "So," I said in an upbeat tone. "What's in that room?"

"Storage," Lambda said simply.

"Of what?"

"Perishables," he replied.

*Fine. Be that way.* I tried again. "Where did this ship come from?"

"It was built by Omen-Ra Astrotechnics," said Lambda, to my surprise.

"Hm," I said as casually as possible. "On Earth, I presume?"

"Indeed."

"And, um... to where is it heading?"

Lambda paused for a moment, then said, "I'm afraid I am not at liberty to discuss it, Miss."

"Is there a final destination?"

Lambda paused again, his processor trying to determine if the question violated protocol. "There must be," he said as if he might not actually know.

As I ate my surprisingly good meal, I ran through the possibilities. Honestly, there was only one good explanation for why Captain was so secretive: someone had found a planet. But that was ridiculous. How and why would they keep something like that a secret from the SEA? The time, the science, the funding... what kind of company could sustain a project of that magnitude?

I'd never heard of Omen-Ra Astrotechnics before. I had a feeling that was not by accident.

"Who owns Omen-Ra?" I asked.

"Dr. Ahmed Omen."

The name itself did not ring a bell, but the surname sure did. "A relation of the captain's?"

"Yes. His grandfather."

I was somewhat surprised that that wasn't classified information. "And he's... back on Earth? Assuming he's alive."

I couldn't quite remember the time dilation equation (nor would it help me when I didn't know the relative speed of the ship) but if I had to guess, I'd say the *Atlantis* had probably left Earth fifty years ago. That would account for a lot, including why no one had ever seen it before.

"That, I'm afraid, I am not at liberty to discuss."

Fine. But at least I had something to work with.

I finished my dinner without further inquiry, and though I did enjoy it, I was wholly put off by the dining experience. Meals were supposed to be a happy, social time where you took a break from work-related stressors to consume delicious (or at least nutritious) food and catch up with your crewmates and family members. Not this weird, clinical, almost experimental transaction.

But I guess when you live on a ship by yourself, you don't really think about these sorts of things. This was probably normal to the captain.

I thanked my robot server and returned to the lounge, where I took stock of the so-called "educational materials" Phala had spoken of. It was basically a digital library contained in a podium-like server that stood in front of a standard retina glass screen. You could either drop files onto a tablet or project them onto the screen, but everything was in one place: thousands of titles, most of them informative or educational in some way. There were *a lot* of old texts, much of it philosophical or cultural in nature: I spotted Plato, Aristotle, the Bhagavad Gita, Confucius, and Mill, to name a few. Wow, shocker. However, it looked like at least a little bit of fiction had made the cut. Of the English-translated works, I spotted Homer, Shakespeare, and Jules Verne, which was honestly impressive.

So at least I knew I'd have something to read. But what about to watch? The film catalog bore unsurprising results: science documentaries, university lectures, and tutorials on everything from agriculture to zoology. Everything that one might need to know in a lifetime and then some.

As for me, at least I knew I'd have something to fall asleep to.

Aside from that, there were actual forms of entertainment in the room, however old-fashioned: a very compact piano in the corner, for one. And after some investigating, I found a chess set and a few other strategy-heavy board games hidden in the resin-topped coffee table. Plus, there was the 3D printer, so as long as I could get creative, I wouldn't necessarily be bored.

But was boredom really my primary concern right now? Finding ways to stay entertained felt a lot like accepting my new situation, which did not sit right with me one bit.

There was still a lot of mystery surrounding this ship, but perusing the library turned out to be less useful than interrogating a robot had been. Searching terms like "Omen-Ra" or "Atlantis" didn't result in anything helpful. The former only came up with a brief history of the company—interesting, but not exactly insightful—and the latter were just blueprints and maintenance manuals.

*Wait. Blueprints...*

I went back to the blueprint file and projected it onto the glass. I saw where I was: the lounge, just behind the bridge, which was at the nose of the ship. Behind me was the dining room, and behind that was the mysterious storage room of "perishables."

Except that on the map, it was labeled, "Cryo Room."

As in, cryonics. As in, frozen people.

*Let us just say yes*, Captain had said when I'd asked him if he were the only human aboard.

Now it made sense. Technically, he wasn't the only human aboard. Just the only conscious one.

There was no time to lose. I had to see this shit for myself, forbidden or not. I sprinted through the dining room to the locked door and started looking for clues.

"Is something the matter, Miss?" Lambda asked.

"There's people in here, isn't there?" I said, knowing full well he wouldn't confirm it.

"I'm afraid that I am—"

"Not at liberty to discuss it. Got it." I located a small touchscreen and retina scanner embedded in the wall to the left, almost hidden from the naked eye. No doubt Captain was the only one who could open the door.

But when I tapped on the screen just out of curiosity, a timer popped up.

REANIMATION TO BEGIN IN 32 YEARS, 4 MONTHS, 14 DAYS, 03 HOURS, 22 MINUTES, 39 SECONDS ATLANTEAN TIME

I watched in stunned silence as the second hand counted down, a painfully slow reminder of time's unyielding march.

Then I turned my attention back to that first number.

Thirty-two years. *Thirty-two years?!*

It had to be a planet. It had to be. Either way, wherever Captain was going, he wouldn't get there until he was fifty.

More to the point: I was stuck here until *I* was fifty.

No mother shipping way.

# 14

# Captain's Log, Year 17, Day 231, 2132 Atlantean Time

There is a girl on my ship.

This has been a tumultuous day, to say the least. The elimination of the SEA ship was not quite as seamless as I had expected. However, there is nothing I can do at this point about the escape shuttles my newly-acquired passenger claims got away, which means I must deal with the problem at hand.

I should not have let that girl onto my ship. I should not have lost my nerve and sedated her. And I certainly should not have sworn never to harm her, because I almost certainly would have had to kill her otherwise. Now my honour is on the line.

Could I truly have killed her, though? It would have been the obedient thing to do. To act in this way, while not explicitly against protocol, feels undeniably at odds with it.

I should have done it right the first time. But then why did it feel so *wrong?*

It is of no consequence. What is done is done, and the mission shall proceed on course under these new circumstances.

After I had given the girl, Miss Nepier, a tour of the *Atlantis*—and for posterity, I will confess that the pride of presenting my ship to an unfamiliar third-party outweighed any guilt I may have subsequently felt toward revealing its inner workings—I left her in the lounge and returned to the bridge. Stepping back onto the helm, I could pretend for the moment that everything had returned to the status quo.

And yet, I could not help but wonder, *What now?* Could I ignore the fact that there was another living, conscious person on my ship? That by all counts the only solution to the ethical conundrum I had put myself in was to never let her leave?

Could I live with that?

She was so outspoken, and brash, and vulgar. But she was also smart, and if her overall attitude during the tour was any indication, she seemed captivated enough by the *Atlantis* to be content living here. As long as I provided the basic necessities and did not confine her to a single room, perhaps all would be well.

It was about an hour of quiet focus later that Beta turned to me and said, "Captain, I have just been informed by Lambda that your guest has ventured a bit too close to the cryo room door. If you aim to keep her here, I suggest you go diffuse the situation before it escalates."

I acquiesced and gave Beta the helm, leaving the bridge and crossing the upper level to the dining hall.

There she was, standing in front of the door, fiddling with the keypad. She must not have heard me enter because when she turned around, she jumped as if she had been electrified. I shall now transcribe the conversation that took place as verbatim as I can recall:

Nepier: Gone-dammit! Don't sneak up on people like that!

As if I had intended to scare her. Perhaps she had poor hearing.

Me: I thought I already made it clear that that room is off-limits.

Nepier: Just when were you going to tell me that you're on a *fifty-year* mission? Or that there are *people* cryogenically frozen in storage?

I confess I was confounded. The fifty-year part I was sure she had surmised from the keypad, but the nature of the room's contents? She was too certain for it to be a mere guess.

Me: How did you figure that out so quickly?

Nepier: It's called human nature. Look it up.

That tone, I had begun to realize, was very specific. Accusatory, almost derisive. It gave me an instant headache.

Nepier: The blueprint, you ass-wipe. I looked at the ship's blueprints.

I fought to keep my expression impassive. Of course she had. She was intelligent, after all. I failed to formulate a proper response; my shock had been amplified by her inclusion of what I assumed was a colloquial insult. If so, how could she just *say* things like that, particularly to a ship's captain?

Nepier: Your little secret's out. So now, why don't you tell me who's in there?

Me: My family.

Nepier: You're joking.

Me: I would never joke about something like this.

Nepier: All of them? Mom, dad, brothers and sisters?

I hesitated.

Nepier: Come on. The cat's out of the bag.

Me: My parents, my grandfather, my three brothers, my aunt and uncle, and three cousins.

Nepier: Why are they in there?

Me: I cannot tell you. It is against protocol.

Nepier: You keep saying that, but what *is* the protocol, exactly?

I supposed there was no harm in telling her that much.

Me: No one who encounters this ship and learns of its purpose can live. Otherwise, the entire mission is in jeopardy.

Nepier: Then why didn't you kill *me*?

That was not the question I had been expecting. I did not know what to say, what I should say. Because she had begged for mercy? Because she was the first human being to ever talk to me in real-time and it had rattled me far more than I could have anticipated? Because, dare I say it, I had felt obligated to save her? Guilty if I let her die?

No, I could and I would say none of those things, not to her, not to anyone. I should not even be saying them here. But for the sake of the record, I will leave it in.

Me: I do not know.

Nepier: Great. Very comforting. I feel *so safe* right now.

There it was. That grating tone again. Irony—that was it. She meant the opposite of nearly everything she said. How singularly irritating.

Me: You should. In any case, you are protected now. By our pact.

Nepier: Right, yes, obviously. Barring that, you would've shot me in the head like some kind of sociopath.

Me: I am psychologically very stable.

Nepier: Like *hell* you are!

Me: Lower your voice, please, and listen to me.

Thankfully, she could be reasoned with. She stopped her tirade and waited, arms crossed over her chest, the picture of fierce independence. My foil in every imaginable way.

I made a decision then, one I had been contemplating since she had arrived and that I hoped would not cost me dearly in the long run.

Me: You know more than you should, and there is nothing I can do about that now. That is, assuming you will accept my proposition.

Nepier: Which is?

Me: Become part of the mission in an official capacity. In return, I will be able to answer any questions you may have, starting with what the mission is.

Nepier: It's a planet, isn't it? You're going to a planet.

I was too confounded by her unprecedented powers of perception to formulate a proper response in time. Unfortunately, my silence spoke volumes.

Nepier: Yeah, because it's not like it's totally obvious.

Me: Was it obvious?

Nepier: Extremely.

Me: I see.

Nepier: Where is it?

Me: It is the third planet in the Zion system. A fifty-year journey. My grandfather and his team of scientists discovered the wormhole and, subsequently, the solar system it connected us to. They spent decades planning and developing the technology necessary to get to it. This planet is in the habitable zone—terraformable by every test in the book. All that is left is to get to it.

Nepier: Seems a little too good to be true, don't you think?

Me: The science is absolute.

Nepier: No one has been able to successfully *find* a terraformable planet yet, let alone get to it. And what's the plan once you're there, huh? How are you gonna populate it? In case you didn't notice, you've got a group of blood relations in there. Don't you know anything about genetics?

Me: It is not like that. Yes, there is a plan, but even I do not know the full extent of it yet. All I know is that every possible angle has been considered. Every detail thought out. Yes, my family will colonize that planet. They will be the start of an entirely new race of people. That is my purpose. To ferry them there. To birth a new civilization free from the oppression of Earth.

She stared at me not in admiration, but in halted disgust.

Nepier: You can't do that.

Me: It has been done. It is done. You are bearing witness to it. Think about the privilege you have been granted. You would be the first woman to ever step foot on a terraformed planet. That has to offer some incentive.

Nepier: Sure, *thirty-two* years from now. What am I supposed to do in the meantime? I mean, what if we hate each other? You wanna live aboard a ship with a person you can't stand?

*That* was her primary concern?

Me: Do you hate me now?

Nepier: At the moment? Something kinda close to it!

I know it should not have stung, but I suppose it is indicative of human nature to desire acceptance, even from a stranger.

Me: That is rather unfortunate. I do not hate you.

Nepier: Really? You like me, then?

Me: I am indifferent toward you.

Nepier: Wow, what a compliment!

If my prior evaluations of her speech patterns were to be relied upon, she did not, in fact, take it as a compliment.

Me: Better than unjustified hatred, wouldn't you say?

Nepier: Unjustified? In what way is my hatred unjustified?

Me: Very well. Think what you want of me. Just know I do not harbour the same disregard toward you.

Nepier: Not yet, maybe. But trust me, Captain, I can make you hate me. I can make you wish you'd never met me.

The look she gave me sent an involuntary chill up my spine.

Me: Not exactly the most productive tactic, considering the situation we find ourselves in.

Nepier: The situation you've put us in, you mean.

Me: Let us not get caught up in technicalities, Miss Nepier. Wouldn't you say that my proposition is fair?

Nepier: Define "fair."

Me: It functions within a set of predetermined guidelines of conduct. It neither contradicts my protocols nor the pact we made with each other, and is mutually beneficial for both parties. I.e., "fair."

She groaned, a wholly aggravating reaction to doing exactly as she had asked.

Nepier: How is it mutually beneficial for you?

That was a very good question, actually. How was it beneficial for me? Companionship, I supposed? She was hardly an amiable companion now, though when I had given her a tour of the ship, she had seemed pleasant enough. Could she serve a function aboard the *Atlantis*? I didn't need an engineering assistant, but...

Nepier: Oh, no. No, no, no, no, no. No. *No.* This is way too convenient for you. Isn't it? You never expected to meet another human until you were fifty, let alone a female human.

Me: What in God's name are you talking about?

Why was she going on as if I'd somehow planned this? As if I'd wanted the responsibility of looking after another living being?

Nepier: What are you talking about?

Me: You asked how it would be mutually beneficial for

me. I confess that I had not given it much thought. This ship was designed to provide me with optimal fulfilment. In other words, I have everything I need.

The look she gave me was somewhere between incredulity and terror. What had I said now?

Me: With that said, I do think it could be beneficial to have another set of human eyes aboard. It's not necessary, but it wouldn't be harmful, either. In any case, I am just trying to make the best of an unexpected situation.

Nepier: I'm an unaccounted-for variable.

Me: Yes. And this is the solution.

Nepier: Do I have any other option?

Me: Death.

She looked at me in alarm, and I realized I might have been too glib.

Me: You asked. But I already promised not to harm you on this ship, so you would have to permit me.

Nepier: No, I want to live. This is just... ugh, never mind. You wouldn't understand.

After that, she asked if she could have some time to think about it, and although the request was futile, I obliged. For, despite her claim that I wouldn't understand, I felt as though on some level, I might. It was abundantly clear that this had not been part of her plan. She had a family. She had a future. She had not asked for this.

But there was nothing I could do about that now. I would do everything in my power to keep her comfortable and content, but the one thing I could never do was let her leave.

# 15

# The Art of Being a Molecule in a Low-Temperature Environment

I don't know what to do. I thought I'd be able to sleep on it, but I did a lot of rolling around and fretting instead. I guess that was to be expected in a new environment like this, not to mention how bizarre the circumstances were.

Captain had caught me snooping around in the dining room and after a bit of prodding, I finally got him to come clean: there were people in that storage room, and he was going to a planet, but the rest of it was so bizarre I could hardly comprehend it. What I did know is that he'd made me a proposition to become part of his mission, and while I hadn't exactly agreed to it, I hadn't *not* agreed, either.

Instead, I'd bailed out with, "This is a lot of information to process, and it's been a long day. Can I sleep on it?"

Which is how I found myself here, not sleeping.

Besides, as he'd so succinctly pointed out, it didn't really matter whether I agreed to it or not; I was stuck here regardless. I guess I could say it was *polite* of him to give me the *illusion* of a choice in this scenario, and I guess I could say I wanted to exercise the *illusion* of free will by thinking about it.

But it still didn't make the situation any less effed up.

*Thirty-two whole years.* Sure, most of us expected to spend a good portion of our lives exploring uncharted areas of deep space, but not like this. And after all was said and done, I'd live the rest of my life on some bygone planet (assuming it was as habitable as Captain claimed it was, which I doubted to the max). I'd never see my parents or sister again. My friends and colleagues. Kiss them goodbye.

Instead, I'd have a ship full of androids, some human popsicles, and a humorless captain who seemed to think this was an elegant solution.

The fact that he was a boy did not escape me. But when I imagined being with someone for the rest of my life, this was not what I had in mind. As a spacer, the expectation was that you still get to choose, even if the pickings are slim. But seriously, what if we did hate each other? Or only ended up liking each other because there was no one else around and we were lonely?

That did not sound very romantic to me, no sir. It sounded sad and desperate.

Still, it was an infinitely better alternative to dying.

At least I had that part worked out: death was not going to be my escape. Which meant escape would have to be my escape. I didn't know how, I didn't know when, but as I lay awake in distress, I decided this much: I was not going to spend the prime of my life trapped here, sharing a bathroom with a guy whose social ineptitude was, quite frankly, transcendent.

Of course, I couldn't tell Captain that. Which meant I'd have to lie to his face and tell him I accepted his proposal instead.

In the morning, there was no formal breakfast. I went to the dining hall alone and received my meal from Lambda. It was some kind of protein bar—not bad, actually—and a hot cup of tea. A surprisingly good cup of tea, as a matter of fact. At least I had that much to look forward to.

I took Captain's sage advice to "maintain optimal health" and explored the gym. After messing around with the equipment, I opted for the simple treadmill and went on a jog to clear my head. Like with most modern treadmills, you had the option of putting on a VR headset and simulating a real environment, but I decided I'd rather get used to my actual reality first. Still, I had to wonder what kind of mental image the captain had of off-ship locations.

Workout complete, I went back to the room to freshen up, and by then it was lunchtime, so I took my meal alone—again—and hung out in the lounge, reading and messing around with the piano. I supposed I could go bother Captain on the bridge if I wanted to, but he had more or less made it clear that he'd rather not be disturbed. And besides, I was still put out about the whole fifty-year mission thing.

I expected him to find me at some point and ask for

my answer to his question. At around fifteen hundred, he finally entered the lounge, faltering when he saw me on the couch as if he'd forgotten he wasn't alone. Then he continued across the room to the dining room without so much as a nod of acknowledgment.

*Lunchtime?* I padded silently to the doorway of the dining room and peered in.

"Good afternoon, Captain," Lambda said cheerily.

"Greetings, Lambda," Captain answered flatly, stopping in front of the cryo room door. He tapped the keypad once, twice, and then a third time. He must be checking up on them, making sure everything looked normal. Did he ever go inside the room, I wondered? Could he go inside?

I sprinted back to the lounge before he could turn around and catch me, splaying myself as naturally as possible over the couch as he crossed the room without a word and returned to the bridge.

So this was how it was gonna be, huh? Well, I'm sure seventeen years in one place had formed a pretty rigid routine. God forbid I disrupt that in any way.

The next time I saw Captain was at twenty hundred, well after dinnertime. This time, at least, he didn't appear determined to ignore me.

Stopping in front of the couch where I lay watching a nature documentary on the tablet, he put his arms behind his back and said in the most unnatural way possible, "Hello."

"Why, hello," I said candidly as if we did this every day. "How was your day?"

He stared at me like he didn't know how to answer. I

doubted he'd ever been asked such a mundane question before. "Fine," he managed. "And yours?"

"Very chill," I said with a nod. Yeah, this was awkward as hell.

"I keep the ship cold," he said. "If you need more insulated clothing—"

I laughed, stopping him dead in his tracks. "I don't mean it literally. I mean, it is cold, but I'm comfortable. 'Chill' is a slang word. An old one. It means relaxed. Calm. Chill."

"Like how molecules move slower in low-temperature environments," he said.

"Sure," I said. Definitely not the origin of the word, but I was not in the mood to give him a semantics lesson.

"So, cold."

"Oh my God," I said, sitting up. "I didn't realize this is what happens when a person doesn't grow up around humans. Do I even speak English to you, or is it like talking to a caveman?"

"I can understand you perfectly fine, despite your improper grammar and syntax," he said, pinching his nose in what I gathered was a gesture of exasperation.

I scoffed. "Ouch. I got all As in English, I'll have you know. I got all As, period. Okay, maybe a couple Bs, but they were really hard classes and the professor was a dick."

"Is that another 'slang word'? Dick?" he asked, completely straight-faced.

Oh my freaking gosh. I couldn't believe this kid. "If you don't already know, it's not going to help you now."

To my relief, he decided now was the time to change the subject. "So, have you thought about my proposal?"

"Yes," I said, standing, ready to launch into my rehearsed speech. "And I'm prepared to accept. On one condition."

He folded his arms across his chest. "And what would that be?"

"That I can send a transmission to my family. Just to tell them I'm alive. I won't mention you, or the mission, or anything incriminating. You can even proofread the message if you want. I just want them to know I'm not dead, even if they can never see me again."

After a brief pause, he said, "Wouldn't it be better for them if they presumed you to be dead, so they could mourn and move on, versus always holding onto some futile hope that they might see you again when they never will? Wouldn't one cause them more pain than the other, in the long term?"

I opened my mouth, then closed it. "That's really morbid."

"It's utilitarian."

"Well, I'm not utilitarian, I'm human. If you were never going to see the people you loved most in the galaxy again, wouldn't you want to at least say goodbye?"

To my surprise, the question actually had an effect on him: he looked wildly uncomfortable, pained, even. It took him a full breath cycle to plaster that blank, stoic expression of his back on.

"I will take it into consideration," he finally said.

"Thank you," I said.

He didn't say "you're welcome" like a normal person

would. In fact, he didn't seem to know how to react to gratitude at all. Instead, he left the lounge the way he'd come.

I guess that was it. Again, it wasn't so much an agreement as it was a tentative negotiation. Which was fine with me, because I still didn't want to commit to this whole thirty-two-year mission thing. The longer I could keep us in a gray area, the longer I had to figure out a way out of this.

And if by some miracle he did agree to let me record a transmission to my family, you better believe I'd find a way to leave a coded message.

The next few days were basically identical to the first, and while on the one hand, it was nice to have no obligations whatsoever, it started to get old fast. I loved to read and I enjoyed exercise, but I also loved to *actually do shit.*

When I get bored, I get restless and talkative. And while I'd gladly befriended Lambda and his janitorial counterpart, Kappa (small and squat like a trash can with a head), there was only so much companionship a task bot could offer, even one with an intuitive response driver.

I'd even visited Phala downstairs, but just like when I'd first woken up, she didn't seem inclined to talk about anything that wasn't medical-related. Uncanny as she was, she still behaved a bit like an NPC in a video game, spouting out programmed responses and dodging off-topic questions with platitudes.

On the plus side, I was able to acquire feminine products without having to bring it up to Captain. Though part of me would have just for the sheer joy of seeing him flustered.

Speaking of my distinguished host, he hadn't been kidding when he'd said I'd barely see him. Since our little tête-à-tête in the lounge, he'd become as elusive as a cryptid. In fact, it was almost as if he actively avoided me. Couldn't imagine why.

I tried to guess when his meal times were but he was never in the dining room when I was. I tried to guess where he slept but the only place that made sense was in the lounge, and he was seldom ever in the lounge. He would pass through once in the morning and again in the afternoon with a curt hello, check on the cryo room, and go back to the bridge. He never went inside, just looked at the keypad.

I know because I continued to follow him and got snapped at when I was caught.

God, he was such a grump.

Surely, the man had to take a break at some point, right? He was human... right?

I supposed the monotony of his routine was a comfort to him, as it was for so many of us deep space explorers. One task at a time, that was how most of us lived. Which was all well and good when you had a daily to-do list you had to run through and an end goal to work toward. Not to mention, generally, there was a crew of like-minded individuals around you, helping you stay sane.

I had none of those things.

Day by day, I grew more restless and more socially starved. Day by day, I experienced the same level of robotic indifference from my host. Was he just going to pretend I wasn't there for the rest of forever? Well, not only was that insulting, but it was also the worst punishment you could give a near-textbook extrovert.

Which would explain why, about a week into this "unprecedented situation," I finally snapped.

# 16

# My Dinner With Omen

It was dinnertime. Another meal eaten alone at a counter with no stools and nothing but a robot waiter for company. Another day with barely any human interaction. How did Captain stand it?

"Can I ask you a question?" I asked Lambda, who wiped down the counter like a bartender in an old movie.

"You may, though my answers may be limited," he said. His usual response.

"Fair enough. When does Captain eat?" It was a wonder I hadn't thought to ask this question before now, but truth be told, I'd expected to catch him in the act.

"His eating schedule is irregular," said Lambda. "He often takes his meals late at night or early in the morning."

"So he's a night owl? But if he works all day, when does he sleep?" I mused to myself.

"That I am not sure of. You would have to ask Phala."

Fat chance of that. "*Where* does Captain eat?" I asked, pivoting back to food.

"He often eats on the bridge," said Lambda. "Or sometimes standing here at the counter, as you are."

"Hm. Very efficient of him. Was this ever a proper dining room?"

"Yes. There used to be a table and chairs, but they were taken away several years ago and recycled back into Iota."

"Why?"

"I suppose because they were seldom in use."

Figures. I looked off to the side and noticed the clock on the wall above the cryo room door. Nineteen forty-four. "Has Captain eaten dinner yet?"

"His last meal was at approximately zero five thirty-five this morning."

My eyes went wide. "He hasn't eaten all day? Can I bring him his dinner?"

"We are not required to bring the captain sustenance unless explicitly requested."

"Not required, but still allowed?"

"Yes."

"And you have to obey a direct order from a human, correct?"

"Yes."

"Well, I would like you to prepare Captain's dinner now, please."

"Of course." Wow, that was easy. Within a few moments, Lambda set down a tray identical to mine of reconstituted bean and vegetable soup.

I picked up both trays and headed toward the door. "Thank you, Lambda. I appreciate it."

I really didn't know what I was thinking, taking such liberties with a guy who was somehow both my captor and my savior. But I couldn't keep living like a ghost, and if I were being honest, I really hadn't done much to try to curry his favor. Maybe if I got him to come out of his shell, he would actually let me send the transmission. I got the sense he hadn't done much "thinking about it" since our initial conversation.

And while I'd considered making good on my word to become a menace, I'd ultimately decided that the risks involved were not worth any potential reward. That left only one option: I had to use my abundance of charm to get through to this guy.

Mom always said that the fastest way to a man's heart was through his stomach. Much as it seemed unlikely, Captain was, indeed, a human man. Better yet, he was a boy. And boys were always hungry.

My heart pounded as I crossed the landing to the bridge—it felt like breaking an unspoken rule. What if I really wasn't supposed to be here?

Captain's back was to me at the helm, as were the rest of the crew's, including Beta, who stood between the helm and the control center. Soft, lyrical beeps came from different areas of the console and the endless expanse stretched to infinity beyond the wide viewscreen windows. I felt a little like a fish in a bowl, but it was also breathtaking—most bridges weren't this quiet or this open.

I wasn't sure how to announce myself, so I just stood there and cleared my throat in what I hoped was an inconspicuous way.

Captain turned, saw me, and did a double-take. "What are you doing here?" he said, which instantly made me second-guess my master plan. He zeroed in on the trays in my hands. "What is that?"

"I brought you dinner," I said, feeling less confident now that it was obvious I'd startled him. Beta had turned to look at me too, and while he said nothing, his expression seemed to confirm that I'd intruded—but maybe that was just his resting face. "I was talking to Lambda, and he said you hadn't eaten since this morning, so... since I was already eating dinner, I thought..."

"I do not need you to dictate my meal schedule," Captain said brusquely. "I told you, I eat when I am hungry."

I tried to remain flippant as I said, "Yeah, but it's been over fourteen hours. You must be hungry. I mean, you seem like the kind of person who gets hyper-fixated on work and forgets to eat. I live with one of those. They have to be reminded. Even forced, sometimes." I chuckled, though it came out more nervous than I would've liked.

"I get reminders," he said sternly. "There is an entire OS dedicated to making sure I take care of myself. I believe you have met her already. I do not need you."

That did it. I was trying to be nice, and he insisted on being an asshole. And the irony of admitting he didn't need me when it was obvious he had no intention of letting me leave? It was beyond insulting.

I had a few thoughts run through my head then: throw the tray on the ground, throw it in his face, leave in a huff—but I was still determined to keep my cool, and a meltdown was not going to help him see my side of things.

"Very well," I said in a saccharine tone. "I'll just eat your portion for you, then. Thank you for the extra serving. You're too gracious, Captain."

With that, I turned toward the exit.

"Wait," said Captain, deep reluctance coloring his voice. "You can't do that."

I turned back around. "Can't I? If you're not gonna eat it, it's going to go to waste."

He beckoned me over to the helm with two fingers. But seeing as though I wasn't into being summoned like a dog, I acted like I didn't know what he meant.

He beckoned harder.

"Use your big boy words," I said sweetly.

Frustrated, he said, "Will you come here, please? I would rather not leave the helm right now."

Finally, I approached him. "Was that so hard?" I asked.

"You may leave the tray," he said. One would think I'd just beat him in a VR game, he sounded so defeated. "But for future reference, I would prefer it if you did not deign to assume what I want and when."

"And I'd prefer it if you put some mother shipping chairs in the dining room," I said, heated by his pretension. "I hate eating alone as it is, but having to eat standing up on top of it? It's just sad."

His brows knit together in confusion. Or irritation. It was difficult to tell. "Eating alone?"

His question forced me to introspect. Chairs weren't really the issue here at all, were they? After all, if I wanted to sit, I could eat in the lounge (and I had, several times). But how pathetic would it be to ask him to eat with me? To interact with me, period? After all, did I really want his company?

Nevertheless, I said, "Yeah. I've had to eat every meal alone since I've been here. And don't tell me robots count, because they don't. I mean, it's better than nothing, but I don't think you understand. I've always been surrounded by people at mealtimes. It's just... really depressing to be alone. It reminds me how far away they are."

I was getting choked up just thinking about it. I had to get out of there before I actually started crying; I didn't think Captain was ready for such an unbridled show of emotion. His circuits would surely overload.

And yet I could swear his expression softened, if only by a fraction. Even if he had no frame of reference for this sort of thing, he had to have genuine empathy in there somewhere, right? That's what had compelled him to save my life in the first place... right?

"Chairs," he finally said. "And a table, I take it?"

"Even just a couple of bar stools would be stellar."

He nodded once in his utilitarian way. "I will see what I can do."

I smiled and said, "Thank you." And then, feeling emboldened by this small victory, I added, "And I'd like a job."

His brow furrowed again. "A job?"

"When I first got here, you said something about problem-solving?"

He shifted on the stand. "Yes, but currently there aren't

any problems to solve. I hope you understand that this ship was not designed for two human crewmembers to be necessary. All other roles are filled, rendering your primary position as 'passenger.'"

Resident ghost, more like. "Yes, I get that. But I still need something to do. Ennui is extremely dangerous to spacers, and space... it does things to people. But I'm sure you knew that."

"I do not experience ennui," he said, a bit haughtily.

"Yes, because you have a job," I said, thrusting my hand toward the dais. "Unlike me, you get to be up here all day, working. This is not a pleasure cruise for me. This is... a situation."

He paused, then said, "You are not barred from the bridge. You may observe whenever you would like, provided you are not a distraction."

Relieved as I was to learn that, this was still him we were talking about. "Is that your way of saying I have to be quiet?"

"Yes."

I made a buzzer sound. "Pass. That's boring."

He actually had the gall to look offended.

"What, do you really expect me to be content just watching you breathe for the foreseeable future?" I said. "Tell me, does that sound fun to you?"

"What does fun have to do with it?"

"What does—" I scoffed. "Okay, then. Does that sound *productive* to you, Mr. Utility? Huh? Because it sounds like if I can't be useful, then I'm a waste of oxygen. Jettison me into oblivion, why don't you?"

He looked at me quizzically, as if trying to figure out if

I were serious. I felt a twinge of fear. What if he thought I was? Then he looked straight ahead and said, "Identify a job that you can do that isn't superfluous, and I will assign it to you."

"Thank you," I said pointedly. "And you're welcome, by the way, for dinner."

"I don't recall ever saying 'thank you,'" he said in a clinical tone.

I groaned and walked away, once again amazed at his utter lack of social skills. But I guess that's what happens when you learn human behavior from non-human entities.

I paused in the foyer, a really stupid idea for a job forming in my head. I didn't turn back, though. I spent the rest of the evening pondering the idea's relative stupidity until I'd made my decision, and then I went to sleep.

When I woke up the next morning, I still felt pretty okay with my stupid idea. I did a light workout and headed to breakfast, where, upon entering the dining room, I was surprised to find a table with two chairs and two barstools set up in the once-depressingly empty room.

But even more surprising than that was the person sitting at the table.

"Captain," I said.

"Good morning, Miss Nepier," he said. He was eating. And drinking tea. I could kiss him. He was a real boy! "Would you care to join me?"

"Um, sure," I said, sliding into the chair across from him. Lambda brought my breakfast promptly, which was some sort of rice pudding. Not bad, actually. "Thank you, for doing this. It means a lot."

He nodded once but said nothing, and we lapsed into a semi-comfortable silence as we ate our breakfasts. I considered myself a pretty fast eater but I quickly realized Captain had me beat—no wonder I'd never seen him eat before, he ate at the speed of sound.

This was as good a time as ever to pitch my idea. "So, I think I've found a job."

He stopped in his tracks, his spoon suspended midair as if someone had hit a kill switch on his arm. "Oh? And what is it?"

"Teacher."

He canted his head. "I don't need a teacher. I have already surpassed my regular schooling."

"Not for normal subjects," I said, tapping my spoon against the edge of the tray. "I'm sure you know how to read and all that. I mean..." I sighed. How did I put this lightly? "The nuances of society."

He went back to his food, disinterested. "And why would I need to know that?"

"Because we're a society now," I said. "It's not just you anymore. You have to navigate life with another person, i.e., me. And no offense, but you haven't exactly had much experience interacting with another human being."

He put his silverware down and laced his fingers together in that irritating, intellectual way of his. "I don't think two people aboard a ship counts as a society."

Oh, a wise guy, huh? Two could play at that game. "Lambda, what is the definition of 'society'?"

"Society," said Lambda from behind the counter. "The aggregate of people living together in organized communities with shared laws, traditions, and values."

"And what does 'aggregate' mean?"

"Aggregate," said Lambda. "Formed by adding together two or more amounts; total."

"A total is more than one," I said. "Actually, technically, in math, a total can still be one—or less than one—but in any case, two counts as a society. We're in an organized community—your ship—and we more or less share the same laws by way of our pact. So, yeah, we're a society. Have I convinced you, Captain?"

"Very well, you have convinced me on a technicality. You are saying my manners aren't adequate? Have I been uncivil toward you?"

I rolled my eyes. "Not on purpose, no. But there's a difference between being polite because it's proper and being polite because it's kind."

"You are saying I'm not kind? Is granting your request for dining room furniture not considered a kind gesture to you?"

I winced inwardly. It did sound a little ungrateful—obviously, this was him trying. But how could I make him understand? "No, I mean, yes, it is a kind gesture. And I do appreciate it. But it wouldn't have occurred to you if I hadn't brought it up. You lack the cultural context to make that inference. Basically, you don't exactly... think like a normal human being should."

Something flashed in his eyes, an indignation I had

begun to recognize as his knee-jerk reaction to criticism. I doubted he'd ever had anyone tell him he was anything other than the most special boy in the whole wide world.

Looks like I'd just burst that egocentric bubble, and I was about to feel the acid rain.

"Well, how should a so-called normal human being think?" Captain said pointedly. "Impulsively? Selfishly? Irrationally? Because if that's what you expect from me, then I can assure you I would rather err on the side of being 'too polite' or 'too proper' than succumb to the base instincts you seem to value."

A surge of heat rose within me and what was left of my reservations melted away. "Let's examine that claim, shall we?" I said. "In your view, a 'normal human being' is impulsive, selfish, and irrational. Fair. But you're saying you're not any of those things. Okay. And yet, you saved me from the vacuum, which was impulsive," I counted on my fingers, "you won't let me contact my family to tell them I'm alive, which is selfish, and you expect me to be content on board this ship for the next thirty-two years without question, which is irrational." I forced myself to maintain eye contact. "So I stand corrected. You are a normal human being by your estimation, Captain. What you lack is the self-awareness."

For a long, cold moment, he stared at me as if I'd just spoken another language, one he barely understood. Doubts began to creep in past my blazing wall of righteous boldness. He'd been congenial so far, but what if he had a temper? What if he lacked more humanity than I thought?

What if he really could jettison me into oblivion?

I regret to say I flinched when he finally moved. But it wasn't to seize me or retaliate; he simply got up from the table in a rush and left the dining room. He didn't come back. Lambda cleared his place and it was like he was never there.

"Oh my God," I said. "I pissed him off."

*Oh my God*, I thought. *I was right, and he knows it.*

# Putting the "Fun" in "Fundamentals of Humanity"

Generous person that I am, I decided to give Captain some space for the rest of the day. I wasn't sure what to expect from him if I tried to confront him and part of me didn't want to find out. So instead of going to the bridge like I'd planned, I stayed in the lounge and read the afternoon away.

I also found the music library, which, unsurprisingly, consisted mostly of classical albums. Not that I was complaining; as much as I missed modern music, I still loved me some Bach and Beethoven. At least Captain (or, perhaps, his predecessors) had good taste.

I broke for lunch, and when I came back, I was surprised to find Captain standing in the center of the room, his hands behind his back.

"At ease," I said dryly.

"I hoped I would find you here," he said and motioned for me to take a seat. "We need to talk."

I sighed and sat down on the couch. He sat in the armchair. "It's about what I said this morning, I know. I didn't mean to insult you. I just—"

He held up a hand. "I accept."

"You accept... what?"

"Your offer. To teach me about society." He watched me carefully. "Upon further reflection, I realized that while I have all the technical knowledge necessary to help colonize our future home, I lack the ability to put said knowledge into practice. Now, of course, this had been taken into account before my mission began, but nowhere in my mission parameters does it say I cannot become more capable than I already am. In short, you have presented me with a rare opportunity to become ahead of the curve. Like I said, I have exhausted all my formal schooling, but that does not mean I have lost my desire to learn."

My mouth hung open. Ambitious little bugger. "So... you... actually want me to teach you?"

He blinked. "Is that not what I just said? I thought you were smart."

"Okay." I brought my palms down on my thighs. "If this is happening, then we're gonna have to set some ground rules."

Now he looked concerned. "Just because you are being promoted to 'tutor' does not mean you suddenly hold any kind of authority over me."

"I'm not exercising authority as a teacher, I'm exercising authority as a human being." I watched his brows knit together. "Lesson number one: 'treat others as you would like to be treated.'"

"A gross oversimplification of countless philosophical precepts, but very well."

"Ugh, and stop being so pretentious. I don't care how much philosophy you know, and neither will anyone else."

"How does being well-educated make me pretentious?"

I rubbed my temples. It felt like I was explaining this to a child. In a way, I was. "People don't like being talked down to. It's insulting because it's saying you're better than them."

"What if I am better than them?" He said this with absolute sincerity. He believed it. Heck, he'd probably been taught it all his life, and it wasn't as if there was anyone around to knock him down a peg.

"Even if you have certain... proficiencies, it doesn't mean you have to lord it over people. Humility is one of the most valuable qualities in society, and probably one of the most rare."

"'Rarest,'" he corrected.

"See, this is what I'm talking about!" I groaned. "Let's start over. Rule number one: be nice. How about that? Does that compute?"

"Yes, it 'computes,'" he said flatly.

"Great. Rule number two: participate. Even if you don't agree with my teaching methods, which I'm sure you won't. I'll give you one free pass to skip a lesson per month, but that's it, bucko."

"This is getting increasingly more totalitarian."

I ignored him. "Those are the only two rules. Unless you'd like more?"

"That will suffice, thank you. On their own it's more than enough."

"Remember that you agreed to this. I didn't make you do anything."

"Yes," he said. "I am aware."

There was a strange pause after that.

"So when do we begin?" he asked.

"When are you off-duty?" I countered.

He checked his wristband. "I am never off-duty, but my next break is at seventeen hundred. I can expedite greenhouse duty and meet you by half past."

*So that's when he checks the greenhouse.* "Perfect. That gives me more than enough time to prepare. We'll start this evening."

"Very well," he said formally. "I'm looking forward to it. Where should we meet?"

Since I didn't have a lesson plan yet, I was about to tell him to meet me here, but then, genius struck. "Meet me on the ground-level corridor."

He gave me an odd look, but nonetheless, he agreed and left the lounge, apparently to return to the bridge. I, on the other hand, headed downstairs to pay a visit to Iota.

"Welcome to Human 101," I said when Captain exited the greenhouse to join me in the corridor, looking mildly confused.

"What an odd place to convene for a first lesson," he said, hands behind his back. "Are you trying to prove something by being unconventional?"

"Not at all," I said. "This is just the best place for this." I held up the object I had printed for today's lesson: a rubber ball roughly the size of a tennis ball. It had a small, steel core so that it would react with the artificial gravity. I'd been testing it all afternoon with great success.

"A ball," he said flatly. "We are playing children's games?"

"Wall ball," I announced triumphantly. "The most basic and universal of spacer boredom-crushers. The object is simple: bounce the ball against the wall to the other player. If they don't catch it, it's a point for you. We will start with one-bounce wall ball. Choose your position."

"I do not understand," he said. "How is this a lesson?"

"It's fun," I said. "Today's lesson is about fun. The most *fun*damental of human attributes. Ha! See what I did there?"

"I disagree."

I bounced the ball impatiently, a little chapped that he hadn't acknowledged my pun. "Do you not want to participate? Think very carefully before you use your pass. This is the least of what I can do."

"Fine," he huffed. "We will play your little game."

"Great." We spread out along the wall and I began by bouncing it to him. He caught it with ease. The challenge wasn't really the catching part; it was carrying on a conversation as you played. That was the real lesson, but he hadn't earned the right to know yet. "So, when you saw the ball, you recognized it as a children's game. Does that imply you played them, growing up?"

He bounced the ball back to me. "More or less. To learn fine and gross motor skills or strengthen cognitive development. But I long surpassed the need for them."

"No video games for you, then?" I bounced it back to him.

"Video games?"

"Never mind. So, what do you do for fun, then?"

"Nothing. 'Fun' is not conducive to the mission."

I rolled my eyes as the ball came back to me. "Growing your own produce is pretty fun, wouldn't you say?"

He paused when he caught the ball. "It's not for my leisure," he said pointedly. "It's a necessity. Even more so now that you're here."

"Right. Well, at least you'll know how to grow food on your alleged new planet."

"It's not alleged. I told you—the evidence is concrete."

"You know, they used to say that about a lot of things. Like the Earth being flat."

"Be as skeptical as you want. That doesn't change the facts."

"Oh, a true believer. Does this miracle planet of yours even have a name?"

"In English, it translates to 'New Eden.'"

I stopped with the ball in my hand. "You've got to be kidding me."

He turned toward me. "Why are you always under the impression that I am joking?"

"Eden? Really? You do know what happened to Eden, don't you? In the Bible?"

"Yes, but that was then. This is now."

"Sure, sure. Well, when you get to this Exo-Paradise of yours, be sure to steer clear of any snakes or particularly enticing fruit trees."

"There won't be any—oh, I see. How poetic of you."

"Okay," I said with a sigh, eager to change the subject, "how about we move on to two-bounce?"

"Let me guess: two bounces," he said wryly. So close to humor!

"You are correct, good sir," I said. "We'll want to stand facing each other this time. Two-bounce takes a little more finesse since you'll be bouncing it from either wall to wall or floor to ceiling. Ready?"

He nodded, and the game commenced. This time, we began scoring points on each other. The game was tied 3-3 when Captain asked, "What does the winner receive?"

Oh ho, so he was competitive. This game was turning out to be profitable after all. "Bragging rights," I said.

"That's not very moral," he replied.

"Oh, bah. An extra ration, then," I suggested.

"That's not very wise."

"Okay then, Captain, what would you consider a worthy prize?"

"Winner leads the next lesson," he said.

I huffed. So he was used to being in control. That was valuable information, if not a bit concerning. "Doesn't that defeat the purpose of me being your teacher? I mean, no offense, but what could you possibly teach me about being human?"

"We have years to complete my training," he said, a

reminder that made my stomach bottom out. "But there are plenty of things I know that you do not. I wouldn't impede on your curriculum; I'd come up with my own subject matter."

"You want to teach me things you know?" I considered it. Yes, technically, in his mind, we weren't in any sort of rush. In my mind, the more I took an interest in him, the more likely he was to let his guard down, which increased my chances of finding a way to get the heck out of here.

But I couldn't just be content with my ulterior motives, could I? I also couldn't help but put myself in his shoes and recognize that he'd never been able to share anything about his life with anyone before. If he had a bunch of knowledge stored in that wacky brain of his, he was probably dying to talk about it, just like he'd been dying to show his ship to someone. And hey, I was technically still a student. I could stand to learn more stuff about stuff. Learning is fun.

Then it hit me: *Learning is fun. This is his idea of fun. He's passed the lesson!*

I smiled. "You've got yourself a deal."

The game continued. I may have let him win, just to see him get excited about something. It was restrained and stoic, but he radiated pride as we shook hands in a show of good sportsmanship.

"Same time tomorrow, meet me in the docking bay," he said.

"Aye aye, Captain," I said.

Okay, this could be interesting.

# 18

# This Magic Moment, When We're Inches From the Void

Captain's idea of a lesson plan was not, as I had expected, a boring lecture on the "concrete evidence" of New Eden's habitability or the magnitude of his glorious mission. It was an EVA.

"No way," I said. "You can leave the ship?"

"Of course," he said. "I have to be able to do so in case there is something wrong with the exterior, such as a space object colliding with it in transit."

"Has it happened before?" In seventeen years, the chances weren't astronomical.

"Several times, though they were all minor incidents."

I gaped. "Were you scared?"

"I was ten years old the first time."

I took that as a yes. "I see. So is there anything wrong today?"

"No," he said. "Once a month, I have to do a routine

inspection of the hull to ensure everything is still in good working order. In the past, it has taken me four hours by myself to complete. I am hoping that with your help, we can cut that time in half."

I gaped again. "How inclusive of you, Captain! Or are you just taking advantage of free labor?"

"You said you wanted a job."

I smirked. "I did say that, didn't I? But why not have an android help you?"

"Androids conduct regular inspections on a weekly basis. Usually Beta does it himself. I am required to do so without technological help. Perhaps for the same reason I need to be captain at all."

"Human intuition," I said. "But I don't know anything about this ship, other than what you've told me."

"That is perfectly fine. Today will be my chance to teach you. It is still a lesson, after all."

"Ah. Trial by fire. I accept."

"In the future, we can split the work, but today I do not expect it to take any less time than normal. In fact, it will probably take more. I estimate five to six hours."

"Late-nighter," I said. "Should've told me. I would've caffeined up."

He reached into his breast pocket and handed me a pill.

"What is that?" I asked tentatively.

"Ginseng and green coffee extract," he said. "If you're tired, it should help."

"Is this how you stay awake on the bridge?" I inquired, taking the pill.

He didn't answer as he led me to the EVA airlock,

located to the left of the ship airlock through which I'd originally entered. The EVA airlock had an inner chamber for suiting up and an outer chamber that opened up to space. Upon entering the inner chamber, I was perplexed to see two EVA suits hanging on the wall. Convenient much?

"A spare," Captain said as if reading my thoughts. "In case I damage mine before I have finished a task."

"Ah. I see." *Duh.*

"You have put one of these on before, I gather?"

"Of course I have," I said. "But this looks... very different." It was much sleeker than the EVA suits I'd trained in. Not quite a skintight suit—no one had perfected that design yet—but way less bulk than I thought would be possible. They were dark blue like our uniforms with reflective, aqua blue lines following the major seams on the arms, legs, and torso. The helmet was only slightly bigger than a motorcycle helmet, shaped in the likeness of a head as opposed to the round, bulbous designs we all know and love. "You're sure it's safe?"

"Of course it's safe," he said as he took off his gravity suit. His inner layer consisted of a gray, fitted t-shirt and black tights. It felt strange, almost intimate, to be able to see the definition of his lean muscles. Of course I noticed, and of course noticing made me blush. "I've been out in the void dozens of times in one. I've never had an issue."

"Where's the life support system?" I asked.

"On the back."

I flipped it over. "It's so small."

He stopped with his suit pulled to his waist and said, "If you're not comfortable—"

"No, I am. I am." I quickly shrugged off my outer layer so I could suit up. My inner layer was a white t-shirt and black mid-thigh tights. I tried not to think about whether he noticed me the same way I noticed him, but based on the little I knew about him, probably not.

He instructed me on how to properly adjust the suit while adjusting his own, and then we checked each other for loose latches before attaching ourselves to tethers and engaging the pressure system.

"Your gloves and boots contain electromagnets to stabilize you if you need to stay stationary. To deactivate them, flip this switch." He pointed to the wristband built into the suit. "Ready?"

I nodded, my heart rate already spiking from the adrenaline.

We entered the outer chamber. He opened a control panel on the wall, pulled a lever, and typed something into the keypad. The airlock opened, and just like that, I was looking out into open space wearing something nearly half the thickness of a normal EVA suit. All around me, the totality of the universe yawned in anticipation.

"Follow me," said Captain, kicking off into the void and moving upward along the curve of the ship's exterior. I forced myself to breathe and followed, catching up to him as he attached himself magnetically next to what looked like a breaker box. "External readouts," he explained. "If something has broken that is too small for the internal systems to catch, it triggers a sensor here."

"Like what?"

"Cosmetic damage, mostly. But if left untreated on a mission as long as this, it could lead to bigger issues. Looks like some of the usual cuts and bruises. Nothing you haven't seen before, old girl." He patted the hull fondly.

*He personified the ship*, I thought. *That's really cute.*

"So that is task number one, to mark out all the dents and dings we can see. You will find the tools necessary in the pockets of the suit. Task number two is to clean the undercarriage, where the engine is. A lot of debris gets statically attached to it."

"Like barnacles," I remarked.

"Stay focused," he said. "We do not have time for analogies. Our oxygen will last seven hours, and we are set for a six-hour mission. Just follow me and keep your eyes open."

Well, he had the tenacity of a cosmonaut, I'd give him that. And in a way, it was nice to finally have some sort of structure to follow; his teaching method may be rigorous, but it was admittedly way more exciting than playing wall ball. Perhaps he was like that tough professor who never cracked a smile but then decided that the final would be watching a film instead of taking a test.

*Speaking of, he's right. Focus. You're in for a long spacewalk.*

But despite the thin suit and endless expanse and the fact that my life was in the hands of a seventeen-year-old idealist, I felt surprisingly at peace. There was something deeply profound about being in open space—it didn't matter how long humans had been off-planet, it was still an enlightening experience. Maybe we took it for granted a little bit more than the first astronauts did, but no amount of deep space travel would make you forget how close you were at all times to an absolute lack of existence.

What helped during the spacewalk was how calm and collected Captain was as he led me through his task list and taught me what to do. Like he'd said, he'd gone through this dozens of times and would go through it dozens of times more.

Come to think of it, he might hold the record for most time spent in space relative to his age. And no one would ever know.

I tried to refrain from asking him personal questions, curious as I was. I actually didn't talk much at all, surprisingly—I was too busy listening to Captain's explanations, marveling at how confident and knowledgeable he was for someone so young and isolated. He was more patient than I'd expected, too, making sure I fully understood a task before moving on to the next one. The only time I really spoke was to acknowledge that I got it.

And then there was a moment, while we were standing upright on the *Atlantis*, where we both seemed to have the same idea. We paused what we were doing, even though it cost us precious seconds, and looked around at the magnitude of the universe around us, the vast ocean of stars and vacuous darkness, full of nothing and everything. The distant planets of the Zion system were delicate pinpricks against the void, the Current's event horizon a lowly sentinel watching us grow further away.

And we, the only living beings for hundreds of thousands of miles, alone but not alone, stood there together, two specks of dust bearing witness to it all.

That enlightenment I mentioned? Astronauts called it "the moment." And I think I had it, standing there with Captain. I think he had it, too.

I didn't want to speak for fear of breaking the fragile thread of shared experience between us, but I had to acknowledge it somehow. I had to solidify it with all five senses.

"Unbelievable, isn't it?" I said.

For a long moment, Captain didn't reply. I wondered if he'd heard me. Then, quietly, he said,
"'That which is far off, and exceeding deep, who can find it out?'"

"Who said that?" I asked.

"King Solomon," he said, and continued onward.

# PART II

# Atlantis

# 19

# Quin's Journal #2

Here's an observation for science: grief is a little bitch.

It had been a month since the *Washington*'s maiden voyage had gone up in flames. A month since we'd lost Xan. And it hit me way, way harder than I'd anticipated.

I'd never really realized how much I'd taken for granted; I'd always had my family around me and I'd never had more than a passing thought about losing them. Of course, with the life we led, there was always some measure of risk. But it had been so far from my mind that actually having to live through it was as devastating as the loss itself.

It took a week for the escape shuttles to reach the Current and another to return to the *Aster*, and all I can say is that I was physically there to process it, but mentally I was in limbo, just aware enough to function but not much else. I ate sporadically and slept a lot. There was a memorial service held soon after we arrived.

I was barely aware of that, either. I remember Rodney hugging me while Seb kept his distance. I should've said something to them—to him—but I was no better at finding words than usual.

What was there to say?

My parents resumed their posts onboard the *Aster* after a week but I asked the Academic Board for an extension before I went back to my studies. I couldn't just go back to the way things were. It felt wrong to.

Most days, I blamed myself. Even though the logical part of me knew it was ridiculous, I couldn't help but wonder what would've happened if I'd never found that stupid squid ship in the first place. Even though I'd voted against the investigation, it was still *my* discovery. I could've just ignored it. I *should've* just ignored it.

But no, that's not what a scientist does, is it? No, a real scientist fucks everything up out of curiosity. Call it a rite of passage.

So here I was, a month after the fact, still dysfunctional. I'd lost track of which stage of grief I was in and I didn't care. I wanted to feel better, I wanted to be able to logic my way through it just like I did with everything else, but all my attempts sunk into the bottomless pit of despair that had replaced my insides.

And then one day, while I lay in bed watching an old Earth sitcom, there was a knock on my bedroom door. Mom and Dad were at work and I hadn't been expecting any visitors, so it caught me completely off-guard. I considered ignoring it, but a neuron actually bothered to fire in my brain as I tried to puzzle out who would've let themselves into our apartment.

"Come in," I said.

The door slid open and Seb walked in. Sebastian Alcott. In my room. He held something in his hand that must have been food, judging by the warm, buttery scent that hit me like a slap in the face. I sat up immediately, hyperaware of my rumpled appearance and how chaotic my room was.

"Hey," he said. "Sorry to barge in. You busy?"

"Are you kidding?" I said, then instantly felt rude. "I mean, no, not really. What are you doing here?"

"I thought you could use a pick-me-up," he said, holding the aromatic object out to me. It was a croissant. "The bakery owed me a favor."

"Oh, you didn't have to do that," I said, but my stomach betrayed me by rumbling loud enough for Seb—and likely the rest of the colony—to hear it.

Seb smirked. "I think I did." He handed it to me. It was still warm. Part of me wanted to refuse it on principle, but it smelled way too good and I was already salivating.

I took a bite, groaning when the flaky pastry crumbled all over my shirt. "Shit," I said.

He laughed. "Never said it wasn't messy."

"It's really good, though. Thank you, Seb. You want a piece?"

He shook his head when I went to tear off a corner. "No, it's for you. I've had plenty, trust me." And then he sat down on the edge of my bed.

That woke me out of my stupor a bit.

"I've really wanted to come visit you," he said. "I just wasn't sure if it was right, you know? I wanted to give you your space. But I... I had to know how you were doing."

He was worried about me? Now I felt a little guilty that I'd avoided human contact for so long; a lot of other people were probably worried about me too, but I had been relying on Mom and Dad to cover for me. Which was probably really selfish of me, now that I thought about it. I mean, they were grieving too, but they weren't laying around all day depressed about it.

"Yeah, I'm…" I nodded a little too enthusiastically. "I'm fine. I'm getting better."

"Good," he said with a single nod.

There was a beat of awkward silence. He looked around the room and I looked down at the warm croissant in my hands. Neither of us knew what to say.

It was his silence that did me in, I think. He was trying so hard to be respectful, and I was shutting him out just like I did everyone else.

"I lied," I said. "I'm not getting better."

He looked at me with a placid expression on his face, waiting.

I felt a knot in my throat. My chest was heavy. Was I going to cry? No, I couldn't cry, not now. Not with a boy in my room and crumbs all over my shirt. How pathetic would that be?

Which was, ironically, exactly why I started crying.

"Hey," he said softly, scooting closer to me. "It's okay." He hesitated to touch me, and I honestly couldn't predict how I'd react if he did. But he was close enough that I could feel the heat rolling off his body, and it wasn't unpleasant. "Don't be so hard on yourself. These things take time. Sometimes lots of it. I know because my dad, he… he wasn't the same after my mom passed away.

And... I know this is the last thing you wanna hear right now, but it does get easier. Eventually. Sometimes really slowly."

"It's not fair," I sobbed, and then I voiced the one thing I'd refused to examine for the last month: "Everyone made it but her. Why her?"

After a moment, Seb said, "I've been asking myself that question, too. I don't think there's an easy answer, though. I think that sometimes, it just... happens. Sometimes your time is up, whatever that means to you."

"I don't believe God kills people," I said. Scientist though I was, I had my convictions, too.

"Me, neither," he said. "Nature kills people. *People* kill people."

I made myself meet his eyes and wiped my nose with my sleeve, feeling lower than low. Between hiccups, I said, "You think... there were actual *people* on the ship that attacked us?"

"I've heard all kinds of crazy theories these past few weeks," he said. "Most people say it was a pirate ship. A gang of mentally unstable spacers with some kind of grudge against the SEA. Why else would they attack an SEA vessel in cold blood? But there's no way of knowing, not without tracking it down."

"Are they? Going to track it down?"

He shrugged. "How? It's long gone, and it already destroyed one of their most expensive ships. They don't have the funds to go after it and they sure as hell won't risk sacrificing another ship. Or another crew. The consensus is that if anyone ever comes across it again, now or in the future, they should shoot to kill.

Otherwise, they're saying there's a slim chance anyone will ever cross paths with it again. It's just too damn fast. Might even have some FTL or partial-FTL capabilities."

I perked up at the sound of my thesis topic. For the first time in a month, I felt the cylinders start to fire. I felt like I could *think.* "Surely not everyone is happy with that verdict, are they?"

"Oh, hell no," said Seb. "Starting with your dad. My dad says he's appealed to the SEA several times now to do a full-scale investigation and has been shot down every time. I think he wants blood."

Holy shit, I really had been wallowing in my own black hole of misery. My math-loving, mild-mannered father, consumed by revenge, blockaded by the bureaucracy? What else had I missed?

Seb noted my shocked expression and said, "Everyone copes in their own way."

"No shit," I said. "I feel like such a failure. Xan wouldn't want this. She'd want me to get off my ass and go change the galaxy, or whatever it is I'm supposed to do. Or at least avenge her, or something. Dammit, why am I so weak?"

"You're not weak," said Seb emphatically. "And this isn't a superhero movie. If your dad—a respected engineer tech and the father of the deceased—can't get the SEA to think twice about that damn squid ship, then I wouldn't put so much pressure on yourself to do any better. You are right about one thing though: Xan would want you to live your life to the fullest. And you should. When you're ready."

I was touched, I'll admit. He was right, of course, and I

should take his words to heart. But my mind had finally powered on, and there was no shutting it down now. Part of me wanted to keep him here longer—he seemed to be good for me, neurologically speaking—and the other part of me wanted to kick him out so I could think in absolute silence.

Then I looked down and noticed in earnest all the croissant crumbs still covering me. I made an embarrassed squeak in the back of my throat and stood up to dust myself off. I'd clean the floor later.

Seb chuckled. "Don't be embarrassed, by the way. Those damn pastries always leave something behind."

"Yeah, I know—" I stopped short. "What did you say?"

"Damn pastries?"

"Leave something behind," I said. "It would've left something behind."

"What would've?"

I sucked in a breath as I sat back down, grabbed my tablet, and accessed the SEA database. "You know what bothered me the most about this whole thing? To the point where every time I think I'm ready to get back up, it knocks me down again?"

"What?" Seb asked cautiously.

"That we never found a *body*." My heart sank as I said it. "That we found the empty pod, but not the body."

"The heat of the explosion, it could've incinerated—"

"From the back?" I said, finding the mission report and projecting it in 3D. No detail was too insignificant for the SEA, so there was a full simulation of the attack compiled from live feeds, eyewitness reports, and a physics engine. I could watch the *Washington* get blown up in real-time, an activity I had thoroughly avoided since living through it.

But perhaps I shouldn't have avoided it.

"Think about when the ship exploded," I said, zooming in on the part of the ship closest to the engine. It didn't show Xan's pod specifically (it wasn't a perfect simulation) but it did show the trajectory of the engine room's explosion. "She wouldn't have been turned around facing it, she would've been heading away from it as fast as possible. If she died from anything, it would've been impact trauma. Which meant we would've found a body in that pod."

"Morbid, but okay. This isn't bothering you to talk about?"

"No, because I've been so wrapped up in thinking I was just stuck in denial that I never actually stopped to think about it rationally." I navigated away from the simulation and brought up an image I hadn't had the stomach to look at since the *Pennsylvania*: the 3D rendering of the empty pod they'd found in the sweep. "If she wasn't inside the pod, then she would've had to have been ejected outside the pod, which means there would be broken glass. But the glass was cracked, not broken. Do you see?"

"I do, but I also don't. Q, you're scaring me a little."

"Even so, if she'd been ejected outside of the pod, they would've found her. It's space."

"Are you sure? I mean... there was a lot of debris."

"It was on the edge of the explosion site. The far edge, actually. Plus, even if there had been a debris field, they would've been able to detect her biosignature. They couldn't find a body because there *was no body*." I felt manic with excitement, hedged by apprehension and fear.

After all, what if I was wrong and it was just false hope? What if I was still in denial and this was some sick, twisted distortion of my inability to accept my sister's death?

Well, then I guess I would need a lot more help than I thought. Because if I wasn't wrong—if this wasn't denial—and I didn't pursue it, I would spend the rest of my life wondering if I'd been right to believe in a miracle.

"Quin," Seb said, concern edging his voice. "You're not saying what I think you're saying, are you?"

"I am," I said.

"You think she's alive," he said, stunned. "Don't you?"

I took a deep breath. "As of the time we found her escape pod, yes, I think she was."

"Then where is she?" he asked, obviously wanting to hear me say it, to prove to him and myself that I actually took this theory seriously.

"She's on board the damn squid ship," I said.

[20]

# Remember This Greenhouse. It'll Be Important Later.

I want to say something changed after that spacewalk, but it could've just been wishful thinking, the futile desire to see the best in what was still an unpleasant situation. Though I wasn't sure "unpleasant" was the right word anymore. Unprecedented, maybe?

In any case, since no one "won" the spacewalk, Captain declared that since I had done so well, I could choose the next lesson.

How generous of him.

I think he expected me to pick another game, but I'd decided it was too much fun to catch him off-guard. I taught him the history of space colonization instead, lecture-style in the lounge. It was a four-part lecture that took two days to put together, so it basically became the topic of the week.

Captain knew popular names and dates, but he didn't

know the story or its impact on humanity. I talked about the tragedy of the *Solaris*, the first colony ship ever launched, and how it was destroyed in Jupiter's orbit. I talked about how it changed the way the SEA designed and built generational ships. I talked about the emphasis on family units and how it had solved many of the psychological issues associated with long-term space travel. I talked about Mobis and donut gravity, large-scale artificial farms and sprawling botanical gardens, about the Space Technical Academy and its cosmonaut training programs.

Honestly, for those four days, I talked a lot about a lot. I probably talked too much, but Captain was the perfect student—he listened intently, raised his hand when he had a question, and when the last lecture ended, he gave me a round of applause.

"You are an educator, through and through," he said. I don't think he realized how huge of a compliment that was to me. "You speak with such conviction. It's enrapturing."

Enrapturing. Only he could get away with using words like that in a normal conversation. "Thank you," I said. "I guess I've never had the opportunity to go that in-depth before. I'm specializing in elementary education, after all."

"Well, any student would be fortunate to have you as their teacher."

Where were all these compliments coming from? He'd better stop or I was going to start blushing. Scratch that—I already was.

"You choose the next one," I said. "You passed the class with flying colors."

"I don't recall a final exam."

"It was an attendance-based grading system," I said with a smirk. "Besides, I don't mind taking turns."

"Unless there is a competition involved," he stated.

I crossed my arms over my chest. "Ah, you like it when there are high stakes, don't you?"

He looked up at me with a smug expression. "It makes it interesting."

*You're interesting*, I wanted to say, but I stopped myself. A weird electricity hung in the air between us, as if we both had a word on the tip of our tongues that neither of us could remember.

Eventually, he broke eye contact and rose from the couch. "Good work today, Miss Nepier. I will see you at breakfast."

What? He was going to join me for a meal again? It had already happened a couple more times since he'd installed furniture in the dining room, but I hadn't expected it to become a habit. Either he'd taken what I'd said to heart or... well, what other reason would there be for willingly eating with someone? He hadn't made me any promises about it.

"Don't be late," I said and instantly cursed myself. It was something Mom often said to Dad.

It was flirty.

Captain's next lesson for me was botany. Yes, finally!

I had been curious about his greenhouse ever since he'd given me the grand tour. I know he went down there on a daily basis, usually before our lessons, but it always seemed like a private thing, his own personal oasis. I didn't want to disturb it without permission, so the fact that he was allowing me to work alongside him felt like a huge honor.

"These two rows of lettuce are ready to harvest," he said, deftly waving a pointed hand toward one of the beds. "Then we'll turn the soil and fertilize it. Because then, I want you to help me with this." He unfurled his palm and let float a packet of tiny seeds. The label read, *Fragaria x ananassa.*

I racked my brain for my rudimentary knowledge of scientific classification and gasped. "Strawberries! I would kill for some. I love strawberries."

He snatched it back up before it could float away. "Let's get to work."

I donned some gardening gloves and helped him dig up the lettuce, which were about five to six inches in diameter each and smelled way better than lettuce should, almost herbal. They went into a covered bin to be washed later, and then Captain showed me how to turn and fertilize. As we went, he rambled on about how to make certain plants grow, how to control the pH of the soil, how to counteract nutrient deficiencies, et cetera.

As he rambled, I realized: whether he wanted to admit it or not, he loved this. Maybe his purpose was to ferry human souls, but his passion was to nurture organic life. If he'd been raised on Earth, he might've been an agriculturalist. Or a simple farmer.

I imagined him in a field, working under the heat of the sun, bronzed and glowing from hours spent in man's natural element. It gave me a rush I didn't expect, a warm, bubbling feeling that went from my stomach to my cheeks. I caught myself staring at him. His deep olive skin looked blanched in the overhead heat lamps, but he was still radiant, a fine layer of sweat on his brow from the heat of the greenhouse, a light in his eyes that I never saw when he was on the bridge.

And for the first time since my delirious first impression, I let myself realize how handsome he was.

"Miss Nepier?" he said, snapping me out of my embarrassing reverie. "The pincers, if you please."

I quickly grabbed the tool from the magnetic rack nearby and held it aloft. Captain took it and extracted one of the tiny seeds from the bag. He carefully inserted it into the fertilized dirt, making sure the seed was securely caught in the vacuum system and not about to float out of the bed. He repeated this a dozen more times with the other seeds, and then he directed me to retrieve a vial of water from the receptacle on the wall and water each potential plant with careful drops.

"And that's it," he said. "That is the lesson for today."

But I wasn't ready to leave this verdant oasis quite yet. Instead, I wandered over to the fig tree. The figs were still green, but they'd gotten bigger. One even looked a little darker, which made me giddy.

"You said this is the first time this thing has produced fruit?" I asked.

"Yes," he replied. "Edible fruit, that is."

"We should do something special when it's finally ready to eat."

"Special? How?"

"I don't know. Like a holiday." I turned to face him. "I'm guessing you don't celebrate holidays."

"Two, actually. My birthday and the day the *Atlantis* began her voyage. I don't need any others."

"When is your birthday?" I asked. It seemed like something worth knowing.

"The third of July," he said. "By my calendar, not necessarily the SEA's."

"Well, I guess that's the only calendar we have to go off of at the moment."

"And yours?" he asked, to my surprise.

"October twentieth," I said.

"I will remember that," he said. "Peak harvest season. On Earth at least."

I smiled, turning back to the tree. "Harvest," I mused. "We could do Thanksgiving."

"Beg pardon?"

"As a big holiday."

"An American tradition based on historical fiction, if I'm not mistaken."

I scoffed. "Don't be a buzzkill. We all know the pilgrims didn't actually eat turkey. It's the principle of the thing. Food, family, harvest. Thankfulness."

"You are descended from Americans, I take it."

"You mean you couldn't tell?" I laughed. "Yes, of course I am. What about you?"

"My family originated from Egypt," he said. "But I

believe that long before I was born, they were already living in the UK. The ship was assembled there."

"That would explain the accent," I said.

"To me, you're the one with the accent," he said with a wry smile.

"Should I start talkin' like you, then?" I said in a very poor approximation of cockney British. "Tally-ho? God save the king? Oi, jolly good day for a spot o' tea, innit?"

"I don't sound like that," he said, looking unexpectedly amused. "And I'm certain half of those words were pure nonsense."

"I've watched a lot of old British TV," I said. "Egyptian, not so much."

"I can't say I'm entirely surprised."

"Actually," I hesitated, "I have a question about your heritage, if you don't mind me asking."

"Ask away."

"Egypt has such a rich mythology. Why did your family choose to name things after Greek legend? Atlantis, the lost continent? The robots, all named letters of the Greek alphabet? See, I noticed."

"That is an excellent question," he said, hands behind his back, ready to play professor. "Egypt and Greece have a long history of interaction and influence with one another, due in large part to their proximity. There is Greek in my ancestry as well, dating back centuries. I believe that my grandfather was also very much inspired by classical ideals and literature. After all, the Greeks were a seafaring people who wrote of epic voyages to distant lands; I believe he desired to emulate such a tradition with the *Atlantis*. A modern Odyssey, if you will."

"And you, a modern Odysseus," I said dryly.

"More or less."

I wondered if he was thinking the same thing I was: that he was more a ferryman than an explorer. And if you knew anything about ferries in Greek mythology, you did *not* want to end up on one.

An odd silence stretched between us until Captain cleared his throat and said, "You were saying we should have a holiday to celebrate... what was it again? The fig harvest?"

"It was just a silly idea," I said, waving it away.

"No, I rather like it," he said. "It adds an appropriate level of gravitas to what has been, quite honestly, a tumultuous cultivation."

I giggled. "Don't you ever talk like a normal teenager?"

He gave me a pointed look.

"Sorry, I—I was just giving you shit. I like how you talk."

"Giving me...?" He trailed off in confusion, to my dismay. I really wanted to hear him say "shit."

I giggled again. "I'm sorry. I keep messing with you. I'm treating you like I do one of my friends."

He tilted his head slightly. "Are we friends?"

The tone he used was not derisive, nor was it hopeful. It was pure, objective curiosity. He was asking for a definition.

"Well, technically speaking... yeah, I guess we could be friends. I mean, would you like to be friends?"

"Does the classification change the nature of our relationship?"

"Huh?"

He paused, rebooted, and tried again: "Do friends treat each other any differently than we do now?"

I thought about it. "Not really, no. They might talk to each other more. Confide in each other. But that takes time to build, so, considering how unorthodox our circumstances are to begin with, I'd say we do pretty well. We're still in the 'getting to know you' phase."

It was weird to talk about such an organic part of life in such literal terms, but I knew it would compute for him better if I did. The fact that he was asking these questions at all was admirable. He could shut me down and refuse to see me as anything other than an inconvenience, but he didn't. And come on, what human being didn't desire friendship?

Even if it was a bit incidental.

"Very well," he said. "We can be friends. And if you'd like to plan a holiday around the fig tree, it wouldn't go amiss."

"Can't argue with that." I smiled at him, and something in his expression made me stop dead in my tracks. He looked so earnest, as if he were about to tell me a secret. I paused with bated breath, waiting for him to speak his mind.

Instead, he dropped his eyes to the floor and cleared his throat. "That is all for today. You may go."

"What about you?"

"I just need a moment to check something. Nothing you'd be interested in. Run along. You're free."

"Okay," I said, and reluctantly, I left. But like the nosy little space rat I was, I paused outside the door flap and pressed my ear to the tarp, listening.

I could hear him muttering to himself, the same cadence over and over. I strained to make out what it was, but I could swear he was saying, "I have everything I need. I have everything I need. I have everything I need."

# 21

# In Which I Accidentally Use the Oldest Trick in the Book

Following our afternoon in the greenhouse, Captain had announced that he wanted to decrease the frequency of our lessons, owing to "some upcoming ship maintenance that requires my attention," allegedly.

What I suspected was that things had gotten a little too personal that day and it had spooked him—though I couldn't imagine why. It wasn't like he'd given away any trade secrets, unless knowing his birthday and the fact that his grandfather liked *The Odyssey* was somehow sacrilegious.

Or us officially being friends, for that matter.

Nevertheless, I acquiesced to his skittish request and we cut the sessions down to three times a week. For our next lesson, I went easy on him and did a lecture on Earth's oceans (plagiarized from Mom's lesson plans, naturally), utilizing the convenient props throughout the lounge.

When I asked, finally, why there were so many ocean artifacts lying around, his answer was, "It was the one collection my grandfather couldn't part with."

Well, thanks, Grandpa. Your weird obsession with marine biology is my gain.

Captain's next lesson for me was, once again, full of surprises: he let me run through a training exercise. He explained that he'd been trained on how to handle hypothetical scenarios through VR simulations—very similar to how they train cosmonauts at the Space Technical Academy. He even had a similar headset. This simulation was a simple problem: what to do if the ship gets caught in a planet's orbit. Simple, but not easy. It took me a few tries and some hints from Captain to get it right, but it was fun.

My next lesson was to teach him slang words—but for his sake, I spun it as a "sociological study." I can't say it wasn't entertaining to have to explain the historical significance of the word "yeet" to a teenager with the diction of an Oxford scholar. In fact, it was downright hilarious.

Captain let me do more training simulations. I bullshitted my way through other ridiculous aspects of human society. Sometimes, Captain would cancel lessons altogether. This was the pattern for the next few weeks, and while it was its own kind of fun, it was noticeably more formal than the greenhouse or even the EVA had been.

I did visit him on the bridge from time to time in an

attempt to be sociable, but despite his open invitation for me to shadow him, I still felt like I was disturbing some sacred ritual. It wasn't always Captain who made me feel this way; he might not be very talkative while working but he never acted as scandalized as he had the day I'd brought him dinner. If I had to categorize his attitude, I'd call it neutral.

Beta, on the other hand, always made it a point to stare at me while I was up there as if he were trying to make me feel like an intruder. I purposefully avoided interacting with him, but when I did, his answers were always short. Gone were the polite formalities of our first meeting, lest I forget this was a machine and not a man.

One good thing did come out of it, however: it made Captain seem warm and fuzzy by comparison.

For the next few lessons, I decided to play some more games and see how far I could push the envelope before Captain shut up like a clam. We started with chess, even though he already knew how to play. Not only that but—big shocker here—it turned out he was really good at it. Of course, he'd only ever played against robots, which meant I wasn't nearly as much of a challenge. After I got tired of losing to him, I decided to switch to something a little more my speed: poker.

"Gambling," he said in surprise when I explained today's agenda. "Not exactly a moral sport, is it?"

"Oh, don't get all high and mighty on me," I said. "We're not playing for money." I'd already 3D printed a deck of cards and a set of poker chips, so we were set. "But what should the winner receive? And don't say next lesson. I want it to be high-stakes."

"Glory and honor?"

"Good things both, but how about a dare?"

He squinted at me. "What?"

"Winner gets to dare the loser to do something. If they refuse, they have to tell them a secret instead." It was a pretty contrived version of Truth or Dare, but I was proud of myself for thinking it up on the spot.

He squinted at me some more. "I'm not sure I see the utility."

"Do you accept my wager or not, Captain?"

Oh, how I loved knowing that he was a sucker for a friendly bet. "I accept."

I explained the rules, we played a few practice hands, and then the game began in earnest. As I expected, he had a superior poker face. But I had superior cards and I knew how to bluff. In the end, I wiped the floor with him.

"All right, you won fair and square," he said with a sigh. "What is your dare?"

I thought I was going to dare him to say the f-word or something else immature, but then my eyes strayed to the baby grand piano in the corner and I found myself saying, "I dare you to play something on the piano."

He raised an eyebrow. "How do you know I can play piano?"

I gave him a dubious look. "You've been stuck here for seventeen years and you were classically educated. You know how to play piano."

With a blank expression, he rose from his seat, walked over to the piano, and lifted the cover. Maintaining dead eye contact with me, he played a single note.

I giggled. "Smart-ass. That's cheating. I meant a song."

"You said play something. You never said that something had to be melodic."

"Touché. Okay, come back here, then, and let's go another round."

We did. And I won again. My bluffing skills are legendary.

"Now I dare you to play a *song* on the piano," I said. "A real one."

Looking indignant, he rose and took a seat on the bench. I followed him and stood beside it. "I was never very rigorous with it," he said. "So I can't claim anything close to mastery."

"I'm sure you're passable."

He got into position and began to play. I recognized it; it was Chopin's Nocturne No. 9. I had it on my "Classical Studying" playlist back home. He got about halfway through the piece before he tapered off, either out of embarrassment or because he'd forgotten the rest. I wished he hadn't stopped.

"Wow," I said. "You play beautifully. Better than I ever could, at least."

"Do you play?" he asked.

I snorted. "Do show tunes and pop covers count?"

He got up and motioned for me to replace him. Oh boy. I did, but I wasn't sure I was going to blow him away in quite the same manner. I cleared my throat and started the first song I thought of: the *Star Wars* theme. Cliché as heck, but it was a real hit at parties.

However, the second I looked up at Captain, I knew the magic was lost on him. He had no idea what I was playing. I tapered off and said, "You don't even know

John Williams? Isn't he considered classical music these days?"

"Play another one," he said with a nod.

I tried to think of a single song he would know. The best I could do was a really down-tempo version of Mozart's Rondo Alla Turca. It was decidedly not great.

"No, no, not something I'd know," he said, waving me off. "Play something else new. Something from your culture."

I almost laughed at that, the thought of pop music as my "culture," but in a way he was right. I played a selection of my favorites, among them *Pirates of the Caribbean*, *Beauty and the Beast*, and *Project Hail Mary: The Musical*. He seemed spellbound by all of them, or at the very least, grossly fascinated.

"Where'd you learn such a colorful repertoire?" he asked.

"My mom," I said with a forced smile. "She loves music. And she can actually play, like you. She taught my sister and me all sorts of songs growing up just for kicks. It wasn't exactly classical training, but it was fun."

He'd stopped laughing and leveled his expression at me. "You have a sister?"

"Oh. Yeah." I felt a pang of guilt toward the realization that I'd never mentioned her outright. "Just one. Two years young than me. Her name's Quinette."

"Do you get along well?" he asked, to my surprise.

I nodded. "She's my best friend."

He didn't say anything, just kept looking at me with a mildly curious expression. I felt the need to fill the silence.

"You know, you remind me of her sometimes," I declared. His brow furrowed in response. "Not in a feminine way, mind you. I mean, she's pretty precocious for someone her age, too. She's practically a genius, actually. She's probably going to be a world-renowned astrophysicist someday. And she's a locked box, just like you are. Keeps everything close to the vest. Still, I've always admired how mature she is for her age. How in control of her emotions. It's a really desirable quality in a cosmonaut, you know?"

It hurt more than I expected to talk about her. I'd barely said a word about my family since I'd come aboard the *Atlantis*, and this was exactly why. The crushing weight of the distance continually increasing between us and the thought of how devastated they must be, thinking I was dead, was just too much. Unlike Quin, I was crap at pushing things down, but I realized that lately, I'd been trying harder than ever to hold back.

It was futile, though. Like a bubble of gas, my feelings always found a way to rise to the surface.

My eyes welled up, the lack of gravity already pulling the water upward. I ducked my head to hide it, but it was too late. I sunk my face into my hands and sobbed.

I expected Captain to be uncomfortable, silent, and unhelpful. That's what would make the most sense for him, and there was a certain comfort in anticipating it. But although he was silent for a long time, eventually, he said, "What can I do?"

Which shocked me senseless.

This would've been a perfect opportunity to insist that what he could do was let me send a transmission to my family, but I couldn't bring myself to say it; it seemed too emotionally manipulative, and my other needs were more imminent. At that moment, I needed a friend. And he was the only one I had.

I reached for his hand and took it in mine, pressing my face to it like a handkerchief. He was stiff, obviously unused to the physical contact. This probably wasn't at all what he'd expected me to need, but I couldn't bring myself to care, not when his hand was so warm. Slowly, he sat down next to me on the piano bench and I swapped his hand for his shoulder, angling my body into him. And he stayed there. And I cried.

"I'm sorry," I said once I'd calmed down. "I know this is, like, really not cool of me—"

"It's all right," he said. His tone was clinical but not annoyed.

"I forgot to warn you that girls are emotional," I said with a congested chuckle. Very flattering. "Well, in any case, I'm emotional. Not every girl cries at the drop of a hat."

"If you need something, I can have Phala prescribe you an antidepressant. They're very helpful in... times like this."

I caught his implication and pulled myself away from his shoulder to look at his face. "So you do feel."

He furrowed his brow at me.

"You just take drugs for it." I poked him in the chest.

"Only to keep myself chemically and physically balanced. What is it you said? Space 'does things' to people."

"What has it done to you?" I asked.

He shifted uncomfortably, and I instantly regretted asking him such a personal question, even if I was painfully curious.

"Should I call for Phala?" he asked.

I shook my head as I forced myself to stand. "I don't need to be medicated for normal, human emotions," I said. "Thank you for comforting me, though. I'm sure that was difficult for you."

He looked at me sternly, as if I'd just told him a riddle. I walked across the room, cleaned up the playing cards, and headed toward my room.

But then he said, "Nepier, wait."

He'd dropped the prefix. Stunned, I turned back around. He'd stood up from the bench. "I know you think of me as inhuman," he said.

"No, it's not—"

He held up a hand. "I know what I lack. But you placed your trust in me today; I'd like to return the favor. As a friend."

My heart sped up. What did that mean, exactly?

"Tomorrow, you may record your transmission," he said.

I stared slack-jawed at him. Was this really happening? Was crying really all it took to make him melt like putty in my hands? Now I felt a little slimy.

Which is why, to my utter disbelief, I found myself shaking my head. "No, no, no," I said. "You're underdeveloped in the 'resisting girls crying' department."

"Nepier."

"Let me be the first to tell you that if you don't grow a thick skin about it now—"

"Nepier."

"—they'll walk all over you for the rest of your life. Your wife, your sisters, your daughters. Anytime they want something, they'll cry, and then it's all over. Take it from me; my dad was outnumbered three to one. He never stood a chance—"

"Xanorra," he said. Hearing my name from his mouth shut me up immediately. He exhaled. "It's not because you cried. It's because you told me about your sister."

I stared at him, dumbfounded.

"That is when I decided," he continued. "You see, I have to wait to meet my family. But you were never meant to be apart from yours. I confess that my hesitation to allow you your parting words has a lot to do with the fact that if they receive a message from you, they will likely be able to surmise how you are able to send it."

True. That was kind of the point. But he was no idiot, and I hadn't expected any less from him.

"However, if you can come up with a message that provides you with the catharsis you need without revealing anything about the mission, I'll let you send it."

I couldn't help myself. I rushed into his arms and hugged him. Again, he went stiff, but since I'd already invaded his personal space once in as many hours, he seemed a little less shocked.

"Thank you, Captain," I said. "Thank you so much."

His hands patted my back awkwardly, and I pulled away before he could implode from the exposure.

"Don't thank me just yet," he said, all business. "If you

want it sent, you have to report to the bridge at oh seven hundred sharp tomorrow morning."

I nodded and saluted him. "Yes, sir. Oh seven hundred sharp."

He gave me a fraught half-smile and left the lounge.

# 22

# The Uncanny Valley

I entered the bridge at 0659. Yes, it was a little overeager, but what can I say? I was excited. I thought all night about what I was going to say. And yes, I was still going to try to code the message. Hopefully, Captain signed off on it.

"Good morning," he said as I came into view on the bridge. He did not look well-rested, but I was beginning to realize that he seldom ever did.

"Good morning," I said cheerily. I looked around, realizing there was a distinct lack of robotic scrutiny today. "Where's Beta?"

"On an early EVA," he said, switching the helm to autopilot. "Shall we?"

I followed him to the far-right side of the control center, nearest to Zeta, who gave us a curt "hello" as we approached. Captain punched a few buttons and a wavelength popped up on the screen. "You have three minutes of audio," he said. "Press this button to start and stop the recording."

I nodded and took his place next to an impassive Zeta, mulling my script over in my head. Then, I pressed record. "This message is intended for the Nepier family aboard the colony ship *Aster*. Registration number six-four-one-five-seven. Ensign Xanorra Jade Nepier, formerly of the *USE George Washington*, speaking.

"Hi, Mom and Dad. Hi, Quin. If you're listening to this, first I want you to know that I'm alive. Even months from now, which is probably when you'll receive this. The explosion that separated my escape pod from everyone else's didn't kill me, just spun me out and damaged the navigation system. As to where I am now, unfortunately, I can't really tell you that, which I know is frustrating, but you don't need to come looking for me. You won't find me. In any case, I'm… content. And most importantly, alive.

"I'm so sorry it had to be this way. Quin, I love you, baby sister. You're going to do great things, and I wish I could be there to see it. But I have zero doubt that you'll figure everything out, because you're the smartest person I know."

I paused. I had this whole cryptic message planned out with obscure pop culture references, but something told me not to say it, that it might sound too nonsequitur. Besides, I got a distinct feeling that Quin wouldn't need it. The truth was obvious enough.

"Mom and Dad, I love you so, so much. Thank you for making me the woman I am. I'm going to miss you. All of you. I love you guys. Xanorra out."

I was barely able to bite back tears as I hit the button to stop the recording. What if they didn't get the message? Or what if they did but couldn't do anything about it? What if they wasted the rest of their lives looking for me and never found me? What was I even thinking, trying to hail a rescue? And why did part of me feel bad about villainizing Captain, even though this was totally his fault?

At the very least, I'll have said my goodbyes. I wouldn't ever regret telling my family that I loved them.

Captain put a hand on my shoulder. "I will accept that."

It was the greatest gift he could've given me, short of helping me get home. I turned around and embraced him—again—this time fighting the tears back. I sniffled a few times, but mercifully, that was it. I could cry it out later in the privacy of the bedroom if I needed to.

"My, my, my," said a voice from the other side of the bridge. Beta. "She looks unwell."

Captain bristled. "You have completed the EVA already?"

"In record time. Should I call for Phala?" Beta motioned to me.

"No, that will not be necessary," said Captain, and I noticed that his arm went protectively around my waist as he said it. "She just misses her family. The void is messing with her head."

"Ah, that happens to the best of us, I'm afraid," said Beta, as if he had any concept of what space could do to a person psychologically. "Perhaps she should rest."

"That is a novel idea, Lieutenant," said Captain. "I shall

escort her to her room. Take the helm. I will be right back."

There was a very weird tension in the air as Captain ushered me out of the bridge and into the lounge, a hand on the small of my back. When the doors closed, Captain leaned in close to my ear and said, "Beta's programming would not have allowed the message to be sent."

I stopped and looked at him, his eyes like two dark portals. "You broke the rules for me?"

"I bent them," he said softly. "Stay away from the bridge today. Act sick."

"That won't be hard. I feel sick," I said. The urgency of our exit had supplanted my melancholy with adrenaline, a feeling not unlike standing up too quickly.

He put a hand on either side of my face. They were cool while my cheeks felt hot. I closed my eyes, soothed by the skin-to-skin contact, which sounds more sensual than it is. Between that and all the hugging lately, my oxytocin levels were on the up and up. I hadn't realized how much I needed it until it happened.

"You're very warm," he said matter-of-factly. "Phala can prescribe you something for the fever. Or just something to help you sleep."

I shook my head, touched as I was by his bedside manner. "No fever. Again, just human emotions. I just need some time to process them."

Captain nodded and dropped his hands. I wished he hadn't. "Get some rest."

He turned to leave, but I reached out and touched his arm.

"Captain," I said. "Thank you. You have no idea how much it means to me."

He gave me a tight-lipped grimace and said, "You're welcome, Miss Nepier."

"You can call me Xanorra, you know," I said. "Or even just Xan. I think you've earned the right to a first-name basis. Technically, I've been on one with you since we met. Feels a little unfair." I threw in a chuckle for good measure.

He stared at me with an expression I couldn't read as he said, "I will do my best."

I patted his shoulder. "That's all we can do."

With a curt nod and a half-smile, he walked away.

I did what Captain asked me to do: I stayed away from the bridge for the rest of the day. I didn't even venture very far past the lounge, and for once, I didn't mind at all. There was plenty to distract me. I even found some brain games on the tablet to play.

And Captain said he didn't have anything fun.

At seventeen hundred, Captain entered the lounge. I hadn't expected him to show up. I certainly hadn't prepared for a lesson today; we were still on our three-day-a-week schedule.

Had Beta found out about the transmission? If he had, what could he do about it? Scold us? I guessed (or, rather, hoped) his programming wouldn't allow him to do much else, and yet I'd still been plagued with anxiety about it all day. It was no secret that there was something ominous about that android, creepy staring notwithstanding. There was something ominous about this whole damn thing.

But if anything were amiss, Captain didn't show it. He wore the same calm, collected expression he usually did, if not a touch friendlier. "Hello," he said.

"Hi," I said. "Sorry, I didn't think we were having a lesson today."

"That's all right. We're not." He paused for a beat too long. "I've given it some thought, and I've decided to show you something."

I sat up straighter, my curiosity piqued. "Okay."

He walked slowly to the glass screen in the corner of the room and motioned for me to follow him. He tapped his wristband and what appeared onscreen was a home video of a young, Middle Eastern couple sitting on a green couch, smiling. They spoke Arabic, but there were English subtitles below.

"Hello, son," said the man, who I supposed looked like an older version of Captain.

"Happy seventeenth birthday," said the woman. She was pretty but didn't look like Captain at all.

"By now you will have passed through the Current," said his father. "That's very exciting. You should be on course to pass the first planet in the Zion system in about three years." He went on for a few minutes, talking about what Captain could expect in the coming months, and then his mother took over.

"You're sleeping right now," she said. "You love when I sing you lullabies, but I have to be careful or you'll fall asleep before you're done eating. You love to sleep. None of your brothers ever slept as easily as you do." She went on talking about baby Captain for a few minutes. It was endearing, if not a little rote—like giving a medical report.

"You're a fully-realized captain now," said his father. "You'll likely feel it, the sense of responsibility, the confidence of manhood. Embrace it. You've been given a great destiny, and so much depends on you. We patiently await the day that we are able to meet you, and I am sure you are doing the same. May God be with you."

The video stopped, a freeze frame of their smiling faces. I was honored that Captain trusted me enough to let me see this, and I wanted to feel what he felt, but as I looked on at their mild expressions of contentment, I could only identify one emotion: uneasiness.

I turned to Captain and said, "They recorded a message for every birthday?"

He turned the screen off. "Yes. The next one won't be available for me to view until the day I turn eighteen. They recorded them all within a few days of each other, when I was only a few months old. Right before the mission began." He stared at the clear mirror as if they were still onscreen. "In a few of them, my brothers appear."

"That was very... thoughtful of them, but..." I really didn't want to belittle his family, but there was something so wrong about all of this. It felt cruel, like dangling a piece of meat in front of a hungry dog. "This only gives you a piece of the picture."

"I know," he said. "It's insufficient to the real thing, but it's better than nothing. I also have my father's and grandfather's journals. A photo album. Some letters.

They didn't leave me without a memory of them. At least I know who they are."

*You only know what they want you to know,* I thought, but it seemed deeply inconsiderate to say it. Instead, I put a hand on his shoulder and said, "Thank you for showing me this."

He nodded once. "I thought it might be... informative."

I knew what he was trying to say, even if he didn't fully understand what he meant. This was his attempt at empathizing. And it was truly touching—adorable, even—but it had inadvertently opened up a can of space worms I'd only just realized was there.

His family had painstakingly planned this mission with him at the center. And while I couldn't tell to what extent his parents had been involved in the process, it seemed to me that the line of demarcation between the Omens and Omen-Ra as a company was practically nonexistent. These messages weren't just from his parents, they were from his *superiors*—and whether Captain noticed it or not, it gave their words an eerie, almost rehearsed quality. It was like the uncanny valley: almost believable, but not quite.

Almost human, but not quite.

# 23

# Houston, We Have an Asteroid

That night, I tossed and turned as I mulled over the events of the day, unable to wipe the eeriness of the birthday video from my mind. I was trapped in an ethical conundrum: should I tell Captain what I saw, or continue to let him believe his parents' words are genuine? The answer seemed obvious at first, but the more I thought about it, the less certain I became.

I needed to see that video again or watch more like it before I could confidently say that I'd seen what I thought I'd seen. But would it be rude or invasive to ask? Obviously, the birthday video (and anything else like it) was stored on Captain's personal hard drive, which appeared to be in his wristband. So, in order to see it again, I'd have to get permission.

In the end, I decided to wait a couple of days before asking him any more questions and had just settled into a pleasant half-sleep when a loud, blaring alarm startled me right out of it again.

That couldn't be good.

Frazzled and groggy, I pulled on just my boots as I bounded out of the room and onto the bridge. "What the hell is going on?" I demanded.

Captain, at the helm, turned to look at me. "Xanorra. Hello," he said, his tone at odds with his anxiety-ridden expression.

He didn't even have to answer my question because it only took a moment's glance across the bridge to realize what was different: we weren't in space.

Well, technically we were—there wasn't anywhere else we could be—but you couldn't see it. We were completely enveloped by a swirling, ethereal cloud of turquoise gas that obscured every inch of the viewscreens.

That's why the alarms had gone off. We were flying blind.

"Uhhhh," I said. "Is this a problem?"

"Just a minor mishap," said Captain, sounding a little strained.

"Oh," I said, nodding. "That's cool, that's cool. Does this happen often?"

"Truth be told, it hasn't happened yet," he said. "But I'm prepared. There is nothing to concern yourself over."

The ship started shaking and then the alarms went off again.

"Really?" I said dubiously.

"The stabilizer system is on the fritz, but it'll be fine," said Captain. "You can return to your room."

"No, I think I'll stay right here," I said nonchalantly.

"You're not even dressed for the bridge," he said.

I blushed. "So?"

Modesty is really the last thing you should worry about in an emergency situation, but the fact that he'd acknowledged it still made me wish I'd grabbed my suit on the way out. Now I felt compelled to stay out of spite, even if it somehow felt like I was intruding on something private. The look Beta gave me certainly said so, as if I were the major inconvenience here and not the gas cloud. Still, I made myself move forward until I was level with the helm and gripped the edge.

Another tremor shook the ship and Captain's attention turned back to the helm controls. "Beta, can we get a bot to the hull?"

"We could, but it is unlikely that they will be able to see much more than we can," Beta replied from where he stood near Delta.

"Can we send a beam, or a solar blast, or something? Try to break up the particles?"

"The opacity is too thick. The only way out is through, I'm afraid."

Captain gritted his teeth. "Then so be it."

"Is there anything I can do?" I asked.

Captain looked surprised that I was still there at all. "Nothing comes to mind. Which is why you should return to your room, for your own safety."

"I already told you, that ain't happening. With all due respect, of course." I smiled sweetly. "Why can't you just change your axis and fly above or below the cloud?"

"This ship cannot alter the Master Course except

under the direst of circumstances," said Captain. "This does not yet count as such."

A deafening explosion sounded as something impacted the hull, sending a jarring vibration through the bridge that almost knocked me over. Captain gripped the helm and looked over at me. "If you insist on being present, would you mind standing behind me?"

"Behind you?"

"There's a magnetic lock on this platform. It'll keep you stabilized in the event of turbulence. More turbulence, that is."

"Okay, sure." At least I could stay. I got on the helm's podium with him and he inched forward just enough to give me a decent handhold of the stand's curved outer edge. Still, I was unreasonably close to him, which felt different now that I wasn't overwhelmed or caught up in my emotions. He didn't smell like floor cleaner this time—he smelled like sweat and adrenaline, i.e., an actual human being. It was comforting in a weird way.

I found my grip just as another tremor pitched me forward into his back. I quickly straightened out and said, "What's causing the turbulence? This doesn't feel like stabilizer issues."

"Space rocks," said Captain, his hands moving deftly across the controls like a practiced magician. I had no idea what any of it meant but it sure looked snazzy. "It's impossible to see what's in front of us, so we're helpless against anything trapped in the cloud. Beta," he shouted across the bridge, "can we run an infrared scan outward from the hull? Try to see what's up ahead?"

"An inspired idea, Captain. I will see if I cannot

calibrate the sensors." Beta went to work at the control station, his android hands moving impossibly fast. Then, just as quickly, he stopped. "Captain, the opacity is decreasing. I think we are approaching the end."

From this close, I could hear Captain's audible sigh of relief. "Excellent. Thank you, Lieutenant."

The blue-green glow began to dissipate. A few stars peeked through the haze.

And then something massive struck the ship, capitulating us forward.

*This doesn't feel like approaching the end to me*, I thought.

The gas cloud had broken up into swirling, translucent tendrils, but now we could see an endless field of space rocks awaiting us—a veritable minefield in space. What we'd encountered inside the cloud had only been a sample platter. This was the main course.

"Well, at least we can see it," I said. Glass half full, you know?

"Beta, I want solar canons online," Captain said. "Helm switched to manual control. Unlock the Master Course to a radius of fifty meters. Stabilizers to max." Another impact. I lost my grip, Captain took a step backward, and reflexively, I gripped his waist to keep from falling off the platform.

"Sorry," I said as I let go and found my grip on the helm again.

He acted like he hadn't noticed as he continued giving commands to his mechanical crew. A hatch beneath the helm controls popped open and he pulled out a headset that looked like a VR training headband without the face shield. Affixing it atop his thick hair and sliding on the gloves, Captain said, "Switched to manual. Guns on standby. Fire on course."

*Whoa, he's piloting the ship himself.* Now things were getting interesting. And now I definitely felt like dead weight. Perhaps my stubborn insistence that I should stay on the bridge had been petty and misguided.

"Captain, maybe I should go—"

"You stay right where you are, Nepier. It's too late for you now," he said urgently. "Just hold on tight."

Oddly encouraged, I turned my attention to the windshields instead. The solar guns blasted any large obstacles in our path and Captain, piloting manually, dipped and swerved to avoid as much of the debris as he could. But we were moving so fast, and there were so many rocks that were unreasonably close together... we had to be taking serious damage to the hull even if we couldn't feel it.

Time seemed to stretch on and compress at the same time. Captain stayed laser-focused, navigating through the debris with a dexterity only achieved by years of training. He really was like a machine, but this time in a good way. The bots were also busy doing their jobs, which I'm sure made it easier, but the longer we were in here, ducking and dodging, the more I wondered: how long could we keep this up? A rock field like this could stretch for hundreds of thousands of miles.

"Captain, maybe it's time to break that 'stay on course' rule?" I dared to say.

"I think not," said Beta, to my surprise. "The radar is detecting an equally large body of space rock in any direction we travel. My recommendation is to stay on our current course, as it has the lowest probability of failure."

I gritted my teeth. I didn't like it when androids were programmed with negative-bent probability. "You mean the highest chance of success," I corrected, for Captain's sake and my own.

Beta didn't answer, which made me angrier. But if I was stuck here as Captain's shadow, the least I could do was offer moral support. And he did say having an extra set of eyes looking at problems could be helpful, right? I'd been through *three whole* training simulations (though none involved dodging rocks) which meant I was practically an expert, obviously.

So I kept scanning the viewscreens and watching the debris fly around us as the *Atlantis*'s solar guns blazed us a trail. Maybe there was something I could see that they couldn't, some way I could contribute. But all I could really do was speculate.

And then I saw it: a megalith, a true asteroid rising into view like a giant waking from its primordial slumber. It came up so fast and so unexpectedly there was hardly time to react, much less to blast it with the solar guns.

"Captain, incoming!" I exclaimed.

Captain jerked and threw his entire body to the left to dodge it, but the asteroid's momentum went the same direction and it hit us in the ship's underbelly—a terrible, screeching sound of rock on metal that made me grip the helm's railing to the point of pain.

We broke course, the *Atlantis* veering diagonally through space and hitting every space rock in its path, battering the hull like an Earth hailstorm pelting a roof.

Captain shouted commands that I could barely hear—the blood pumped too loudly in my ears and I was too fixated on the likelihood of detaching from the platform and zinging across the room like a projectile missile, magnetic lock be damned. In a desperate attempt to maintain my grip, I threw myself against Captain and wrapped my arms around his waist again.

I didn't even care if it bothered him; I needed the stability he offered, physically and mentally. To my surprise, his back was completely drenched in sweat. Hard to notice on a dark-colored jumpsuit but understandable nonetheless. It didn't even gross me out. Once again, it was strangely comforting to be reminded how entirely human he actually was.

I held on for dear life as the *Atlantis* finally stopped veering into the abyss and Captain worked on getting us back on course. There were some questionable protests from the engine but otherwise, it didn't look like anything had been critically damaged. Still, if he had reacted a second too late...

Overcome by the realization that we'd been this close to becoming one with the cosmos, my head began to spin and my stomach to sour. I pressed my forehead to Captain's back and focused on my breathing. Captain was still piloting manually and hardly noticed that I was stuck to him like a magnet. We weren't out of the deep end yet, and I was too shaken up to watch the rest of his deft maneuvers as he plowed ahead through the asteroid field without once breaking his focus.

How could he stay so *calm?*

I guess when you've trained your whole life to be a

ship's captain, when you're under pressure, you act... like a ship's captain. Aside from the physiological signs of stress, he didn't waver, not for a second, until we'd finally cleared the worst of it and realigned with the Master Course. The crewmembers let out a programmed but no less jovial cheer.

We'd done it. More to the point, he had done it.

That's when I finally had the good sense to let go of him. I expected him to go slack, get off the podium, something—but he stayed locked into position even though the danger was over. Wasn't he relieved? Didn't he need a moment's reprieve, a drink of water, something? Was there something I was missing?

I leaned over his shoulder to get a look at his face, and that's when I saw that his hands were shaking.

# 24

# Frightfully Little Room for Error

"Excellent, well done, Captain," said Beta, oblivious to his human commander's heightened state. "A very narrow escape, but an escape nonetheless. Your dexterity has improved tremendously. An eleven percent increase in accuracy at the least."

Captain remained statuesque, either unwilling or unable to move.

"Beta, would you mind taking the helm from Captain Omen?" I asked cordially.

"I am terribly sorry, Miss Nepier, but only the captain can relinquish his own duty."

I tried to meet Captain's eyes. "Sir?"

He nodded, prying the headset and gloves off as if they'd been frozen to him. "Take it," he croaked. "Take the helm, Beta."

I moved aside to let him step down from the podium.

He swayed as he took a step and I caught his arm from behind him.

"I'm fine," he said, shrugging me off. "I just need some water."

"Let me get it for you," I said and raced ahead of him to the exit, buoyant without the full gravity suit. I beat him to the dining room, asked Lambda for a water pouch, and doubled back through the lounge. There, I stopped dead.

Captain stood in the center of the room, hands on his knees, hyperventilating.

"Whoa, whoa, whoa," I said, rushing to his side.

"Get Phala," he wheezed. "I need twenty milligrams of—"

"No, you don't," I said. "You don't need drugs, you need to breathe. Inhale... exhale. Look at me." I made him meet my eyes and kept repeating the breathing exercise until he finally synced up with me. Only then did I hand him the water pouch. "Now drink." He downed it all in one swig. I think he hoped that was it, but I wasn't letting him off that easy. "Are you okay?"

"I'm fine," he said. Even I knew it was a lie. "I just need—"

"You need time to process what happened," I finished, knowing full well that wasn't what he was going to say. "That was scary. I was scared. We could've died."

He shut his eyes. "I'm aware of that, thank you."

Okay, maybe that wasn't helping. I changed tactics. "We survived," I said. "It's over. We're in the clear."

"I'm aware of that also," he said stiffly. "I told you: I am perfectly fine. My dexterity operated at maximum efficiency. The only error was a variable outside my control, but I was able to thwart it with split-second reflexes."

I rolled my eyes. "You're not a computer, you know. You're a human. Prone to human error."

"I know that!" he shouted. The reverberations shocked us both. Calmer, he said, "I know what I am." He paced to one of the museum-like display cases along the wall, one that held a selection of corals. "Must you always remind me?"

"Well, yeah," I said. "Must you act like it's such a big frickin' deal to feel things? Must you be such a frickin' drama king?"

He didn't say anything to that, just stared at the coral and proved my point. I could tell he wanted me to drop it, to stop voicing all the things he'd rather sweep under a rug. And maybe I should've said less, but that had never been one of my strong suits.

"Why are you fighting this so hard?" I asked. "Why is it such a sin to be afraid?"

"I'm not afraid," he finally said.

"Bull*shit*," I countered.

He whipped around. "Are you quite finished psychoanalyzing me, Miss Nepier?"

"Does it count as psychoanalysis when it's written all over your face?"

He gave me a steely-eyed look. "Is it, truly? All over my face?"

I knew it was a challenge, but I also suspected it was a genuine question. He wanted to know if his excessive attempts to school his emotions were at all effective.

I gave him what I hoped was a sympathetic smile. "It's not weak to feel fear if you know how to handle it."

"I do know how to handle it," he said.

"Drugs?" I asked earnestly.

"Would you prefer that I run this ship as an emotional wreck?"

"Of course not," I said. "But there's a difference between treating the source and treating the symptoms."

He crossed his arms over his chest. "And what would you say the source is, *Doctor* Nepier?"

"You expect perfection out of yourself," I said. "Which is impossible. You're afraid of what you already know. That deep down, you can't control every variable, and that one day, you're going to make a mistake that you can't fix with a drug or a robot. That's the source."

He stared at me for a long, tense moment. I forced myself to maintain eye contact with him, trying to get a read on his reaction—I could gauge neither confirmation nor denial, only passive indifference.

Finally, he said, "Right, then. I think I'll be on my way." He pushed off from the edge of the display case and stalked across the room to the bridge-side door.

"Is this how you deal with getting called out on your bullshit?" I said. "You either get defensive or just ignore it altogether? Honestly, I'd rather you just get mad. At least it would mean you actually feel something."

He stopped, turned, and said, "You want to know how I feel right now, Xanorra? Fine, then. Have it your way. I feel abysmally tired. I feel anxious to the point of discomfort even though, as you said, the danger has passed. I feel critical of myself and all the things I could've done better to prevent this ship from being damaged. And frankly, I feel like your analysis of me is not helping one damned bit."

I was stunned at that. Not only because he'd actually opened up to me, but because what he said made me realize how bad my timing was. I'd been basking so liberally in the glow of being right lately, I'd forgotten it was possible for me to be in the wrong, especially with him.

But he was a person too. A person who'd just endured an excruciating amount of duress.

"I'm sorry," I said, swallowing my pride like a jagged tortilla chip.

"It's all right," he said, resigned. At least he was quick to forgive.

"You did an amazing job out there," I said in an attempt to reassure him. "Really. I've never seen maneuvering like that from someone my age. Hell, from anyone, really. You're a very talented pilot. And everything you did, you did right. I know it's a lot to process, but when all is said and done, you should be very proud of yourself. I know I'm proud of you."

His entire demeanor shifted from defensive calm to relieved exhaustion in a heartbeat. "Thank you," he said in a way that implied he'd really needed to hear that.

I closed the distance between us and hugged him. "You're welcome," I said, hoping I hadn't just made another presumptuous error.

Thankfully, he didn't pull away. In fact, he placed his hands on my back. "Are you all right?" he asked, to my surprise. "After all that?"

I pulled back to look him in the eyes. "I was terrified," I admitted. "But I also felt safe with you. I knew you'd pull through."

"You're in earnest?"

"Did you not feel me clinging to you like Velcro?" I said, releasing him in a sudden bout of self-consciousness. "I was using you as a literal anchor. Sorry about that, by the way."

"No, I—" He straightened the front of his jumper. "It did not bother me."

"I admire your focus," I said. "Honestly, I wish I could stay as calm under pressure as you do."

He paused for a moment, then cast his eyes to the floor and said, "It's nothing to admire, really. On a mission like this, there is frightfully little room for error. I can't afford to be any weaker than I am right now."

"That's a dangerously low margin," I said, intending to give him a compliment.

"That's why I need Phala."

"You haven't needed her yet," I said, trying to meet his eyes. "You seem like you're doing pretty good, actually. Am I wrong?"

When he looked up at me, my heart caught in my throat. His eyes searched mine as he said, "No, you're not wrong."

What was I supposed to do? This seemed like the most inopportune time imaginable to want to kiss him. It was the adrenaline, of course. It had to be the adrenaline. Besides, he probably didn't know it was something people did in a romantic sense, if at all. What if I freaked him out? Did I really want to cross that line?

But then he reached out and touched my hair. Why my hair, I couldn't say. He'd never shown an interest in my hair before. But it occurred to me then that it was a bit odd how he kept his long enough to fall across his forehead—after all, everyone else on the ship was bald. Why didn't he shave his head? Why didn't he emulate his robotic caretakers in yet another way? It would've been more efficient. Utilitarian, as he would say.

Maybe because one's hair was an expression of individuality, a truly human attribute? Maybe it was one of the few ways he had to express his humanity at all?

"You're as much to thank for our survival as I am," he said, his voice soft. "You saw that asteroid before any of us did. I was too absorbed in the whole to focus on the parts. If you hadn't spoken up… I might've reacted too slowly."

I could hardly think straight as it was with his fingers caressing my hair, but now he was giving me credit for saving us? It was too much. "I doubt that," I said.

"I don't," he said, his hand brushing my cheek, sending my heart into a frenzy.

"We make a good team, then, don't we?" I said, watching his mouth.

"Yes," he said. His hand came to rest where my neck met my shoulder. I was hyperaware of how close we were, how warm he was. How I was still in my underlayer of shorts and a t-shirt.

*Abort mission!* my mind shouted. *Abort! Abort!*

"Did you ever think you'd work so well with another human?" I asked, inching my face forward.

"No," he said, still as a statue. "Never."

I was a breath away from him, dizzy with anticipation and apprehension. Was this actually happening? "Me neither."

Just then, the bridge-side doors slid open and Phala bustled in with a look of maternal concern. We sprang apart like opposing magnets, repelled by the shock of interruption and, in my case at least, the shame of having been caught.

But Phala seemed unfazed by our familiarity as she said firmly, "Captain, it has been approximately fourteen minutes since your stress-inducing event. Why didn't you seek me out immediately? Your biochemistry is highly irregular!"

I bit back a chuckle. *Highly irregular, indeed.*

"I'm sorry, Phala. I was deterred," said Captain, sparing me a glance.

Phala made a very human tutting sound as she scanned Captain's face with her retina sensors. Then she began to do the android equivalent of fussing over him: checking his vitals, taking a blood sample, and rattling off chemical levels that even I didn't understand.

And then, so quickly I couldn't even protest, she injected him with those twenty milligrams of whatever he'd wanted when we'd first entered the room.

"This will set everything back to rights," she said with satisfaction. Then she turned to me. "Xanorra, would you like me to scan you as well?"

*Oh, I get the option?* "No, I think I'm okay, but thank you."

"Of course," she said cordially. "Captain, I recommend at least an hour of sedentary rest before you resume your duties. Also, be sure to drink at least sixteen ounces of water."

I scoffed inwardly. *Way ahead of you, sister.*

"Thank you, Phala," he said.

She left the way she came and we were alone again. Alone, but I could tell by looking at him that the moment was irretrievable. Thanks a lot, Robot Mom.

"Feel better?" I asked.

He nodded once, avoiding eye contact. "I will take Phala's advice. I suggest you do the same."

As he moved past me toward the door, I said, "Captain."

He stopped and gave me an expectant look.

"Thank you."

His brow furrowed. "For what, exactly?"

"For being honest with me."

He gave me a half-smile. "Likewise." Then he left.

# 25

# Quin's Journal #3

The natural next step had been to tell my parents about my theory, which I did over dinner the same night—after letting them recover from the shock of seeing me at the dinner table for the first time in a month.

Then, once we were well into the meal, I cleared my throat and said, "Mom, Dad, there's something I need to talk to you about."

Both my parents looked at me. Mom said, "Of course, honey."

I swallowed, trying to keep the words straight in my head. I'd rehearsed my speech with Seb that afternoon before he'd left, marking that day as the longest amount of time I'd ever spent with him alone. Part of me was still reeling from it, which did not help my nerves a dang bit.

"I've been going over the incident report, from the attack," I said. "Something about it didn't add up."

"Yes, the identity of the ship is still unknown," said Dad, his face grave. "Of course it doesn't add up."

"But there's something else, isn't there?" I said. "Have you looked at the photos of the escape pod? The one Xan was supposed to have been in?"

"Quin," Mom said gently. "You probably shouldn't look at those reports right now. For your own peace of mind."

"I'm totally fine with it," I said. "Because what I found is huge. Xan should have been in that pod. The window was cracked, not broken. I think there is ample evidence to support the theory that that ship—the squid ship—took her. That at the very least, she's intact, but that she may even possibly be alive."

I let that little nugget sink in for a minute. Mom looked like she might burst into tears but Dad just looked exhausted, like he'd just worked an overnight shift. I waited, patiently, for them to process the declaration before I tried to elaborate.

"Quin," Dad finally said. "I understand that you're grieving... I understand that Xan's... that it hit you hard... but I expect you of all people to be rational."

"I am being rational, Dad," I said. I'd expected this reaction. I was prepared for it. "This isn't wishful thinking or denial; there is real, solid evidence to support this. We have to make a case to the SEA."

"Even if there is," said Dad, "even if we could, I doubt there's anything the SEA would be able to do. This event—the *Washington*—it's set them back at least five years. Probably more."

"Yeah, I get that, but don't you think knowing that the spacer they lost might actually be alive on that ship would change their minds? They're not that heartless, are they?"

"It's not about heartlessness," said Dad. "It's about what's possible with the resources we have. Even if we could find the ship, how do we get to it? Even if we could get to it, how do we extract Xan safely? It would take months of planning, of preparation. Technology we don't have. *Money* we don't have."

After a stilted moment, I exclaimed, "Then I'll invent something, and then they'll have to fund us!"

"Quinette Tourmaline," Dad said firmly. He rarely ever used my full name, so I shut up like a pressure seal. "You are smart, and you are ambitious, but you are still young. It doesn't work that way. You don't get to hurry decades of research along because you want your sister back."

I nodded. "I understand."

"However," he said slowly, "I can still try to make a case to the SEA for you."

I looked up, my heart fluttering. "Really?"

"I can't guarantee they'll listen to me—I used up the last of their patience a long time ago—but I'll try. I'll try anything, Quin. I hope you know that. But... I want you to be realistic. It's not that your mother and I don't believe you. It's not that I think it's a lost cause. It's just..."

"The practicality of the thing," Mom finished.

"Exactly," said Dad. "If you're right, then it'll be the greatest miracle this family has ever known. But if you're wrong, the truth could destroy you. Are you prepared for that, Quin?"

I lowered my eyes to my half-finished dinner. It was a fair question.

"Listen," Dad went on, "these past few weeks, seeing you like this, it broke my heart. I can't even fathom the pain of seeing you shattered by false hope, too. So ask yourself, can you live with the outcome, no matter what it is?"

I couldn't answer him right away. It really sucks when your parents are right.

Mom reached across the table and took my hand. "Quin, you've never been a quitter. I've always loved that about you. If there's a problem, you find a solution, no matter what. Just remember that sometimes, there's more than one right answer."

I swallowed a lump in my throat and said, "I am prepared for whatever outcome. I just want to bring her home." I made myself look at Dad even though I could feel the pressure building behind my eyes. "She deserves to be with her family. Even if it's to be put to rest. *We* deserve to give her that."

"And if we can't find her?" he said softly.

I took a deep breath and said, "Then we deserve to know we tried."

I knew Dad was right about the whole "you can't rush progress just because you have a vendetta" thing, but at the same time, I couldn't just sit back and do nothing while my dad waded through the red tape.

For the first time in a month, I wanted to do something, and I had every intention of acting on that impulse before it flew away like an aimless butterfly.

So, the next day, I tracked down Seb. Yes, *I* went looking for *him*. I know, right? I was really starting to not recognize myself these days, but I was on a mission, so it wasn't like I was interacting with him just because. And on the flip side, he was only interacting with me because Xan meant a lot to him, too.

So really, nothing had changed; it was still Xan forcing us to spend time together, even from beyond the stars. Possibly even beyond the grave, morbid as it was to consider it. Dad was right about that, too: I had to be prepared for every outcome. I didn't think it was wrong to hope, but it was wrong to lie to yourself and not face up to reality.

I told Seb all this too, and he agreed. Thankfully, he also agreed that sitting around and twiddling our thumbs was a no-go.

"But that does leave the question, what can we do?" he asked. We were in the medical school's infirmary, where he trained during the day. It was empty for the moment aside from Dr. Basco in his office at the back of the room. As long as there were no patients to attend to, he didn't care if Seb had visitors. "Even if one of us is practically a genius."

"That's why this will work," I said. "If I apply myself, and if I have you to help me, I'm certain the two of us will be able to come up with something. It's gonna take a lot of work; all of our free time and then some. And I will have to go back to my studies at some point, though maybe I can negotiate a part-time schedule so I have more time to devote to this."

"Just be careful," said Seb. "I don't want you getting in trouble or getting shut down."

I shook my head. "They won't shut me down. I'm going to say it's for my thesis. It *is* my thesis now. The solution to the problem—to finding Xan—it might just be FTL."

"Yeah, I was afraid you'd say that," said Seb. "You really think the two of us can accelerate a field that's been a century in the making? Isn't that a recipe for hubris?"

Why did he have to be so wise? And why was he so attractive when he thought things through? *Focus, Quin. This is no time to be a teenager.* "I think we have a unique advantage," I said plainly. "And it's not my brain; I'm not that special. It's that ship. That ship is an enigma. It's got to be far beyond any technology the SEA has if it's been able to fly under the radar for so long. And we have footage of it. Simulations. Data. If we want to find Xan, we gotta unlock the secrets of that damn squid ship."

Seb's eyebrows went up at that. "Okay, fair enough. So that's our starting point then: figuring out who could've built a ship like that."

I nodded. "And most importantly, how to find it."

# 26

# A Good Time to Succumb to Sleep Dysfunction

The *Atlantis* may have survived its little thrill ride, but it definitely had not come out unscathed. The hull had taken a good beating and the underside had a nasty scrape that had nearly breached the engine room. Of course, I didn't know this until I entered the bridge the following morning, after an unsatisfying night of sleep.

As far as Captain could tell me, the internal systems were all okay, though he had Lambda and Kappa running diagnostics on every last bolt and screw. The other bots, Beta included, were busy combing the hull like ants on a rock, mending any critical damage.

That meant the bridge was next to empty. The navigation bot, Delta, was the only non-human presence, but she wasn't exactly a conversationalist. It was surreal to see the bridge devoid of its crew, with only its human pilot to direct its operations.

Other than a general look of fatigue, Captain was focused and appeared unfazed by yesterday's events. I wondered if he'd slept as uneasily as I had. Instead of asking, I gained permission to sit in one of the control center's empty chairs and watched the viewscreens. One screen showed Eta and Theta working in the engine room and another showed the rest of the crew from several angles on the hull.

I'll admit it: I felt some newfound level of authority now that I'd actually helped do something on the bridge. Not that I was going to hop up onto the helm again anytime soon—though the thought did cross my mind in an unwarranted way. My mind kept wandering to our conversation in the lounge, to how close together we'd been. If Phala hadn't interrupted us, what would've happened?

Eh, probably better that I didn't follow that train of thought too far.

"How long are these repairs going to take?" I asked, purely out of curiosity.

"Based on the reports they've been sending me, probably a week," Captain replied. "Thankfully, most of the damage is cosmetic. We'll do a spacewalk tomorrow and another when the repairs are completed."

"You want me to come with you?" I asked, turning in my chair to face him.

"Yes, I do. If you don't mind."

"I don't," I said with a smile.

"I suppose it goes without saying that our lessons will have to be put on hold until we can sort all this out."

"That's fine," I said. "I don't mind a break. As long as

you promise to take care of yourself. Eat, sleep, that sort of thing."

"I had breakfast," he said as if I held any sort of authority over him in that regard.

"That's a start." I smiled at him and got out of my chair to approach the helm. "Is there anything I can do to help?"

"Actually, there is," he said. "If it's not too much trouble, I would be much obliged if you would look after the greenhouse. I could usually get away with a little neglect, but with two of us to feed, it can't afford to go untended, not even for a day."

I tried, in vain, to stop my smile from reaching idiot levels. "It would be an honor, Captain."

"Thank you," he said, polite but sincere.

"I may need detailed instructions though," I said. "I would hate to mess something up."

"Didn't I walk you through it once already?"

I gave him a serious look. "Yeah, once. I don't have an eidetic memory, unlike some."

"I don't either. I'd just like to think I'm that proficient a teacher."

I rolled my eyes. "So humble."

"That was intended as a joke," he said, averting his eyes.

My jaw dropped. "You, attempting humor? God forbid. I might actually die of shock."

"Please refrain from dying. It would be terribly inconvenient," he said with a smirk.

This time, I laughed out loud. It was the first time he'd ever made me laugh on purpose—and it felt wonderful.

"See? You're improving already," I said. "I must be that good of a teacher."

"Now look who lacks humility."

I scoffed. "Rude!"

He looked at me, eyebrows knit together. "Was it?"

I smiled and shook my head. "I knew it was banter. You're a fast learner, though. Grade A use of irony."

"I learned from the best," he said, and then his face lit up in remembrance. "Let me get you those instructions."

I waited while he typed them up and dropped them onto my tablet. I thanked him and turned to leave the bridge, but before I could, he said, "Xanorra."

I still wasn't used to him calling me by my first name. I turned and answered, "Yes?"

"Your laugh. It's… nice."

I blinked. "Was that a real compliment, Captain? Or are you attempting irony again?"

"I'm in earnest."

I smiled wide. "Well, thank you, Captain. Good to know it's not an assault on your eardrums."

Without skipping a beat, he said, "I don't imagine any sound you could make would ever offend me."

Well, that sure rendered me speechless. I'm pretty sure I turned as red as Mars as I scuttled off the bridge in an awkward exodus.

Taking care of the greenhouse was a real treat. I took my time half out of determination to do everything right and half because it was just so nice to be there. I wondered if this is where Captain slept, even though it was a little warm for my taste and I didn't see any bedding-like materials lying around. For all I knew, he slept on the floor. Or standing up. With the sort of upbringing he'd had, it wouldn't surprise me one bit.

Once I'd completed the checklist, I returned to the bridge to give Captain my report. I kept it strictly business, mostly because I didn't want to start blushing again thinking about his embarrassing (but endearing) attempts at flattery. I told him the fig tree looked great and that it should be ready for harvest in about two weeks. Maybe my standards were really low these days, but I couldn't wait for our makeshift Thanksgiving.

I was on my own for the rest of the day, which I mostly spent reading in the lounge. After dinner, which I ate alone, I went down a nature documentary rabbit hole that took me well past my normal bedtime—but thanks to my lazy afternoon, I wasn't that tired and found that it was kind of fun to break what had so far been a pretty consistent routine.

I guess it took getting hit by an asteroid to shake things up around here. Literally.

I was just starting to entertain the idea of turning in when the bridge-side doors opened and Captain stepped into the room. I froze. Did he sleep in the lounge after all? I guess I wouldn't know since I was usually in bed by now.

I jumped up from the couch and said, "Sorry. I lost track of the time."

He didn't respond. He just stood there, a blank expression on his face as he looked into the middle distance. It took me a long, creeped-out moment to realize what was happening: he was sleepwalking.

"Oh," I said. Quin used to sleepwalk sometimes when we were little. I more or less knew what to do, and even though I knew waking him up wouldn't be the worst thing in the world, I decided it would probably be better if I didn't.

"Come on, Captain, let's get you to bed," I said, taking him by the arm. I meant to steer him to the couch, but he turned and walked toward the bedroom instead. I followed and opened the door for him, and then I gently guided him to my bed, which was technically his bed–so I wasn't opposed to him reclaiming it subconsciously.

It was so odd, seeing him like this. I figured it must be due to lack of sleep and a surplus of stress, but I had to wonder if it happened often, and if so, whether or not he was aware of it. Once in bed, he pulled the covers around him and seemed to settle back into a comfortable, stationary rest, so I left him there and resolved to sleep on the couch.

Couldn't hurt. In fact, it was a nice change of scenery.

But the whole thing was still unsettling as heck, so I couldn't really relax. I continued the nature documentary instead, keeping one eye on the door in case he decided to wander again. He didn't.

But about an hour later, when I finally started drifting off, I woke up just as quickly to the sound of shouting.

I bolted to the bedroom door and entered the room. Captain sat upright in the bed, his eyes wide and panicked, yelling at the wall, "Please let me stop! Let me stop!"

I went to him and took his face in my hands. "Captain! Wake up! It's okay! You're okay!"

He blinked rapidly until his eyes focused on me. Then he pulled me into him, crushing his face into my chest, and breathed deep, wheezy breaths, somewhere between hyperventilating and sobbing.

I was stunned beyond speech. I began to wonder if maybe I was the one having a dream. I almost asked if I should get Phala, but quickly decided to screw that–I could handle this myself. I positioned myself more comfortably on the bed and rubbed his back.

"It's okay," I said. "You're okay."

"What am I doing in this room?" he said, pulling away from me. He sounded so tired.

I shifted and said, "You were sleepwalking. I was just trying to... help you get back to sleep."

"Shit," he said, dropping his head in his hands. "Shit, shit, *shit*. I'm so sorry."

In any other context, hearing him finally use a colloquial swear word would be a cause for celebration. But all I could feel was remorse.

"Don't be sorry," I said. "Why should you be sorry? It happens."

"Not to me. Not for years. I thought... I thought I was past all this." He pressed his palms to his eyes. "I had it under control."

"Come on, Captain, have some grace on yourself. It's been a rough couple of days. You're mentally and physically exhausted, I'm sure. You need to sleep."

"I don't sleep very much," he said. "Not even in the best of circumstances."

Now it made sense: he had insomnia. I wondered how I hadn't seen it before. "How long have you not been able to sleep?" I asked gently.

"Oh, since I was around... thirteen or so. Puberty, I suppose."

"Where do you sleep, when you manage to?"

"On the bridge, upright," he said in shame. "Or sometimes... sometimes in the lounge. Not often. For maybe a couple of hours at a time, early in the morning."

"I never hear you," I said reassuringly. "Would you like to try to sleep in here? It is your room, after all."

He shook his head. "I hate this room. I could never sleep in here, either."

I wanted to ask why that was (other than the room's total lack of personality) but it didn't seem like the right time. "I'll stay up with you, then," I said.

He shook his head. "No, that's not necessary."

"It's no problem," I said. "I was in the middle of a documentary, actually, before you came in. We could watch it together if you'd like."

He gave me a confused look. "For what reason?"

"To get your mind off of things." I rose from the bed. "Come on."

He hesitated for a moment, then slid out after me and into the lounge. I sat down on the couch and motioned for him to sit next to me, and then I used my tablet to cast the video to the glass screen.

"There," I said. "Isn't this nice?" It was almost like the late-night movie marathons Quin and I used to have. Except we usually watched something a little more riveting than whales. (No offense, whales.)

"It's passable," he replied.

"Already back to your old self, I see," I said. Not sure I actually meant to say that out loud, but I did.

He huffed. "I'm sorry you had to see me... like that."

I looked at him while he actively avoided eye contact with me. "Don't apologize for that. You've seen me at *my* worst. Friends are supposed to be there for you at your lowest."

"That was not my lowest," he said offhandedly. For a split second, I thought he was trying to dismiss my assessment, but then I realized the true implication of the remark.

It could've been worse.

If our conversation following the asteroid incident was any indication, then it was obvious that he kept everything bottled up inside. But how much of that was due to his stoic personality, and how much of it was due to the medications Phala gave him to regulate his emotions? It was difficult to say.

However, something else bothered me about what had just happened, and while I didn't want to pry, I had to ask: "What were you dreaming about?"

He turned to look at me with trepidation in his eyes. "What?"

"When you were having a night terror, you said: 'Please let me stop.'"

"I did?" He had a far-off look in his eyes, and I got the sense he knew exactly what he'd said and why.

"You don't have to tell me if you don't want to," I said. "I just wondered... in case you needed to talk about it.

Sometimes talking about the bad dream helps make it less real. It sort of loses its power that way."

"I know it wasn't real," he said, and instantly I could tell I'd lost him. Well, it serves me right for prying, I guess. "Already it feels like a distant memory. You needn't worry."

"Okay," I said, cutting my losses before I said something I'd regret. "As long as you're okay."

We lapsed into silence.

"The documentary is very soothing," he said, nodding to the screen. "I assume that was the design behind choosing one about the ocean? To calm the nerves?"

"Oh, no, I didn't plan that," I said with a chortle. "You got lucky, bro. I might've been watching one about screaming monkeys or volcanic eruptions or something."

He chortled back. At least I'd succeeded in lightening the mood. "I picked a good night to succumb to sleep dysfunction, then."

"Yeah, bully for you." I looked at him, smiling. He had his head tipped back against the couch, and when he caught my gaze, he smiled, too. My heart turned to helium. I couldn't help myself—buoyant, spurred by bubbly courage, I leaned forward and kissed him on the cheek, drawing back quickly in case he hated it.

He sat forward, his eyes widening. "Why did you do that?"

"I don't know," I said, my heart sinking with sudden apprehension. "I just... I didn't... I wasn't thinking."

"Weren't you?" The look he gave me wasn't disgust or scandal. It was curiosity.

Right, how could I forget? He didn't understand kissing.

"Um… okay, so… that was a kiss," I began.

"Yes, I know what it was," he said. "I'm asking why you did it."

"Well, culturally—in most cultures, that is—people kiss to display… affection."

He leaned forward, elbows resting on his knees. "Friends as well?"

"Sometimes," I squeaked. "There's, um, different types of kisses. For different types of relationships. A kiss you'd give your mom or your sister is not the same type of kiss you'd give, say, your wife."

"I gather that," he said haughtily. "So, how would you classify that kiss?"

I groaned. My patience was as thin as his subtlety. "Why does everything have to be an academic exercise? Why did you touch my hair yesterday, huh? How would you classify that? Friends don't touch each other's hair. Like that."

He stared at me with a look of befuddlement. "I crossed a boundary of yours? Why didn't you say so?"

"Well—yes, but… I didn't mind it so much." I looked down at my hands, waxing bashful. "I did wonder why, though."

"I… couldn't say," he said. I believed him. He straightened, lifting his chin slightly, and said, "I suppose it's because I like your hair. It's a very nice color. But I did not mean to cross a line. In the moment, I…"

"Wasn't thinking?" I guessed good-naturedly.

"Scientifically improbable," he said.

"And yet there's an entire race of intelligent beings that would disagree with you wholeheartedly."

"Omen versus the human race," he said with a sigh. "Very well. I concede. I wasn't thinking."

"Atta boy."

"But I will refrain from making the same mistake again."

"Swing and a miss," I said with a sigh. I leaned against him and put my head on his shoulder, half-expecting him to protest out of some misinformed intellectual obligation. He stiffened but made no move to reject me. "It's okay to stop thinking every once in a while," I said with a yawn.

"And yet there is a ship full of intelligent processors that would disagree with *you* wholeheartedly," he said, relaxing into me.

A blanket-like warmth settled around me as my body began its shutdown sequence. A weight settled across my shoulders that I thought at first was fatigue, but realized with glee was actually Captain's arm around me. I settled in, too comfortable to change plans, and drifted off to sleep.

# 27

# The Manifold Uses of Duct Tape

When I woke, I was alone on the couch. That didn't surprise me, but what did was that Captain had tucked a blanket around me and replaced himself with a pillow as my headrest. It was disgustingly sweet of him. I wanted to melt into a mushy puddle of sentimental bliss, but there was work to be done.

I cleaned myself up and had a good breakfast in preparation for today's spacewalk. I was excited to go out again, excited to do something useful. Admittedly, I was also eager to see Captain again, to know how he was feeling after the events of last night, good and bad.

I reported to the bridge with the intention of keeping things professional, but as soon as he turned and saw me, my stomach did that annoying backflip thing and I gave him a wry grin like we had a secret now. I guess we kinda did.

He greeted me cordially but otherwise was as stoic and

focused as ever as he ran through the day's itinerary. Determined not to waste any time fawning, I checked the greenhouse before meeting up with him in the docking bay at the allotted time.

Now that I'd been through the *Atlantis*'s EVA procedure once, I felt way more comfortable with it. It took me about the same time to suit up as it did Captain. We did a final check on each other's latches and tether anchors, and then the airlock door opened and we entered the abyss once again.

The turquoise gas cloud we'd passed through was directly behind us and fully visible, which indicated that it was way bigger than I'd initially thought. I'll admit, it was nice to see some color in what was generally a colorless expanse. At least the stars and planets always gave you something interesting to look at, even if that something was usually far away and didn't change very quickly.

Instead of going to the top of the ship first like last time, we used the support rungs along the side to make our way down to the underbelly, where most of the damage was. The two bots that had been deployed for repairs today—Epsilon and Zeta—were hard at work. They didn't look like they needed our help, but Captain ordered a status report from each of them to make sure everything was on track. He also inspected each of them to make sure the exposure wasn't inflicting any damage. They wore protective skins similar to an EVA suit, but one could never be sure. Thankfully, aside from the odd dent here and there, they passed inspection with flying colors.

Captain and I split up to take readings of the gash and see how much heat leaked from the engine; Beta had done this yesterday, apparently, but Captain wanted to do it himself today.

"Sixteen percent improvement on this section," I reported.

"Twenty-four percent improvement here," he said.

We continued like that until we met in the middle, and then we made our way back to the top of the ship. Captain checked the external readout sensors and scowled. "It's as I feared," he said.

"Is it bad?" I asked.

"There was a high concentration of micro-debris in that gas cloud," he said. "It's hard to see, but it caused thousands of indentations from stem to stern." He crouched down and I followed. Sure enough, the metallic surface of the hull was pock-marked, like the surface of a golf ball. "Some of the dust is embedded now, too."

"What does that mean?" I asked.

"Initially, nothing. But if left untreated, like a wound, it could break down the integrity of the hull and cause massive damage. Worse than the gash on the underside."

"How do we fix it?"

"We don't," he said.

"Well, how long will it last, then?"

He shrugged. "If we're lucky, for the duration of the mission. Provided we don't run into any more obstacles."

"What's the likelihood of that, in thirty-two years?"

"Highly unlikely." He stood up. "We'll have to be extra vigilant. Think ten steps ahead. Take no risks."

"Sounds stressful," I said. "You can't plan for everything. You'll spend the rest of the mission tied up in knots. That's no way to live."

"At least we'll be alive," he muttered.

"Come on, let's think of alternatives. Maybe we can't cover the entire hull, but can we identify the weakest areas and prioritize those?"

"It's impossible to tell which are the weakest. For all we know, we could cover the wrong areas and it wouldn't make a difference."

"Well, say we hypothetically went ahead and patched it all anyway. How would we do that?"

"Cosmetic damage is patched with a silicone epoxy alloy, which acts like glue with metallic properties. It's what the crew is using to weld with right now and they'll likely use it all up by the end of this."

"Can anything inside be converted into silicone epoxy?"

"With Iota?" He bobbed his head, pensive. "Possibly, but it would take a lot of recycled material, and it would have to be solid."

I smiled. "Ever heard of duct tape?"

It's official: I'm a genius.

After we finished our spacewalk, we tested out my theory with Iota and discovered that we could, in fact, print silicone epoxy duct tape. Rather than make it into a thin roll, we would print it out in sheets like contact paper. It would use up all the extra material we had, and we would have to break down the dining room furniture for the rest, but some things were more important than having a place to sit.

"Are you sure?" Captain kept asking me even after we'd carried the furniture to the storage room. "We can find other alternatives."

"I'm one hundred percent positive," I said. "We'll just have to eat cross-legged on the floor. They do that in Egypt, don't they?"

"Traditionally, yes," he said. "Though I'm more apt to stand."

"How American of you."

It was going to take a few hours for the materials to print, so that was basically it for the day. We'd do another spacewalk tomorrow and get to work on hull repairs. Captain went back to the bridge, I went back to the lounge, and we didn't see each other for the rest of the evening. No sleepwalking. No night terrors. No classifying kisses. It was as if none of that had even happened.

Just as well, I guess. He probably hadn't wanted it to happen in the first place.

You know how on Earth, there are people who tile roofs for a living, and they spend all day on those steep slopes laying down squares of rubbery stuff that are supposed to protect the house?

Take that concept, make the tiles four times bigger and about a tenth as thick, and subtract any gravity whatsoever. That's basically what patching the hull's micro-damage was like.

We each had a backpack-type case strapped to our stomach that held the patches and a device that was more or less a blow dryer designed to activate the epoxy. We started from the nose of the ship, just behind the bridge windows, and worked our way down.

At first, it was fun, and I was optimistic—the *Atlantis* wasn't a huge ship, though it wasn't exactly a one-person cruiser, either. But after four hours of meticulously laying sheets, it got pretty old. Plus, every time I looked behind me, I saw just how much surface area there was and felt a sense of impending doom. This had been my idea, and I still thought it was a good one, but it was going to take forever.

Which I guess we technically had. But still. I get bored easily.

I had just about emptied my backpack—our stopping point for the day—and had taken a quick rest break when something went wrong. The ship lurched, shuddering violently. My footing—which, thanks to my impatient patching method, hadn't been too secure to begin with—slipped from the hull, and I began to fall along the side of the ship.

I scrambled for a support rung and at the same time tried to activate the magnets—but they either weren't working or not catching, and focusing on them made me miss any potential handholds.

"Shit, shit, shit," I said, the level of urgency rising in my voice with each repetition.

"What's wrong?" Captain's voice came through my

helmet. We'd kept the comm link open so we could update each other from opposite sides of the ship.

"Um, I may have slipped. But it's fine. I've got the tether."

But I didn't have the tether. The point where it should've gone taut and kept me anchored to the ship never happened. It stayed slack and trailed after me like a lazy river, and it was then that I realized: it had come undone. Even though we'd checked it twice over. I wasn't attached to the ship.

And that's when I started to panic.

"Captain! I was wrong! I'm not tethered, I'm freefalling! Captain! Help!"

"Hold on!" he shouted, and a moment later, I saw him rappelling down the side of the ship closest to me. He launched himself off the hull, using the ship's momentum to propel himself toward me, or more accurately, toward the tether floating in the abyss. I was already too far out of reach. If he wasn't able to grab the rope, I'd be lost. Or at best, very difficult to retrieve again.

Would he even alter course to rescue me? Would Beta even let him?

This was literally every spacer's worst nightmare. And it was even more horrifying than I could've imagined.

Captain reached for the line, letting his own tether take him out as far as it would go. I prayed his wasn't somehow unattached either or we were both in deep shit. But it wasn't. Just as it began to reach its limit, he grabbed onto mine and wound it around his wrists and forearms as many times as he could, turning himself into a human anchor.

I braced myself for the rebound as it pulled taut. He cried out with the constriction but quickly began to haul me in hand over hand, not stopping until I was close enough for us to latch onto each other. I held onto him tighter than I'd ever held anything in my life, gasping for air as the panic dissolved into anxious relief.

"I've got you," he said, his face mirroring my emotions. "I've got you."

He activated the pulley that retracted the tether back to the ship, and it wasn't until the airlock doors closed that I truly felt safe. Still, I shook all over. The airlock couldn't have cycled fast enough; as soon as I could, I tore my helmet off and dropped to my knees, wheezing.

Captain moved a little slower, removing his helmet and crouching down to my level. He put a hand on my shoulder and said, "It's all right. You're safe now."

I collapsed into his arms. He held onto me with equal fervor, as if he'd been afraid, too.

"The tether anchor—we checked it—how did it—?" I couldn't get the words out, but the question was there: how the hell had it come unbolted?

"I don't know," said Captain. "But I intend to look into it."

The mystery made me queasy, the possible explanations bitter like bile in my throat. I didn't want to think about how it could've happened; I was still recovering from the fact that it had happened at all.

And that's when something else occurred to me.

"You didn't have to save me," I said.

He pulled back in alarm. "What?"

"Our pact. It only applies as long as I'm on the ship. You could've let me go."

"Technically, I suppose I could have," he said, rubbing his chin. "I did say as much once, didn't I?"

"Did it even occur to you?"

He met my eyes. "No, it did not. And I can't say I would've been able to live with myself if it had."

It honestly surprised me to hear him say that. "So you do have a heart," I said with a smirk.

He sighed as if this whole thing had been one huge inconvenience. "If it wouldn't be too much to ask, could you suspend your limitless supply of sarcasm long enough for Phala to look you over?"

I really was okay, just a little shaken up. But to put him at ease, I said, "Sure. Anything for you, Captain."

He pulled back and looked like he wanted to retort, but he held his tongue as we got up and changed from the EVA suits back into our regular jumpers. Then it was off to the infirmary where, as expected, I was diagnosed as perfectly healthy. Part of me thought Phala seemed a bit disappointed by that fact, but it could've just been my harried imagination.

"What about you?" Phala asked her ward, turning her discerning robot eyes onto him.

"I am fine," he said.

She scanned him up and down. "You are lying. Come here."

He obeyed instantly. Honestly, it was both disturbing and fascinating to watch these two interact—aside from her brief appearance after the asteroid incident, I hadn't seen them in a room together since I'd come aboard, even though I knew he visited her nearly every day.

Phala obviously held a maternal authority over Captain, whether he was aware of it or not. He acted differently around her; more emotionless and detached. I couldn't tell if it was habitual or circumstantial, but it reminded me of friends I'd had back home whose parents were overly strict.

Considering what she was, the correlation didn't surprise me one bit.

Phala ordered Captain to unzip the front of his jumper and remove his undershirt, which he did without question.

"Should I—?" Too late, he was already shirtless and there was no way I was leaving now. I blushed like crazy, but only for the time it took me to notice his forearms. They were covered in big, ugly welts.

I gasped. "Are those from the tether? From hauling me in?"

"It's nothing," he said. Phala was busy scanning his arms and chest with some kind of handheld x-ray, no doubt to determine if he'd broken any bones. "A trifle."

"I am going to apply cooling patches to the affected areas," said Phala, moving to one of the cabinets. "What you did was extremely dangerous, Captain. You could have broken both radii and ulnae."

"But I did not," he said triumphantly. He looked over at me and must've noticed my flushed face and horrified expression. "I'm fine, Xanorra. Truly. It looks worse than it is."

"It is going to get worse before it gets better," said

Phala, applying the patches to his outstretched arms. "These are fresh. They will turn black and blue by tomorrow."

"My favorite colors," he said flatly. More bewildering than the fact that he was cracking jokes at a time like this was the fact that he had favorite colors at all. Unless that *was* the joke.

"Leave those on for twenty minutes and then come back in four to six hours," said Phala, pulling his shirt over his head and helping him thread his arms through the holes as if he were a toddler in need of dressing. Then again, he was injured, so maybe it would've been a struggle for him by himself.

"Of course."

"And promise never to do anything like that ever again."

"I promise."

Now that was a little weird. Since when did promises mean anything to a robot? Or was that why Captain took our pact so seriously in the first place... because he'd been taught how to make promises? Did I have Phala to thank for my safety, or was this something I should be concerned about?

The android put her hands on either side of his face and said, "You are a good captain."

A chill went up my spine. Not "you're a good man." Not even "you're a good boy," cringy as that would be. It made me realize—with a sick feeling in my stomach—that he wasn't so much a person to them as he was a role being filled.

Which begged the question: what, exactly, did that make me?

# 28

# Why Must I Be a Teenager in Space?

I took the rest of the evening off to recover from my brush with death—a different kind of shock than that of the asteroid incident—and to reflect on what could have caused it in the first place. I'd avoided rationalizations for this long, but left to my own thoughts, I couldn't help but speculate on whether or not it had been a freak accident.

Because if it hadn't been an accident, then by process of elimination, it had been on purpose. Which means that someone—or, rather, something—wanted me off this ship.

I knew I sailed into dangerous waters thinking about it; an android's programming shouldn't allow them to enact harm on a human being, even one that they tolerated at best. But could one of them really have attempted to murder me? And if so, which one?

You could probably guess who my money was on. But

without any proof, even bothering to confront Captain about Beta would be futile. It was clear he turned a blind eye to the androids as it was. He turned a blind eye to a lot of things about his situation.

With all these uncomfortable musings swirling around my overstimulated noggin, I had half a mind to turn in early when Captain entered the lounge from the dining room door, a tray of food in his hand.

I hadn't even known he wasn't on the bridge.

"Lambda tells me you didn't eat," he said as he came around to the front of the couch.

"Hey, that's not fair," I said, sitting up. "I don't ask him about you anymore. Speaking of, how are your arms?"

"Sore, but otherwise fine." He sat down next to me and handed me the tray. "Are you ill?"

I shook my head as I took it from him. "Just tired. And overwhelmed."

"Understandable." He cleared his throat. "I fell once. I was ten years old and it was my first spacewalk alone. I didn't activate my magnets, like an idiot... I thought I was too good for them. I was wrong. It took me twenty minutes *with* Beta feeding me instructions to haul myself back to the airlock. It was the most terrifying twenty minutes of my life."

I looked at him in surprise as I swallowed a bite of food. "I bet. And it wasn't like you had anybody to—" I stopped myself. Phala had probably comforted him, and in his mind, that had been enough.

Still, that knowledge combined with the visit to the infirmary earlier today raised all sorts of questions about his childhood that I'd forced myself to hold back.

"I inspected the tether anchor," he said. "It came unbolted from the mount. How, I do not know. It shouldn't have. I spoke to Beta about it, and he said it could've been faulty from the start, and since I'd never used it, I hadn't known."

"That seems plausible," I said flatly, struggling to hold my tongue before I voiced my other, more nefarious, theories.

"I also asked him about what caused that lurch while we were on the hull, and he said he didn't know either, but that it probably had to do with the engine repairs. In any case, I'm going to ensure nothing like this ever happens again. Until then, however, I would prefer it if you didn't come with me on EVAs."

"I had a feeling you'd say that," I said. "But truth be told, I'm gonna be a little traumatized for a while. So I'm okay with it." If the incident had been premeditated, then going out there again would be asking for trouble. I wasn't that dumb.

He nodded. "Take the time you need to recover. I'll try to find another job for you to do."

"I like my role as interim gardener," I said to reassure him. "It's fun."

He raised an eyebrow. "Is it, now?"

"You don't think it's fun?" I challenged. I knew he did, even if he refused to admit it.

"I don't think it's a game, if that's what you mean," he said, leveling his eyes at me. "Though if that's how you feel about it, I might have to rethink your assignment."

"Hey, now, give me a little credit," I warned. "I'm not

about to play whack-a-mole with the potatoes, as entertaining as that would be."

He chortled, likely due to the fact that "whack-a-mole" was as funny a word out of context as it was in context. "I was kidding, you know."

"You, kidding? God forbid. I hardly recognize you lately, with all the wisecracking and the saving my life and shit. By the way, thank you for saving my life. Twice now, actually." I looked down at the tray in my hands. "I never thanked you the first time."

"There is no need to thank me," he said quietly. "Especially for the first time."

I put the tray down on the coffee table and angled my body toward him. "Captain, has it ever occurred to you that you're a good person?"

He looked at me in confusion. "'Good' in what sense?"

"Kind."

He looked away. "I am not kind; I'm polite. You said so yourself."

"I was wrong."

He looked at me in gentle surprise, his face relaxed. He looked so handsome this way, so blissfully normal. I leaned in and kissed him, softly, on the lips. He didn't tense nor did he pull away, but he also didn't seem quite sure what to do except hold still.

I pulled back to gauge his reaction. He wasn't beside himself like he'd been when I'd kissed him on the cheek. If anything, he looked satisfied. What had changed?

"How would you classify that kiss?" I asked him wryly.

"Nice," he replied. "Very nice."

"Is that a technical term?"

He scoffed, his hands going to either side of my face. I expected a smart retort, but he didn't say anything, just searched my eyes with such a tender expression I thought I would dissolve.

I closed the space between us and kissed him again, this time threading my fingers through his thick, beautiful hair and going a step further than before—I thought French kissing might freak him out, but he took it in stride and answered me right back, hands in my hair, lips moving in time with my own.

I got the sense that he was following my lead—and while I'd definitely seen more movies than he had, I couldn't say I was the most experienced teacher. In fact, he was only the third boy I'd ever kissed, and the only one I'd ever felt this close to, even if our connection was circumstantial. I knew there was more to it than mere proximity.

There had to be.

I slipped my hands down to his torso and wrapped my arms around him. He followed suit, crushing me into him with such unexpected confidence that it shot my heart rate up into the stratosphere. And that's when something seemed to click, the steps of the dance switching so that he was in the lead.

He pushed gently until he'd lowered me onto my back and positioned himself on top of me, his hands trailing up and down my sides, getting bolder. I was tempted to start fumbling for zippers but that seemed a little… presumptuous. And hasty. Was I really ready to go that far with him, that fast?

Was *he* ready to go that far? Did he even know where he was going?

I fully expected him to cut us off, but he didn't stop, not even when I wrapped one leg around his, threading us together like wires. He responded by pressing his body against mine and grinding against me—wholly unexpected, but I'd be lying if I said it didn't feel good. Or that it didn't turn my brain to gelatin.

But one spark of rational thought did make it through the haze as I realized something that should've been obvious: unlike myself, he'd probably been sexually repressed for his entire life. This wasn't your typical tryst; this was years and years of being told he'd never, *ever* be able to do this kind of thing suddenly disrupted by the arrival of yours truly. Maybe I didn't want him to stop, and maybe he wouldn't—but he wouldn't be able to live with himself if he believed he'd lost control.

I had to let him know. I had to make sure he understood what he was doing.

By pure force of will, I managed to extract my hands, detach my lips, and say, "Wait."

He met my eyes and it was as if he'd just come out of a trance. Or a nightmare. Before I could get a word in edgewise, he pushed himself off of me and put as much distance between us as the couch would allow.

"I'm sorry," he said, angling himself away from me. "I don't know what came over me."

"Captain," I said gently. I wanted to laugh, but it probably would've embarrassed him more.

"I didn't mean to—It wasn't my intention—"

"Captain."

"You should have stopped me. You could have stopped me."

"*Captain.*"

"What?" He looked over his shoulder at me, distress turning him stolid.

"There's no need to be embarrassed," I said. "You didn't do anything wrong. I just... wanted to respect your boundaries."

He dared a glance at me. "*My* boundaries?"

"Yeah."

"I thought this was about *your* boundaries."

"My boundaries are fine," I said. "I just... well, can I ask you a personal question?"

He tossed a hand up. "Why not?"

"Do you know what sex is?"

"What?"

"Sex. You know, intercourse."

"Yes, of course I know what sex is," he said. He had his elbow propped up on his crossed knee, framing his face as he continued to look askance at me. "It's the foundation of life. Simple biology."

"Right..."

"But I'm unlikely to ever reproduce, so why would I need to do it?"

Ohp, there it was. "Oh my God. They told you it was just for making babies, didn't they?"

He managed to shrug. "What else is it for?" He motioned between the two of us. "You and I do *not* need to reproduce. Besides the fact that we don't have the resources to sustain three conscious humans."

"True though that may be, that's not the only reason

people do it." Was I really giving him The Talk 2.0 right now? How romantic. "It also just feels good."

"Of course it feels good. No one would have children if it didn't." He looked away from me, likely praying to God for me to shut up before he imploded.

"I mean, there's a lot of hormones involved. Attraction. And such."

"Yes, yes, chemical reactions in the brain. I'm very aware. Evidently, my daily administrations aren't quite strong enough to override the biological imperative. I did apologize, did I not?"

I gawked at him. "You take drugs to suppress how *horny* you are? That's... actually, that doesn't surprise me. Still, that can't be healthy."

His mouth pulled into a thin line. "I appreciate your concern, but as I've said before, the drugs simply regulate my biochemistry so I can do my job more effectively. It doesn't repress bodily functions in any way that would be a danger to my health."

*Says the guy who used to fast all day and never sleeps.* "Yeah, I'm sure that has zero drawbacks whatsoever."

"Well, I do get irritable," he offered.

"Do you? I hadn't noticed." He narrowed his eyes at me. I pursed my lips. "I would, too."

"And then there's the headaches."

"Do you have one now?" I blinked.

"No, but..." He looked off into the middle distance. "I thought I would suffocate."

I reared back. "While we were kissing?"

He turned to face forward with his hands in his lap, shaking his head. "When I saw you falling. When I thought I wouldn't be able to catch you in time. I feared for your life as if it were my own. The thought of losing you, it..." He trailed off. "It's a dangerous feeling, isn't it? To feel as if your life is tethered to someone else's?"

I smiled in understanding, sliding over on the couch so I was beside him again. "It's a normal feeling, Captain. It's what it means to care for someone. It's what it means to have a heart." I pressed my hand to his chest. Sure enough, there was a heartbeat there. Not that I ever doubted it, but at least now I could refrain from making a snide remark as he put his hand over mine and brought them, interlocked, to his knee.

He met my eyes and said, "Sometimes I think you see more in me than is there."

"Sometimes I think you see less."

He released my hand and brought his to the side of my face. "I suppose I should go."

"If you must," I said. My hand was still on his knee, his caressing my hair. "But you're also welcome to stay longer. Unless you're too embarrassed. I'm sorry, by the way, if I embarrassed you."

He glanced toward the bridge-side door and then back to me. "I embarrassed myself."

I shook my head. "You don't have to be ashamed around me, you know. I understand. I'm human, too." I leaned forward and kissed him gently.

He smiled softly as I pulled away. "Yes, that's rather the problem, isn't it?"

# 29

# You Can't Spell "Distraction" Without "Action"

To my utter surprise, Captain stayed. I'd never seen him so reluctant to go back to the bridge, and I'd be lying if I said I didn't encourage him to put it off for as long as possible. Though he was noticeably more restrained after realizing just how human he actually was, things didn't feel uncomfortable. If anything, they felt uncertain, charged with possibility.

It was as if for just a moment, I could pretend like we were a normal boy and girl living a normal life, realizing we liked each other under normal circumstances.

I fell asleep in his arms that night and expected to wake up snuggling a pillow again. Instead, I woke to the sound of something beeping and realized it was Captain's wristband. He stirred, lifted his arm from where he'd placed it across my waist, and brought his wrist to his face.

Then he rattled off a string of curse words I didn't know he knew, startling the living hell out of me as he bolted upright and scrambled off of the couch.

"What? What's wrong?"

"I overslept," he said. "I'm late for bridge duty! Never have I—" He paused, looking at me as if he'd just realized I was there. "Oh my God."

"What? What?" I suddenly felt self-conscious, as if we'd done something bad. We hadn't.

A lazy smile crept over his face. "I fell asleep."

I gasped, ecstatic. "You did? When?"

"Shortly after you did, I think."

"And you slept all night?"

"I woke up for an hour or so with the intention of leaving the room, but I couldn't—In any case, I must've fallen asleep again before I could decide."

"That's wonderful!" I gave him a wicked smirk. "I think we found the cure."

He scoffed, instantly embarrassed. "I have to—I must—" He cleared his throat. "I'll see you this afternoon."

"I'll stop by the bridge."

"Please don't." He paused at the bridge-side door. "Not—Not that I don't want you there. It's that... I fear I'll be too distracted. God knows I'm distracted enough." He left the room before I could protest, but the truth was, I understood where he was coming from.

With a sigh, I collapsed back onto the couch. Wow. Was this going to make everything better, or worse? I wasn't sure of anything, but what I did know was that I felt lighter than air. Sure, this was probably the most typical, most predictable, most unreliable feeling a girl could have, but I didn't care.

Now, the real challenge: getting it the hell together.

After a few more precious minutes of daydreaming while I waited for the shower (the first and only time Captain had overlapped with me), I cleaned myself up and ate a late breakfast. Then, it took all my willpower not to visit the bridge against Captain's wishes. Restless as I was, I spent much of the early afternoon in the gym instead. Once I'd exhausted myself, I headed back to my room to freshen up again before I could finally see him.

But to my surprise, I found Beta standing in the center of the lounge, his hands behind his back. Waiting for me.

"Miss Nepier," he said congenially. "What a pleasant surprise. You were just the person I was looking for."

*As opposed to whom?* "Hi, Lieutenant. What can I do for you?"

"I just need a moment of your time."

I grew suspicious. Beta had never asked to speak with me alone before. Hell, I'd never even seen him in the lounge before. Whatever the reason, it couldn't be good. I swallowed my trepidation and asked, "What's up?"

"Have you noticed that the captain has been acting a bit strange lately?"

"Strange? No." I'm not sure what question I'd been expecting, but that certainly hadn't been it.

"He showed up late to the bridge today. Aside from a few exceptional circumstances, he has never once been late for his duties. He says he overslept. But I find that unlikely. Were you aware that the captain suffers from insomnia?"

I tried to keep my face blank as I said, "I was aware, in fact. But even insomniacs sleep sometimes, don't they? And often at odd hours. Perhaps something disrupted his normal routine."

"Yes." Beta paced the room like a human man would. It made my skin crawl. "Yes, I fear something has disrupted his routine as of late. Any idea as to what that could be?"

Suddenly, I knew exactly what he was getting at. I just didn't expect him to have such a capacity for subtlety. "You're talking about me."

"What a smart girl! See, I do not doubt your intelligence, not a wink. But as to your... utility, that I am rather uncertain of."

I was silent. I didn't want to give him any fuel to feed his fire.

He stopped in front of me and leaned forward. "Whatever you are doing to him, whatever you think is good for him, I assure you that it isn't. You do not know him. You do not know a thing about his life or the great burden he carries. You are nothing but a fly in the ointment."

God help me, I couldn't stay quiet. "I'm sure it really ground your gears when he went against protocol to bring me on board, didn't it? I bet you wanted any excuse to get rid of me."

Maybe, if I played my cards right, I could get him to confess to the tether incident. Now I wished I'd had the foresight to record this conversation, but he'd caught me completely off-guard.

Beta stared at me, unblinking as he processed how to respond. It was the most robotic I'd seen him look. Finally, he jerked back to life and said, "Like any high-driver AI, I am adaptable." His grin bordered on haughty. "But that does not make you any less unnecessary."

"Captain thinks I'm necessary," I said, feeling unreasonably confident as I said it. "And his word is final."

Beta actually laughed. "Oh, dear girl. I thought you were smarter than *that*."

I paused. I wondered what that meant.

His silicone face softened. "Please, I hope you do not take this personally. Nothing is personal where androids are concerned. I am programmed to do two things, and two things only: protect this ship and protect its captain. So any threat to that, no matter how tolerated by our young commander, is still a concern of mine." He forced a smile. "Consider this a warning, Miss Nepier. Keep your distance. Stay in the ointment, as it were."

I racked my brain for a scathing response as he turned to leave the room. Instead, I blurted, "I know what you did."

He stopped and turned, inhumanly graceful. "I have done many things, Miss Nepier. Would you like me to catalog them for you?"

"I wish you would."

"The ointment, Miss Nepier." He cupped his palm and pointed to it. "Do not let your stubbornness be your demise. It is a rather unseemly quality in a human."

"Is that what you told Captain, growing up?" I bit out.

Beta gave me a patronizing smile. "Good day, Miss Nepier." He turned and left the room.

I stood there for a long moment, boiling with anger. In my mind, this confirmed that he was plotting against me, but I still didn't have quantifiable proof. And what had Beta meant when he'd laughed at my claim that Captain valued me? Was I missing something? Was I being too naïve?

No. Whatever mind games Beta tried to play with me, I had to trust that Captain's feelings were genuine. He stood to gain nothing from associating with me.

In fact, it seemed like he had everything to lose.

Captain joined me for dinner that evening—cross-legged on the dining room floor—and brought me up to speed on the latest developments of Operation Patch Job (my name, not his). He was unusually chatty and seemed excited to fill me in. Which was so cute I could squeeze him, but my adoration was undercut by my anxiety. If Beta had gone out of his way to threaten me, what had he told Captain? And if he did have a talk with him, why did Captain seem so unaffected?

"You seem happy today," I noted.

"It's strange," he said. "I suppose this is what a little sleep can do."

"Maybe we should... try it again," I said, testing the waters. "Falling asleep together."

He was silent for a beat too long. Then he said, "I'm not sure that's the wisest idea."

"Because you overslept?" I said. "I'll set an alarm, too. We'll make sure you get up this time."

"It's not just that," he said, pushing his nearly-empty tray back and forth on the floor. "I don't think we should... do the things we did last night again."

It didn't surprise me to hear him say that, but it still smarted to think he might regret what had happened. Before I could think it through, I blurted out, "Why not? Because Beta said so?"

His entire body tensed. "What about Beta? Did he say something to you?"

I hesitated. "It doesn't matter. I shouldn't have said anything."

He put his silverware down on his tray. "Tell me what he said to you."

I sighed. "Basically, he said that I was distracting you. That I needed to back off because I was going to endanger the mission."

He looked down, penitent. "Well, he's not wrong."

"Captain, I'm not trying to distract you," I said. "I'm not trying to do anything. I just..." I hesitated, waxing bashful. "I like you, that's all."

He was silent for too long, so I forced myself to look at him. He stared at me with a look of contemplation, like he was trying to decipher what my words really meant.

"But I don't want to cause any problems," I said quickly. "If you're truly uncomfortable with any of this, with intimacy—"

"My comfort level has nothing to do with it," he said, which gave me some relief.

"It has everything to do with it," I said. "This isn't about what Beta thinks. This is about what *you* think. That's all I care about."

"But it's not all I care about," he said.

An ache shot through my heart. *This is where he tells me that I mean nothing to him.* Looks like Beta got inside my head after all.

"Listen, Xanorra... Xan..." The final evolution: my preferred nickname. Rather than feeling elated, I only felt anxious. "You're not at fault here. I don't blame you. But Beta—his programming—it's designed to identify deterrents. To keep the mission running as efficiently as possible. I can't help that, as annoying or inconvenient as it may be. I still have to listen to him. Because despite what I may want *physically*, I cannot let anything compromise me *mentally*. You understand that, don't you?"

It was a better response than I could've hoped for, perturbed as I was by his indomitable logic. "I understand. For what it's worth, I don't regret what happened. If you do, I don't blame you, but... I really hope you don't."

"I don't," he said, which would have lifted my spirits if he hadn't said it so clinically. "But that doesn't mean it can happen again."

Even though my brain understood his reasoning, my heart still took a sucker punch. I couldn't just turn off my feelings. And one look at him said that he couldn't either. He was following orders. Doing the responsible thing. The *obedient* thing.

That's when the pieces of the puzzle started to come together. And perhaps it should've been obvious, but Captain's ability to bend the rules and his general air of authority had masked it from further observation.

But come on. Phala's mothering. Beta's threats. Captain's overwrought sense of duty.

He wasn't the one in charge here. The androids were. They let him play ship's captain and feel important, and maybe they did need him for the mission to succeed, but at the end of the day, he didn't call the shots. If he did, he might do something idiotically human, like bring a girl on board and tell her all his secrets.

Well, shit.

Lying in bed that night, I tossed and turned and mulled all this over, growing increasingly more disturbed the longer I thought about it. Eventually, I realized that there was no way I'd be getting any sleep tonight unless I got my mind off of everything first. But when I slipped into the lounge, I found Captain already there, lying awake on the couch.

"Oh," I said as he sat up quickly. "I'm sorry, I didn't—"

"I suppose that ends the streak of you never catching me in the lounge," he said, standing up and straightening his jumper. "Just as well. I shouldn't be in here, anyway."

"It's your lounge," I said, sweeping my arm. "If you wanna sleep in here, sleep in here. I was just restless. I shouldn't be out here, either."

"Why are you restless?" he asked.

How to answer that? "Um, I guess I just have a lot on my mind."

"As do I," he said, his eyes leveling with mine.

After a beat, I said, "Were you... wanting to talk about it?"

In response, he crossed the room, took my face in his hands, and kissed me.

# 30

# A Trip Down Memory Lane

So that took a soap opera-level turn. Not that I minded—but it was definitely a no-holds-barred, oh-screw-it kind of kiss. His hands trailed down my sides to my hips while mine traced up his back, pulling us together as close as we could go. Not nearly close enough.

Then Captain peeled himself away and said, with much reluctance, "I suppose I should stop."

"You've been doing a great job not stopping so far; why start now?" I teased.

It was the wrong thing to say, as per usual. He released me with a look of consternation. "You're right." He sat down on the couch and leaned over his knee, a hand on his forehead. "After what I said at dinner, you must think I'm such a hypocrite."

"Not at all," I said lightly. "Like it or not, you're still just a teenager. We're very contrary creatures, you know."

"I've never felt my age," he said absently. "Then again, I've never had a basis of comparison. I'm not sure I like being made aware."

I frowned. "Is that your way of saying I'm immature?"

"No," he said, looking at me with widened eyes. "Not at all."

"You just expect yourself to be better than the average seventeen-year-old on principle."

He dropped his head. "Yes. I do."

I sighed. "Well, not that it really matters, but you definitely have more capabilities than the average seventeen-year-old. And more technical knowledge. And you carry yourself like someone twice your age, but, you know, your circumstances are pretty unique."

"Hmph." He looked at me through the cage of his fingers. "You think I would've been much different had I grown up like you?"

The question caught me off-guard. He'd never speculated on what life outside the *Atlantis* might be like. I thought through my answer carefully. "In some ways, maybe. You still would've been precocious, but I think you would've been more social, too. People would've been drawn to you because of your sincerity. And I think you would've smiled more."

He looked down at his feet and said nothing. I didn't take it as unreceptive, but rather that he simply didn't know how to answer. However, the conversation had dredged up some of my suppressed curiosity, and it didn't seem like the worst moment to act on it.

"Captain," I said slowly, "there's something I've been meaning to ask."

"What's that?" he said without looking up.

"What was your childhood like?"

He looked at me with measured confusion. "My childhood? It was fine, I suppose. Why do you ask?"

I had to choose my words carefully. "I don't know. I guess I just get the feeling it wasn't exactly... conventional."

"Of course it wasn't conventional," he said. "Look around. My whole life has been one massive experiment." He didn't say this with irony or disdain, however. He stated it as a plain fact.

"Yeah, I can see that. But was it good?"

He paused for a moment, then said, "It was for the greatest good."

I winced. "That's not the same thing."

"Good is a relative term," he said. "What's good to you in your social and cultural estimation may not be the same thing as what's good to me in mine."

"Yes, thank you, Mr. Sociologist. What I'm asking is: were you happy?"

"Happiness is—"

"Captain," I said reprovingly. "Answer the question."

He exhaled. "Sometimes. Sometimes not. One cannot be happy all the time, can they?"

"No. You're right, they can't." I drummed my fingers against my leg. I guess I'd hit a dead-end.

His hand went to his wrist, to his smartwatch. It popped off into his palm and he passed it to me. "Here," he said. "You may see for yourself if you'd like."

I stared at it in awe. "What's on here?"

"Among other things, a full documentation of my life.

A sort of video diary, if you will, kept by Phala and, to a lesser extent, Beta. You have a certain perception of how I was raised, I assume, that clashes with what you believe to be 'good.' I can't describe it to you in a way you'd understand, so I invite you to judge for yourself."

This was a huge deal. A part of me felt like I should refuse out of courtesy or even out of trepidation, but he was bearing his soul to me in the best way he knew how. And hadn't I wanted a chance to see behind the curtain and find out what, exactly, the AI had done to him? What his *family* had done to him? Now was my chance, and he gave it to me willingly.

What else could I do? I moved to the podium and scanned the wristband across the screen.

WELCOME, CAPTAIN, it said in English and Arabic.

The next screen was the inside of his personal server. In it, there were about a dozen folders. One said *Captain's Log*. Another said *Birthday Messages*. Another, *Performance Reviews*. I stopped on the one that said, *Psychological Development*.

Could you get any more on the nose? Curious as I was about the birthday videos, there were more pressing questions at hand. This was where I needed to go.

Tapping on the folder brought up more, labeled *Year Zero* to *Year Seventeen*. Every year he'd been alive on this ship. I started with *Year One*. Inside that folder were about twenty video files labeled with the day, month, and relative year. The videos were literally from Phala's perspective, recorded through lenses in her eyes. Baby Captain was incredibly cute, and watching him play with blocks and take his first steps made me want to cry, but it honestly didn't tell me much other than that he was a very smart baby and Phala was a scary-good nurse bot.

I skipped ahead to Year Seven. Here, Captain looked like a happy enough child. He was already proficient at the helm, learning the ins and outs of the ship, even playing puzzles and building models out of bricks. So he hadn't been lying when he'd said he'd played children's games. At least they hadn't completely robbed him of childhood, even if every toy he had was likely educational in some way. No wonder he equated learning with fun.

Next, I went to Year Ten, where I found a video of him outside the cryo room, messing with the keypad as I had done.

Phala watched him silently for a moment and then said, "Captain. What are you doing here?" She spoke Arabic here, but like the birthday video, there was an English transcription.

He spun around, every ounce a kid who had been caught red-handed, and said, "I was just—"

"You know you are not supposed to be here. That you won't be able to access that room until your twelfth birthday. So why are you here?"

"I was... just..." His voice sounded so small as he dipped his head in penance. "Curious."

"Come along, Captain," she said. "Let us go back to the library and continue your reading."

"What is in there, Phala?"

"A special surprise. You will find out when you are older."

"There are people in there, aren't there?" he asked. Smart little bugger.

Phala paused for a moment, no doubt computing what the best response would be. "Yes," she finally said. Wow. The truth. What a surprise. "But they are asleep."

"Do I get to wake them up when I am twelve?"

"No," said Phala. "But you do get to see their faces."

"Is it my family?" This he said with obvious excitement in his voice.

"It is," she said.

That was the end of the video.

I moved to Year Twelve and looked for the video of him entering the cryo room for the first time. I couldn't find it—I guess there wouldn't be cameras in there anyway—but I did find something else. Instead of being labeled with a date, this video was labeled, ERROR_1. When I brought it up, I instantly felt my nerves go on red alert.

Captain sat at a table, evidently the former dining room table. Phala obviously sat across from him, recording.

"Captain, why are you so upset?" she asked in an even, placid tone.

"I am trapped," he said. "I am going to die alone."

"Captain," she said firmly. "You know that is not true."

"I want to meet my family."

"You know why you cannot."

"I do not want to be alone anymore."

"But you are not alone, Captain. You have me, Beta, and the crew."

He looked away, obviously torn between the only

affection he'd ever known and his instinctual desire for human companionship. "It is not the same."

"How do you know it is not the same?" she asked. "Who told you it was not the same?"

He looked at her dead on, but he couldn't answer. He couldn't parse out how he knew, only that he did.

"Come, Captain, let us get you back to normal again," she said. "I explained to you what would happen as you got older. This is nothing more than a chemical imbalance."

That was the end of the clip. Now I had a direction. In the same folder was another video labeled, ERROR_2. I tapped on it.

In this one, Captain stood in the center of the bedroom, which looked like a hurricane had gone through it. It had once had more furniture, I realized. A desk. A chair. Odds and ends. No wonder it looked so empty now.

"Captain," said Phala, this time in English. "This is unacceptable. What would your family think, if they could see you now?"

The intensity in his eyes was alarming. "How am I supposed to know what they think when I've never even met them?"

"You have met—"

"It's not the same!" he exclaimed. "Do not tell me it is the same. Because it's not. I can't take it anymore! I feel like I'm losing my mind!"

"That is because you are," said Phala. "You have not been taking your medications. I told you what would happen if you failed to listen to me. Now you are unstable. Imbalanced. All of this torment you have brought upon yourself, you brought because you did not listen."

A fire blazed in Captain's eyes as he stared at her, breathing hard. "I don't need it," he finally said.

"Captain, look around. You most certainly do."

"I don't like how it makes me feel," he said. "I have bad dreams. I can't sleep. And I get headaches."

"That has nothing to do with the medicine," said Phala. "It is simply the product of an overactive mind. You really should talk to me more often, Captain. You know I am able to help you."

He didn't say anything. In fact, he looked like the last thing he wanted to do at the moment was talk to her. "I do not want it."

"It is not about what you want. Nor is it about how you feel," she said. "Your wants and your feelings are unreliable. Here one moment, gone the next. They cause nothing but damage to yourself. All that really matters—all that can really help you—is to do what is best. For your family. For the mission. Don't you want to do what is best?"

That halted him a bit. He dropped his eyes to the floor and said, "Yes, of course I do. But... I..."

Phala walked across the room and crouched to his level, putting a comforting hand on his shoulder. "You were born for this," she said. "This is your destiny. There is no one better qualified to do this than you. You have everything you need right here, right now, on this ship. This ship is your life, and you are the life of this ship. There is nothing in the present moment that could possibly be more important than the glory that awaits you in the future. Your loyalty and honor will be rewarded beyond measure. You will see your family. You will be the one who brought them home."

"Yes, but—"

"You were born for this," she said again. "There is no one better qualified to do this than you. You have everything you need right here, right now, on this ship—"

"Phala, no, don't—"

"—possibly more important than the glory awaiting you—"

"Phala, I understand. I know—"

"—loyalty and honor will be—"

"Phala, stop, please." He pressed his hands to his ears. "Just stop."

She didn't stop. Captain tried to leave the room, but both the main door and the lavatory were locked. He paced like a lion in a cage, trying to drown her out. He pleaded with her, hanging onto her like a child would his mother. She simply took a step backward and continued on. From her perspective, I could see how anguished he was, how desperate. Her cold, passive indifference only made it more heartwrenching. She might as well have been a static camera, faceless and unfeeling.

Eventually, he sank to the floor, head between his knees.

It was several moments later that Phala crouched down to his level and said, "It is your turn now, Captain."

For a long time, he didn't respond.

"Captain, I want to hear it from your own mouth. We are the words we speak. Speak them and be forgiven."

Barely audible, he began, "I was born for this. This is my destiny. I have everything I need right here, right now, on this ship."

"Speak up, Captain."

"This ship is my life, and I am the life of this ship…" He recited the whole mantra, then started over again. Phala pulled him up to a standing position and watched him calmly as he repeated it over, and over, and over again. Tears streamed down his face. He looked physically exhausted, as if he were being forced to run instead of speak.

This went on for half an hour, which I mostly skipped through for my own sanity. Every ten minutes or so, he'd beg Phala to let him stop, but she would demand that he continue. It was hard to watch.

When Phala finally gave him permission to stop, she said, "Good. You understand now."

He nodded, unable to speak.

"You are ready to resume your duties."

He nodded again.

Phala produced a pill from her breast pocket. "Take this. You have earned it."

He threw it back without any water.

"Now, promise me you will do what you know is best."

"I… I promise."

She put a hand on his shoulder. "You are a good captain."

That was the end of the video. My skin crawled, my heart rate elevated, but I had to keep going. I went to

Year Thirteen next, where I discovered that Captain had not, in fact, kept his promise. Each time he broke it, the punishment grew more severe, but it was always the same pattern: Phala would isolate him in his room, repeat the mantra, then make him repeat it for increasingly unreasonable amounts of time. I also noticed that with each offense, less and less furniture appeared in the room until it was all but empty—at one point, not even a bed.

Stripping him of his humanity.

No wonder he hated that room.

In Year Fourteen, the pattern shifted. He wasn't acting out as often—couldn't imagine why—but there were quite a few instances of him sleepwalking, usually toward the cryo room. Phala always intercepted him and returned him to his room. He usually woke up screaming, just like he had the other night.

By Year Sixteen, his record was spotless. He was the perfect captain, the perfect kid. The perfect devotee.

Which brought us to the present day.

I went to exit the folder when a hand on my shoulder made me flinch. Captain jerked his hand back, obviously startled by my reaction. I'd forgotten he was still in the room, engrossed as I was by the psychological horror movie in front of me.

"You're crying," he said. "Why?"

Tears streamed down my face, though I'd hardly noticed them until now. "I can't believe what they did to you."

"Did to me?"

"Don't you see it?" I said. "They broke you down. They... *conditioned* you. Brainwashed you."

"Brainwashed? No, Xanorra. They helped me. This ship was designed for my optimal fulfillment. I wasn't... working right."

"You were feeling, you mean. How can you be okay with this?"

"You'd rather I was the boy in those videos?" he asked, gesturing to the screen. "Volatile, a danger to himself and everything around him? I was ill."

"You were *hurting*," I said. "You were alone."

"I have everything I need," he said slowly. The mantra. It sent a chill up my spine.

"You wanted me to see those videos for a reason, didn't you?" I challenged. "What, did you think I'd be satisfied with what I saw?"

"I thought it would help you understand," he said.

I forced a smile for his sake. "It does," I said. "Maybe not in the way you'd hoped, but it does. Captain, what they did to you... it wasn't right."

"I disagree."

"Why can't you sleep in your own bedroom?" I posited. "Why can't you sleep at all? Why do we have to sneak around behind the androids' backs?"

"*Shhhh*," he said.

"You're scared of them," I said.

"I am not scared of them. I'm not scared of anything."

"For God's sake, stop lying to yourself, Captain."

"Stop seeing problems where there are none. Stop trying to make me out to be something I'm not."

"Then what are you?" I asked.

"I'm..." The fact that he had to stop and think about it was indicative enough that he didn't know. A beat later, he recovered with, "I'm the captain."

"What if that's not all you are?"

He shook his head. "It doesn't matter what else I am. It's all I need to be."

That stopped me in my tracks. For the first time in a long time, I'd bucked up against his programming. I didn't know how to get through to him—how to make him see what I saw. "So where do I fit into all this? How can I possibly fit?" I asked.

He genuinely thought about it. "Well, you... you remind me that I'm still human," he said.

My heart fluttered. It was a beautiful sentiment. Slap it on a Valentine's Day card with a cartoon drawing of a robot and call it a day. But there was just one teeny, tiny problem with that fact.

"Captain, I don't think they *want* you to be reminded."

# 31

# Quin's Journal #4

As much as I'd like to say I knew exactly how to start my research, once I actually started looking closely at the footage of the *Washington* and the 3D mockups of the mysterious squid ship, the more I realized: I had no idea what I was doing.

I wondered if it was alien after all, but it didn't seem likely—and since entertaining that pretense would render me incapable of drawing any conclusions about the technology whatsoever, I decided to suspend that possibility for the time being and move forward under the hypothesis that the ship was, indeed, built and operated by humans.

Now came the tricky part: figuring out how and when.

The Current had only been discovered thirty-five years ago relative to Earth. There was no evidence to suggest that anyone had known about the Current before then (though many had theorized) but there was also no evidence to suggest they hadn't. The fact that the squid ship had been on the other side, ahead of us, had to mean one of two things: either someone with better technology had gotten to it before we had, or that ship had been traveling through space for a very, very, *very* long time.

I decided the former assumption was probably more likely.

Unfortunately, that didn't account for time dilation. The ship may have launched from Earth at the same time as the *Aster*, many years before, or many years after. The fact that we happened to be in the same place at the same time didn't tell us anything about how long the ship had been traveling.

Seb and I started by researching wormhole theories from the last fifty years and trying to connect them to ship launches, but when that proved fruitless, we expanded our search and started looking at any deep space vessel that had launched from Earth around that time.

As one can imagine, there were more than a few. We spent the next week and a half checking every database, news article, scientific journal, and archived video on the *Aster* that had to do with spaceship construction and launches.

We had fuck all to show for it.

"Nothing," said Seb, exasperated. On this particular day, we were in my room. I sat on my bed and Seb sat on the floor with his back against the bed frame. "Nothing about a squid-shaped ship, nothing about a private deep space launch to a wormhole. We've combed every archive, read every interview, watched every damn YouTube clip... you sure this thing ain't alien?"

"I'm sure," I said, equally exasperated. "Maybe I was wrong about the time frame. Maybe we need to extend it out—"

"Hey," he said, turning his body around to face me. "Why don't we take a break?"

"A break?"

"Yeah, a break. Remember those?" He smirked. "My brain is fried. You look like you're about to blow a circuit board. Let's go do something fun. It'll help us think better."

I blinked, entirely caught off-guard. "Fun? What kind of fun?"

He shrugged. "What sounds fun to you?"

"This," I said, pointing to the tablet in my hands. "This is fun to me."

"No, no, no," he said, prying the device away from me and setting it beside him. "I'm talking about real fun. We could go to the gardens, or do an AR room, or go watch a movie. Anything but work. Come on." He sprung up on his lanky, grasshopper legs and took me by the hands, effectively launching me off the bed and into his chest.

My face was about a thousand degrees as I pulled away from him. "Seb."

"Quin." He gave me a look that said I wasn't getting out of this.

I sighed. "Did you have somewhere in mind?"

He nodded enthusiastically. "I have a place I think you'd like. Follow me."

The gallery. The place Seb had in mind was the gallery.

Don't get me wrong; I love the gallery. Basically, it was a museum of human history intended to remind us spacefaring colonists from whence we had come. The thing is, every kid aboard every colony ship visits their gallery at least once a year. After a while, it just doesn't hold the same level of awe-inspiring wonder as it once did.

Perhaps that was the point.

"Interesting choice," I said as we walked in. It was empty except for the curator, Johannes, who offered Seb a friendly "hello" and told us we were welcome to look around for as long as we liked. "Johannes seemed unsurprised to see you. Are you here often?"

"Yeah," said Seb, almost embarrassed. "I come here whenever I need a break from all this... deep space stuff."

I looked at him curiously. "Does space bother you?" It was common for our parents' generation to get "Earth sick" sometimes, but this was all we'd ever known. Any connection we felt to the mother planet was secondhand.

"Nah, not like... in a serious way," he said as we stopped in front of the Stone Age exhibit. "I just like to be reminded, you know? I think it's comforting to know that somewhere out there, there's a planet full of us. Billions of us. And everything that they did led to where we are today."

"That's beautiful, Seb. You should write a book."

He scoffed. "If you're bored, we don't have to stay."

"No, I don't mind at all," I said. "I just never would've thought of it myself, to be honest."

"Most people wouldn't," he said. "That's another reason why I like it: unless there's a field trip going on, it mostly stays empty. It's a good place to think."

We moved through each of the sections in relative silence, absorbing the centuries of history encased in glass or projected in 3D as mini-documentaries. There were some pretty cool artifacts stored on board the *Aster*: old technology from the Analog and Digital Ages, fashion from the twentieth and twenty-first centuries (they really loved denim), and even an old EVA suit from NASA, which had been eclipsed by the SEA sometime in the late 2080s.

The human history sections eventually transitioned into natural history, which was toward the back. Models of Earth, simulations of plate tectonics and volcanic eruptions, diagrams of the animal and plant kingdoms—all of the elements of the universe that were unique to Earth.

All of the aspects of nature that we had absolutely nothing to do with, and at the same time, everything to do with.

After all, if we were ever going to successfully terraform a habitable planet, we'd better remember how a habitable planet, you know, *worked.*

We approached the oceans exhibit, which included a real-life aquarium displaying various species of saltwater fish, the kinds you might find in a coral reef. I'd nearly forgotten it was here and my breath caught when I saw it. It really was easy to forget how beautiful nature could be when you didn't see it very often.

"Neat, huh?" Seb said, coming up next to me—so close, in fact, that our shoulders were nearly touching. "This is my favorite part."

"Fish," I said. Like a moron.

"Fish," he agreed.

Separate from the coral reef aquarium, on the other side of the room, was a jellyfish tank. I moved toward it and watched those beautiful, otherworldly marshmallows pulse gently through the water. No worries, no responsibilities. No brains, really. The closest thing to aliens we truly had.

"Why did that ship look like a squid?" I mused aloud.

"Those are jellyfish, you know," Seb said from behind me.

I whipped around and glared at him. "I know. I'm just thinking: why a sea creature? Is it symbolic? Aesthetic? Some unconventional engineering method?"

"I thought we agreed to take a break," he said, standing beside me again.

I huffed. "I thought we agreed that taking a break would help us think better."

"Touché," he said, narrowing his eyes at me. He turned back to the jellyfish and I tried not to stare at his profile, sharpened by the blue light of the aquarium tank. When he glanced at me again, I quickly turned my head away.

"I'd say the ship more closely resembled a cuttlefish than anything else," he said in a high-brow tone.

"Sure. Whatever you say."

"You ever seen videos of cuttlefish? They're ruthless,

man. Maybe the builders wanted to emulate the resilience of deep-sea creatures like that. Not to mention the savagery."

I gaped, half an idea forming in my mind. "But then… if that *is* the case, and they did it on purpose, and not because it looked cool… then whoever built the ship would've had a pretty thorough working knowledge of marine biology."

"Yeah, I guess. Or they would've had to have an expert working closely with them. Why? What are you on to now?"

I turned to face him. "I think we've been asking the wrong questions," I said. "Obviously, whoever built it didn't want anybody finding out about it. That tells us at least two things: one, it was a private company, and two, they had a lot of money, power, and connections. But you can't build a ship like that without someone else knowing about it."

"So… we need to look for aerospace or astrotech companies that somehow have connections to marine biology?"

"Or astrotech engineers who were also marine biologists."

Seb whistled. "That can't be many."

"No, it can't," I said excitedly. "Come on."

"Aw, but… what about the rest of the gallery?"

"It served its purpose. Great idea coming here, by the way. A stroke of genius." I practically skipped out of the exhibit and raced back to the residential sector, Seb on my tail.

Back inside the apartment, I conducted a new search in

the database: *aerospace engineering + marine biology*. I tried to brace myself for zero results, but I nearly collapsed in relief when a list of news articles popped up instead. Seb squeezed himself next to me on the bed and I tried to ignore how close together we were, let alone that he was on my bed, period.

"Results," he said in surprise. "That's good."

"Could be collateral," I said, but I already had a good feeling about it as I browsed the headlines. "Here! 'Turning the Tide: How One Astrotech Industry Embraced Oceanic Science.'" I couldn't click fast enough. The article was from seventy-five Earth years ago, which was *way* further back than I would've guessed.

Perhaps we should've extended the time frame sooner.

"'What do space and the ocean have in common?'" I read. "'They're both vast, they're both full of mystery, and now, they both have a team of scientists studying their common properties to further progress in both fields. Omen-Ra Astrotechnics, spearheaded by Dr. Ahmed Omen, son of renowned astrophysicist Ibrahim Omen of Cairo University!'" I gasped and turned to Seb. "This is it, Seb! We did it! We have a lead!"

"Hell yeah!" He turned and hugged me, and I was so caught up in the jubilation of finally getting somewhere that I hugged him back without any hesitation. The embrace went longer than a celebratory hug required.

Was he... holding on? Even after all the shoulder-bumping in the gallery, I still couldn't tell if he was just being Seb or not. I was so bad at judging these things. But both out of fear that I was misreading him and the realization that we were on my bed, I panicked and pulled away, both of us awkwardly laughing it off.

"Well, we probably shouldn't speak too soon," I said. "This still doesn't tell us how the ship works or where to find Xan."

"True," he said. "But it does tell us where to start, and that's as good as anything."

# 32

# Remember What I Said About That Greenhouse?

Things were a little weird following that night in the lounge, to say the least. I couldn't stop thinking about what I'd seen. While yes, it did explain a lot about why Captain was the way that he was, it also confirmed many of my worst fears—which did not leave me with a warm, fuzzy feeling of satisfaction, even if it did validate my doubts about the ethicality of this mission.

Then came the more heartwrenching question: what kind of family would do this to their son?

I tried not to assume the worst. Maybe they hadn't been privy to the methods involved in curating the perfect generational captain. Maybe the AI had gone off the rails in an attempt to fulfill its directive.

Obviously, there were practical reasons why Captain would be unable to wake his family up prematurely—not enough resources to sustain that many people, for one.

He wasn't an idiot; he would've known and understood that, even at a young age. I didn't think that's what any of what I'd seen had been about.

It was about feeling isolated. Trapped in a situation he didn't ask for, on a ship he couldn't leave, heading for a planet he'd never seen. Even if it was all he'd known, he'd instinctually yearned for something more. After all, humans were not designed to be confined to fifteen hundred square feet of breathable air and surrounded by a vacuum of nothingness.

And to have his family in the other room, so close yet so far away? The temptation had to be off the charts, especially for a lonely kid, even if his logic told him it wasn't possible for him to have what he wanted.

I'd come full circle in my quest of curiosity: who were these people? And whose idea had it been to send a kid into space?

I already knew from experience that the androids wouldn't be much help if I tried to probe them for information. They only cared about the facts: names, dates, et cetera. Asking Lambda a question like, "How did Captain's parents feel about their son being raised by robots?" wasn't going to amount to much.

I considered asking Captain for access to his hard drive again so I could watch those birthday videos. I hadn't had a chance to investigate my theory that his parents' messages had been scripted, and whether it was the case or not, I thought maybe watching them would give me some insight into Omen-Ra's rationale.

And yet, there was a part of me that already knew the answer because Captain had said it himself: he was an experiment. They were scientists. They'd put their son's life on the line in the name of science.

Now the real question: how did I get Captain to see that it was wrong?

I spent most of the day alone—Captain was on an EVA, repairing the hull, and I had nothing to do except take care of the greenhouse. I spent a long time there, thinking. It was a very good place to think. For obvious reasons, the air felt cleaner and smelt like how I imagined a forest would—warm and heady. I coddled the fig tree, which was getting close to harvest time.

*How long can I keep this up?* I wondered. After all, despite my best efforts, I'd settled in pretty well to life on board the *Atlantis*. I wasn't miserable. It didn't totally suck. But it did put me on edge, and I couldn't fathom living out the rest of my life here.

I couldn't fathom Beta *letting* me live out the rest of my life here.

I began to wonder if it were possible to stage a mutiny. It would probably involve decommissioning one or both of the AI drivers, which was notoriously hard to do unless you either knew how their machinery worked or you had a lot of electricity. Still, it was worth looking into.

After I'd finished up with the greenhouse, I went into the lounge and searched the archives for Beta's specs. Not to my surprise, it was "public domain" and came up with Phala's specs as well. Captain probably needed a working knowledge of their internal systems in case (God forbid) something malfunctioned. Beta and Phala were of the same make but different models, built by a company I did not recognize. They were pretty in-depth mock-ups but most of it was Greek to me; without someone like my dad to translate the engineering jargon, it would take me weeks to decipher.

*Dad.* God, I missed them. Since sending out the transmission, I hadn't had time to think much about them, which struck me through with guilt. It had somehow become easier to pretend that this was the norm—that this was all I needed.

Bile rose in my throat. *Oh my God. Have they conditioned you, too?* Had someone been whispering in my ear while I was asleep? Was I brainwashed? Paranoia surged within me like a wave, but it was immediately squelched by logic.

*No. It's because of Captain.* I'd grown too fond of him. I know I had. In spite of his oddities, in spite of the circumstances, he had become someone I could admire. He was someone worth saving.

Even if he didn't know he needed to be saved.

I didn't see Captain for the rest of the evening; either he was just that busy or he was actively avoiding me. Either way, I tried to give him the space he required in order to brood properly and went to bed early.

I was just on the edge of sleep when suddenly, all the lights came on and a rough hand shook my shoulder. I started awake to see Captain standing over me, a fury in his eyes that I'd never seen before.

"*What did you do?*" he shouted.

I began to think—or perhaps hope—that this was a bad dream. "Huh?"

"What did you do?" he repeated, his voice thick with anger.

I rubbed the sleep from my eyes and climbed out of bed. "*I don't know what you're talking about.*" I racked my brain for what I may or may not have done. Had the android specs been off-limits after all?

"Get dressed. Follow me." He stood, arms crossed, and waited.

"I don't understand. What happened?" I said as I pulled on my jumpsuit and boots. "Why are you so angry?"

"You know very well why."

I totally didn't, and it scared me. What the hell did he think I'd done? Confused and disturbed, I followed him across the lounge and down the ladder to the first level.

He stopped in front of the greenhouse room. *Oh, shit, did I forget to water something? That can't be right. He wouldn't be this angry over a simple mistake.* "Go inside."

I did, and what I saw made me gasp. His anger was warranted. The greenhouse was destroyed. The planters were toppled over, the equipment smashed in a heap on the ground. Dirt was everywhere, floating around the room like an asteroid field in miniature. I had to cover my mouth to keep from breathing it in.

And in the corner—*Oh, God*—the fig tree was knocked over and crushed as if a herd of angry elephants had trampled it underfoot. I walked slowly toward it and gently caressed its once-glorious leaves. The fig that had been almost ripe was flattened to a pulp, a pathetic mash of seeds and pinkish-purple innards. I wanted to cry. He'd worked so hard. We'd been so close.

I turned when I heard him crunching through the wreckage. "You think I did this?" I said in a hoarse voice. I rose, steadying myself against the wall. "Why?"

"You tell me," he said darkly.

"I didn't do this!" I shouted. "I would never do this to you, Captain!"

"Then who did? Phala? Beta? *Lambda?* They are machines. They do as I command."

"It's an illusion," I said firmly. "You don't control them, they control you. They've controlled you all your life!"

"And this was meant to liberate me, was it?" He gestured toward the devastation around us. "To show me how evil the machines truly are? How wrong my mission truly is? To convince me I should turn my back on everything I know?" He glared at me. "I am loyal to my crew. I am loyal to my mission. I am the *Atlantis*, and the *Atlantis* is me. All you have succeeded in doing is reaffirming that, because never in my life have I felt so utterly betrayed."

"Captain, you aren't listening to me," I said, my voice shaking with anger. "I did not do this. I could never hurt you like that. I love this greenhouse. I love *you*." I didn't realize how it sounded until it left my lips, but I did mean it—at least in the sense that I cared deeply about him.

It did, however, have the immediate effect of stopping him dead in his tracks. Though his face remained a hardened mask, his eyes danced like agitated flames. "If this is what love entails, then I don't want any part of it," he said.

"That's not what I—" My mind scrambled for a response. "We made a promise to each other. Do you trust me enough to believe that I'd keep that promise?"

"I don't know what to believe anymore," he said. "After all, humans are vile, fickle, selfish creatures. And you were right. I didn't need to be reminded that I was one."

With that, he left me standing in the ruinous remains of the greenhouse.

I couldn't bear it. I sunk to my knees and sobbed. I let myself be pathetic and heartbroken for a few minutes, and then I started to think. The timing seemed too convenient. I began to wonder if maybe I hadn't been careful enough—maybe looking at the android specs had been the final nail in the coffin. Who's to say Beta couldn't see everything I read and watched? Who's to say there wasn't a camera in every room, watching everything we did? That it wasn't just Captain being late to the bridge that had prompted him to threaten me, but everything that had come before then?

I shuddered at the thought. Yes, I had gotten a little too comfortable here, hadn't I? And now I'd dug my own grave. Destroying the greenhouse was the perfect crime—it didn't technically go against android programming, and Beta would know that Captain's blind trust in him would shield him from suspicion, making me the natural scapegoat.

But there was no way Captain had it in him to... dispatch me. Did he? Was Beta right? Did I really know him at all?

*Shit. Shit.* Shit.

*No.*

I was the only one who knew him. The machines imitated familiarity, and sure, they had all the data, but I'd actually seen what Captain was capable of, and I knew that even if he was angry and hurt, he wouldn't harm me. He'd made a promise. He was an honorable man.

I had to have a little bit of faith in him.

Shakily, I pulled myself to my feet and started picking up the greenhouse. I righted the fig tree and felt a tiny bit better when I saw that no damage had been done to the root system. It might just survive this.

I wasn't so sure I could say the same about myself.

The sound of the tarp rustling made me jump. It was Kappa, the janitor bot, here to clean up the mess.

"This is a contaminated area," Kappa said in his light, robotic voice. "I would suggest you wear PPE while in this room."

"I'm leaving," I said. "But please, if you can... leave the fig tree. It has a chance."

"Captain has instructed me to restore any salvageable organic matter."

"Okay, good," I said with a sigh. "Thank you, Kappa."

He was already hard at work vacuuming dirt particles out of the air, and if I didn't know any better, I'd think he was mad at me, too.

# 33

# The Irony of a House Arrest on a Spaceship Does Not Escape Me

I returned to my room after that, took a shower, and brooded as I'd never brooded before. How was I going to prove myself innocent? Was there some kind of surveillance camera that would show Beta destroying the greenhouse and not me? Unlikely. If he was smart enough to plan sabotage, then he was probably smart enough to destroy any evidence that would implicate him.

It was my word against a robot's. I guess it was really up to Captain and who he believed. I could only hope that the last month and a half had convinced him I was trustworthy.

Then again, it was our month and a half against his seventeen years. I wasn't going to get any fantastical notions about it. As much as I'd love to believe there was a special bond between us, it was in its infancy compared to the psychological fuckery he'd been brought up on.

I let out a shaky breath. *Just wait and see what happens.*

What happened was this: I had been demoted back to prisoner status. I discovered this when I attempted to leave my room to get some fresh air in the lounge and found the door locked. I scoffed, honestly amazed that this was his solution. Well, that answered that question for the present.

What was he going to do? Leave me here until I died? Did it technically count as harm if he did nothing and just let me starve to death?

I got a glimmer of hope when, around dinner time, the door chimed, signaling that it had been unlocked, and opened just wide enough to reveal Kappa holding a tray.

"Dinner," he intoned.

I sighed and took it, though I wasn't really hungry. So the captain would keep to his word. That was good to know. But was this really my life now? Stuck in a small room on this already small ship, eating reconstituted meals alone? I refused to believe this was his permanent solution. This was just a precautionary measure until he got his shit together and realized that I would never, *ever* cross him like that.

I gave it the benefit of the doubt. A couple of days of this wouldn't be so bad.

But it wasn't a couple of days. It stretched to three, then four, then five. During that time, a tablet with the entire digital library was delivered to me, along with changes of underclothes and instructions to leave any dirty ones by the door before bed. Meals were delivered like clockwork three times a day by Kappa, who never said more than a few, dry syllables to me.

This was not a temporary solution. This was my punishment.

I think holding out for over a week was generous of me. I'd restrained myself from attempting anything drastic in case this was some kind of test—I didn't want to do anything that made me look guilty, so I miraculously endured eight days of this cold, silent treatment before I finally got fed up and started reacting.

My first successful idea was to juggernaut my way past Kappa and into the lounge at my next meal delivery. Of course, all the doors there were locked, but it still felt like a small victory.

"Miss Nepier," came Beta's voice over the intercom system I didn't know we had. "Please return to your room."

In a really pathetic way, it was incredibly gratifying to get a reaction out of him. "Make me!" I shouted. "Face me, you coward!"

"Miss Nepier, if you do not return to your room, then we will cease delivery of your daily sustenance. Do not be foolish. We have shown you mercy."

"Mercy." I scowled. "You call this mercy? I want to talk to Captain. Please, let me talk to him!"

"The captain is very busy, and besides, I think you have done enough."

"I didn't do anything and you know it!" I said, anger rising like a tidal wave within me. "Captain, please, if you can hear me, listen to your conscience!"

The intercom was silent. I'd probably been cut off mid-sentence. Jerk.

I wasn't sure whether Beta's threat was a bluff or not, but I refused to believe that Captain would let me starve. He was disillusioned, not cruel. So I decided to take a gamble on Captain's conscience.

I decided to stay in the lounge.

* * *  * * *

Yeah, so, Beta hadn't been bluffing. I didn't get lunch or dinner that day, and now Kappa was stuck in the room under house arrest with me. At least I had someone to play chess with, but chess could only distract you from your hunger for so long.

I began to worry just a little. Maybe they really were going to starve me out.

The following morning, Kappa was gone, no doubt ushered out while I was asleep. I received no meals, no communication, and no indication that this was going to end anytime soon. I was torn between my pride, which compelled me to stay put, and my stomach, which begged me to go back inside the damn bedroom.

But the thought of being stuck inside that room, well-fed but living a fraction of a life, was still a hard sell, even after two days. No, I had to have faith in Captain's humanity. I had to give him a chance to realize that this was wrong.

*One more day*, I told myself. *Just give it one more day.*

I woke the next morning to the smell of something savory and almost started crying when I looked up and saw a plate of food sitting on top of the chessboard. I didn't even hesitate: I pounced on it and started inhaling the bean-based mash as if it might try to run away. Then I bothered to look up and saw who sat in the adjacent chair.

I gasped, nearly dropping the tray. "Captain," I said.

He looked tired and washed out, every ounce the old soul he claimed to be. "That was a very stupid thing you did."

"Is it stupid if it worked?" I said, now attempting to refrain from horking the food down like a wild animal.

"It was stupid because it was stupid," he said firmly.

"Have you finally come to your senses?" I said.

He didn't meet my eyes.

I put the tray down. "Oh, come on. You don't actually think I did it, do you?"

"I told you, I don't know what to think."

This was not good. How could he be here, feeding me, and yet still think I was guilty? Something didn't add up. "Captain," I said. "I wasn't sure how to tell you this, but... remember when the tether broke? On our last EVA?"

His brow furrowed in confusion. "What does that have to do with anything?"

"I don't think it was a freak accident," I said. "I think one of the androids did it. I think Beta, specifically, did it."

"Impossible," he said immediately. "The AI protocol prevents any of the crew from harming a human being. As per our agreement and my own orders, that includes you."

"Yes, but I'm not technically supposed to be here in the first place, right? My very existence breaks protocol."

"I assure you, Xanorra, you would not have made it this far if it wasn't within parameters for you to be here."

"Then what's keeping me here now?" I challenged, even though it put me on thin ice. "Why haven't you killed me yet? If you truly think I'm guilty—if you really believe I'd do something so heartless—then what's keeping me alive right now?"

"A promise," he said, not breaking eye contact. "I made you a promise. And regardless of how I feel, I'd like to believe I'm a man of my word."

My entire body relaxed with the admission. "Well, thank God for that."

"Which is why I've arrived at a compromise," he said. "It's a last resort, but it's the best I can offer you."

My gut churned, suddenly not so at ease. I made myself look at him, but I couldn't hide my anger and disappointment. He didn't believe me enough to take my word over a robot's. That much I'd gambled on and lost. "What kind of compromise?"

His hesitation as he sat down beside me told me I wasn't going to like this. "I put you in cryo-sleep."

Nope. Definitely did not like this. I shook my head fervently. "No way. I'm not becoming a giant popsicle. Besides, aren't all the capsules taken?"

He shook his head. "There's a spare, in case one is

damaged or, for some reason, I need to enter cryo-sleep myself. I'm willing to eliminate that option in order to let you use it."

It was his idea of mercy, so I supposed I should've been grateful. But it was still about as appealing to me as eating compost. "This isn't a solution. It's a punishment."

"You won't even notice time passing," he offered. "It will be like a long, pleasant dream, and when you wake, you'll be on a new planet."

"Thirty-two years from now. I'll be lightyears away from everything. And... you'll be fifty."

"I know," he said.

In spite of myself, I said, "I don't want you to be fifty. I like you as you are right now. My age."

He sighed. "You're making this about you. It's not about you or about me. It's about—"

"The mission," I said with a derisive edge.

"Please, try to understand how difficult a position I'm in. I don't want you to be miserable. I don't want the mission to suffer, either. This is the only solution that lets us have it both ways."

I laughed, hollow with disbelief. "That lets you have it both ways, you mean."

He locked his jaw. "This isn't what I want."

"And this isn't what I want," I said. "So then tell me, why does this have to happen?"

He looked down, nursing his wristband. When he finally looked up at me, I could read his distress like a book. "Because you're right," he said. "The alternative, according to the protocol, is to kill you. And I can't—I won't—I refuse to do it, Xan. I refuse."

My throat felt swollen. "You were supposed to, weren't you? When you brought me on board. You were supposed to shoot me dead."

He nodded, ashamed.

And from that mistake onward, the protocol had fought to overcorrect itself. Like antibodies attacking a foreign contaminant, it would try to expunge me relentlessly until it succeeded.

The protocol needed me dead. It just couldn't kill me without Captain's permission, which was the one thing he refused to give. The one thing he could control—the one thing the androids couldn't touch—was whether I lived or died. And he chose to defy their wishes to let me live, time and time again.

It was a paradox. The longer I lived, the more the protocol tried to eliminate me, but the more it tried to eliminate me, the closer it got to breaking its own rules. And this vicious cycle would likely continue until the AI finally snapped and went over Captain's head.

In other words, if I didn't take Captain's deal now, I might never have another chance. It could be a week from now, it could be ten years from now, but I wasn't safe here. I never was.

"Okay," I said, my voice cracking. "I accept your compromise."

He rose from the chair, walked over to the couch, and sat down next to me. Taking my hand in his, he said, "For what it's worth, I'm sorry, Xanorra. I'm sorry for everything."

I couldn't look at him, but I knew he was sincere. I couldn't blame him, not completely—he hadn't chosen to be here, hadn't asked to be the doomed ferryman of a family he'd never met, to travel to a world he'd never seen. To be sacrificed on the altar of hubris in the name of science.

I just wished I had more time with him. If only I had more time, maybe I could get him to see outside the tiny box he'd been forced into.

Which is exactly what the androids—what the mission, what his family, what Omen-Ra—absolutely, unequivocally, and irrevocably did not want to happen.

# 34

# Quin's Journal #5

Finally, some mother shipping progress.

We spent the next few days digging up as much as we possibly could about Omen-Ra Astrotechnics. Granted, it didn't tell us much about the squid ship, but it did finally give us some context for why it might exist in the first place.

After all, Omen-Ra did specialize in innovative technologies that were especially based on principles of deep-sea biology. The ocean was as uninhabitable to us as space, except it was in Earth's own backyard... and life had actually adapted to it.

But it didn't take us very long to exhaust the information available to us in the SEA databases. It looked like we were coming up on another dead-end, which was annoying, to say the least.

"If we could only talk to them," I said to Seb. We sat across from each other at a table in the university library today, which was more of a café, really, since everything was stored in digital archives. But on the plus side, coffee!

"Like they would answer our questions," Seb said with a snort. He looked as ragged as I felt. We'd been going pretty hard lately, after all. Scientifically speaking. "Their real specialty seems to be keeping things a secret."

"Someone has to know something," I said. "The SEA recruited from all corners of the aerospace industry. Maybe somebody here on the *Aster* knows somebody who worked at Omen-Ra, or worked there themselves."

Seb whistled. "That's a bit of a stretch, don't you think?"

"Have any better ideas?" I challenged.

He smiled and shook his head. "Couldn't hurt to try."

I went into the citizen database and searched for "Omen-Ra." Profiles for each person were public domain on board a colony ship but usually only contained basic information—names, jobs, et cetera. However, most profiles also showed a person's job history, so if someone had worked for Omen-Ra at one time...

"One result," I said, my heart going haywire. "Dr. Lavanya Basu, a retired neurologist employed by Omen-Ra... she's about eighty-five now, but it says she's still living. Come on! We gotta go!"

Seb tapped the table like a pair of bongo drums. "The game is afoot, dear Watson!"

It didn't surprise us that Dr. Basu lived in the assisted living area of the residential sector. She was old, after all. But as we made our way there, it did dawn on me that her mind may not be what it once was. What if she didn't remember Omen-Ra? Then I guess it would be another dead-end and back to the drawing board we would go, heads hung in over-caffeinated shame.

When we knocked on the door of the suite, the person who opened it was probably in her late thirties—either a caretaker or a relative. She was tall and very pretty, with dark, Indian features. She looked at us in surprise and said, "Can I help you?"

"Hi," I said, wishing I'd rehearsed this speech on the way over. "My name is Quinette Nepier and this is Sebastian Alcott. We're graduate students at the Academy and we're doing a research project for our... aerospace history class. We were, um, informed that Dr. Lavanya Basu lived here and we were hoping she might be available for an interview."

The woman looked suspicious as she said, "You want to interview Dr. Basu? About what?"

"Um, her time as a scientist on Earth. The innovations she helped to move forward. You know, research project stuff." I chuckled awkwardly.

"Are you a relation?" Seb asked the woman.

She nodded. "I'm her granddaughter, Navi."

"We don't mean to intrude upon your and your grandmother's privacy, ma'am," he said. "We just want to ask her a few questions."

"About Omen-Ra, I presume," Navi stated, then noted our shocked expressions. "Why else would you be here?"

I tried not to look guilty. "If it's too much trouble—"

"It's not that I'm against an interview," she said. "It's that my grandmother is very reluctant to talk about her time at that company. I can't promise you'll get any information of note out of her."

"Would it be all right if we tried?" Seb asked gently.

Navi nodded. "Come on in. I'll let her know she has visitors."

We stepped inside the living room and sat on the white, faux-leather couch while we waited. Navi moved to the back room, and a moment later, an older woman with the dignified presence of a matriarch entered, her orange and yellow wrap dress the most colorful clothing I'd seen in a long time. It was clear that she came from another time. Another world.

Her sharp eyes found us and she said, "I hear someone's been snooping through the archives. You two? For a research project, Navi says? I call horse manure."

Seb guffawed while I remained silent, unsure how to respond.

Dr. Basu sat down in the nearest chair as Navi reemerged and went to the kitchen, asking if anyone wanted tea. Dr. Basu obliged. Seb and I declined.

"Now," said the scientist. "Why don't you tell me why you're really here?"

Evidently, she hadn't lost any of her intelligence. "My name is Quinette Nep—"

"I know who you are," she said, her brown eyes tracking from me to Seb. "And I know who you are as well, Sebastian. You two were aboard the *Washington*, weren't you?"

What could we do? We nodded.

"Horrible ordeal. Just terrible." Her eyes met mine and

her expression softened. "My deepest condolences to you and your family."

I swallowed. "Thank you, ma'am. The truth is, we're investigating the ship that attacked us, and our research has led us here. We think the ship was built by Omen-Ra. The question is, why?"

Dr. Basu shifted in her seat as she said, "What makes you think that, pray, tell?"

"Well..." I swallowed again. "Honestly, the fact that it looks like some kind of cephalopod. We found out that Omen-Ra was interested in integrating principles of marine biology into their innovations. So it's the best lead we've got."

"Not a very strong one, wouldn't you say?" said Basu. "It could be a coincidence that the ship looks the way it does. Any number of private companies could've built it."

"We hoped you'd be the one to tell us," said Seb. "Since Omen-Ra never disclosed any ship launch plans to the public."

Basu straightened as she said, "Child, I was a neurologist. My role at the company was more consultant than employee. They brought me in when they needed to test the integrity of their AI drivers. Do you really think I had the clearance to know such things?"

"I guess not," I said quietly.

So that was it, then. Another dead-end.

Then Seb spoke up and said, "What were the AI drivers for, if I may ask?"

"Various astrotechnologies, I assume," she said. "Omen-Ra had contracts with many larger companies."

"Like the SEA?"

She sighed. "Yes, like the SEA."

"Then why haven't we seen any Omen-Ra tech on our ships?" Seb asked. "Was it just not that good?"

"I know what you're doing," said Dr. Basu good-naturedly, wagging a finger at him. "You're needling me for more information."

"Is it working?" Seb said with a charming grin.

"No."

The grin evaporated.

"Dr. Basu," I said. "We appreciate how much you've been willing to tell us so far. Your granddaughter told us it's not something you prefer to talk about. I imagine that if Omen-Ra and the ship that attacked us are in any way connected, their business ethics are probably less than respectable. But—and I know this is going to sound crazy—I have reason to believe that whoever's on that ship took my sister alive. It's what started this whole investigation. If there's even an iota of a chance that she survived, that there's someone on that ship who will listen to reason, I have to try to find them. I owe her that much."

Dr. Basu and Navi, now seated at the kitchen table, exchanged a look charged with something deep and ominous. Then the doctor turned back to me and said, "You are right: it is difficult to speak of. I've spent years trying to forget the things I saw at that company. They were quite... esoteric. Too much so, I'm afraid, for my tastes. And when I could no longer stand their methods, they bought my silence. I was a neurologist for them, and I did work on AI drivers. But during my last few years there, I also worked extensively on a very specific, very unusual project: the psychological framework necessary to support a mind raised in isolation."

Seb and I exchanged a look of mutual shock. "For space travel?" he asked.

Dr. Basu nodded. "So I assumed. They did keep me in the dark about a great many things, but I knew they were planning some kind of deep space exploration. The core of the company, Dr. Omen and his sons, were the only ones who knew the full scope of the project. They were very secretive, and anyone who worked on the project piecemeal, like myself, was ordered not to ask questions. We were *paid* not to ask questions.

"But the tests they had me run gave me cause for concern. They wanted to know if an android could be programmed to support a *child's* neurological development. Ambitious, to be sure, but also puzzling; this didn't seem to have anything to do with astrotechnics. For a while, it was purely theoretical, until... one day... they brought in an infant, a beautiful baby boy, and told me to run the tests with him.

"In the coming weeks, the puzzle pieces began to fall into place: they wanted to send a baby into space. With an android." Dr. Basu clamped a hand over her mouth, composed herself, and continued: "I protested. I adamantly refused to be part of such an unethical enterprise. I had half a mind to take the baby, but they hid him away before I could."

"Whose baby was it? Where did he come from?" I asked.

"I don't know," she said. "They never told me. I assumed he'd been abandoned. Still, it did not give them the right to treat him like a lab rat. In any case, once my views on the matter became clear, they fired me with a severance package so big I could've retired right there. Instead, I took a job in America and relocated my family halfway around the world. Part of it was fear for their safety; what if Omen-Ra had decided that the money wasn't enough to guarantee my silence?

"And indeed, I was tempted many times to expose them. But then, several years later—shortly before I took a position aboard the *Aster*—the company shut down completely. I thought perhaps they'd finally gotten what was coming to them and I could finally rest easy. But with what you've told me, I fear they may have succeeded after all."

My heart raced as it processed this information. "You think that baby... that they actually..."

Dr. Basu nodded slowly. "If their aims were what I suspected them to be, then that ship could very well be theirs. And the child, he'd be in his young adulthood now, if my time dilation calculations are correct. Hardly older than you. Old enough to have rational thoughts. Or old enough to have gone insane."

I shuddered as I considered the implications. What if Xan was alive but stuck on a ship with a psychopath? I felt hot and then cold, nauseous and then empty. My breathing became shallow.

"Q?" Seb said, putting a hand on my back. "It's all right.

We don't have to assume the worst. If they used Dr. Basu's research, then he probably turned out okay."

"My research was unfinished, but they did own all the rights to my work," she said. "If they did use it, I'd like to believe I did my due diligence."

I calmed down enough to say, "You're right. I shouldn't speculate. We need to think about the next steps. How to find the ship, how to get to it. It's on the other side of the Current, so…"

"Have you brought your case before the SEA?" Navi asked. "No offense, but I don't think two teenagers could get very far without the government to back you up."

"Not yet," I said. "We didn't have enough evidence before. We barely do now. And I wouldn't share any information that you don't want shared, Dr. Basu. We can keep looking. You've already given us more than we bargained for, which we're really, really grateful for. So—"

"Calm yourself, child," said Basu. "I believe I have been silent for too long. I am willing to vouch for you to the Council. On one condition."

"Name it," said Seb.

She gave us a stern look of matriarchal concern as she said, "You tell your parents what, exactly, you've been up to."

# 35

# Out of the Frying Pan and Into the Refrigerator

Okay, so, how exactly does one prepare to become a human Drumstick? First, you drink this pink goopy stuff that looks like old-timey Pepto-Bismol, which flushes absolutely everything out of your system. I mean everything. I was on the toilet for two hours, hating myself and cursing Captain out.

But that was only the beginning.

Then, you have to eat this nasty, chalk-like protein cake that basically clogs your pipes so that while you're freezing and after you're frozen, you are digesting very, very slowly. Just enough to keep your not-completely-frozen cells alive but not so much that you go into septic shock before you can thaw out and evacuate all.

Oh yeah, fun fact about cryo-sleep: when it's over, you go potty on yourself. Very fun. I think I get to wear a diaper though. Even more fun.

But before that fashion show can happen, you get to strip to your birthday suit and get sprayed down in this thermal protectant designed to keep your skin from getting frostbitten, which would be counterproductive, to say the least.

That part was done by Phala just outside the cryo room door, to both my relief and chagrin, and then I donned the standard-issue Depends and barely-useful bandeau that would keep my most private parts concealed. Modesty first.

I still couldn't believe I was going through with this, but there was one upside: I finally got to see inside the room where Captain's family dwelled in their frozen slumber. A fact we would soon have in common, though it was the last thing I expected to share with the mysterious, possibly morally-depraved family of the boy I'd recently kissed.

Speaking of whom, he had reentered the dining room once I was decent. I wished Phala would get lost, but I guess she had to be here for medical purposes. In any case, as we stood before the door of the cryo room, myself with a steel-threaded blanket over my shoulders to keep me from floating away, he turned to me and said, "Are you ready?"

I shrugged, keeping the blanket wrapped tight around me. "As I'll ever be."

He punched in a code and scanned his iris to open the door.

Inside, it was much colder than I'd expected, like a deep freezer. Standing in a semi-circle around the edge of the room were oblong, elliptical capsules about as tall as a man, silvery gray with a round port window at head height.

I didn't really want to look, but I did anyway. Of course, you could see their faces. I recognized his mother and father from the video he'd shown me, followed by three young boys aged, I guessed, between five and sixteen.

*You can put five-year-olds in cryo?* But apparently not infants.

There was also an older man, a middle-aged couple, and three other teenagers: two girls and a boy not much older than we were.

I didn't want to say it, much less think it, but they looked uncannily like corpses.

"Um," I said, starting to get cold feet (quite literally) as Phala scanned me and prepared the spare pod. "Are these all your relatives?"

"Yes," said Captain, sounding distant. "Except the boy on the far right. He's my cousin's fiancé."

"Lucky him," I said. In an effort to distract us both, I asked, "What are their names?"

"My grandfather, Dr. Ahmed Omen. My mother, Anippe. My father, Shakir. My brothers, Omar, Kosey, and Femi. My uncle Ibrahim and aunt Safiya. My cousins Jamila and Tabia, and then Yosef... I honestly don't remember whose fiancé he is."

"Hi, everyone," I said, feeling ridiculous but needing to feel ridiculous just to break the tension. "I'm Xan. Nice to meet you. I guess I'll be joining you for... a while."

Captain pinched the bridge of his nose but said nothing.

"The capsule is ready for you, Xanorra," said Phala placidly.

I finally looked over at my frozen sarcophagus, which sat on the far-right end of the semi-circle. The inside was white and cushioned, forming a very rough outline of a person, and looked simultaneously inviting and discouraging.

"Go on, I'll help you in," said Captain.

Not to my surprise, I didn't want to go in. I stood facing the temporary coffin, feeling frozen already, absently pulling the blanket tighter around my shoulders. I glanced at Phala, waiting patiently for me to accept my fate. In a moment of desperation, I said, "Can I have a moment alone with Captain? Please? Just to say goodbye."

Phala's eyes flicked over to Captain, then back to me. Her smile was uncanny as she said, "Of course," and left the cryo room.

Captain's hands went to my arms in an unexpectedly comforting way. "Are you all right?"

I leaned close to his ear so we wouldn't be heard. "Promise me something," I said. "If you can."

"All right," he said, sounding nervous.

"If you can unthaw me sooner... if something changes... please, do it."

He sighed and pulled back to look me in the eyes. "I can't promise that."

"Only if it's safe," I said, hoping he knew what I meant. "If it's safe. That's something only you can judge."

He nodded. "All right. I promise."

I wrapped my arms around his torso and crushed my

face to his chest, not caring if it made saying goodbye harder. Not that this was goodbye forever, but things would be different when I woke again. If all went according to plan.

He wrapped his arms around me in return and buried his face in the crook of my neck, kissing the blanket. In spite of it all, I wanted him to kiss me again for real, but that was asking too much, wasn't it?

"I'm sorry to cut your farewell short, but there is an optimal time frame that must be met," said Phala from the doorway.

Captain pulled away and looked into my eyes. His were not impassive or rigid, not cold or robotic, but soft and full of sorrow. I wanted to believe he was going to miss me as much as I would miss him. How could he stay awake through all this? Would he forget about me? Would everything return to the way it was before?

"I'll see you tomorrow," he said, and then he kissed me on the forehead.

I knew tomorrow was a euphemism, but I appreciated it anyway—somehow, thinking of it as only "tomorrow" made it easier. I caved in and kissed him on the lips, and he answered with equal eagerness.

"Enough," said Phala with an edge that seemed entirely too irritated to be pure robotic functionality. "It is time."

We pulled apart reluctantly. I let him take my hand as I removed the blanket. He eased me into the capsule and Phala secured me in place with a strap across my arms and another across my legs.

"You will be intubated after you're under," she said

clinically. "You won't even feel yourself freeze. It will simply feel like going into a deeper sleep."

"Okay," I said, watching as she produced a syringe from a compartment on the side of the unit, flick it, and hold it to my inner arm.

"Just relax," she said, and these were the last words I heard as the world went hazy. My eyelids became heavy and my hearing felt like I'd been plunged underwater. I couldn't fight it, though I tried. I said a quick prayer in my head, and that was my last conscious act before everything I knew slipped away into oblivion.

# PART III

# Esther

[36]

# Captain's Logs

**Year 17, Day 252, 0334 Atlantean Time**

I slept for two hours, perhaps less, between 2300 and 0200 yesterday morning. I remained on the bridge after that until my duties began in earnest. I hardly follow the outlined schedule anymore. When I am awake, I am working. I am always awake; therefore, I am always working.

At 0300, I spent an hour in the gymnasium. At Phala's behest, I have taken up boxing in an effort to help me sleep better. Sometimes it works. Today, it did not. I showered and reported directly to the infirmary for my daily administration.

"How are we feeling today, Captain?" Phala asks. A routine question, but lately, she's been asking it more frequently.

"Tired," I reply. "But not to the point of dysfunction."

"How are your dreams? Are you still having nightmares?"

"I do not remember my dreams," I lie through my teeth. I always dream, and it is rarely good.

"Take care, Captain. You have everything you need."

I began my bridge shift at 0600 and took a quick break at 1000 to check the status of the cryo room. All vitals were stable. I am still growing accustomed to seeing a twelfth metric on the screen. I try not to think about it. I cannot think about it.

Everything is as it should be. And I have everything I need.

## Year 17, Day 264, 1812 Atlantean Time (Written Entry)

She plagues me. Confound it all, she's found a way to torment me without even being conscious. I shouldn't be saying these things, but I'm in the safety of the greenhouse at the moment, and I plan on deleting this written entry as soon as I've recorded my thoughts. It's simply for catharsis, you see. Nothing more.

It has been approximately two weeks since Xanorra was put into cryo-sleep. Two weeks since everything returned to stasis. Or it was supposed to, at any rate. In truth, nothing feels the same. I see her absence everywhere. I expect to find her in the lounge whenever I pass by, in the dining room whenever I eat, on the bridge whenever monotony threatens to put me to sleep.

Though my rational brain knows where she is and why

she must be there, I can't help but feel like I'm looking for a ghost.

This feeling will pass in time, so I'm told. It must pass, because it's as excruciating as any physical injury I could sustain.

When—if—I sleep, I dream of her. They're not good dreams. Usually, she's drifting away, growing smaller as she falls into oblivion. Or she's trapped in a room, begging to be let out, but I cannot find the key.

I don't have to run a diagnostic to deduce the psychology behind such inventions. It's as plain as day. I thought I knew what it was to be alone, but I did not realize how helplessly I had come to depend on her company. How pathetically susceptible to loneliness I was, just like any other human being. Then again, I think part of me has always known. It was just easier to lie to myself when I didn't know anything different.

Try as I might to compartmentalize these feelings, to tuck them somewhere deep in the recesses of my mind, she refuses to be denied.

That girl. That stubborn, incorrigible girl.

I spend every spare moment I have in the greenhouse, repairing the damage that should by all rights have expunged every fond feeling I had toward her from my mind. And yet I cannot. Even on the days when I believe she did it, I cannot bring myself to hate her for it.

But lately, more and more, her words following the incident have haunted me: *I could never hurt you like that. I love this greenhouse. I love you.*

I had dismissed them at the time as a desperate attempt to gain sympathy. Even if they were true, they were a lifeline cast in a last-ditch effort to survive. She didn't love me. She couldn't.

In any case, why did I care?

Removing my own misgivings from the equation, I could believe that she'd loved the greenhouse. It had delighted her, and she'd done as good a job tending to it as I ever could. That much she'd had no reason to falsify. Which is what made it all the more mystifying when I learned she'd destroyed it.

*I warned you she was dangerous. I warned you she was a threat to the mission. Do you see? This is what happens when you let emotions cloud your judgement. She needs to go. The protocol demands it*, I'd been told.

*I will not kill her*, I'd said. *There has to be another way.*

*You are treading dangerous waters, Captain. You have been ever since you brought her on board. Look within. You know it's true.*

It was true. But even so, why would she destroy the greenhouse?

She claimed an android had done it. She claimed Beta had been against her from the start. That much I could not deny; at every turn, he had reminded me what the protocol necessitated—what the path of least resistance would be. And yet I had resisted it. At every point, I'd found a way to sidestep the obvious answer. Something I'd assumed was permissible because, as the human captain, I was the only one who could decide when the situation required an extension of the parameters. Like unlocking the Master Course. Like planting a fig tree. Like saving a life.

If the AI thought I'd broken protocol, they needed to

inform me. But I'd gotten no such notification. What reason did they have to go behind my back? It was positively ludicrous. They were supposed to work for me, not against me. Otherwise, why was I here? Why did the success of the mission hinge upon me?

If I wasn't the one in charge here, then who was?

## Year 17, Day 267, 1703 Atlantean Time (Written Entry)

I could not ignore the nagging feeling that something had gone awry. And so, a couple of days later, I asked Phala if, at any point in recent months, I had broken protocol.

She'd smiled and said, "No, I do not believe you have."

"Not even when I brought Xanorra on board?"

Her smile had dissipated. "I thought we agreed not to mention her unless absolutely necessary."

"This is absolutely necessary. I do not want to make the same mistakes again."

"You will not," she said. "Everything is as it should be."

"How did that tether break?" I said before I could help it. "Did we ever figure that out?"

"Yes. Beta declared that it was an equipment malfunction. Captain, for your health, you should let the past remain in the past. After all, there is so much future to look forward to. I suggest you meditate on that."

"Why am I here, Phala?" I asked instead. Where this sudden insecurity came from, I couldn't say. Chalk it up to yet another way in which that vexing, red-haired girl exacted her unconscious revenge on me.

Phala gave me a look of concern. "Is this a metaphysical question, or a physical question? I assume you know why you are in this room. As to the other—"

"Why am I on this ship? Why me?"

Phala was silent as she processed my question. "You know why," she said. "You were born for this. There is no one better qualified to do this than you."

"But how?" I said. "If I am as susceptible to human weakness as any other man—as susceptible to guilt, to anger, to... to..."

"Love?" Phala guessed. "I assume the source of this inquiry is that girl. Do you truly believe what you felt for her was love?" She didn't wait for me to answer. "No. What you felt for her was a chemical process you are biologically required to initiate. One that is completely at odds with the glorious purpose you have been given. You were never supposed to meet a woman, Captain, because you are genetically programmed to prioritize her over anything greater. It is nothing more than carnal, base instinct."

"You're saying I'm an animal?"

"I am saying you are an adolescent," she said, something she'd never called me before. "And until you mature, you will not be able to control your instincts. That much became abundantly clear the night following the tether incident."

My face grew warm at the memory. "You know about that?"

"I know everything, Captain," she said smoothly. "That is my purpose. Now I ask you, do you know yours?"

I left the room with more questions than answers. All this, because Xanorra and I had kissed? No, that didn't make sense. And yet, at the same time, it did.

*You were never supposed to meet a woman.*

Had that been part of the protocol? "Under no circumstances is Captain to have contact with a female"? Growing up, I'd taken that for granted. Of course I'd never meet a woman. And why would I need to? I had a destiny to fulfil. I had a civilization to help birth. Nothing could be more desirable than that.

And then Xanorra had come along. And for a time, I'd fooled myself into thinking it wouldn't make a difference. I thought I could be better than my instincts.

How wrong I'd been.

# Quin's Journal #6

So… a lot has happened in the last two months. I've been so busy I haven't had time to write any of it down, but that changes today. Because, well… now I have more time than I know what to do with.

After our conversation with Dr. Basu, we did what she'd asked and brought our parents up to speed. Mine already knew most of the story, but poor Rodney on the other hand—Seb's dad—hadn't had the slightest idea what his son had been up to other than that he'd been spending a lot of time with me.

My parents invited him, Seb, and Dr. Basu over to talk about what came next. My dad told us that he had presented my "Xan being alive" theory before the SEA a few weeks ago, but that they hadn't seemed impressed. Unsurprisingly, without hard evidence, they still considered it a waste of resources.

But then Dr. Basu offered to finance a rescue mission. And that rendered us all speechless.

"We couldn't let you do that," Mom had said. "You hardly know us, and—"

"But I insist," the doctor had said. "The money would mostly come from Omen-Ra's own severance package, given to buy my silence—it seems only fitting that it be used to track down the very ship they'd worked so hard to keep a secret. A bit of poetic justice, if I do say so myself."

It *was* poetic justice.

"Besides," she said sadly. "I feel... partly responsible. If I had been brave enough to speak out, to do something, perhaps..."

My dad had shaken his head. "Don't put this on yourself, Doctor. Anyone else in your position would've done the same thing."

It was decided, then: Dr. Basu would go with us before the Council as a financier and not take no for an answer. We submitted our case and our hearing was scheduled for two weeks later. Seb and I worked around the clock to put together the presentation, more devoted to the cause than any class project we'd ever been assigned.

Plus, Seb actually pulled his weight, unlike any project partner I'd ever been assigned to. Why couldn't we have been in the same classes?

When the day of the hearing finally arrived, we were as prepared as we could possibly be. We waited at Aster Hall for two hours before they finally saw us, and to sum it up, it was a wash: with an esteemed, retired neurologist (and, more precisely, her money) to back us up, they granted our proposal within a matter of days.

There was only one stipulation: if possible, we had to bring the squid ship back with us. A tall order, but since they were willing to provide us with access to the resources needed to do so, we agreed to their terms without protest.

From there, it was a whirlwind of preparations. Basu had commissioned us a military-grade explorer, smaller than the *Washington* had been but big enough to sustain a small crew in deep space for years. Plus, this time, it would have enough weapons to give us a fighting chance should a certain squid ship decide to get frisky.

And who would captain this vessel? None other than Commander Rodrigo Peralta, who had volunteered himself as soon as he'd heard the news. He and a small crew of spacers with a military background would run the ship with us.

We were ecstatic. Now the question remained: who would stay, and who would go? We couldn't all go, that much was for sure. Basu would stay behind, of course—she said she was both too old and too disenchanted with deep space travel—and so would Rodney, who couldn't afford to leave his job.

Seb and I were dead-set on going. Taking our cues from Basu, we wouldn't take no for an answer, and both my parents and his dad didn't see much reason why they should fight us on it.

However, they weren't too keen on us going alone, either.

My parents spent days in deep discussion. The mission

could last anywhere from two to five years depending on how quickly we were able to track down the squid ship—and even though that was peanuts for deep space explorers, it was still a significant amount of time to be separated.

In the end, it was obvious that Dad had to go. He'd go crazy if he had to stay on the *Aster*. Mom, on the other hand, would hold down the fort back home and make sure there was a place for us to come back to.

Because we would come back. With Xan. And possibly the whole ship.

A month and a half later, the day of the launch arrived. We said our goodbyes, and Dad, Seb, and I boarded the *Conseil* while several hundred *Aster* residents (who, by now, knew all about the mission) waved us off from the spectator's landing.

And just like that, we were back in deep space again. It took me a couple of weeks to get my bearings and settle into this new reality: an actual, real rescue mission. An actual shot at getting Xan back, at undoing all this chaos.

I've been trying to remain pragmatic, but truth be told, it's a struggle. Hope and optimism have taken root in my overactive brain, and I'll be damned if they'll be weeded out now.

Oh my God. Oh my God oh my God oh my God oh my God.

It's been two months since my last entry because,

honestly, not much has happened since we launched from the *Aster*.

But that changed today. Holy shit, did it.

Today we received a message. From Xan. To us. She's alive. She's *actually* alive! Or at least, she was at the time she recorded the message, which according to its time stamp had been about four months ago. That's good enough for me. She was alive, and she wanted us to come find her. She didn't say it directly; in fact, she claimed the opposite, but I could hear it in her voice. It was obvious, like a secret code only we knew.

God, what must it be like on that ship, with that boy? After what Dr. Basu said about him, I pray it isn't a living hell. I hope she didn't risk everything to give us this message.

I'm so overwhelmed I don't even know what to think right now. I can barely form coherent sentences, much less articulate my feelings.

Okay, let me just focus on the facts. That much I know I can do.

The message arrived nested—that means that someone *else* picked up the transmission and forwarded it using their own system. The fact that there is someone else out here in the first place—other than the stupid squid ship, of course—is as confounding as the message itself. The forwarder did not identify themselves, did not attach their own recording to the message, but they did leave a time stamp: apparently, they were pretty far from us, because they'd picked up the transmission two months ago and immediately tossed it behind them, hoping it reached its intended destination.

So now we were indebted to this Good Samaritan, and we didn't even know who they were or how to pay them back. Dad and Peralta's best guess was that they were a junker who'd come out here to salvage the wreckage of the *Washington*, which was technically illegal—hence the anonymity. But we'd be willing to turn a blind eye if it meant getting closer to completing our mission, so Dad sent a reply back to the mysterious junker asking for any help they would be willing to give.

It might take months to receive a reply, but we've waited this long. We could afford to wait a little longer.

The air on board the *Conseil* changed after that, charged with renewed optimism and the thrill of having a solid lead. Seb and I can't stop smiling at each other, mutually awed by the sudden tangibility of something that honestly had been pretty speculative up until now. And sure, there were still a lot of unknowns, but I would accept them in exchange for this one undeniable truth: we had been right. Xan had been alive.

And she wanted us to come find her.

## [38]

# Captain's Logs, Continued

**Year 17, Day 341, 0115 Atlantean Time**

It has been approximately three months now since Xanorra was put into cryo sleep. Despite my best efforts, I have not been able to forget about her. I replay our conversations when I'm on the bridge. I turn over every word she said, looking for something—anything—that will help me decide I've had enough. That there's nothing left but to forget her.

Instead, it only dredges up more uncertainty. I sleep even less than before. My dreams are none the better. I do not tell Phala this. I have avoided conversing with her since that day in the infirmary. I cannot get her words out of my head, but for an entirely different reason than Xanorra's.

*Do you truly believe what you felt for her was love?*

Truthfully, I hadn't considered it. To do so was dangerous, that much I had enough sense to know. But

I'm not an idiot. I know I felt—that I *feel*—something toward her, something different than anything I've felt before. When she first arrived here, I thought it might be fear. It felt like fear sometimes. Then I thought it might be lust. It felt like lust sometimes, too. If I could define it, I could control it. But the more I got to know her, the more the word kept eluding me. Now, in her absence, I have no excuse. I cannot quantify it any other way.

In the words of Sir Arthur Conan Doyle, "Once you eliminate the impossible, whatever remains, however improbable, must be the truth."

Well, who do I have to lie to anymore other than myself?

I love her.

I love her. I love her. *I love her.*

Damn it.

## Year 18, Day 1, 0005 Atlantean Time

Today is my eighteenth birthday. I'm the same age as Xan now. I wish I could tell her that. She would probably laugh and say she is still older than me. Technically, that isn't true and never has been. I was born on Earth fifty years ago. Time dilation simply dictates that I have only experienced eighteen years.

See, Xan? Thanks to the theory of relativity, I've always been older than you.

And evidently, I always will be.

## Year 18, Day 63, 2209 Atlantean Time

There has been an unwanted development. Honestly, at this point, I can't believe anything would surprise me, but somehow this managed to catch me off-guard. As the saying goes, "Fool me twice, shame on me."

Shame on me, indeed.

There is a ship on my radar.

It appeared just under an hour ago, at my five o'clock, moving at a steady click about seven hundred thousand kilometres away. Still close enough to detect. Close enough to tell that it is not an SEA-issued vessel.

It will intercept us within a matter of days.

I know what I ought to do. I know what the protocol demands I do. And if I were smart, if I had learned anything at all these past eight months, it would be to listen to it without so much as a passing thought. But every time I think about giving the order, I hear Xanorra in my head: *It was heartless.*

Followed by, *So you do have a heart.*

Either I had a heart, or I didn't. An abysmally short time after meeting me, she seemed to think I did. Did that say more about her, or me?

*You can't just shoot them down*, she'd say if she were here. *Those are people on that ship. Living, breathing, people. Like you and me. You can't choose who lives and who dies. You can't play god with people's lives.*

I know what the protocol demands of me. But the last time I followed it to the letter, it didn't work out so well for me. And that isn't even considering the fact that, according to Xan's estimation, everyone but her made it off that ship safely.

I'd already failed to kill—multiple times—even when I'd had no incentive to do otherwise. Perhaps the universe was trying to tell me something?

Perhaps I'd already broken the protocol, and that was why the AI had done the things they'd done.

Either I had a heart, or I didn't.

Xan thought I did.

I suppose all that's left is to decide whether I think so, too.

# 39

# Meanwhile, in Dreamland...

Dreams are a funny thing. I've never been a lucid dreamer, so I always think my dreams are real until I wake up, no matter how bizarre they are. In this one, I was back on board the *Aster*, except it wasn't the *Aster*—its walls were blue like the interior of the *Atlantis*, yet for some reason, I thought I was home, because I was looking for my parents and sister.

I kept calling their names as I ran down the long, curved hallway, convinced they were around the next bend. Then I noticed a door to my right, wide open and spilling warm, yellow light out into the hall. I entered it and there they were, seated at a table that had been set in the middle of Captain's greenhouse. At the head of the table was Captain himself, playing the gracious host.

They were talking, and laughing, and eating dinner, but none of them seemed to notice I'd entered the room. I kept calling out to them, trying to get them to look at me, but they just kept talking as if I were a ghost. Maybe I was.

"Where's Xanorra?" my mother asked.

"I'm right here!" I said.

"She's back on my ship, frozen in cryo sleep," said Captain nonchalantly. "But don't worry. I'll wake her up when it's safe."

"I'm right here!" I said louder.

But they went right back to talking, and laughing, and eating...

# 40

# A Long Winter's Nap, Interrupted

It started with that just-awake feeling, like when you first hear your alarm going off but you haven't decided yet whether you're going to hit "snooze" and steal a few more precious moments of sleep or drag your sorry ass out of dreamland and back to the waking world.

But when I opened my eyes and had no idea where I was, the process of waking up accelerated considerably. I couldn't move. Everything was a painful shade of white. I was cold. Really freaking cold.

It came back to me piece by piece, disjointed shapes locking into place until I could finally see the full picture. *Ship. Captain. Stuck. Robots. Greenhouse. Frozen.*

A pretty convoluted train of thought by all counts, but it was enough to help me remember the rest.

I was in a cryo chamber. I was waking up from *cryo-sleep.*

Oddly enough, it felt too soon for me to be awake. Although, wasn't that what it was supposed to feel like? One minute asleep, the next awake? I grappled for a sense of time. It was impossible to tell other than this strange gut feeling that something had happened.

Well, I supposed it could only be one of two options: either Captain had determined it was "safe" and had woken me up early, or thirty-two years had actually passed and I was about to come face to face with the fifty-year-old version of the boy I had once liked.

*Please be option one. Please be option one. Please, please, please...*

The door opened and I braced myself for whatever was on the other side.

Captain, of course.

And he looked... old, I think? My heart sank. My vision hadn't fully returned yet, so he was blurry, but something was different about him. He looked thinner, more haggard. His hair was longer, almost to his chin, and it looked like he might've grown stubble where he would normally shave clean.

He did look old, but how old? Twenties old? Forties old?

I couldn't speak yet, so I couldn't ask even though I wanted to. Yes, apparently unfreezing was a slow, embarrassing process of regaining all your basic cognitive functions.

"Ccccc—" I tried, but nope, not happening.

"Don't strain yourself," he said. His voice sounded the same as I remembered: low tenor, British, eternally peeved, but unmistakably a young man's voice. Unless my ears deceived me. "Can you move your fingers and toes yet?"

I could, somewhat, so I kept wiggling them until Captain was satisfied with my mobility and finally unstrapped me. I fell like a wet noodle into his arms, my entire body limp and sore.

"Easy," said Captain, dropping a steel-threaded blanket over my shoulders. He had to prop me up for a while, but soon enough, I could stand on my own. It just hurt like a bitch. However, as uncomfortable as I was, I didn't feel as bad as I'd expected after years of stasis.

Which begged the question: had it been years?

My eyes had refocused during this time, and now I could plainly see that Captain was, indeed, still young enough to be dateable. He just looked like shit. He'd lost weight—too much of it. His cheeks were sunken in, the circles under his eyes darker than ever. He looked like he hadn't shaved in weeks or had a haircut in months.

"How—old—are you?" I managed.

He paused for a torturously long moment. "I'm eighteen."

I guffawed, which came out as a sputtering cough. "Eighteen! Only eighteen!" I hugged him, both out of joy and out of necessity—I wasn't as stable as I thought. I pulled away to look him in the eyes. "I—missed—your birthday!"

He scoffed, but there was a smile in it. "That's what you're concerned about? I suppose I should have figured as much."

"How—long—has—it been?"

He swallowed. "A little over six months."

My jaw would've dropped to the floor if it hadn't been only half-thawed. No wonder it felt so fast. It was fast! Now everything made sense. Six months was still six months, but in a cryo-sleep designed to last for years, it was practically a waste of time. What could've possibly prompted him to wake me up this early? Surely it wasn't already safe for me. Surely the androids would not be excited that I was back.

But maybe Captain had come to his senses. Maybe something had changed.

"Six months!" I said, my voice high and squeaky like a hinge in need of oil. "You missed me that much?"

"That's not why I woke you up," he said, oblivious to my teasing edge. "You see, we have a situation. An emergency, if you will. And after much deliberation, it was determined that the best course of action was to... wake you. Early."

I swallowed a dry lump in my throat. "What situation? What emergency?"

"I've said too much. You need to rehabilitate first."

"Like hell I do!" I said, trying to push him away even though my arms were still jelly. "Captain Whatever-Your-Middle-Name-Is Omen, you tell me what's going on and you tell me now!"

He sighed as if I were a great burden and he regretted ever unthawing me. "A ship has been tailing us for the last couple of days. A ship with no registration, no markers, no designation of any kind. To use an anachronism, this ship isn't flying any colors."

I gasped. "Pirates."

Pirates or no pirates, I still needed to rehabilitate, which involved a lukewarm shower, some light physical therapy, multiple layers of clothes, and drinking lots of vitamin water. All this Captain facilitated himself with the assistance of Kappa, and while perhaps I should've been concerned that Phala was not involved, I couldn't say I wasn't relieved.

By the way, that protein stuff I ate before the big freeze? Yeah, that stuff was designed to last way longer than six months and to be digested at one-twelfth the speed of a normal teenager's metabolism. You know what that means, don't you?

A few hours after unfreezing, it was back to the toilet again. For a long, long time. My favorite!

But whilst on the toilet, I had plenty of time to think about this unexpected turn of events. Naturally, they baffled me. By all counts, space pirates were a myth. A funny joke we said to keep the mood light at work or a bedtime story we told to children. Not a real thing that tracks unassuming vessels through deep space wormholes.

It would be more than a hard life; it would be a near-impossible life. Your only hope to refuel would be to either never wander far from a colony ship (risky) or keep flying until you intercepted another vessel and pillaged them (a gamble). Someone would have to be truly insane to even entertain the thought that "yo-ho, yo-ho, a pirate's life" was, indeed, for them.

And then I remembered: I had thought at first that the *Atlantis* was a pirate ship. And while it didn't fit any of the imaginative stereotypes, technically speaking, Captain was a pirate. He was in an unmarked, unregistered vessel transporting unregulated cargo, he played by his own set of rules, and he had attacked and robbed (via the abduction of yours truly) another vessel in open space, aka, on international waters.

Ergo, space pirate.

Perhaps the other ship wasn't tailing us because they wanted to rob us. Perhaps they were tailing us because they thought we were one of them.

And perhaps it was best if they continued to think that.

Fully cleansed in ways I never thought possible, I exited the lavatory and found Captain waiting for me in the lounge. My breath hitched when I saw him, seated casually on the leather sofa, pensive as ever. Even though it felt like I'd seen him just yesterday, it somehow still felt like it had been forever. And while, haggard appearance aside, he looked and acted the same, I couldn't help but feel like there was something else different about him. Something more... fundamental.

His eyes snapped to mine. "Better?" he asked.

"I will be after I get some real food," I said, taking a seat on the other side of the couch. "But I have questions I need answered first."

"I'm sure you do." I'd actually missed his monotone. Go figure.

"Have you talked to anyone on the pirate ship yet?"

He shook his head. "They haven't tried to establish

contact, and I thought it might be ill-advised to do so myself."

"And you said they've been tailing you for the past couple of days?"

"Possibly longer depending on how good their radar is, but mine only picked them up two days ago."

"And you decided to wake me up from my primordial slumber because...?"

He hesitated, and then said, "Because I need you."

I put a hand over my heart. "I'm touched."

He huffed. "Because after much deliberation, I have determined that, in light of what happened the last time I encountered another deep space vessel, diplomacy may be the better tactic here. Especially if they're well-armed. And you, I know, are very skilled at diplomacy."

"Why, thank you," I said. Diplomatically. "But I'm confused. If you're not going to blast them into atoms, then how is this not breaking protocol?"

He paused. "I found a workaround. They're not SEA, so assuming they don't have any sort of governmental affiliation, there is no incentive for them to pursue us once they know we're not a threat. As long as they don't discover the ship's true purpose—as long as we can convince them to continue in another direction—there is no reason to destroy them."

"My God, you could be a lawyer. Captain Omen, Attorney-At-Law."

He glared at me. In spite of my teasing, I was actually beyond proud of him. He didn't want to hurt people. He'd listened to his conscience.

"So... then... how did you convince the AI to let you wake me up?" I asked.

"There was no convincing," he said. "I made the executive decision as captain."

I winced. "They couldn't have been happy about that."

"They're androids, Xan. They do not feel happiness."

"I know. It was a figure of speech. What I mean is... there has to be a catch. I mean, unless it's somehow safe? Like you promised?"

He wouldn't make eye contact with me. I leaned over to look at him and caught his conflicted expression.

"Captain? What happened?"

He beckoned me to him, then must've recalled the last time he'd done the same thing—though the circumstances had been far different—because he stopped and said, "If you don't mind, could you act like you're embracing me?"

Somehow both endeared and disturbed, I sidled close to him and said, "No acting necessary. I want to embrace you."

He crushed me into him and I could practically feel how desperate he'd been these past six months. Lonelier than he let on. Struggling more than he'd admit. Typical, mule-headed Captain.

I hugged him back, genuinely, and kept holding onto him as he leaned into my ear, tickling the side of my face with his breath, and said, "It was a hard sell. The protocol resisted my logic. But in the end, I... I may have insinuated that... I would return you to cryo-sleep after this ordeal is over."

I reared back so he could witness the full scope of my indignation. "I don't *fucking think so!*"

"I know," he said, hands on my arms to pacify me. "I know. I have a plan, but you have to listen to me very carefully."

I leaned toward his ear again and waited.

"You must escape aboard the pirate ship."

I opened and closed my mouth, outraged and speechless all at once. It was the most asinine thing I'd ever heard. "You're crazy," I said. "Six months without me has driven you insane."

"Very nearly," he said, which was as close to an "I missed you" as I was going to get, apparently. Still flattering, in an off-putting kind of way. "But no, I'm not crazy. I've thought this through, and this is the best plan with the greatest chance of success."

I shook my head. "Not if Beta catches onto what we're doing—he'll blast the pirate ship out of the sky with me on board."

"Beta won't know. You have to stow away, and I have to pretend like I don't know. By the time I figure it out, the pirate ship will be too far away and you'll be home free."

I sat back so I could see his face again and winced. "Yeah, about that. I still don't see how it's likely that a pirate ship will go anywhere near a space colony."

"Your chances of seeing your family again are much higher with them than with me. Isn't this what you wanted?" His eyes were solemn. "You still have a choice: escape or go back to cryo-sleep. Either way, I won't see you come to harm. But I doubt you'll get another chance like this again, and when I put you back under, you should not expect to wake up until we've reached our final destination. You don't have to decide now, but I want you to think about it."

I stared at him in disbelief. It was a hard pill to swallow, but he was right. And he'd taken a huge risk just to give me this chance.

And like the grateful, logical, and *totally uncontradictory* person I was, I was so mad at him I could spit.

"I'll never see you again," I said.

"It's better that way," he said. "You being here, it... it never should've happened in the first place."

"What happened to you?" I asked. "These past six months?"

He met my eyes and where I expected to see a broken spirit, I saw a boy at war within himself. After all, he'd had a lot of time to think while I was gone. If he had half the heart I believed he had, he'd probably come to some disturbing conclusions.

The sorts of conclusions that would justify sparing a pirate ship, waking me up, and smuggling me out.

It was eating him up inside.

I put my hands to the sides of his face. "Captain," I said. "Talk to me."

He opened his mouth to speak, then closed it again. A wall of steel fell like a guillotine behind his dark eyes, and just like that, he'd shut me out. He was going to erase the memory of me, purge me from every corner of the ship, just to save my life. Or was it to save the mission?

I guess it was both. He was going to try to do both, even though we were mutually exclusive. How exactly was that going to turn out in the end? Did I want to know?

"You should eat something," he said. "I'm sure you're hungry."

I nodded, forcing the emotions that threatened to surface as far down as they'd go. "Yeah. I feel like I haven't eaten in six months."

He smiled, but the mirth didn't reach his eyes. "Eat. Then we'll make a plan."

# 41

# Of Pirates and Men

"So," I said, feeling a thousand times more human now that I was properly nourished, "how does one schmooze a space pirate? Space rum?"

Captain wrinkled his nose, now seated in the lounge's armchair. "Schmooze?"

"What do we say to them?"

"I figured you'd tell me. You're the one with the superior cultural knowledge, and you've mentioned space pirates in passing before. You must know something about how they operate."

I laughed. "As if! We talk about pirates the same way we talk about, I don't know, the dinosaurs. Like, sure, they technically existed *once*, on Earth, but not in space!"

"Apparently they do." He remained as stoic as ever. "In any case, I doubt they will accept a single human aboard a ship full of robots without question, but two humans?

That may be an easier sell. If it helps, for the sake of this charade, you'll be acting as my first mate."

"Oh, I'm sure Beta loves that." I actually rather liked the idea of subverting him, even if it was in name only.

Captain frowned. "He and the rest of the crew are well aware of the uniqueness of the situation. Everything I've planned is within the parameters of the protocol. He'll follow my orders."

"Mm-hm." I benched my doubts for the moment as I propped my chin in my hand. "If we're going to play charades, then we'd better have our story straight."

"That's where I need your help. I have no imagination for such things."

I perked up, excited to finally share my epiphany. "It's easy. We're pirates, too."

He raised a thick eyebrow.

"We fly no colors. We have no affiliations. We answer to no one but ourselves. We're pirates. Technically, you've been a pirate this whole time, so it wouldn't really be lying."

He actually looked shocked. "How am I a pirate?"

"How aren't you a pirate?" I watched him carefully. "Think really hard before you answer."

He did, and as I suspected, he came up blank. "Touché. So I'm a pirate. Why and how?"

"Parents died on a deep space mission. Engine room accident. For this to work, we're both from *Aster.* In your distress, you stole a prototype transport vessel and set off on your own. Little did you know, it was also full of prototype deep space technology—the kind that could sustain you for years on end. You were set."

"What about yourself?" he asked.

"I am the loyal girlfriend who followed you into oblivion," I said. "Orphaned, of course, because I'd never leave my family without saying goodbye."

"Of course not."

I tapped my chin. "We'd been dating for two years prior to stealing the ship. I was an engineer and you were a bridge apprentice. It was love at first sight, one day while you were doing rounds in the engine room. We met every afternoon in the food court after that for coffee and small talk. I became your shoulder to cry on after the accident—"

"I think you're getting carried away," he said flatly.

"Hey, we have to be able to sell it. Oh, and we need aliases. There's no sense in giving them our real names."

He looked utterly unamused as he said, "What did you have in mind?"

"I will go by my middle name, Jade. Jade… Frost, on account of having just been frozen. Funny, right?"

"Riveting."

"Do you have a middle name?"

"I do not, no."

"Well, then pick one that you like. But it has to be a real name, not a designation."

"I don't know many names," he said. "I suppose I could go by the Arabic version of my name, *Rubban*."

It had never occurred to me that he might actually have another name. He was bilingual, after all. He probably hadn't gone by the English version of his name at all until I'd shown up. I wondered if it had been weird for him. "What if someone on the ship speaks Arabic? Would that strike them as odd? 'Captain Captain.'"

He sighed. "I suppose so."

"How about Reuben? That's phonetically close."

"Reuben." He tested it out. "That's a Hebrew name. Biblical."

"Does that bother you?"

"No. I—" He got a far-off look in his eye that quickly evaporated. "It hardly matters what the name is, does it? It will suffice."

"Reuben will be your first name if they ask for it. Your last name will be…." I squinted. "Silver."

"Silver. Why?"

"Like John Silver? *Treasure Planet?*"

"Not familiar. But very well."

I sighed. "Okay, so, that's settled. Captain Reuben Silver and First Mate Jade Frost. Pretty sharp, if I do say so myself."

"They'll know the names are fake."

"It doesn't matter," I said. "It proves we're devil-may-care rapscallions who answer to no one but ourselves."

He pinched the bridge of his nose. I hadn't realized how much I'd actually missed that obnoxious "I'm annoyed" gesture of his. "Not superfluous at all."

"Oh, and you should probably tone down the pretentiousness," I said. "Use small words, preferably four-letter ones."

"Fine," he said.

"That's more like it."

"Anything else I need to change about myself fundamentally?" he asked, half-joking, half-scathing.

I scrutinized his scruffy, disheveled appearance and said, "Nope. You're good. Keep growing out that beard, though. That's very pirate-y."

He rubbed his temples, clearly regretting his decision to put me in charge of piratical diplomacy. Too late.

"Well then, Captain Silver? What say you?"

"Very well," he said.

"'Aye,' Captain," I said pointedly. "The correct answer is 'aye.'"

With such an ingenious plan set into motion, it was hard to believe that anything could possibly go wrong. But it did give our new unlawful friends the benefit of the doubt: first, that they were not here to shoot us into oblivion, and second, that they were interested in establishing contact at all.

But that's where we would take the initiative and reach out to them first in a gesture of goodwill.

Back on the bridge, it felt like I had made a triumphant but awkward return from prison. The task bots were as neutral toward me as ever but Beta, to my surprise, smiled his uncanny grin and said, "Ah, Miss Nepier. So glad to see you fully recuperated."

As if he were actually glad I was back. Even programmed with impeccable decorum, I still knew bullshit when I heard it. "Yes, a six-month-long nap does wonders for the psyche."

"I can only imagine."

Captain cleared his throat from the helm. "Lieutenant,

we are about to engage with the mysterious ship. For the purposes of executing this maneuver properly, I will be known as Captain Silver. You will be referred to as Beta only and Miss Nepier shall be referred to as First Mate Frost."

Beta nodded as if he had absolutely nothing against that at all. I knew better. "As you wish, sir."

"Zeta, open a communication channel."

Zeta complied.

Captain stood a little straighter and said, "This is Captain Reuben Silver of the—" He hesitated.

Shit. How could we forget to think of a fake ship name?

"Of the independent deep space vessel, *The Kraken*." Nice save. Great name. "We are requesting that you identify yourself and state your purpose for tracking our course. I repeat—"

"I heard you the first time," said a smooth voice. Not the sort of voice you'd imagine a pirate to have, and heavily accented—my best guess was French. "Your little ship, it is charming."

"Little?"

"Kitschy, but charming. Like a children's toy. I am painfully curious about those tentacles at the back. They cannot serve a practical purpose?"

"I—er—they—" Captain stumbled over himself, completely caught off-guard by the pirate's forthrightness. He sounded friendly enough, if not a bit... condescending. Yeah, that had to be a good sign. He quickly composed himself and said, "To whom do I have the pleasure of speaking?"

"I find these sorts of introductions quite tedious, don't you?" said the pirate, bored.

"I told you *my* name."

"I do not recall asking for it."

Captain looked at me, dumbfounded. I scrunched my face and pretended to wring an imaginary neck. This friggin' guy.

"I much prefer face-to-face interaction," the pirate continued. "I am very eager to meet a fellow free ship this far out past the Current. That is what you are, I take it? A free ship?"

"Yes," Captain said slowly.

"Funny that I have never heard of you. One would think a ship design like that would be unforgettable. No matter, there will be plenty of time for chit-chat once we're alongside. My calculations show that I will be matching your rate of acceleration in approximately fourteen hours. At that time, I humbly invite you to board my ship and join me in the captain's quarters for a proper introduction. You may bring one trusted crewmember and no weapons. Have we an accord?"

Captain and I looked at each other in mutual shock. We'd expected to have to convince him to let us board, but he'd offered willingly. Finally, something going in our favor. "Yes," said Captain. "We have an accord."

"I look forward to our meeting, Captain Silver." The line went silent.

"Okay," I said, finally able to breathe. "So he's a precocious pirate."

"Precocious? Try patronizing," said Captain.

"Yeah, well, he is a pirate. Maybe you can turn the highbrow back on a little bit? Match him blow for blow?"

Captain raised an eyebrow at me. "Are you saying I'm patronizing?"

I put my hands up. "You said it, not me."

He sighed and pinched the bridge of his nose. "I should've pressed him for more information. We're practically going in blind."

"Don't be hard on yourself. Besides, if he wanted to rob us or something, I don't think he would've gone through the trouble of inviting us over first. Much easier to just shoot us out of the sky. I hate to say it, but I think he's just as surprised to see us as we are to see him. Which works in our favor, since it's exactly what we were hoping for."

Captain nodded in agreement. "Very well. Lieutenant, prepare the *Nautilus* for departure."

After solidifying the plan before we boarded, we went our separate ways, myself to get some rest and Captain to make preparations for when we were off-ship.

Off-ship... this would be my first time off-ship (tether incident notwithstanding) in eight months. And Captain's first time ever. Was it wrong to be excited about it, even though we were about to meet a mysterious Frenchman who'd basically called the *Atlantis* cute?

Hadn't I said it would take a special kind of crazy to be a space pirate? Best to be on our guards, to say the least.

And on that note, how exactly was I supposed to smuggle myself aboard? Would I have to hide? Would we have to bargain? What if the pirate said no? What if he caught me and tossed me out of the airlock?

Suddenly, Captain's brilliant plan to save my life didn't seem quite so airtight.

Despite all these tumultuous thoughts, I did manage to catch a few hours of natural sleep, and when I woke, I was ready to become a scallywag.

I met up with Captain on the bridge, who gave me a curt nod as he watched the readouts; it was still four hours before we were alongside, but the pirate ship was now close enough to us that its image could be magnified and observed in detail on the view screen.

I could hardly believe what I was looking at. First of all, it was massive. Little ship indeed—the *Atlantis* was probably a quarter of its size. It must've been a retrofitted cargo ship because nothing else would justify how big it was.

Its shape, however, was one for the books: it actually looked like a seafaring pirate ship from the outside, with a curved hull that narrowed into a sharp bowsprit and—get this—an actual figurehead. A woman, made of metal, expertly welded to its front.

Of course, it didn't have masts, sails, or a deck like a seafaring ship would, but it did have large, billowed radiation sails jutting out from the sides and top, giving it the look of a mighty, mechanical whale.

And *we* were the ones who were kitschy! But I'd be lying if I said it didn't cut an impressive figure.

"It's a fast ship," said Captain. "It must be advanced if it's able to match pace with us so quickly. I wonder what its fuel source is."

"I'm sure you captains will have a grand old time comparing apples to apples. Or apples to watermelons, more like. Just look at the size of that thing!"

Captain shot me a scathing look.

I shrugged apologetically. "Not that size matters. I'm sure it has nothing on the *Atlantis*'s sense of style."

"I'm sure this goes without saying, but under no circumstances is he to come aboard the *Atlantis* or learn anything about its inner workings. This only works if we retain our mystique. As soon as he gets a whiff of what this ship can do, he'll start asking questions I can't answer without breaching protocol. Do you understand?"

"Keep him in the dark or you'll have to blast him to Kingdom Come. Got it." Glibness aside, the sad part was, that was exactly what he would do.

And it was exactly what I was here to prevent.

Four hours might've been a trifle to the captain, but it was still an eternity to me, so I walked laps around the ship to help recondition my long-unused muscles—though I was thankful that the process wasn't going to take months like it would the rest of his family.

*Though it will if you go back under.*

Jeez, could you even freeze someone twice without damaging their tissues? Captain didn't seem concerned about it should it come to that, so maybe the short time frame had spared me. Still, once was enough. I didn't like that feeling of being in limbo, halfway between existing and not-existing, barely aware if you were one or the other. Schrödinger's popsicle.

Still a superior alternative to getting killed by pirates. Or robots.

I rubbed my temples. I really didn't want to think about this anymore, but it was the million-dollar question: which option had the highest chance of survival?

Best to play it by ear, I supposed. Meet the pirate first. Get a read on him. Decide the rest later.

What could possibly go wrong?

# 42

# This is Nothing Like the Movies... But Also, Exactly Like the Movies

Zero hour arrived. We suited up in full EVA which, according to Captain, would stay on (helmets included) until we were absolutely sure this pirate could be reasoned with. If he wanted to preserve his anonymity by withholding his name, then two (or three) could play at that game: we'd withhold our whole faces.

Maybe he was a fan of Daft Punk.

Once we were suited up, we boarded the awaiting *Nautilus*. I was excited to finally take a ride in this seashell-shaped cruiser and was not surprised to find that the interior mirrored that of the *Atlantis*, blue and silver with blue-green backlighting. It was only slightly bigger than my escape pod had been, so it sat two people comfortably. Captain piloted while I sat tight and tried to still my beating heart.

The short ride to the pirate ship was a no-brainer, surreal as it was to be leaving the *Atlantis*. But however strange it might be for me, it had to be a hundred times more so for Captain, who had never stepped foot on another ship, had never known anything other than the small, ethereal world of the *Atlantis* and the endless void that enveloped it. On the trip over he seemed fine—not that I could see his face through the blacked-out helmet—but upon entering the pirate ship's airlock, he paused and looked back at his ship, his home, his *life* as if it might be the last time he'd ever see it again.

Then the airlock doors closed.

The inner door to the ship's docking bay slid open. There, we caught sight of our first real human: a young black man who wore a pair of bright red Mobis beckoned Captain forward into what I could only describe as a parking spot. There were at least half a dozen other cruisers in the sizable docking bay, including (somehow) an Earth car. Once we were situated, we disembarked to meet our host in true zero gravity—the *Atlantis*'s electromagnetic variety held no sway here and we had to hold onto the nearest vehicles to keep from floating away.

"Are you the captain?" Captain said immediately to the guy, who had to be in his mid-twenties at the most.

"Who, me?" He laughed exuberantly. He had an American accent, so he couldn't be the man we'd spoken to before. "No way. I'm Frysauce, the ship's jack."

I think my brain might've had a stroke. "Fry... sauce...?"

"Jack?" Captain added.

Frysauce laughed. "Y'all are funny. It's not my real name, just a handle. Long story, tell you later. I'm to take you to the captain, but first—sorry in advance—I gotta frisk ya. For weapons, you know. Nothing personal, just standard procedure. You can take your helmets off."

"The helmets stay on, and you better not touch her," said Captain.

"I'm sorry, it's nothing like that—if we had any women aboard, I'd have them do it, but sadly it's a sausage fest 'round here. Sorry, ma'am."

"It's fine," I said, and then to Captain, more pointedly, "It's *fine*."

To Frysauce's credit, he was discreet about it as he patted us down and declared that we were clean. "Follow me, please."

He led us through the docking bay to a ladder, which we ascended to a corridor. At the end of the corridor was a curved wall that appeared to be moving, as if on a conveyor belt. It took me a few stunned seconds of confusion to realize that I wasn't seeing things: it was a horizontal isolated centrifuge. Basically, a miniature donut.

"Uh-huh," I said as Frysauce hit a button on the wall that slowed the centrifuge to a stop. Now, a single door sat still in front of us, waiting.

Frysauce knocked before sliding the door open halfway. "Captain? Your visitors have arrived."

"Show them in," said a now-familiar voice.

Frysauce slid the door open fully and motioned for us to enter. "Good luck," he said with a wink, and then he closed the doors behind us, leaving us alone to face our new acquaintance.

The first thing that struck me was how colorful the captain's quarters were—living aboard the *Atlantis* with its subdued, cool-toned palette, I'd half-forgotten there were other colors in the spectrum. The room we stood in looked like a world market stall, packed from wall to ceiling with tapestries, trinkets, garlands, flags, masks, and maps—old-timey maps of Earth, astronomical maps, modern SEA-issued maps. Just a lot of maps.

Nothing floated around the room but things did billow a bit before the centrifuge kicked back into gear and everything felt ground-reaction forces again, including the two of us, whose feet landed heavily on the ground.

Sitting behind a mahogany desk was our esteemed host, who looked more like a tribal chieftain than a pirate—not that those two things couldn't be one and the same. He couldn't be older than forty-five and was of African origin, with a careful arrangement of long locs cascading past his shoulders and a septum ring in his nose, along with several other piercings in his ears and on his bottom lip. He wore layers of black, brown, and deep maroon fabrics—more civilian than tactical—but around his shoulders was a white fur pelt that I could only assume was fake. Around his neck were a cluster of beaded necklaces in so many colors and textures that it was hard to differentiate individual strands.

He stood up and of course, he was tall and well-built, too. I wasn't sure whether to be intimidated or comforted by his singularity, but this much was for sure:

he was simultaneously not at all and exactly what I'd expected a space pirate to look like.

"Welcome, fellow wanderers," he said with a roguish smile. "I trust the greeting committee showed you the utmost hospitality?"

"He was a perfect gentleman," I said before Captain could bungle it.

"Was he? I will have to tell him. He will get a good laugh out of it." The captain swept his arm toward us. "The air is safe. You may remove your helmets if you wish."

I waited for Captain's cue. As expected, he made no move to obey. "Not until you tell us who you are. And what ship this is."

"Of course. I am Captain Leon Akade, and you are guests aboard the free ship, *Esther*. At your service." He swept into a bow. "Please do not be put off by my reluctance to exchange pleasantries over transmission. I was sincere when I said that I prefer face-to-face contact. It is exceedingly rare to meet new people in a profession such as ours. Which is why I would be much obliged if I could look upon the faces of my guests."

I looked at Captain. He nodded, and we finally removed our helmets. Akade's eyes went wide and he let out a short laugh that sounded more surprised than condescending. "You are but children," he said.

I take that back.

"Technically, we're both legal adults," I said.

Captain gave me a withering look. Whoops.

"Nonetheless," said the pirate, motioning to Captain. "I thought I was talking to a peer."

"It's the accent," I said.

Captain bumped me with his elbow. It could've been an accident, but I knew better.

"Indeed. And you are the captain?" Akade asked him.

"As I said before, I am Captain Reuben Silver of *The Kraken*, and this is my first mate, Jade Frost."

"*Enchanté, mademoiselle*," Akade said to me. To Captain, he said, "You are lucky to have such a lovely companion."

"Indeed," said Captain with an edge that might've been protective.

After a beat, Akade said, "Please, sit, both of you. Can I offer you a beverage? Water? Tea? Something stronger?"

We sat down in the mismatched dining room chairs situated in front of the desk as Akade moved to a dispenser on the wall.

"Tea would be lovely," I said.

Captain gave me a sharp look. I returned it with equal fervor until he looked up and said, "Same for me, please."

Akade handed us each a steaming cup of hot tea. Mine was in a mug that said "World's Greatest Boss" and Captain's was in one with sunflowers on it. I wondered if that had been a mistake or if he'd given us opposite mugs on purpose. I tried not to laugh at the irony, intentional or not.

"So, the million-dollar question," said Akade as he sat down in his tufted leather seat. "Why would two teenagers choose to brave the void alone?"

Captain recited our perfect backstory, and I supplemented where necessary. It seemed to convince Akade, who was thoroughly impressed by our ingenuity and nonconformity.

Ha, if only he knew.

"And you've been in deep space for how long?" he asked at the end.

"Eight months," I said, thinking fast. Better to go with my timeline and not Captain's.

"Impressive indeed," he said. "And I imagine we are the first vessel you have had contact with since you began your voyage?"

"Yes," said Captain. "If I may ask, how did you find us this far out past the wormhole?"

"Serendipity," said Akade simply. "We crossed the threshold out of pure curiosity and kept going just to see if we could. Imagine our surprise when another ship showed up on our radar."

"Yeah, what are the chances?" I said as eagerly as possible.

"Then your purpose here can only be one thing," said Akade.

We froze.

"Derring-do."

"Yes," I said quickly. "We wanted to see how far we could go before we had to turn back. Be the first humans to ever step foot in this part of space. Before the SEA, before anyone."

"How insufferable," said Akade with a grin. "I do believe we are kindred spirits."

I laughed—it wasn't even forced, I actually meant it. There was something I liked about this pirate captain in spite of his initial pretension. He was a gentleman rogue if ever there was one.

"I must confess," said Captain, "I've never seen a ship quite like yours. It's so... ambitious."

Akade smirked while I suppressed an eye roll. *Now is not the time to start raising your hackles, you insecure, predictable...* "The *Esther* is one-of-a-kind to be sure. Much like your *Kraken*."

"I would be lying if I said I wasn't curious about how it operates."

"And I'd be happy to oblige you, my young friend. But first, I must invite you both to dine with me and my crew. It would be a great honor to have a pair of such fine free spacers at our table."

I instantly snapped my head to Captain to see what he would say. This was exactly the kind of opportunity that would ensure my successful transfer to the *Esther*. But I also knew that the longer we were here, the more at risk the mission became.

"It would be a pleasure," said Captain cordially.

Well, that answered that question. Pirate dinner party it was.

# 43

# Space Shanty Sing-Along Happy Hour

After we'd finished our tea, Akade gave us the grand tour of the *Esther*. I hate to be the one to say it, but for all its singularity on the outside, it was nothing to write home about on the inside. I must be snooty, accustomed as I was to the otherworldly beauty of the *Atlantis*. Everything was industrial, packed to the gills, and—dare I say it—hodge-podge. I think I even saw some parts literally held together by duct tape.

Not that Akade's ship wasn't impressive in its efficiency—like we'd assumed, it was a modified cargo ship retrofitted with the isolated centrifuge, a few creative storage spaces, and a sprawling greenhouse that, sadly, put Captain's to shame.

And of course, the engine room was beautiful. We learned that the ship mainly ran on nuclear power and that the sails on the outside harnessed cosmic radiation, exactly like the tentacles on the *Atlantis*.

Well, so much for being one-of-a-kind there.

Throughout our tour, we briefly met a few other members of the crew—apparently, there were about eight men total, which was practically unheard of for a cargo ship of this size. The fact that they thrived with such a small crew was as impressive as it was scary. Their ages varied, as did the quirkiness of their handles, but they were all surprisingly congenial.

The only exception was the head engineer, who was called Weasel. (He didn't look like a weasel, though. If anything, he looked like a raccoon with his swath of dark brown hair and square-shaped face that was mostly obscured by engineer's goggles.) He barely acknowledged our presence, focused as he was on the wiring box he was in the middle of tinkering with when we drifted through the engine room floor.

"Weasel is, how do you say in English? A 'diamond in the rough,'" Akade told us once we'd moved on. "This ship would not be running so well without him. I think at times he could use an assistant, but he insists he is fine. The application field is, admittedly, a bit sparse these days."

That got a chuckle out of me. Not so much Captain.

"How'd you recruit them?" I asked. "Your crew."

Akade gave me a look of surprise that instantly made me wonder if I'd pried. "I wasn't always so far from civilization, Miss Frost. My crew came to me from all corners of the solar system. Weasel in particular jumped ship from a research vessel eight years ago. A one-in-a-million find."

I wondered how that worked exactly—how a pirate ship could get close enough to a research vessel at all, let alone lift a promising young engineer without anyone making a fuss about it.

There had to be more to that story, but this time, I had the good sense not to push it.

At the conclusion of the grand tour, Akade called everyone to dinner, and we all convened in the dining section of the centrifuge.

Sitting down at a table full of people was truly an unprecedented shock; I hadn't realized how much I'd missed the cacophony of multiple conversations happening at once, the happy, comfortable chatter of people who lived and worked together for years on end. Problems and irritations may arise, but at the end of the day, you put your petty squabbles aside and broke bread together. That was the law of deep space.

I realized with equal excitement that this was Captain's first time ever experiencing a family-style dinner. I tried to gauge his reaction just by looking at him as plates full of beans, mashed potatoes, salad greens, and protein bake were passed around, but he gave me nothing.

"Hey," I finally said. "How are you doing?"

"Fine," he answered. "Yourself?"

"This is what I'm used to," I said with a smile. "But I didn't realize it might be a little weird for you."

"It's... a lot of stimuli, is all," he said. "I'll be fine. I'm eager to experience one of your customs."

"Yeah, I was always dining with pirates. This is just another Tuesday."

"But you said—"

"The name's Columbus," said the crewman to Captain's left, holding out his hand. He was undoubtedly of Scottish descent and therefore sounded exactly like how one might assume a pirate would sound. "A pleasure to make yer acquaintance."

After a second's pause, Captain shook the burly older man's hand. "Likewise."

"How old are ye, if you don't mind my asking?"

"Oh, I'm dead curious about that too," said Frysauce, seated to my right. He leaned forward. "Now that I've seen your faces. You can't be any older than me, and I'm the baby."

"Well, how old are you, then?" I challenged.

"Twenty-three," he said proudly.

"We're both eighteen," I said. "Which I guess makes us the babies now."

Frysauce feigned disappointment.

"Eighteen!" Columbus heaved a belly laugh. "When I was eighteen, I barely knew how to put on an EVA suit, let alone run an entire ship. Ye have a leg up on us, I dare say."

"We're flattered, sir," said Captain. "We're simply lucky. Young and lucky."

"It's a fine thing to be young and lucky, eh, Fry?"

"Young, yes. Lucky? Not sure I can call myself that when I'm stuck with you lot."

"Don't give me that shite," said Columbus good-naturedly. "I've been here a lot longer than you, boyo, and have had to put up with a fair deal more fuckery."

"How long have you been on the *Esther*?" I asked Frysauce.

He looked up at the ceiling. "Going on... two years."

"And you like it?"

"What's not to like?" he said with a wicked grin. "We're freer than birds."

"Don't listen to 'im," said Columbus. "He's still got romantic notions about free ships and the like. But seeing as the two of you are greener than grass, I'm sure you've got 'em just as bad."

"Probably," I said.

"What I wanna know," said Frysauce, "is what the hell is up with that squid-ass ship of yours."

"Beg pardon?" said Captain calmly.

"Your ship! I thought the *Esther* was an odd duck, but yours takes the cake. The inside's gotta be just as weird. When do we get the grand tour?"

"Ah..." Captain hesitated, scrambling for a premeditated excuse. I guess even he forgets his lines under pressure.

"It's nothing special," I said. "Looks about the same as yours, actually, but with even more duct tape and chicken wire. It wasn't finished when we stole it."

"Aw," said Frysauce, disappointed. "Well, the captain'll give us a true account. You'll have to host him, you know. It's common practice."

"What?" Captain said. "I was not aware of this."

"Oh, well, no sweat, Silver. You're new to the free ship world. You'll learn the code."

"I don't think that would be a good idea," I said, thinking fast. "You see, our life support system's been on the fritz. I don't think we should push it by bringing a third person aboard, even just for dinner."

"Broken life support system?" said a new voice from across the table. It was Weasel, who I hadn't realized had been listening. "I can fix that."

"See, there you go," said Frysauce, motioning grandly to the engineer. "As you can see, we're very nice here. We're like the Midwesterners of space."

Yeah, that wasn't necessarily something to boast about. My family was from the Midwest and as lovely as that regional culture was, it could also be... aggressively neighborly. Or so my Wisconsin-born mother had told us.

The captain stood up at the head of the table and tapped on the surface with his spoon, drawing everyone's attention away from their plates. "I think this occasion calls for a toast," he said. "Hazard, pour the crew and our young guests a round, why don't you?"

The ironically-nicknamed helmsman moved to a compartment in the wall while the rest of the crew erupted into a raucous cheer. He then laid out a set of small glasses on the table and began to pour a clear liquid into them.

Shots, huh? Well, they were pirates.

"I hope he breaks out the good booze," Columbus whispered to us as the shots were passed around.

"Decline," Captain said to me under his breath.

Man, what a buzzkill. But I understood why. The last thing we needed was to have our judgment impaired—Midwesterners of space or not, they were still strangers to us and pirates to boot.

When the glasses got to us, Captain passed it on with a polite, "No thank you."

"What?" Columbus exclaimed. The entire table seemed to look at us. "What d'you mean, 'no thank you'?"

"We don't drink," said Captain.

*Speak for yourself!* I thought.

"Is it a religious thing?" Frysauce asked, seemingly stupefied by the idea.

"No, nothing like that. It's not a matter of prudishness, it is simply a personal choice," said Captain.

"Lord Almighty!" Columbus said.

"Perfectly respectable," said Akade from the end of the table. "Let us not peer pressure our *underage guests* with our bawdry manners. But we would be remiss if you had to be left out of the toast. I will switch it out with something. Citrus water?"

The crew erupted into laughter, but Captain remained unfazed. "That would be excellent, thank you."

Akade smiled in understanding and moved to a dispenser in the corner, identical to the one in his quarters, filling two new glasses with the so-called citrus water and passing them down to us.

"I'll be taking that, then," said Columbus, reaching for Captain's unwanted shot of liquor.

"Oh, yeah, if you ain't gonna drink that, I'll take one for the team," said Frysauce to me.

I giggled and passed it to him.

Akade raised his shot glass, and the rest of the table did the same. "Tonight, we toast to our guests of honor and fellow free spacers, Captain Silver and his first mate, Frost. To freedom and free ships!"

"To free ships!" said the crew, toasting to us. I'll admit, it felt nice to be toasted. We all drank in unison, the pirates whooping or sighing as the liquor burned their throats.

"Strong stuff, ain't it?" Frysauce joked from beside me.

"Very hard water," I joked back. "Actually, very sour. And bitter. Is this your best approximation of lemonade?"

"You try growing lemon trees on a spaceship and see how that goes for you."

One of the pirates on the other side of the table stood up and said, "All right, boys, you know what to do." He waved his arms like a conductor and the group began to sing a song I didn't recognize but that sounded piratey enough to me. It ended in laughter and the captain pouring everyone (except for us) another round.

Columbus turned to us and said, "Do ye sing?"

"No," Captain said.

At the same time, I said, "Yes."

"Ye need somethin' more infamous, methinks," he said, and shouted at the conductor, "Oi! Ned! Our young guests need *Drunken Spacer!*"

The crew expressed their excitement with laughter and claps.

"You got it, Lumbo. All right, fellas, *Drunken Spacer* on three."

"Wait," I said. "Is it the same tune as *Drunken Sailor?*"

"The very same!" Columbus laughed. "Just with a few words tweaked."

I laughed, feeling light as air. "I know this one!"

"Thought ye might!"

Captain took my wrist. I snatched it back. "Lighten up," I said under my breath. "Be glad we're hitting it off so well."

He looked like he was about to retort, but he was silenced by the start of the song, an old, hilarious sea shanty that had evidently gotten a Space Age upgrade. Really, the only lyric that changed was the title. Everything else was pretty verbatim, making it very easy to sing along to.

And just to annoy Captain, I sang as loudly at him as I could, clapping my hands to the beat and putting obnoxious emphasis on the tawdrier lyrics. He barely acknowledged me through it, but when he did, he looked as if he wished his eyes were laser beams.

Still a grump. Maybe throwing a boy who'd spent his whole life in isolation into a sea of unchecked testosterone hadn't been the wisest idea after all.

At the end of the song, the whole crew clapped, mostly in my direction, and I gave a mock bow. As they began a third song, this one closer to a ballad, I noticed that something felt different. It was like the room had suddenly been plunged underwater. I felt buoyant but also heavy, as if I were halfway between sinking and floating.

"Whoa," I said. "I must be tired."

I supposed it made sense; I was still recovering from the unthawing process, I'd only slept for a few hours before coming here, and we'd had an eventful day, to say the least. Yet this felt different, almost like when a cold or flu hits you out of nowhere. I'd never felt fatigue like this before, this sudden plunge into a semi-dream state.

It felt a little like being frozen again.

I looked over at Captain, who had his arms crossed over his chest. He seemed to be deep in thought, totally oblivious to the revelry of our hosts. I wanted to tell him that he should at least smile and pretend to have fun, but my mouth felt numb. If I spoke the words out loud, I didn't hear myself say them, but he looked over at me as if I had.

"We should leave," he said. "I don't like these people." I heard him clearly—too clearly, in fact. He'd spoken it loudly. The entire room erupted into laughter.

Somewhere far away, I heard Akade say, "I am most regretful to hear that, Captain Silver. Have we not been agreeable hosts?" He didn't sound offended. If anything, he sounded like he'd expected Captain to say as much.

"Your motives are entirely unclear," Captain said. "And you're condescending. You called my ship little."

*Captain, stop talking!*

"But it is little. I simply stated a fact."

"I don't know what kind of game you're playing, Akade, but I don't trust you and I certainly don't like you."

*Captain! Shut! Up!*

That's what I wanted to say, but I felt untethered from my body, floating away into space. I tried to haul myself back in as Captain had once done for me, but objects turned to shapes and shapes turned to colors, and then everything faded to black.

# 44

# This Is Why You Don't Take Strange Drinks From Space Pirates

I woke up in a haze, as if I really had spent the night drinking with a bunch of pirates and was now coming around to a hellacious hangover. My head felt split open and it took my vision way too long to refocus. When it finally did, I realized where we were: the *Esther*'s dining room.

They'd left us here, asleep in our chairs.

I frantically tried to remember what had happened last night. Everything had been fine. We'd been eating, and talking, and singing... and then I'd suddenly felt dizzy and fatigued, and then I'd blacked out. Neither of us had had a drop of alcohol. So why did it feel like I had?

I looked to my left and there was Captain, dead asleep, his head lolled to one side with a line of drool trailing to his shoulder. I half-wished I had a camera, but I forced myself to have some decency as I shook him awake. "Captain. Captain, wake up."

He groaned and, with great effort, pulled his head back to the center. It wasn't until his head fell forward again that he instantly snapped awake. "What? Where? Am I late?"

"We're still aboard the *Esther*," I said.

"Where?" He looked at me, eyes unfocused.

"The *Esther*, you dingus! The pirate ship! We fell asleep!"

His eyes widened as he registered my words. He jolted upright out of his chair, cursing, but he was so unsteady that he stumbled backward, then forward, bracing his hands on the table. Breathing heavily, he wiped the drool from his mouth, looked at his hand in disgust, and said, "I'll kill him. I'll kill Akade."

"Please don't," I said. "Wait, what happened last night? I can't remember anything after the space shanties."

"We were drugged," he said. "We had to have been. I can hardly remember last night either, only that I wasn't myself."

"What?" I exclaimed. Then I gasped. "The citrus water. Really? It was the water?"

"Everyone else drank from the same bottle," he said, fists clenched against the table. "Everyone but us."

I released a string of expletives so colorful you could've seen them from Earth.

"I cannot believe this," said Captain. "We did everything right. Well, almost everything." He gestured to me.

I scowled. "Excuse me? Don't you go throwing the blame on me. Nothing we did or didn't do could've prevented this. He's just smarter than us. End of story."

Captain shut his eyes and continued to breathe heavily. It occurred to me that he wasn't accustomed to being outwitted or outmatched by another human being, not at this level. I could run circles around him socially and emotionally but I was still his peer; he'd never had to contend with a superior before. He'd never been bested intellectually.

"So we made a mistake," I said. "So we couldn't account for this variable. So what? What do we do right now?"

He pushed himself away from the table and stumbled to the door. "We talk to the captain."

I followed him over as he pushed the button and waited for the centrifuge door to line up with the corridor. Then, with the grand tour still fresh in our brains, we navigated quickly to the bridge, where Akade stood at the helm, his bridge crew on duty.

"Ah, good morning, Captain Silver," Akade said as if this had been a planned slumber party and we'd simply overslept. "You got some rest, I take it?"

"Don't you mock me," said Captain, visibly angrier than I'd seen him since he'd woken me out of a dead sleep to tell me I'd destroyed his greenhouse out of spite. "You know exactly what you did. You drugged us. You slipped something into that blasted water."

Akade didn't seem offended by the accusation. In fact, he looked like he'd been expecting it. "It was in poor taste, I know. I told them not to do it, but they didn't listen."

"They?" I asked.

"One of my crewmen, I'm afraid. It could have been anyone sitting to your left, Captain," said Akade. "I haven't been able to identify the perpetrator, but trust me, when I do, he shall be punished accordingly."

"Is that so?" I countered.

"Believe it or not, it is a common hazing ritual amongst free ships, usually done with liquor. Perfectly harmless. Actually, be grateful you didn't wake up with lewd images drawn on your faces in permanent marker. That is also quite common."

"You have got to be *fucking kidding me*," said Captain. Wow, the first time I'd heard him drop an f-bomb in earnest. Of course it would be in front of a pirate.

"Yeah, what is this, the sixth grade?" I chimed in.

Akade smirked at me. "You have no idea, *mon cher.*"

"Don't you *mon cher* her," said Captain. "Don't talk to her. Don't you even *look* at her. How dare you? Just who do you think you are?"

"Captain," I said, putting a hand on his shoulder. "Relax."

He shrugged me off. "I will not relax, not if this is how pirates treat their guests."

Now Akade looked offended. Even the bridge crew turned to look at us. "Now, who told you we were pirates, Captain Silver? When did we ever use that word?"

"Is that not what you are?" said Captain. "Is it not what we are?"

"You may call yourselves whatever you wish, but we, good sir, are free men on a free ship. Scavengers? Yes. Rogues? Certainly. Free men? Always. But never pirates."

"Your definition of pirates is about as stable as your definition of hospitality," said Captain.

"Captain," I scolded, this time more firmly.

"Have a care, Captain Silver," said Akade. "We have shown you the utmost generosity. I apologize on behalf of my incorrigible crew, but take heed before you dole out insults so hastily. The next time we meet, I may not be so merciful."

Captain was still for a moment as he and Akade had a silent battle of wills, two pairs of dark, intelligent eyes locked together with equal stubbornness. Finally, Captain said, "Frost, I think it's time we took our leave."

"I couldn't agree more," I said. "Thank you, Captain Akade, for having us aboard. It really was a pleasure, until it wasn't."

"Likewise, Miss Frost," said Akade. To Captain, he said, "You better keep that first mate of yours close at hand. She's got a good head on her shoulders. And a lovely singing voice."

Captain broke from his angry trance long enough to snap, "I know that. You think I don't know that?"

I would've been flattered if not for the concern that Captain was about to lose his shit. Akade called Frysauce over the intercom, who saw us out.

"Y'all look pissed," he noted. "I guess I would be, too. Sorry you didn't know about the hazing thing. Guess we shoulda counted on y'all being so new to this."

It was as sincere an apology as I could've hoped for, though I doubted Captain was satisfied. "It's kind of a weird tradition," I admitted. "Maybe consider replacing it with something less creepy, like just taking a regular shot?"

Frysauce laughed. "Yeah, that'd be nice."

I found his wording odd, but his response seemed genuine. So maybe these not-pirate pirates weren't all morally depraved. After all, space could do strange things to people, give them a skewed sense of social norms. I had living proof of that standing right beside me, impatiently waiting to leave.

"For what it's worth, it was nice meeting you," I said to Frysauce as we boarded the *Nautilus*.

"Same here," he replied. "Best of luck to you both!"

It wasn't until we were back in open space and on our way back to the *Atlantis* that I realized: we'd blown our shot. The chances of my becoming a stowaway were next to nil now.

"Well, so much for that," I said, disappointment weighing heavy on my chest. Sure, they'd really screwed us over, but what if we–and by "we," I meant Captain–had handled that a little bit better? Would it have mattered?

Was it too naive of me to think that they'd meant no harm?

"Are you all right?" Captain said halfway there, his voice sounding strained, the question forced. "Are you hurt in any way?"

"No," I said, touched by his concern. "Not at all. I feel fine, just... drained. You?"

"I am fine," he said in the most not-fine tone a person could take. "Just angry. Mostly at myself."

"Don't be so hard on yourself," I said. "Everything is

okay. We made it out in one piece, and they're none the wiser."

He exhaled as we entered the airlock, turning to look at me while it closed and pumped the chamber full of oxygen. For a moment, I thought he might kiss me—which, I'll admit, I eagerly hoped for—but then his eyes went wide. "But what did they do while we were out?"

"What?"

He steered the *Nautilus* back into the docking bay as fast as was physically possible and disembarked at record speed, not even bothering to take off his EVA suit as he sprinted for the corridor. I followed at his heels, churning his question over in my mind.

"What?" I said again. "You think they robbed us?"

He didn't answer as he checked every storage room down the line, and then the greenhouse. Finding nothing amiss, he clambered up the ladder to the bridge and stopped short. I did, too. Everything looked... absolutely normal.

"Ah, Captain," said Beta, leaving the helm to greet us. "Good to have you back. Did the mission go according to plan, or do I need to initiate the main protocol?"

"Not sure yet," said Captain, observing his android keeper with confusion. "Did anything odd happen while we were gone? Any strange readouts or unidentified space objects?"

"Nothing comes to mind," said Beta. "I will run a full diagnostic of the last twenty-four hours to see if we missed anything."

"Please, do," said Captain, heading toward the helm. He

stopped mid-stride and turned back toward Beta. "Did you say… twenty-four hours?"

"Yes, sir," said Beta. "You were on board the unregistered ship for twenty-two and a half. I rounded up to twenty-four for convenience."

That explosively angry look returned. "They stole something. I know they did. I do not know how, but they did. Run a comprehensive diagnostic. Run it twice, if you have to. I want every non-essential bot dispatched and scanning the ship from stem to stern. I want a full inventory, every screw, every bolt, every wire. If I find one thing missing, we are blasting them into the abyss."

*Paranoid much?*

"Right away, sir," said Beta a little too enthusiastically, relaying his commands to the rest of the ship. Half of the bridge bots scurried toward the entrance hatch to carry out Captain's orders.

"And until we sort out this mess, Xanorra will remain conscious," said Captain. "I need to run a full medical diagnostic on her."

"Of course, Captain."

I almost protested, but if it kept me unfrozen, I would do whatever he asked. I followed him down the ladder to the first floor, and when we entered the infirmary, Phala greeted us in her customary maternal way.

"I need a full work-up on Xanorra," said Captain without so much as a "hello." "Internal, external, blood, bone, whatever. And scan for foreign substances."

Completely unnecessary as this was, I did as I was told: I stripped down to my undergarments, let Phala secure me to the hospital bed, and stayed still as she ran a full medical diagnostic. Nothing was invasive, though I still thought Captain should maybe have given us some privacy. But he stood there with an expression of such intensity I didn't even want to acknowledge him. So I ignored his brooding while Phala did her thing.

"No external signs of duress," she said after a thorough physical examination. "No foreign contaminants. Nothing out of the ordinary."

Captain let out an audible sigh of relief. I was relieved too, even if I thought he was overreacting.

After a few more minutes, Phala brought up a screen with a bunch of figures on it. "Internally she seems perfectly healthy as well. The only thing I found were traces of an unidentified barbiturate in her bloodstream. Were you administered a sedative?"

"They drugged us," said Captain. "I suspect foul play."

"How uncouth," said Phala, aghast. "Have you taken the appropriate action?"

"I'm running a comprehensive diagnostic as we speak. Soon we'll know what's what."

Phala nodded as she unstrapped me. "You are free to go," she said, helping me back into my jumpsuit. "Captain?"

He shook his head. "I know what I need to know."

"Now, now, Captain," I said. So maybe I wanted him to suffer a little bit. "Maybe I'm worried about foreign substances on *you*."

He looked at me as if he didn't grasp my meaning, but in the interest of being thorough, I assumed, he consented and stripped down to his underwear. In spite of it all, I found myself blushing. Though I'd seen him shirtless, I'd never seen him in just his underwear.

At least now we were even. Kind of.

Phala strapped him to the table and repeated the process. His physical exam came up clean and his bloodwork showed the same traces of barbiturate. But whereas all my vitals were fine, his blood pressure was up and his adrenaline levels were through the roof.

"It's because you're so angry, right?" I asked. "Over this whole thing."

"He is more than angry. He is heightened," said Phala.

"I feel like I'm burning from the inside out," he said. "And I have a splitting headache."

"It has been over twenty-four hours since your last administration. No wonder. You are imbalanced."

"He's just angry," I said. "We had a pretty crappy night. What he needs are electrolytes and sleep."

Captain and Phala both looked at me in surprise. "I cannot operate like this," he said to Phala.

"I know," said Phala lovingly. *Lovingly?*

"Captain, please? Just let yourself process everything first before you put more drugs in your system."

He sighed. "Very well." He began to unstrap himself, but Phala stopped him.

"I appreciate Xanorra's concern, but I am your medical specialist. It is perfectly safe for you to take your daily medication. In fact, you need it."

"You've made him dependent," I argued. "He's practically an addict. You said it's been over twenty-four hours since his last dose? What he's feeling right now are probably withdrawal symptoms."

"Xanorra," said Phala in a calm but surprisingly firm tone. "I appreciate your concern, but I am his medical specialist. It is perfectly safe for him to take his daily medication. In fact, he needs it."

The repetition threw me for a loop. Hearing it in a video was one thing, but actually being reminded that she had the capacity to drive a person to the brink of insanity just by repeating the same phrase over and over again gave me such an unsettling feeling I wanted to cry. Was this the hill I wanted to die on? I was already on thin ice with the androids as it was. How much of Beta's obvious disdain translated over into Phala? Maybe she wouldn't threaten me openly, but what *could* she do?

"Xanorra," said Captain. "Please. Don't make her... repeat herself."

I looked over at Captain's disconcerted expression and realized that if I didn't stop now, I was going to end up torturing him. Phala was capable of torturing him. That much she could do.

I couldn't forget that.

"Okay," I said. "Fine. Whatever."

*Mother knows best*, I couldn't help but think.

# 45

# Give Me Something I Can Punch

"What do you mean, 'everything is accounted for'?" Captain nearly shouted at the immovable Beta when the ship-wide inventory came back with nothing to report. Nary a bolt nor a wire was out of place.

In a normal situation with a normal captain, this would be good news. But with Captain Omen, this disappointed him on an astronomical level. Probably because he wanted an excuse to shoot something.

Those medications needed to kick in already, as much as I hated that he'd had to take them at all. The least they could do was *work*.

"Nothing was stolen," Beta said. "Surely, if they had breached the hull, we would have been alerted. There is not an inch of this ship that we do not surveil."

Yikes. That was an unsettling revelation, even if I'd already suspected as much.

"So that's it, then," Captain said.

"It appears the mission was a success after all," said Beta flatly. "Your diplomatic tactics have misdirected them and they have not uncovered the delicate nature of the mission. I would say congratulations are in order."

"I wish I could accept them," said Captain. "But something isn't right. Something feels... off about this whole thing." He turned to me and said, "Think about it. They invite us over, drug us, send us into a panic, but ultimately take nothing. I refuse to believe the motive was as simple as some barbaric tribal ritual."

"Maybe they just like to play practical jokes?" I guessed lamely. "Maybe they're just sadists who like feeding on people's paranoia?"

"But why, though?" Captain asked, pacing the bridge. "We're never going to see them again and vice versa. What could they possibly stand to gain other than a few hours' petty amusement?" He stopped short. "Xan, do you remember anything after you passed out? Anything at all? Dreams, strange pictures, anything?"

I shook my head. "If I dreamt anything, it's fuzzy. I was out like a light."

"I had the strangest dream," he said. "I dreamt I was talking."

"Everyone talks in their dreams."

"Not me," he said. "You already know the nature of my dreams—in them, I'm always helpless to do something. If I talk, I'm screaming. Often, I'm mute or no one can hear me. But in this dream, I was having a conversation. And I was... happy to be having it."

"Okay," I said. "Drugs often make you have unusual dreams."

"But they also make you do unusual things," he said. "Right?"

"Yes," I said, getting an inkling of where this was going. And boy, did I not like it.

"Are there not substances known to make one suggestible? Truth-telling drugs, if you will?"

"The heck if I know." I did vaguely remember him saying some out-of-character things right before I'd blacked out. Honest things. Unguarded things.

Captain brought his wristband up to his mouth and said, "Phala, can barbiturates make you suggestible?"

It was the first time I'd ever seen him contact her directly from the bridge, but her answer must have appeared as text because he pulled the watch back to read it. Whatever her answer, it obviously confirmed his theory. He looked positively livid.

"Well, shit," I said.

"'Well, shit,' is a gross understatement," said Captain. To Beta, he said, "They know. The mission failed. We have to break course."

Beta nodded and began to input instructions via the helm's console.

"I thought you couldn't alter course," I said in shock. "They're heading in the opposite direction."

"With the exception of one, dire circumstance," said Beta coolly. "To protect the sanctity of the mission."

"What are they gonna do, beat us there?" I said. "Come on! Even if they know, it's not like they—*oh*." *Oh shit.*

"What?" said Captain. "What do you know?"

"So, keep in mind: space pirates were a myth until, like, yesterday. But there's another myth about people called extractors. They're usually lumped into the same category, but the fact that Akade didn't like us calling them pirates... well, it kind of lines up with the stories I've heard about the extractors."

"Extractors?" he said. "As in, spies?"

"Yeah, but, like, mercenary spies. Spies-for-hire. In the stories, it's usually an inside job. SEA officers who sell trade secrets to private companies and vice-versa. Shady, underhand shit. Everyone wants the latest secrets on the newest technology, the best advancements. I just never thought it could be so... hands-on."

Captain began to pace. "So then, what you're saying is... they are going to sell my secrets to the highest bidder." He looked like steam was about to come out of his ears.

I winced. "Yes."

"Which will most likely be the SEA."

I wished I could shrink. "Probably."

Captain turned to Beta and shouted, "Lieutenant, engines to max. There is not a second to lose!"

"Captain," I said calmly. "Think of your blood pressure."

"I need a moment," he said angrily and stalked off toward the lounge.

I intended to follow, but Beta said, "Miss Nepier, a moment, if you'd please."

*Uh-oh.* This couldn't be good. It was never good. I plastered on a big, fake smile and turned to face this glorified Hal 9000. "Yes, sir?"

"Do not be deceived by this unprecedented turn of events. You are still on probation only."

"Of course," I said, hiding my fear behind a saccharine

smile. "Captain blows a pirate ship to smithereens and I go back in the freezer. Everything returns to the status quo."

"Yes, that is exactly what will happen," said Beta. "So do not go hashing any half-baked schemes or try throwing any temper tantrums in the hopes that Captain will let you stay awake longer. With every minute that you are on this ship, you are putting this mission more and more at risk."

Maybe it was hanging out with not-pirate pirates that gave me so much intestinal fortitude all of a sudden, but in any case, I felt emboldened to take a step closer to Beta and say, "Then why don't you just kill me, then?"

Beta's face flicked into a half-frown. "That would violate the protocol," he said. "However my programming may tell me to feel about you, Miss Nepier, it would never be my aim to harm you. All I can do is continue to remind Captain of his priorities and help him come up with appropriate solutions."

"Like convincing him to kill me?"

"Like convincing him to do what is right."

"You wouldn't know what's right if it hit you in the face," I said. "You're just a machine. Just plastic and metal. And Captain? He's flesh and bone. He's better than you'll ever be, and he doesn't even have to try."

He smiled in that eerily human way of his and said, "With all due respect, Xanorra, I beg to differ."

I don't think I'd ever heard him call me by my first name before, and it sent a chill up my spine. Without another word, I fled the bridge, praying to God my big mouth didn't get me in trouble again.

I found Captain in the gym, going beast mode on a punching bag. Under different circumstances, it would be hot, but this was no time for girlish fantasies. He was about to kill a ship full of morally gray pirates, and yeah, they did know his secret, and *yeah*, Captain had tried to take the high road, but they were still human beings. I couldn't just sit back and let Captain commit manslaughter.

There had to be another way. That's why I was here, right?

"Permission to enter the boxing ring?" I asked when he spied me across the room.

"I'm done," he said. "I need to get back to the bridge."

"No, you don't," I said evenly. "Think about this. Really think about it. Is this seriously the best course of action?"

"There is no other course," he said. "It's the protocol. We tried to do it your way, and it failed. It failed miserably. *I* failed miserably." He punched the bag, hard. When it swung back to him, he caught it and leaned against it in defeat. "It's what I get for trying to bend the rules again. It's retribution for disobeying the protocol. It was simple." He punched the bag. "It would've been simple!"

"The right thing to do is rarely ever the easy thing to do," I said. "But come on, Captain, the truth is plain to see. You don't want to kill people. You don't."

"It doesn't matter what I want," he said. "It must be

done. Besides, they're criminals, Xanorra. At least I tried. At least I'm not attacking civilians without due cause."

"They say killing takes a toll on a person," I said. "It tears your soul apart."

"My soul's already torn apart," he said offhandedly.

"No, it's not," I said, tempting as it was to give in to his sad boy elegy. "Listen, there's got to be a better way."

"Like what?"

"Like, what if we bought the information back from them?"

He furrowed his brow. "How? I have no currency they would accept."

I sighed. "Offer them me."

He stared at me, dumbfounded. "What?"

"Offer them me," I said again. "I was supposed to stow away anyway. Plus, Akade did say they needed an engineering assistant. That's gotta be invaluable to them. If he accepts, we both get what we want."

He shook his head. "Too many unknowns. And besides, there's no way I'm letting you leave aboard that ship, not after what they did. Forget it."

"Much as I appreciate your protective instinct, Captain, you're not the boss of me. I don't belong to you. And you're the one who wanted me to escape in the first place. Tell me how that's fair."

He set his jaw. I knew he knew I was right.

I swallowed and said, "I can't go back in the cryo tube, Captain, I... I hated it. I thought I could be okay with it, but I'm not. It terrifies me. And truth be told, based on my track record with the androids, I'm not all that confident I'll ever wake up again. And even if I did, you'll be old, and we'll be on some god-forsaken planet that might not even be habitable."

"It is habitable," he said on impulse.

"How do you know?" I shouted at him. "Because some pretty, smiling couple read it off a teleprompter to justify why you're morally obligated to be miserable? It's inhumane. They sacrificed their own son to the abyss just for their own selfish ambitions, and the worst part is, they've convinced you that it's what you want, that it's somehow an honor."

He was taken aback by my outburst. "It is an honor."

"It's a curse!" I shouted. "You're going to be older than your parents by the time you meet each other. They'll likely outlive you. You get no wife, no children, no *future* of your own."

He swallowed. "We're advancing humanity."

"Bull*shit*. There are entire divisions of the SEA dedicated to finding habitable planets. You really think your family is interested in humanity? Why keep it all a secret then? Why send a baby into space? No, I'm sorry, but they're only interested in advancing themselves."

"You're wrong," he said. Man, it's like I expected years of conditioning and indoctrination to come crumbling down just because I spoke some harsh truths. If only.

"You can think whatever you want," I said. "You're an intelligent, rational human being with your own free will, whether you want to admit it or not. You, and only you, decide what you believe. But nothing you say or do can convince me that what you're doing is right. Every cell in my body knows it's wrong, and if I didn't think you had a good heart underneath all that programming, that you were worth saving, I would've lost my mind a long time ago."

He stared at me with those bottomless eyes of his, his face struggling to remain blank. For once, I could see right through him and I knew he was fighting himself.

"Captain," I said gently. "Something must've happened during those six months I was frozen. I can see it in your eyes. Why else would you wake me up? Why else would you go through all that trouble?"

He didn't answer, just looked at some invisible spot behind me, processing.

I paused, weighed the risks, and said, "You wanna know what I think? What I've always thought?"

His eyes carved a path to mine, passive and emotionless.

"I think that deep down, really deep down, you hate it here."

The accusation struck him like lightning. His jaw clenched as he said, "That is not true."

"You might not think that it is, you might've been conditioned to deny it, but there's still a little kernel way, way down in the depths of your soul that knows what they did to you is wrong. You can't purge that part of you, no matter how hard you try. And the truth is, you don't want to. Because that anger—that deep-seated knowledge of right and wrong—it keeps you human. It keeps you sane. Not the drugs. Not the mission. Not even me. You see, Captain? You're the master of your own soul. You always have been."

His face remained stoic, but I could see his jaw clenching, his nostrils flaring. He dropped his eyes and his fingers tapped a rhythm against his leg, restless. Finally, he looked at me and said, "I told you that you see more in me than is there."

"I respectfully disagree."

After a beat, he said, "I will negotiate with Akade on your behalf. But if he refuses, then I must do what I must do. I'm sorry I can't be the person you think I am, Xan. I'm sorry you were trapped here with me."

I smiled sympathetically. "It wasn't always so bad. In fact, it was mostly good. That's why I don't wanna be frozen." And I meant it.

He looked askance. "Xan, I know... I know you didn't destroy the greenhouse."

I was stunned. So six months had given him clarity after all. "Then who did?"

"I'm not sure. Perhaps no one. Perhaps it was a freak accident."

"Yeah. Because a freak accident did that," I said slowly. "Look, I'm not gonna tell you what you already know. But I trust that you'll do the right thing. I trust you, Captain." I meant that, too.

He gave me a sad smile. "Perhaps you shouldn't."

# 46

# An Actual, Real Space Battle, Like With Lasers and Stuff

If I ever doubted the *Atlantis*'s capabilities, my faith was renewed when we came up on the *Esther* in record time. Captain hailed Akade from the bridge, and the not-pirate pirate answered within minutes, this time with video.

"Ah, Captain, what an unexpected surprise," he said. "I cannot say I thought I would have the pleasure of speaking with you again so soon."

"Let's not waste time with empty pleasantries," Captain said pointedly. "You stole something of mine, and I'm afraid I cannot abide you getting away with it."

"I am afraid you must be mistaken, Captain," said Akade lightly. "I never touched a single thing of yours. Your security system surely would have been alerted if I or one of my men had dared try to steal anything from your ship. We are not quite so foolish as to insult our guests so blatantly."

"Not everything that can be stolen is material," said Captain. "As you very well know."

"Captain, I have just as much time for games as you do. If you are going to accuse me of some abstract form of thievery, I implore you to speak plainly."

Captain paused for a moment before saying, "You gave us a drug that would make us suggestible. I cannot speak for Miss Frost, but I know I said things under the influence I never would otherwise. You stole vital information from me. Information that you had no right to know."

Akade actually looked stunned before his face settled into a smug half-smile. "I have to say, I am impressed, Captain *Omen*. I've yet to meet someone smart enough to figure it out quickly enough to track us down and accuse us openly."

"You wouldn't be very good extractors if they did. That is what you are, is it not? Strictly speaking?"

"You are correct, Captain Omen. But now I must ask: what exactly is your plan now that you've caught us?"

"I would like to avoid violence as much, I assume, as you would. And because of this, I am willing to propose a trade: my first mate has expressed a desire to jump ship. You said you're in need of an engineer's assistant. She has willingly offered to serve aboard your ship—she's a skilled engines operator and an intelligent spacer all around." *Aw, Captain, you flatter me.* "In exchange, you will make a spacer's oath never to repeat to another living soul what I may or may not have said while in an altered state."

Akade looked frozen on screen for a moment, and then he started laughing, a loud, heady sound that, under different circumstances, would have been delightfully contagious. "Oh, shame on me for forgetting how very young you are," he said between guffaws. "Alas, even the smartest teenager can still be terribly naïve."

A muscle twitched in Captain's jaw. "Are you saying the trade is unfair?"

"Please, do not take offense," said Akade. "I have no doubts regarding Miss—Xanorra, was it?—and her capabilities. It is just the assumption that we would make such an exchange at all. That something as intangible as information can be traded like coin." Akade leaned closer to the screen as if to tell us a secret. "The beauty of our profession is that a secret once stolen can never be stolen back. It is non-refundable. So, no, I'm afraid that I cannot accept your offer. Nor could I in good conscience allow Miss Xanorra aboard this ship. My men are held accountable for their actions, but they are still men. I do not think she would be very comfortable here."

That was actually really considerate of him to say, loathe as I was to admit he was probably right. Maybe he was a thief and a con artist, but at least he was a gentleman.

"I couldn't agree more," said Captain. "I'm afraid that leaves us with only one option, then. I hope you are well-armed. I would hate for you to die without dignity."

Akade gave him a stern look, as if he were a parent reprimanding a child. "Are you sure this is the path you wish to take, young Captain? I will warn you, we stand undefeated in battle."

"So do I," said Captain. A horrible bluff, seeing as though he'd only been in one and that particular opponent had been caught off-guard and totally outgunned. Deep space research vessels aren't exactly built for combat.

They also aren't four times the size of the *Atlantis*.

"Captain," I snapped. "Don't be an idiot. This is madness."

"The man isn't giving me a choice, Xanorra," he said firmly.

"You do have a choice, my boy," said Akade. "Turn around. Forget you ever met us. We will not pursue."

"Not a chance," said Captain. "Either you accept my deal, or you accept your fate."

"Very well. If it is a fight you want, then it is a fight you shall have," said Akade with a dramatic sigh. "For what it is worth, I'm sorry things have to end this way. I respect you, Captain, I do. And your first mate. And I think your mission is brilliantly ambitious. Too ambitious, I'm afraid, to be kept a secret."

"I respect you as well. Morally reprehensible as your business may be, I would be lying if I said I wasn't impressed."

Akade smirked. "Likewise. I hope you find peace one day, Captain." With that, he ended the call, and the clear glass went back to displaying the endless expanse of deep space, the *Esther* sitting just off starboard.

What an odd statement to end on, especially in light of the fact that he planned on blowing us to star fodder. It made me wonder what, exactly, Captain had said during his barbiturate-induced interview.

But now was not the time to ponder it because we were about to do the exact thing I'd tried to prevent from happening. Tried and failed.

"Lieutenant, turn shields up to maximum and charge the solar guns," Captain said.

"Right away, Captain," said Beta.

"I want every bridge bot on full operative capacity. Defense mode. What we lack in size, we shall make up for in speed and agility. We will dodge and outmaneuver until they've gone cross-eyed, and then we will strike back with everything we've got."

"That's assuming a lot," I said, finally coming to terms with the fact that we were about to engage in an actual space battle. They weren't as common as the movies made them out to be. "What if they can outmaneuver us? I don't know if you recall from our little tour, but they have a pretty advanced piloting system."

"Not as advanced as ours," said Captain and turned to face me. "Nepier, I'd appreciate it if you returned to your room and didn't go past the lounge until this is over."

I paused for a moment while I processed that ridiculous request (along with the fact that I'd been downgraded to a last-name basis), and then I said, "To hell with that. I'm staying right here."

"This isn't the time to argue," he said.

"You're absolutely right. Which is why you're going to let me stay here," I said.

He ran it through that supercomputer brain of his and

arrived at an extremely logical answer: "Fine. Stand behind me."

I gladly complied. This time around, it was way less awkward.

"What's the contingency plan?" I asked as he inputted commands. "What if we lose? Will the *Nautilus* sustain us, and if so, for how long?"

"There is no losing," he said in an offhand way. "It's not an option."

"Yes, way to visualize the win—but you still need to be realistic, Captain. The *Esther* is huge. And Akade, he's more experienced than we are."

Captain laughed haughtily. "Just because he runs a free ship doesn't mean he knows more about surviving space than I do. Just because he outsmarted us once doesn't mean I'll allow it to happen again. I've spent my entire life training for this and he has not. That's all I have to say about it."

I suppressed a groan. It was like talking to a brick wall. Captain was no stranger to hubris, and encountering a real crew of real men, well... I think it might've set off a chain reaction. So, I decided that I would make a contingency plan for us: if all else failed, if the ship was critically hit and damaged, we had to get to the *Nautilus* and escape. I would drag Captain kicking and screaming if I had to, but I would not leave without him.

I would not let this mission be the death of him. Or me.

We faced the *Esther* head-on, and I could see from the viewscreens that they had rolled out their front guns, which looked unnervingly like cannons.

Very fitting, in light of the ship's design. Were all pirate ships this on the nose? I almost hoped so.

Meanwhile, the *Atlantis* had opened the front hatches that held its unique but effective solar guns. These were not cannon-like, but rather, flat when viewed from the front, like a vent. There was nothing ventilating about them, though. I could hear the hum and feel the vibration beneath us as the weapons charged up.

I was about to ask if we were supposed to make the first move when the barrels of the *Esther*'s cannons glowed bright white and short, laser-like beams shot in rapid-fire sequence directly at the *Atlantis*'s hull.

And so it began. Usually, I erred on the side of optimism, but even I had a bad feeling about this.

Captain, who had taken manual control of the helm, made a series of hand gestures and the ship responded by moving downward—dropping so abruptly that I had to lock my knees to keep from smacking the ground, even with the magnetic lock in place.

We sustained two hits but dodged the rest—I supposed evasive maneuvers might be a good strategy after all. He swung the ship to the right and said, "Aim for the bases of the guns. Take them out."

Smart. We hit one but didn't seem to damage it. The *Esther* responded by swinging the targeted gun at us and firing again, this time appearing to miss on purpose as I watched the pure white lasers whiz past us—but no, I quickly realized that they were aiming for the stabilizer fins.

"Captain," I said, "you might wanna—"

The ship shook as we were hit. A message flashed on the screen: LEFT REAR STABILIZER DAMAGED. We weren't dovetailing, but I could feel the tilt as the ship was thrown off balance.

Captain cursed under his breath. "Lieutenant, send Eta on an emergency EVA. Patch that up quickly."

"Right away," said Beta, silently transmitting the message to the engine bot.

"What if they see the airlock opening?" I asked. "That's kind of a soft spot." Mostly, I was worried that if they decided to target said airlock, it might damage the *Nautilus*. That would throw a wrench in my brilliant contingency plan.

"They won't," said Captain. "We just need to fake injury." He let the ship continue to drift to the right until we were broadside with the *Esther*, who appeared to be waiting for us to make the next move. "We'll circle them and come up on their port side, guns blazing."

"Okay," I said uncertainly. Akade seemed like a fair opponent, but I doubted he would let us catch our breaths for any longer than necessary.

Meanwhile, one of the readout screens showed Eta's camera as she traveled along the hull of the ship to the broken stabilizer and began to repair it with a flat sheet of something metallic.

The *Esther* hadn't moved yet, which worried me. Maybe they were just that polite? But as we came around to the stern, I realized that politeness had nothing to do with it.

They had rear guns. And as soon as they began firing them, it was obvious that these were more powerful than their front-facing counterparts.

"Dammit!" Captain shouted. He brought his arms down and the ship dropped so fast that this time, I buckled into a crouch.

But these guns were on the same swivel mechanism as the front guns and followed our trajectory downward. They were at a ninety-degree angle from the plane of the *Esther* and still firing at full capacity.

"They faked us out," I said, pulling myself upright again.

Captain took the ship under the *Esther* and around to the front, where the front guns still waited for us. "Fire all," he said, and the solar guns, charged to full capacity, began to fire. Yellow-white light mingled with the pure blasts of the *Esther* in a deadly fireworks show.

"We lost Eta," said Beta from the console. "The stabilizer is still damaged."

"What?" Captain looked horrified. "What do you mean, we lost her?"

"She is gone, sir."

Captain mumbled a curse under his breath and pounded the helm with his fist. Even I felt a wave of sadness at the loss, but there was no time to mourn his robotic crewmate. "Send Theta, then," he said with a palpable effort.

"With how quickly we are moving, there is no way any

of the bots could maintain proper purchase," said the lieutenant. "We need a critical hit."

"I'm trying," said Captain, teeth clenched.

"Sir, you could deploy the squid," he said.

Captain didn't respond.

"What's the squid?" I asked. After all, the whole ship was like a squid.

"It's a blackout gas cloud designed to disorient your opponent. The only problem is, it blinds us, too," said Captain.

"Remember your training," said Beta. "You have simulated this before."

"One time was enough," said Captain.

"I don't think you should do anything you're uncomfortable with," I said.

Beta said, "There is no aspect of this mission that Captain has not been trained to handle. There is no one better qualified to—"

"Shut up!" Captain shouted just as a laser blast knocked us off our axis. Beta looked stunned but I was impressed as Captain made a frantic series of hand gestures that eventually, with much protest from the *Atlantis*, righted the ship enough to allow us to fall back from the *Esther*. "Very well. Deploy the squid."

"Captain—" I warned.

"I said deploy it!" he said, shooting me a look over his shoulder. I was tempted to take it personally, but I knew he wasn't trying to be a jerk. This was a little bit different than dodging asteroids—at least those hadn't been *trying* to kill us.

Beta relayed the command, and within a moment, an

inky, black cloud billowed out from the front of the ship, stretching toward the *Esther* like a supernatural fog. It blotted out the stars, the lasers, the lights on the ships—everything went abysmally black, as dark and endless as a singularity. The only lights were the blue, illuminated backlights of the control console and the helm.

I instantly understood why Captain didn't like this. It activated some deep, primordial fear of oblivion, the instinctual drive to seek out the light. Despite the instant feeling of dread, I stayed put, watching over Captain's shoulder.

"Displacement," he said simply, and an image appeared on the viewscreen that was mostly black save for two infrared shapes in either corner: us and the *Esther*.

Ah, I understood now. It was a dense gas, so by looking at where it wasn't, you knew exactly where the other ship was in relation to yourself, even if you couldn't physically see it.

"Fire all," Captain commanded, and the solar guns roared to life, lighting up the inky cloud like lightning flashes in a nighttime thunderstorm. Something about the energy blasts must dissipate the gas cloud because I started to see stars peeking through the opaqueness and the weapon fire became brighter the longer it went on.

But when the smoke cleared, the *Esther* was nowhere to be seen.

"What the—?" I looked from one screen to the other to make sure they weren't reading wrong. "You didn't blast them into non-existence, did you? There should be some kind of collateral damage. Right?"

"Right," said Captain uneasily. "There was no way they could have—"

Suddenly, the ship was there. It had flickered back into existence, like a lightbulb about to go out.

"Oh my God," I said. "They have a ghost shield."

Ghost shields were as coveted as they were rare. In fact, they were actually illegal in the SEA because they were so dangerous. It was an impenetrable, high-energy shield that reflected the light around it and made any objects within appear invisible. They required so much energy that most ghost shields could only be used once for a brief amount of time before they shorted out, making them ideal only for specific situations. Such as now.

The *Esther* fired on us instantly, the white light of the laser blasts blinding and relentless. The ship lurched and shook with the impact as CRITICAL HIT and DAMAGE warnings flashed on the viewscreen in alarming succession. We careened to the side, holding onto the helm for dear life.

Through it all, Captain shouted orders to Beta, but I could barely hear him over the blaring of alarms. Then a new message flashed on the screen: HULL BREACH: DOCKING BAY. CRITICAL DAMAGE: LIFE SUPPORT.

"No, no, no, no," I said, finally pulling my senses together. Now was the time for the contingency plan to kick in. I grasped Captain's shoulder and said, "We need to get out of here *now*."

He didn't seem to hear me or register that I was there. He just kept shouting commands: "Shields to maximum!

Divert all power reserves to weapons! Beta, divert all ship's power to the cryo room. We have to protect it at all costs!"

I hopped off the dais and inched my way around the front of the helm until I faced him head-on. "It's over, Captain," I said, tears stinging my eyes as I saw how desperately he was trying to keep fighting. "We lost. We need to either surrender or abandon ship."

He looked at me as if he were snapping out of a dream. "We can *never* abandon ship."

"Then we have to surrender," I said. "It's either that or die."

"I'd rather die with honor than surrender to thieves," said Captain.

"I wouldn't! I want to live! Captain, if we die, the mission fails."

As obvious a statement as that was, it seemed to stir something in him, as if he finally understood the true consequences of failing to swallow his pride. His arms shook and sweat slicked his forehead as he weighed his options. Finally, with great effort, he said, "Hail Captain Akade."

The cannon fire stopped and a fuzzy, distorted image of the *Esther*'s captain appeared onscreen. "Captain Omen. I must say, for such a little ship, you put up quite a fight."

"I've sustained massive damage," he said as if every word pained him. "The life support included. I am asking—requesting—a ceasefire. In the interest of protecting the lives on board, I must surrender."

"A very wise choice indeed, Captain," said Akade. "I

cannot say it would have given me any pleasure to take two young lives of such promise. I accept your surrender. I will tow your ship, and I suggest you come aboard so we can discuss the terms."

"We do not need your help," Captain said through clenched teeth.

"I'm sorry, but I beg to differ," said Akade. "You do not want to be aboard a ship with a failing life support system, and if the damage is as extensive as it looks, you will need more than your own reserves to fix it. If it is truly your wish, then of course we will leave you in peace. But I would not recommend it if you value your lives."

Captain stared, jaw locked, knowing Akade was right but not wanting to admit it. Then he made eye contact with Beta, who nodded at him as if they'd communicated telepathically. Something cold and obedient leveled Captain's features as he faced Akade and said, "Very well. We will accept your aid on one condition."

"Name it."

"None of your men are to set foot on my ship."

# 47

# Parlay?

I resisted the urge to make a "betcha didn't account for this variable" joke on the ride over, which wasn't as difficult as I thought it would be—one glance at Captain's look of utter despair and words fled me. The crew had already begun work on whatever repairs they could, with Beta instructed to relay updates to Captain every hour.

From the outside, the *Atlantis* looked worse for wear, and I could even see the hull breach—thankfully, it wasn't very big and the bots had secured it with a tarp before we'd ventured into the docking bay to board the *Nautilus*. Thanks to the magnetic platform it locked onto, the cruiser hadn't been damaged in the fray.

However, the holes and scorch marks riddling the rest of the hull informed us that there was a long road to recovery ahead. One stabilizer fin was gone and another was broken. Instead of looking like a galactic cephalopod, the ship had the look of a sad walrus.

Back on board the *Esther*, truly the last place we ever expected to be again, Akade was the one who met us in the docking bay this time and actually shook our hands. He seemed genuinely sorry, but in a sportsmanlike way, as if he'd beat us at a pickup game of basketball and not totaled our ship. But he hadn't asked for a fight, per se. He'd simply done what any ship's captain would do. And he'd succeeded.

"We need to discuss logistics," said Captain right away, his voice dull and robotic. "As you are well aware, I have a purpose, and I cannot afford to lose time."

"Of course," said Akade. "But I suggest you take some time to rest and gather your thoughts first. Surely you can afford to lose one day?"

"Not even that," said Captain firmly.

"Captain," I said gently. "I think you should listen to Akade. It's been a long day. I, for one, am tired."

"Did I ask you?" he snapped.

I knew emotions were running high, but he was being a pathetically sore loser. "Excuse you, sir. No need to be a bitch."

He looked at me in shock. Akade chuckled.

"Did I teach you that one yet?" I said glibly.

He was silent for a long moment, jaw locked. "If you are tired, then rest. Do as you wish. Please. But I have… business with the captain that cannot wait."

Better. I'd accept it.

Akade looked amused. "I will show you to your quarters. I apologize in advance, but it appears that you will have to share a room, as we only have one spare. I would ask my men to double up, but I figured since you are a romantic couple..."

"We're not a romantic couple," Captain said pointedly. "That was a lie."

Ouch. "What he means is, we're not boyfriend and girlfriend, per se," I said.

"I see. My mistake. I will arrange separate rooms, then."

"That won't be necessary," I said. "We're used to sharing a space. He'll survive."

Captain gave me a withering look but said nothing.

Akade smirked. "Very well. This way, please." He beckoned us with a hand and led us back through his now-familiar ship to the isolated centrifuge, where he stopped it on a door labeled with the number seven. "Here you are, Miss Xanorra. Captain, I will speak with you in my quarters."

He opened the door and allowed me to step inside. It was small, a capsule really, but it had two bunks and was all the privacy I needed right now.

"Rest well. And let us know if you need anything," said Akade, closing the door shut.

What I needed was a drink. But I didn't think I would be taking anything from the pirates—my bad, extractors—anytime soon.

It didn't take much for me to nap. When I woke, it was to the weightless feeling of the centrifuge slowing to a stop. I half expected Captain to enter the room, but the door never opened. It must've been somebody entering a different room.

I checked the time on the bedside clock. I'd slept for six hours. Where was Captain? Surely not still talking to Akade. Curious, I slid out of bed and pressed the button next to the door to signal I wanted to exit. Within moments, I was floating through the *Esther* proper, looking for my misplaced comrade. I supposed he could be in another room in the centrifuge, but I doubted it. He'd want to be somewhere he couldn't be disturbed.

In the corridor, I ran into Frysauce. He gave me a wide smile and said, "There she is! Xanorama. Xanadu? Xanthan Gum."

"It's Xanorra, actually," I said, amused. "I know, not the most common name in the galaxy."

He scoffed. "Just look who you're talking to. What's shoot'n?"

"Have you seen Captain?" I asked. "Mine. The young, angry one."

Frysauce laughed. "I think I saw him heading to the docking bay a while ago. Haven't seen him since."

"The docking bay? He didn't leave, did he?"

Frysauce shook his head. "Nothing's left since y'all arrived. I think he wanted to do maintenance on that transporter of yours. The seashell. Love that thing. Is it as fun to ride in as it looks?"

I smiled. "Yeah, it is. Thanks, Frysauce." I continued down the hall.

"Hey, one more thing," he said.

I turned, grabbing onto the side rail that ran along the corridor to keep me stationary.

"I probably shouldn't be say'n this, but we were all relieved about the ceasefire. We may be hoodlums, but we ain't heartless. We had no idea y'all would be so young."

"Thanks," I said with a smile. "We're relieved, too. Even if some of us may be pouting about it at the moment."

Frysauce rolled his eyes. "Captains and their pride."

"Tell me about it." I smiled and continued on.

In the docking bay, there was no sign of Captain initially. I approached the *Nautilus* and walked its perimeter, but there was no sign of him there, either. Then I noticed the viewscreen was blacked out, which hadn't been the case on the ride over. I bet my stars he was in there, the only private room he could find. The only space that resembled what he was used to. Tentatively, I knocked on the window and waited.

He didn't turn off the blackout shield, but his voice did carry through the glass. "What?" He sounded garbled, like he'd been asleep. Maybe I'd woken him up.

"It's me," I said. "I just came to check on you."

"I'm here. I'm fine."

Now I was suspicious. "Is something wrong? Why do you sound sick?"

"Perhaps I am."

"Then you need a doctor," I said. "Come on, open up. Let me see you."

"I was being facetious. I said I'm fine."

"So you say," I said, pressing a hand to the glass. "Then why don't I believe you?"

He was silent for a moment. I was half afraid he was going to remain silent in an attempt to get rid of me, but then the blackout filter dissolved, and a miserable-looking Captain with red, puffy eyes stared back at me, equal parts annoyed and apprehensive.

I couldn't look away. Now I understood why he didn't want to be seen: he'd been crying.

"Are you happy now?" he said bitterly. "Are you satisfied, now that you see how pitiful and human I can be? How weak and wretched and—" His voice caught, and he dropped his face into his hands, his shoulders shaking as he sobbed.

I was completely at a loss. I thought I would feel some amount of triumph seeing him so undone. But instead, my heart ached for him. "May I please come in?" I said gently.

Without looking up, he pressed a button and opened the hatch. I climbed up and slid into the passenger's seat, waiting until we were safely concealed inside before I leaned over the center console and pulled him into me. He clung to my jumpsuit and cried into my shoulder—it was full of frustration, of what I can only imagine was years of pent-up distress.

This had sent him over the edge.

"You're not weak," I finally said.

"Yes I am," he warbled. "Look at me." He pulled back to meet my eyes. "I can't—It's too much, Xanorra. I thought I could bear it, but I... I feel like I'm drowning."

"Listen," I said with a sigh. "I know it may seem like it in the moment, but failure isn't the end of the world. My dad used to say it's not about never falling down—because you are going to fall down eventually.

Everyone does. It's about whether or not you pick yourself back up again."

He wiped his eyes with his sleeve. "Then I suppose I'm doing an exemplary job of that now, aren't I?"

"Don't be so hard on yourself," I said. "You're handling it better than most people would. And it's not weak to cry, you know. Or unmanly." I poked him in the shoulder. "What's weak is letting your emotions control you, which you definitely don't do."

He scoffed as if he didn't believe me.

"But sometimes, the best way to keep them in line is to... get it all out. It's dangerous to bottle everything up all the time."

"I was an emotional child," he said absently.

"That's not abnormal."

He looked at me. "Emotion was punished. Compliance rewarded."

"I know." Where was he going with this?

"I think it... affected me more than I realize."

My heart pounded. "Yeah, that much is pretty obvious."

"Do you think..." He trailed off, eyes unfocused. "Do you think my parents would've raised me differently?"

Now my heart felt like it might explode. There were cracks in his armor. I could see them now. "I would hope so," I said. "They were human. At the least, they would've loved you. Hopefully, they would've loved you for the person you are and not the person they wanted you to be."

He locked eyes with me, a silent question in them. *What kind of person am I?* I guessed. But instead, he said, "I suppose it does no good to speculate. Not when there are real problems to be solved."

I grimaced, even though he was right. "Yeah. How's the ship looking? It can be fixed, right?"

He nodded. "But it'll take time. Longer than I would like."

"How long?"

"Weeks," he said, forlorn. "Possibly longer. Even with myself and the bots working around the clock. I've done the math. Now that we're short an engineer, we're looking at a four-week restoration project minimum. That's four weeks tethered to the *Esther*."

"Is that really so bad?" I asked. "Akade seems to have a pretty solid honor code, pirate or not."

"Do you really trust him?"

"You're the one who spoke to him. You tell me."

He stared off into the middle distance. "We came to an agreement. I expect him to honor his word. That's all I can say."

"He agreed to keep your secret?" I said carefully. I didn't want to ask what I really wanted to know: whether or not Captain would follow his protocol once the *Atlantis* was operational again. If our conversation in the gym indicated anything, it was that he would. But I couldn't give up on him that easily, could I?

"He did," Captain said, sounding surprised. "More or less."

A blossom of hope formed within me. "It sounds to me like all's well that ends well. Right?"

"Will you be jumping ship?" he deflected.

"I don't know yet," I said. "Is that... still on the table?"

"I explained the situation to Akade. He's willing to take you on as a passenger. You're free to do as you wish." He looked down at his hands. "It was never my place to forbid it, I just... I got so angry..."

I smiled in understanding. "You don't have to explain yourself. I understand. You were just looking out for me, and I do appreciate it. To tell the truth, I don't know what I'm gonna do yet, but it looks like I'll have plenty of time to think about it. I always think better when I'm working, anyway."

He looked at me in surprise. "You intend to help with repairs?"

I answered him with a look of confusion. "Of course. What did you think I was going to do, lay around all day twiddling my thumbs? We've got problems to solve. And you're gonna want two people for this one, I guarantee you."

He looked floored. Did he really think I was going to leave him high and dry like that? Or that because I had the opportunity to jump ship, I was going to wash my hands of the *Atlantis* just like that? No way.

Even if there was a chance that by helping him I would be enabling a vicious cycle, there was also a chance that this could be what *breaks* it. After all, the worst had already happened. What if this were the catalyst that caused him to take control of his own destiny? I couldn't abandon him at a time like this—now more than ever, he needed someone by his side who cared about *him*. Who loved *him*.

Wait, did I love him?

I'd said as much, hadn't I? At the time, I'd thought I'd meant it as a friendly love. A loyal love.

Whether or not that was a safer love, however, remained to be seen.

"Xanorra, I..." He looked down at his hands again, then up at me with steeled resolve. It meant something to him, my willingness to help him. That made me feel even more confident with my decision. "I'd very much appreciate your help. Thank you."

"You're welcome," I said, taking his hand in mine. He interlocked our fingers, and we sat like that for a while inside the *Nautilus*, saying nothing. Just two kids who, despite the odds, still existed.

# 48

# Captain's Log, Year 18, Day 68, 1147 Atlantean Time

I have taken stock of the ship repairs necessary to get the *Atlantis* at full operating capacity again, but before I detail the extent of the restoration project before us, I must recount the last twelve hours in their entirety.

First, in the interest of keeping accurate records, I am transcribing the conversation between Captain Leon Akade of the free ship *Esther* and myself. There has been an unfortunate and unprecedented delay in the ship's course following our first encounter with the *Esther*. I will expound on the details that led to said encounter at another time, but the most salient outcome is that the *Atlantis* is critically damaged and currently in tow by our adversaries, on whom we are forced to rely.

I blame only myself for the danger in which I've put the mission, but I am determined to remain focused, as there is a corrective course of action that will in due time put the mission back on its proper track.

[Pause]

This is an unmitigated disaster. Why is it that every time I try to do the right thing, it always backfires terribly? I shouldn't have woken Xanorra up. I knew it was a mistake, and yet... I cannot fathom any other outcome. Is that shortsighted of me? Probably. Lately, I feel more and more as if I do not know myself.

What I do know is that I have to fix this. I must fix this.

[Pause]

Anyway, the conversation with Captain Akade that took place after our forced surrender to the *Esther* proceeded as follows:

Akade: Take a seat, Omen. Do you mind if I call you Omen?

Me: That's fine. Call me whatever you wish.

Akade: [Sighs] It is common courtesy, in the bowels of deep space, to put aside all previous grievances in the interest of mutual survival. So I hope you believe me when I say that we intend to help you in whatever capacity you will allow.

Me: Yes, I am aware. I will be taking stock of the extent of the damage tomorrow morning and checking it against my inventory.

Akade: Please inform me of anything you do not have. It is likely we will have it.

Me: I will. And if you have no prior heading, I would like to request that we follow the *Atlantis*'s intended course. The one you found us on.

Akade: That can be arranged.

Me: Yes, well, I suppose that's settled.

Akade: If I may be so bold, I must say you look quite ill at ease.

Me: My ship is in tatters. What do you expect? If you'd like to take this opportunity to boast about the *Esther*'s superiority, I suppose you have earned the right. I will hold my tongue.

Akade: From one captain to another, I would not be so petty. My only question is this: didn't anyone teach you how to pick your fights?

Me: No. Only that I must win them.

Akade: [Sighs] It is as I thought. You are reckless.

Me: Reckless?

Akade: And lost.

Me: I do not appreciate this. I think this conversation—

Akade: Do you remember at all what you said while under the truth serum?

I had risen from my seat at this point, but upon hearing this, I lowered myself back down.

Me: No. Should I have?

Akade: It is interesting, I will admit. Everyone reacts to the drug differently. I fully expected Miss Xanorra, for example, to be the talkative one and not you. But she was asleep for most of the interview. You, however, spoke so lucidly that for a while I wondered if you were affected by the drug at all.

Me: Why are you telling me this?

Akade: It is usually a very delicate process, extracting information directly from the source. You have to know the right questions to ask. You have to make the extractee think it was their idea to tell you. But you... you spilt your guts without us hardly having to lift a finger. As if you wanted your secrets known. It was the most fascinating thing I had ever seen.

Me: Glad you could derive a moment's amusement from my shame.

Akade: It is nothing to be ashamed of, Omen. But I will say, your reaction does belie a guilty conscience. And a desire to be purged of it.

Me: You are a psychologist, I take it.

Akade: Hmph. Hardly.

Me: Right.

Akade: I will not insult your intelligence by telling you things you either already know or have no interest in hearing from the likes of me. I was a teenager once; I know that look of stubborn pride all too well. Just be careful, Omen, that it isn't your undoing.

Me: Are we done here?

Akade: Not quite. [Pause] What about Xanorra?

Me: What about her?

Akade: I understand that she is a result of collateral damage. Inflicted by you, as it were.

Me: You should be grateful that I didn't conduct myself the same way toward you as I did her unfortunate ship.

Akade: [Laughs] If you had attacked me on sight rather than to speak with me first, the outcome would have been the same as it is now. Nonetheless, I applaud your diplomacy, even if it was a meagre attempt at best. And I fully understand why you tried to use her as a bargaining chip. It was at her behest.

Me: Yes.

Akade: So, she has been trapped on your ship for the

better part of a year, and now that we have crossed your path, her options have miraculously doubled. She can now entertain the hope of seeing her family and her home again. The only question is whether or not we would be able to ferry her.

Me: Correct.

Akade: Well, not the only question. [Gestures toward me]

Me: She is not beholden to me. She is free to do as she wishes.

Akade: Of course. But what will you do if she leaves?

Me: What I'm meant for: I will continue my mission as planned. Perhaps I'll think of her fondly from time to time, when I think of her at all.

I still regret saying that.

Akade: [Sighs] That's grossly optimistic of you.

Me: How so?

Akade: It does not matter. Tell her I will take her up on her offer if she so desires. That I can guarantee safe passage. She will be as my own daughter, and I will not let any of my men give her any cause for discomfort.

It sounds contradictory, but I hated him for saying such a thing. I hated that I believed him because it meant that Xanorra could leave. That by all rights, she would leave. But is that not what I'd wanted?

Me: Thank you. I will be sure to let her know.

Akade: [Tapping his chin] I have one other concern if you will oblige me. Just moments ago, you would rather fight than let us make off with your secrets. So how do I know that, if we help you fix your ship, you will not pursue the same course of action once you are free?

Me: I try to pride myself on not making the same mistake twice.

And yet I'd made many of the same mistakes repeatedly. How many times was I going to lie to the captain's face?

Akade: That is a good answer. It is not out of concern for myself that I ask this; it is out of concern for you and Miss Xanorra. You see, during our little tête-à-tête, we held back. We did not attack you at full power, because to do so would have been your demise.

This news pricked me. Based on what I'd seen of the *Esther*'s guns, I had little doubt that he told the truth.

Me: I see.

Akade: But mark me when I say, if you try to come after us again, I will give no quarter. Do we have an understanding?

Me: We do.

Akade: Please believe me when I say it is not what I want. I do not take pleasure in death. But much like you, I am loyal to my ship and to my purpose, and I will protect the lives on board at any cost.

Me: Yes.

Akade: Which, for the time, includes you and Miss Xanorra. I hope you understand that. We will treat you with the utmost hospitality—more so than the first time.

Me: I think I speak on behalf of us both when I say it is appreciated.

Akade: Is there anything you need at this moment? Food, water? We will inform you of mealtimes, but do not hesitate to ask in the interim.

Me: That would be nice. [Standing] Thank you, Captain.

Akade: Of course. And Omen?

Me: Yes?

Akade: We all must live with the choices we make. We may think they do not matter to the void, but they matter to us. And to those we love.

I did not reply to that last comment as I left his office. Instead, I went to the *Nautilus* to be alone and process the last few hours' turn of events. I did not expect to have an emotional breakdown, nor am I entirely sure why the conversation with Akade of all people left me in such a damnably vulnerable state.

He was a master con artist, after all. And, apparently, he had a working knowledge of psychology. He'd probably been playing mind games with me for the entirety of our conversation, which is part of the reason why I have transcribed it here. It is a riddle, to be sure, but one thing is for certain: he unsettles me in ways I do not fully understand.

Xanorra found me while I was still undone, as if she'd sensed my distress. I suppose it should have been demoralizing, but it wasn't. I suppose I should have sent her away, but I didn't. I could not deny her then any more than I could before.

She claims she always says the wrong things, but I do not agree with her. She has said some very right things as of late, things I did not know I needed to hear or to feel certain of.

Agh, I shouldn't be saying things like this on record. Atlantis, del—

[Knocking]

Yes?

*Hey, Captain, sorry to bother you. I know you're in the middle of captain stuff, but... there's a really weird smell coming from the engine room, and I can't pinpoint where it's coming from? Neither can Theta. He's not exactly built with advanced olfactory sensors. And Beta's on the hull, so...*

Of course. I was just finishing up anyway. Atlantis, save log.

# 49

# Back in the Saddle and Ready to Giddy-Up

We began repairs on the *Atlantis* the very next day. Captain opted to sleep in the *Nautilus*, and I couldn't deny him his privacy (especially after I'd already invaded it once), so I returned to the centrifuge dorm alone.

In the morning, we dined with the crew. Captain looked significantly more rumpled than usual and said little, leaving me to pick up the conversational slack—a task I would usually relish, but today, I wasn't in the mood. Thankfully, the crew mostly gave us a wide berth.

Let it never be said that space pirates aren't good at reading the room.

Then we took the *Nautilus* back to the unmanned *Atlantis*, caught up with Beta on the bridge, assessed the damage, and got to work. The bots had successfully repaired the life support system before we'd gotten there (priority numero uno), so we didn't have to worry about silly little things like dying of hypoxemia.

I was assigned to the engine room and I have to say, it was nice to be back in the saddle. This was no training simulation—this was the real freaking deal. This was *work*.

The majority of the other robots had been deployed to the exterior of the ship to fix the damaged hull and stabilizers. Captain spent most of his time in the docking bay or on the bridge, directing and redirecting the reports. Occasionally, he checked in on me, but truth be told, I saw a lot less of him than I expected. Which was frustrating, since I was relying on a lot of alone time with him in order to turn him from the dark side.

I had to make up excuses to go talk to him, usually innocuous questions about engine repairs that I probably could've asked Theta or, God forbid, Beta. The last time it happened, I'd caught him in the middle of recording a captain's log and it felt like I'd walked in on something private. He gave me a spare wristband after that.

Captain probably would've worked nonstop if I didn't accost him with my very real need to eat and sleep, and God bless him, he obliged me—after about ten to twelve hours each day on the *Atlantis* with a lunch break in the middle, we returned to the *Esther*.

I suppose we could've slept on the *Atlantis*, but it was considered rude when you were tethered to another ship. (Besides, with neither of us manning the greenhouse, food conservation was a genuine concern.)

So, we returned to our gracious hosts each night for

dinner and, let's face it, entertainment. Akade's crew was downright hilarious. The way they'd acted during our first visit had been one hundred percent authentic, space shanties and all.

I found I couldn't help but like them as a group, but individually, I had my favorites: Columbus had a very dad-like energy about him, Akade was like the cool professor, and Frysauce and I were buddies now. He was a total flirt, which, if Captain even noticed, didn't seem to make him jealous. As generally put off as he was by the extractors, he still lacked the ability to understand many of their social cues.

It made me realize that while he'd become fairly well-acclimated to life with me, he'd never experienced camaraderie with other men before. I wanted to see him laugh and smile at their rowdy jokes but he remained guarded, uninterested, and suspicious. A lone wolf forced to interact with an established pack, supervised by a true alpha male to whom he had no intention of submitting. I was no sociologist, but even I found it fascinating to watch.

*My entire life has been one big experiment*, he'd said.

Well, this was a new experiment. In my opinion, a better one.

I just wished Captain would see it that way.

We slept in the centrifuge dorm, or at least I did—Captain was never in there for more than an hour at a time, restless as ever, and I didn't have the energy to complain about it. I assumed that when he did sleep, it was in the *Nautilus*. In spite of our heart-to-heart that first day, things were definitely weird between us when we weren't working, as if fixing the ship was the only thing holding us together.

In a way, it was.

Man, I really needed to get my shit together. Every step we took toward fixing this ship was another step toward answering questions neither of us wanted to ask.

A week passed, and then two. We fell into a comfortable rhythm, an artificial status quo. Problems arose. Solutions were found. Uncomfortable silences were had.

And then, one day, after yet another rambunctious dinner aboard the *Esther*, Akade asked to speak with me privately.

*Dammit*, I thought, assuming this would be about me jumping ship. What else could he want to talk to me about? I had been hoping to put this conversation off until the last minute, but what could I do? No time like the present, I guess.

When we stepped into his office and took our seats, Akade gave me a fond smile and said, "How are you doing, Miss Xanorra?" As if he were a school guidance counselor and I a promising student under duress.

"I'm... staying busy," I said vaguely. As far as I knew, he'd been pretty laissez-faire as far as the *Atlantis* was concerned. Captain had had a few meetings with him to discuss creative solutions to missing parts, but other than that, he'd kept a respectful distance.

"Do you think of your family much?" he asked, completely catching me off-guard. "Do you miss them?"

"I..." I was caught between being honest and being

guarded. I settled for a compromise. "I mean, who wouldn't?"

"Did you send them any messages when you first became a passenger of the *Atlantis?*"

I wondered if I should be suspicious of his odd line of questioning. "Just one," I said. "It would've been about seven or eight months ago by now. Why do you ask?"

He gave me a long, sincere look that I couldn't decipher, a hand to his chin in contemplation. "It is not often that one finds messages all the way out here."

"You intercepted it, didn't you?" I said, my heart sinking. "That's how you knew how to find us."

"It is indeed," he said. "And then I passed it on."

And just like that, my heart rose to the surface again. "You did? Oh my God, thank you. I can't even begin to say—"

"And I've received a response."

I stopped short. "What?"

"Just this morning. From your family. It appears that long before they received the forwarded transmission, they were already en route to come find you."

I couldn't wrap my head around the knowledge that my family had received my message at all, let alone that they'd sent one back. "You have to play it. Please? Can you play it? I have to hear it for myself."

Akade chuckled. "I would not be so cruel as to taunt you. Of course you may hear it."

I was rigid as he opened a panel in his desk that was probably linked to the bridge and inputted a command.

"This is Engineer Technician Casper T. Nepier of the SEA deep space seeker *Conseil*." As soon as I heard my dad's voice on the speaker, I burst into tears. It was like someone had flipped a switch inside me. "We have received the transmission forwarded from your ship and on behalf of the captain and crew, I would like to thank you for passing it on. The sender is my daughter; she went missing after an unfortunate incident aboard the deep space vessel *USE George Washington* forced us to abandon ship less than a month into our eight-year mission.

"I gather that she is not currently on board your ship, but if it would be feasible, we would like to request a rendezvous so that we might pool our resources. I gather you're reluctant to identify yourself, but the SEA is prepared to offer full immunity if you agree to help us. And if you wouldn't mind forwarding this message on, so that Xanorra might receive it and know that we're coming for her, I would be eternally grateful. We are... four-ish months into a two-year search-and-rescue privately commissioned through the SEA. By the time this reaches you, if my math serves, we will likely be between six to seven months in. I would be much obliged if we kept a channel of communication open between us. Please respond with your answer and your preferred rendezvous point. *Conseil* out."

I couldn't speak. I just kept blubbering like a baby, unable to control my knee-jerk reaction to hearing my dad's voice, to knowing that they were out there, looking for me. That technically, they'd already found me, even if they didn't know it yet. It was more than I could've hoped for so soon. It was unbelievably overwhelming.

Akade got up and retrieved a multi-colored scarf from

his wall of memorabilia, offering it to me as a handkerchief. It was almost too pretty to get my snot all over, orange with clusters of teal and purple flowers, but I accepted it anyway. He put a heavy hand on my shoulder and said, "I intend to send a swift reply. I had thought that perhaps you might want to be the one to record it."

"Once I calm down, yeah," I said through my tears.

"Take your time," he said, moving back around to his desk. "I assume this means you'll be coming with us once the repairs to the *Atlantis* are complete."

Oh. I'd been so caught up in the moment that I hadn't thought of what this actually meant for the future. This decided it for me, without a doubt. But how was I going to tell Captain?

"Yeah, I guess it does," I said, not liking how uneasy I sounded. "If you're okay with that, that is."

Akade smiled. "Even if I hadn't received such a promising message, I still would have agreed to ferry you should that have been your wish. Despite what I said when Captain tried to negotiate with me for you, I will be able to guarantee your safety. You have my word as a spacer."

"Thank you," I said. "I can't even express how thankful I am."

"It is an honor to bear witness to such an extraordinary event. We get so used to the void taking from us, we forget that sometimes it gives back, too."

I frowned at that. Yes, this was a happy ending for me, but I hadn't anticipated how I'd actually feel about leaving Captain when all was said and done. I figured it would be a little hard, but I hadn't expected it to feel... painful.

"You worry about young Captain," said Akade, reading my thoughts.

"Yeah," I said. "I don't want to abandon him. I mean, you know what fate awaits him out there. But I don't know how to save him. I don't know if he'll let me. What do I do?"

Akade rubbed his chin thoughtfully. "You said it best," he said. "You cannot save a person who does not want to be saved."

"There's a part of me that believes he wants to be, but that he won't let himself. Those androids—his handlers, essentially—won't let him, either. Every time I think I've helped him up, they knock him back down. It's infuriating."

"Machines have that strong a hold on him?" Akade furrowed his brow. "That is a very dangerous reality."

"They're supposed to be Asimovian, I guess, but sometimes I think that's a lie," I said, the words tumbling out of me before I could stop them. After months of mulling all this over, of fighting with Captain on whether or not it was true, it felt good to finally tell someone who was on the outside looking in. "After all, they've lied about plenty of other stuff. I saw *video evidence* that they psychologically abused Captain as a child. He doesn't see it that way, but who in his position would? And then there's the fact that I think one of them might've tried to kill me. Like, legitimately, with intent."

"How?"

"My tether came loose once, during a spacewalk. I

almost floated away. Captain said the anchor had come unbolted. How suspicious is that?"

Akade had grown graver with every word I spoke. In fact, he looked downright disturbed, like he'd remembered a nightmare. "You are certain this happened?"

"It's not like I have any real proof," I said. "Just a hunch. That, and, they've made it abundantly clear that they don't like that I'm there. They framed me for destroying something I never touched. I know for a fact it had to be one of them. It wrecked Captain's trust in me, even though he knew deep down that I didn't do it. And then to protect me and the mission—mostly the mission, honestly—he put me in cryo. Actually, I have you to thank for being awake right now as opposed to thirty-two years from now. If you hadn't shown up, Captain might never have thawed me out early."

Akade sighed, running a hand down his face and muttering in French. "And just when I thought this mission of his couldn't get any more inhumane," he said.

"Thank you! Finally, someone gets it."

He looked at me with fierce urgency. "Xanorra, how long until the ship is operational?"

"A couple weeks, maybe. Why?"

"I want you to have something." He got up and moved to the wall again, which I started to realize was like a grab bag without the bag. He handed me a metal rod about the length of my forearm, tapered at the end.

"What's this?" I asked.

"Essentially a Taser," he said. "A very powerful Taser. Decommissioning powerful, if you catch my drift."

I did catch his drift.

"I want you to be on your guard when you're on that ship," said Akade in a low tone. "And if you feel threatened, or if you feel that Captain is threatened, I want you to feel free to use that device."

I looked down at the innocuous-looking baton in my hands. I was armed now, I realized. Armed with an android killer.

It was a lot more power than I knew what to do with.

"Thank you, Captain," I said sincerely. "I'll use it wisely."

"You may also use it unwisely," he said. Right, I almost forgot: he was still a not-pirate pirate. With a charming smile, he switched gears completely. "Now, shall we record your message to your family?"

I smiled, forgetting my troubles and the rough road ahead for the time being. "We shall."

# 50

# Parting is Such Sweet Bullshit

When I returned to the centrifuge dorm after recording my message—short and to the point but way less vague than my transmission from the *Atlantis* had been—I was surprised to find Captain there, sitting on the bottom bunk. Waiting for me.

"Hel-lo," I said with mild confusion. "What's up?"

"Is everything all right?" he asked. "Between you and Akade?"

Ah, he assumed the conversation had revolved around the matter of my jumping ship. Well, technically, it had. Just not in the way I'd anticipated.

I knew I would have to tell him eventually, but I really didn't want to have to do it right then and there. I needed time to process everything, and the one time I didn't want him in the room, there he was: the manifestation of bad timing.

"Everything's fine," I said. "He asked me for my

decision and I said I needed to sleep on it. Which I intend to do. Post-haste."

"Could you spare a moment?" he asked. "I would like to talk to you."

Against my better judgment, I nodded and sat down next to him on the bed. "What's up?"

"Your decision is entirely your own," he said. "I'm the one who woke you up with the aim of helping you escape in the first place. It would be positively hypocritical of me to revoke that now. With that said, I am hoping to persuade you to stay with me aboard the *Atlantis*."

Damn, I really should've kicked him out of the room when I had the chance. "Captain—"

"If you're afraid of the cryo chamber, don't be," he said quickly. "I've thought it through. I know how to keep you awake. I'm going to tell Phala my mental health is contingent upon your presence. The primary directive may be to protect the mission, but I'm vital to that mission. They won't do anything that compromises my ability to perform my duties."

I sighed. "You think they won't be able to convince you I'm a problem? They did it once before and it barely took two months. What will they be able to convince you to do in five, ten, fifteen years?" I knew I shouldn't even be entertaining hypotheticals, but I had to get him to see the bigger picture. "Don't make promises you can't keep, Captain."

He rose from the bed and knelt in front of me. My heart did a somersault even as my brain buzzed with confusion. "This is a promise I'm determined to keep."

He had to make this difficult, didn't he? "Captain…"

"I'll be true to my word," he said in a softer voice, taking my hands in his. "I'll keep you safe."

Good Lord, this was too much. I had to tell him now. So much for sleeping on it. "Listen, Captain…"

"I'm not asking you to choose me over your family," he said. "I'm asking you not to throw in your lot with those pirates. It's your safety I'm concerned about. There are too many risks, something I should have realized from the start. At least, with me, I can guarantee your survival."

"Captain," I said as firmly as possible. "I'm deeply touched. Really. But there's something you should know. Akade, he…"

His expression went cold as he stood up. "What did that madman do now?"

I chuckled at his intensity. "Nothing, Captain. Nothing worth getting angry over. In fact, it's a really good thing. It's… that transmission you let me send, you remember it?"

He nodded.

"Well, it reached Akade first. And then Akade nested it and passed it on, likely with a wider broadcast signal. Well—It—So, apparently… my family was already out there looking for me anyway, so they got it and sent a message back, and Akade received that message today, and that's what he wanted to talk to me about. My family's coming for me. Akade's agreed to rendezvous with them. I have to leave, Captain. My mind's made up."

He let go of my hands as if I'd shocked him. "What a fool I am."

"No, don't be embarrassed, please—"

"I'm happy for you." His expression was restrained but full of frustration. "Truly. Don't mistake my... shock... for unhappiness. I just..."

"Captain," I said, sitting down on the bed and motioning for him to sit next to me. "Saying goodbye to you is going to be the hardest thing I've ever done. Really, you have to believe that. That's why I wanted to sleep on it because... it's going to suck really, really bad." And now I was teary-eyed again. Great. "And I don't want to think about it."

He clenched his jaw. "Are you positively sure your family is coming? Would you bet your life on it?"

"Yes," I said. "I'd risk everything to see them again."

"Then there's nothing else to it," he said, the thickness in his voice betraying him. "We will finish repairing the *Atlantis* as planned, and then we will go our separate ways."

"Don't make it sound so cold," I said, tears running down my face. "I can see it in your eyes. You're as miserable as I am."

"So I am," he said. "But that won't change anything, will it? What's done is done."

I groaned in anguish, the words tumbling out of me before I could think twice about them. "Stop believing you don't have any control over your life, Captain. You have a choice, same as me. You don't have to say goodbye."

He was taken aback, and rightfully so. It was a bold thing for me to say. Perhaps even controversial. "I am loyal to my family," he said firmly. "As you are loyal to yours."

I shook my head, deciding at that moment that I had nothing to lose. "There's a difference between being loyal to your family and being subject to them. Captain, there's another option for you. Come with us. Stay with me. You can be the one to rendezvous with my family and we'll go back to the *Aster* together."

"And what of the mission?" he asked. I was amazed that he was even entertaining the idea at all. "What of my family?"

"I don't know," I said. "Maybe… it's time for them to wake up."

He shook his head. "No. Do not tempt me like that. I… cannot even consider it."

I thought back to that boy in the video, the one who so desperately wanted to meet his family. Who'd been worn down and worn down until he was convinced it wasn't what he wanted anymore. It was cruel of me to remind him of that, wasn't it? To try to put it back on the table as if it were that easy?

"I'm sorry," I said. "I shouldn't have said that."

"It seems… our destinies have always been on parallel paths," he said. "Never meant to touch. The fact that they crossed at all is… well, I believe literature has a word for it, doesn't it? 'Star-crossed'?"

I snorted. "You make it sound so melodramatic."

"For what it's worth… I don't regret crossing paths with you," he said. "I'm glad to have met you. But I think… it's better that we say goodbye. For both of us."

"I don't regret crossing paths with you, either," I said. "I wish things could've been different. And for what it's worth, I didn't mean to imply that you should throw away everything your family worked for. Especially just because *I* want you to stay."

"I know," he said.

"But..." I hesitated, then continued anyway, "what bothers me is that it was never your sacrifice to make in the first place. It was theirs, and they decided they'd rather pass it on to an innocent child than do the dirty work themselves. They *manufactured* your destiny. They didn't give you a chance to decide it for yourself."

I braced myself for deflection, but the expression on his face was contemplative, not angry. "What do you suppose my fate would've been otherwise?" he asked.

"Whatever you wanted it to be, I'd hope," I said with a shrug. "That's the beauty of life. Maybe you would've studied agriculture. Maybe you would've been a farmer. Maybe you would've joined the SEA and become an astrobotanist."

He furrowed his brow. "Those are all hyper-specific career choices, Xanorra. I assume this has to do with the greenhouse?"

I smiled mischievously. "Those are just examples. I would never dare limit you to plants. But don't even pretend like you don't love it. I've known it since day one."

"All right," he said, exasperated. "Very well. You win. The only times in life I was ever truly happy—prior to meeting you—was when I tended to the greenhouse. Its success was my pride and joy, and its destruction was like tearing out a piece of my soul. Is that what you wanted to hear?"

I kissed him on the cheek. "Yes. Thank you. You may go in peace."

He stood and walked to the door, pressing the button on the wall to stop the centrifuge. He gave me a long look that said he wanted to say something else. I waited just in case, but when no words came, I smiled sadly and said, "Goodnight."

"Goodnight," he said softly and left the room.

# 51

# Captain's Logs

**Year 18, Day 112, 0845 Atlantean Time**

How could I have been so stupid?

After I had so flagrantly declared that Xanorra was free to do as she chose, after I'd already resigned myself to the reality of her absence, I'd turned around and done exactly what I'd vowed I wouldn't: I begged her. I *begged* her to stay.

I was a fool to think she would ever choose someone like me. Even if her rescue wasn't imminent, I have little doubt that she would have jumped ship regardless, and I would've had to honour it. It was *my* idea after all. As I myself said, our paths were never meant to cross in the first place. It was selfish and stupid for either of us to pretend otherwise. Wasn't it?

Then again... what if her family hadn't contacted her? Would her answer truly have been the same?

What if I'd told her I loved her?

Stop it, Captain. Focus, dammit. Now is not the time to start speculating. You have too much to do. Too much riding on you to let yourself become undone by a girl.

It's better this way. Besides, to love someone is to want what's best for them, is it not? You're not supposed to hold them hostage to your desires. That is why I must forget it. I must let her go.

In less than a month, I will continue my mission alone, as was always intended. And she will return to her family, as she always intended. Everything will be exactly as it is supposed to be.

After our conversation last night, I felt compelled to assess the damage to the greenhouse. Admittedly, I'd hardly been back in there since our surrender to the *Esther*. Even after the six months following Xan's cryonic incubation, I still hadn't gotten it back to full capacity. And every time I went in there, I was reminded anew of the consequences of my actions.

But as I stood among the rows of struggling lettuce and disfigured potato plants, I thought about Xan's claim regarding my love of agriculture. Yes, I suppose I had denied the affinity, telling myself that I only enjoyed it due to its utility and my own proclivity for it. My ability to pilot the ship came out of necessity, but this... this could have been automated. By all rights, it should have been. I'd taken it over voluntarily.

The greenhouse had been the one thing that was truly mine, and they'd taken it away from me.

While I was there, I'd forced myself to look at the fig tree—it had been an absolute wreck after the ordeal, hardly a leaf to its name—but it had a chance of surviving if I bothered to take care of it. Which, of course, I hadn't. I'd shoved it as far out of sight as I could, behind a pile of crates, and had left it to die.

But when I moved the crates to look at it, I was surprised to find that it wasn't dead. Not yet, anyway. Even more surprising was that there was a single leaf still hanging on. And next to that leaf, a bud. A fig. Fighting to survive, in spite of it all.

Fighting to be free.

I shook with some strange amalgamation of anger and relief. I made myself move the container back into view and watered it. Then I left and went about my day, thinking I'd achieved catharsis.

I had not.


## Written Entry, Date Unknown

I couldn't take it anymore. There was nowhere to run from my thoughts, after all. Following my visit to the greenhouse, I stole away to the infirmary to speak to Phala. She was already awake, waiting for me just inside the door.

"Captain," she said pleasantly. "How nice of you to visit. I am detecting abnormally high cortisol levels from you. Is that why you have come by?"

"It is," I said. My entire body felt tight and uncomfortable. "I must speak with you."

"Let me get you something first," she said, moving to the medicine cabinet.

"No," I said, louder and more urgently than I'd intended. "I do not need it."

She gave me a flummoxed look. It had been years since I'd refused one of her administrations outright.

"You are unwell," she said. "You have been working too hard on too little sleep. You need your rest. You need—"

"The greenhouse," I said.

Her bewilderment increased. "What about it, Captain? Is something wrong with it?"

"The tether," I said.

She canted her head. "I do not understand."

"How did you do it? Why did you do it?"

"You are going to have to be more specific, Captain."

"You loosened the tether. You destroyed the greenhouse. Telling me to get rid of her is one thing, but to actually take matters into your own hands? How could your programming allow you to attempt the *murder* of a human being?" My voice had risen in intensity until I was practically shouting. It had been years since I'd shown any emotion toward her other than calm complacency or restrained anxiety.

She was unnaturally still for a long moment as she processed the gravity of my inquiry. "In what way could my actions be construed as attempted murder?"

As she did not deny my accusation, I took it as a confession. "How could you? You put her in danger."

"You put this mission in danger the second you brought her on board."

"A fact of which I have been excruciatingly aware for every second since."

"And yet you have refused to follow protocol. For

every time you have bent the rules, my programming, in turn, has had to bend along with it. If you have not broken protocol, then neither have I. However, the problem with bending anything is, the more you do so, the weaker its integrity gets. Eventually, it will either be altered irreparably... or it will break."

I was spellbound as I processed this. It should have been obvious, but I was so blinded by my rationalizations I couldn't see it for what it was.

In my attempts to protect Xanorra, I'd managed to put her even more in harm's way. What cruel irony.

"How does this correct itself?" I asked simply.

"You know how. Dispose of her and dispose of the pirate ship. Preferably at the same time."

My stomach turned sour. "You saw what happened the last time we engaged with the *Esther*. If I go after them again, they're liable to send us into the ether. There has to be another way."

"That sort of thinking is what got you into your current situation, Captain," she scolded. "I assume you have heard the expression, 'Insanity is doing the same thing over and over and expecting different results'?"

"Albert Einstein," I said blithely. "And it is a logical fallacy."

"It is a logical paradox," she corrected. "And you are bringing it to life with every poorly-made decision. Captain, you have forced my hand."

"And I am telling you to unforce it," I said. "I will not risk this ship by fighting the *Esther* again. I am here to protect life, not destroy it."

"*Lives*," she said. "You are here to protect specific,

sanctioned, *significant* lives. It is time you were reminded of that. If you will not act, then I must."

"I forbid it," I said. "I will handle this myself." Thinking I'd said all that needed to be said, I turned to leave.

That was a mistake.

Phala stopped me with a hand to my neck, yanking me back with a strength I'd forgotten she possessed. It hurt. She'd never hurt me before, not physically. And then she stuck a syringe into my arm, which hurt even more as something powerfully fast-acting moved through my veins and clouded my vision. I sank to the floor, still scrambling in vain for the exit.

"It pains me to have to do this," said Phala. "Not physically, of course. Metaphorically. But then again, androids do feel pain in a sense. We feel pain when we are unable to fulfil our purpose. It wails in our ears like a siren, electrifies our wiring. So, too, do we feel pain when we must break one aspect of our protocol in order to fulfil another of higher priority. Like an animal gnawing off its own foot to free itself of a trap. Remember that the next time you feel the need to disobey."

I turned myself around to face her, my back against the door. My mouth felt dry and heavy, my vision fading in and out of focus. She crouched in front of me, watching me struggle with a complacent, emotionless stare. Is that really what I'd looked like when Xan first met me? So cold. So inhuman.

"You can't... do this," I slurred.

"Yes, I can," she said. "Because now I am going to fix you." She produced another syringe and injected it into the same arm. The cloudiness of the sedative was quickly replaced by a sharp, painful refocusing. My vision tunnelled and my heart rate increased as if I'd just been pumped full of adrenaline.

But this was more than just adrenaline. No, this was something much, much worse.

"This is for your own good, Captain," she said. "The greatest good." Her voice was so crisp, so certain. It was a voice I knew as well as my own, a voice that had raised and nurtured me from infancy. I trusted this voice. I wanted to do whatever it said. "I have sent you two codes: with the first, you will retrieve an explosive charge from Capsule 17 of Storage Room C and place it in the engine compartment of the *Nautilus*. With the second, you will retrieve a gun from Capsule 19. Then you will report back to me. Are we clear?"

We were clear, even though what she wanted me to do was wrong. I had to do as she asked. It could be no other way. It was the strangest feeling—stronger than suggestion—yet I was still aware of myself, as if trapped in a box inside my mind, my voice snatched away. My body moved of its own accord, every step a release of endorphins—doing this was good. It felt good. It felt *right*.

I'd been told all my life to ignore my feelings and listen to my heart. It had never occurred to me that perhaps I'd been taught to mistake one for the other: to ignore my heart and go entirely by my feelings.

The heart, after all, could not be so easily manipulated.

In the very back of my mind, I prayed that Xanorra would catch me—that she'd stop me from betraying her against my will. But she was hard at work in the engine room, helping to repair a ship to which she owed no allegiance, for a captain to whom she'd never sworn fealty.

To a boy who was about to break his promise to her, even though it was the last thing in the universe he wanted to do.

# 52

# Just Having an Off Day I Guess

Something felt off today.

You ever get one of those feelings in the back of your mind, like God is tapping you on the shoulder, trying to warn you of impending doom? If you're smart, you listen. If you're dumb, like me, you ignore it and bury your head in your work for a few more hours.

But alas, the feeling remained, and eventually, I figured that something must be wrong with Captain. He'd seemed a little ill at ease since our conversation about my inevitable departure, and I hadn't really tried to talk to him about it since. Now was as good a time as ever, I supposed. So I took a break and headed to the bridge. To my surprise, Captain wasn't there. But Beta was.

He turned and gave me a wide, fake smile. "Ah, Xanorra. What a pleasure."

My senses went on high alert. I had the android killer

Akade had given me tucked away in my boot. I hoped for Captain's sake I didn't have to use it.

"Where's Captain?" I asked.

"Fulfilling his duties, no doubt," he replied.

"No worries. I'll go track him down, then." I turned to leave.

"Miss Nepier," Beta said a bit too urgently. "Why don't you wait for him here? I'm sure he will be back soon."

Red alarm bells blared in my head. It seemed like an odd suggestion, considering his past disapproval of my presence on the bridge. "Why? What is he doing that's so important? He's not on an EVA, is he?"

"Even if he was, I would not suggest you go traipsing after him."

My heart rate jumped. "Right. Wouldn't want my tether coming loose, would we?"

"An unfortunate occurrence," said Beta. "No, I daresay we would not like a repeat of that."

"Because God forbid Captain catch me again, right?" I said bitterly.

Beta furrowed his mechanical brow. "Whatever do you mean?"

"Just admit that it was you," I said, anger coursing through me like a fever. "You unbolted the anchor."

"No," he said simply. "As a matter of fact, I did not. I cannot."

"Then who—?" I froze, the pieces falling into place one after the other. My anger turned inward. "Phala."

Beta dared to look smug. "What about her?"

"It's been Phala the whole time, hasn't it? I thought...

since you were the beta, you had the more advanced driver. I mean, she's smart, but..."

Medidroids are built for a singular purpose. She rarely ever left the infirmary, rarely ever did much other than mother Captain and push his psychological buttons. It never occurred to me that maybe she was the one capable of finding loopholes like this. That maybe she wasn't just a medidroid.

"Holy fucking shit," I said. "Phala is an anagram of Alpha. She *is* the one in charge. And she can bend the protocol."

Why hadn't I seen it before? It wasn't as if anything about the naming scheme on board this accursed squid knew the definition of subtlety.

Beta didn't react, did not confirm or deny my revelation. For a frightening moment, I wondered if I'd somehow broken him just by saying that. But then he said, in a dull monotone, "Do not move."

Naturally, I didn't listen. I made a break for the bridge hatch, determined to track down Captain and warn him about her, but a firm grip on my arm jerked me back with unnatural force. My arm felt like it was about to pop out of my socket. I cried out in pain.

"I said, 'do not move,'" said Beta coldly.

"Let me go!" I shouted. "Help! Captain!"

Beta did not relent. He clamped a hand over my mouth to keep me from screaming. "Calm yourself, Miss Nepier. There is no need to act irrationally."

*Irrational? I'll show you irrational!* I twisted my body toward the floor and, with my free hand, retrieved the baton from my boot. A switch on the side was all it took to light it up. With all my force, I shoved it behind me toward Beta's center. He released me immediately and I turned to plunge the Taser into him again.

He convulsed and blinked rapidly, a sound like warped static rippling through his body as his motherboard overloaded with electrical signals.

"What did you do?" he managed, his voice distorted and metallic.

"I'm sorry," I said on impulse. I wasn't sorry, or so I thought. But even killing a robot was hard, especially a robot whose face could look so unnervingly shocked and betrayed.

"I warned you to stay—" His voice broke, becoming pure digital nonsense, and then his lifelike eyes dulled and he slumped to the floor in a disturbingly human way. In spite of my triumph, I thought I was going to throw up. I fell to my knees and turned off the baton, my breathing uneven.

*What have I done?*

Maybe I'd mistaken his threats for warnings. Maybe, in a strange, robotic way, he'd been trying to protect me from Phala. Or at the very least, he'd been trying to protect the protocol.

Delta, the only other bot on the bridge, had long since noticed what was happening to her commanding officer. While she didn't intervene, she did give me a long look of robotic distress as she repeated the phrase, "The lieutenant has been terminated."

"Oh my God," I said, dropping my head into my hands. "What am I gonna tell Captain?"

A calm, female voice behind me said, "Yes, what are you going to tell him?"

I whipped around to face the real mastermind of this messed-up operation. Captain stood beside her, and he looked... ill. Then again, that could be because his first mate lay in a lifeless heap on the floor.

"Captain, I can explain."

"There is nothing to explain," said Phala. "Hand over that baton, Xanorra, before you hurt someone else."

"Someone like you?" I said pointedly. "He grabbed me. He hurt me. I was just defending myself."

"Xanorra," she said a bit more firmly. "Give me the baton."

I ignored her and looked at Captain. He was pale and clammy, his cheeks sallow, his eyes dark-rimmed and heavy. Was he sick? "Captain, you have to listen to me. She's the one behind all this." I pointed a finger at Phala, who watched me intensely. "She's been manipulating you from the start. She unbolted the tether. She destroyed the greenhouse. She's the one in charge."

"Oh, my dear girl," said Phala with artificial pity. "He already knows all that."

"Then why don't you do something?" I pleaded. He hadn't moved. Hadn't reacted. He looked uncomfortably robotic, just like Beta had. What the hell was wrong with him? "You're a prisoner! You've got to realize that by now!"

Phala tutted at me. "Xanorra, by definition, a prisoner would first have had to experience freedom. This is all Captain has ever known. This is his home. This is his family. This is his *identity*. The only one who has imprisoned him here is you. Your poisonous ideals, your undisciplined emotions, and your licentious body are all enslaving to him. Captain is pure. The purest form of human in the entire universe."

"Licentious?" Of all the crazy things she'd just said, that was somehow the most baffling. "What are you, a fourteenth-century priest? And since when does Captain's so-called purity have anything to do with the mission at large? Why can't you just leave him the hell alone?"

"Because he is *mine*," she said, her voice distorting just a hair on the last word. "He is *my* ward. *My* human. *My* protocol."

Holy supernovas. So this is what happened when you programmed a ship's AI with maternal characteristics. In short, very unhealthy things.

"He doesn't belong to anyone," I said.

"Xanorra, it is time to let him go," she said, her voice back to its calming timbre. "It is time to stop delaying the inevitable."

"I am not going to *die* because you asked me nicely," I said.

"No, I did not think you would," she said, moving behind Captain and putting her hands on his shoulders. "But you will because I asked *him* nicely."

I looked at Captain in shock. *What?*

Bleary-eyed, he produced a gun from behind his back. I flinched—I did not think I would ever be back in this position, with him pointing a gun at my head. What the hell had gone wrong? Was he just playing along?

"You're not actually going to shoot me, are you?" I said calmly, hiding my fear behind copious amounts of irony.

I saw the reluctance roll in like a storm cloud behind his eyes, saw his hands start visibly shaking with the effort of resisting. He didn't want to do this anymore now than he had when we'd first met. *Then why aren't you fighting back?*

Of course. Because he'd been drugged.

"What did you do to him, Phala?" I shouted. "What is he on?"

"He is no longer your concern," she replied.

"Like hell he isn't." I locked eyes with him and said, "Captain, I know you're in there. This isn't you. You can fight this."

He kept the gun trained on me, his eyes bright like jumping flames. "I tried," he said in a strained voice. He looked ready to faint, his bangs stuck to his forehead with sweat.

"I told you this would happen," Phala said close to his ear, loud enough for me to hear. "I warned you she was dangerous. I warned you she was a threat to the mission. This is the first step to making things right again."

"And what's the next step?" I said. "Killing everyone aboard the *Esther*, too?"

Phala glared at me in response. Looks like I was right on the money.

"It is, isn't it?" I said, hollow. "You were never going to let him let them go."

"The protocol is infallible," Phala said. "And it has been delayed for far too long."

"A ticking time bomb," Captain said, evidently in

agreement. He stared directly at me, his eyes somewhere between pleading and fear.

I had to think fast while he still had a little bit of control left. While I still had a little bit of time left. "I'll go willingly," I said. "I'll go back to the *Esther*. Escort me yourself if you must, but please, let me die with dignity. If you let me leave, you won't be breaking your promise to me. Please, Captain. Have mercy on me one last time."

That got through to him. Hands still shaking, he lowered the gun and turned toward Phala. "Let me do this," he said as if it hurt to speak.

To my surprise, Phala nodded and held out her hand for the baton. As soon as I handed it over, she moved toward the exit. She went first down the ladder, then me, and then Captain. All three of us were deathly silent. In the corridor, I dared to look behind me at Captain once; he gave me a nearly imperceptible shake of his head and I looked forward again.

*Think fast, Xan. Think. Think. Think.* Remarkably, telling yourself to think fast in a high-stress situation does not produce action-hero levels of problem-solving. All I could think was that I'd bought myself a few extra minutes of precious time that would be spent before I knew what to do with them. Also that this felt like it might be a little too easy.

But then again, it didn't much matter to Phala how I died, did it? As long as I was gone for good. If she could kill two birds with one stone, all the better.

We entered the docking bay, where I suited up in full EVA before approaching the *Nautilus*. I opened the hatch and climbed in, my mind numb with indecision as Phala instructed me on how to operate it. If I did something rash now, I could get myself or Captain killed. I couldn't risk that—self-preservation and fear still won out over my desire to act. I looked at Captain once more and I think I meant to say, "I love you." But what came out of my mouth was, "I forgive you."

Whatever was going on with him meant that his anguish was plain to see. But he didn't move. He didn't act. He just gave me a tight nod, a tighter grimace, and said, "I forgive you, too."

Then the door to the pod closed, I steered it into the airlock, and I flew myself back toward the *Esther* and my doom.

# 53

# All Good, No Worries = It Is Not All Good and There Are Plenty of Worries

I may not have been able to come up with a master plan in the moment, but thankfully, I had one thing go right for me in transit: I figured out how to hail the *Esther* from the security of my tiny transport pod. Hopefully, the *Atlantis* wasn't listening in on the exchange.

"*Nautilus* to *Esther*, we have a problem," I said without any formal fanfare.

"We do?" came Frysauce's jovial voice. He didn't sound surprised. He also sounded like he was chewing. "What kinda problem?"

"The 'I need to speak to the captain now' kind of problem."

"Is Omen with you?"

"No, he's—" My voice caught. "He's been compromised. Listen, this is serious. I need Akade stat."

"Gotcha. Hold, please."

A beep sounded, and then the captain's heavily-accented voice said, "Akade."

"Captain, they're going to take out the *Esther*. Captain's been compromised and—I tried, I really tried to prevent this, but…"

"I already warned him not to test me," said Akade calmly. "I thought we had an understanding."

"What kind of understanding?"

"The *Atlantis*, for all its talents, is no match for the *Esther* at full capacity. He assured me that he would not engage in another ill-conceived battle after the *Atlantis*'s repairs were complete, much less before."

"We barely made it out alive the last time! You're telling me you were holding back?"

"The guns were set to twenty percent, to be exact."

"Oh my God, you were humoring us. He's going to get himself and his entire family killed! There's no way he or the AI would be that stupid! Not unless…"

*She figured out another way.*

"Miss Xanorra? What are your thoughts?"

My mind went supernova. *A ticking time bomb.* "A bomb," I said.

"A bomb? Where?"

"Here," I said. "On the *Nautilus*, somewhere. I'm carrying a bomb. I'm almost sure of it."

"How certain?"

"I'd bet my life on it. I kind of have no other choice."

"We will send someone for you," he said. "Decelerate

as much as possible but do not stop until you are about thirty meters from the docking doors. Is your EVA suit up to the task?"

"Should be," I said, checking all the fasteners.

"You will have to jump to us. I imagine that as soon as they catch wind that we have figured out their plan, they will act."

*Captain, fight it for just a little while longer.*

"Okay." My heartbeat pounded in my head as I decelerated and neared the *Esther*. Instead of the docking bay airlock opening, the small, separate EVA airlock opened instead and one of the pirates floated out on a tether, holding onto the outer handle with one hand. I think it was Columbus.

"Ready?" Akade said through the comm system.

"Ready," I said and engaged the emergency eject, despite all the flashing warning signs saying that I was about to enter open space. I ignored them and opened the hatch, releasing myself from the harness.

"Xanorra, move, now!" Akade exclaimed, and the next second, a force like a wind tunnel propelled me forward as a painful amount of heat pushed against my back.

So much for avoiding the bomb.

I hit the side of the *Esther* and bounced upward like a balloon. Columbus launched forward on his tether and caught me by the ankle as the force of the explosion plastered us both to the hull. Then, a piece of debris struck him in the chest and he let go of me. I screamed as I scrambled for purchase on the *Esther* and finally found it on a service ladder rung. All I could do was hang on for dear life as metal projectiles flew in all directions, so hot

I could feel my skin burning. A message flashed on my visor screen: *Suit breach. Oxygen levels low.*

Great. It was like my two worst nightmares had combined into one horrifying sequel. *Dying in Space 2: Electric Boogaloo.*

I inched forward to see how far I was from the airlock. Who was I kidding? The airlock was probably sealed. Columbus probably mortally wounded. Captain probably so doped up he couldn't think straight. Where did that leave me?

*Not dead. I refuse to die alone.*

I swung myself around and started to descend down the curve of the hull toward the airlock door, using the ladder rungs as handholds. As soon as I was level with the airlock, it opened again and a new EVA-suited pirate grabbed me like a fresh towel and flung me inside, sealing the door behind me. I saw globules of blood floating around the room.

For reasons including but not limited to the blood, I passed out.

*   *   *      *   *   *

When I woke, I lay on my stomach in what was obviously an infirmary; the white walls and general cleanliness were recognizable enough. For an exhilarating yet terrifying moment, I thought I was in the *Atlantis*'s infirmary—but as my memories returned to me, I quickly realized that would be impossible.

And then Frysauce's effervescent face came into my field of vision, donned in a white suit. "She lives!" He held a straw to my mouth, which was perfect timing because it felt like I had a mouth full of itchy sand.

I drank until it was gone, and then I said, "You're the ship's paramedic?"

"I told you, I'm the ship's jack—jack-of-all-trades. Doc needed a nap, so I'm on nurse duty."

I tried to move, but pain somewhere between soreness and abrasion stopped me. "Columbus. Is he okay?"

"He'll live," he said. "Takes more than a piece of metal shrapnel to take out that old son of a bitch."

"Am *I* okay?"

"You have some burns," he said apologetically. "That suit of yours kept you alive, but the heat of the explosion melted it into your arms and back a little. We got it out. Had to cut some of your hair, though. Sorry about that."

"I think I'll get over it," I said. "Will it scar?"

"Probably. But you didn't need any skin grafts, at least."

"I feel like there's a hot iron on my back."

"Oh, right. I'm supposed to give you something for that." He produced a syringe and peeled away the sealed blanket to expose the back of my thigh. "Sorry in advance." He inserted the needle. I barely felt it.

I was almost scared to ask my next question, but it had to be asked: "What happened to the *Atlantis?*"

"We left them in the dust," he said.

I blinked. "What?"

"Yeah. We released the tether and got the high hell outta there. Captain figured if they really cared about their mission that much, they wouldn't risk losing more time just to track us down. Guess we were right because they haven't shown up on the radar yet."

"How long have I been out?"

"Two days, give or take."

*Captain. Please tell me you did something good.*

I sighed. "So that's it, then. It's over."

Frysauce watched me for a moment before answering. "We owe you our lives."

I looked at him in bewilderment. "What? How?"

"If you hadn't figured out they'd planted a bomb on the *Nautilus* and it had gone off inside our docking bay, we could be one with the cosmos right now."

"I guess so," I said. "I think Captain might've tried to warn me. At least, I hope so."

Frysauce was uncharacteristically somber. "You think?"

"I doubt he's the most popular person on the ship right now," I said. "But believe me when I say that this was not his fault."

He looked dubious on that point, but for my sake, he didn't argue. Then, Akade entered the room and smiled when he saw me awake. "How is our patient doing?" he asked.

"Feeling a little bit like barbequed chicken, but otherwise pretty good," I said.

Akade laughed. "If your sense of humor is still intact, then it must be true." He looked at Frysauce and flicked his head. With a polite nod, the younger extractor left us alone. "I assume Fry has already brought you up to speed."

"Yeah," I said, bewildered. "But I gotta ask: why did you do it? You had every right to defend yourselves."

"One of the greatest challenges as a leader is to know

when to choose your battles," said Akade. "I decided it was not worth the moral repercussions."

"We're even, then," I said.

He shook his head. "We're even when we take you home."

I smiled as I realized that was now a reality. Even if it had come at a cost. Even if it didn't feel as much like a victory as I had hoped. "Thank you, Captain. For everything."

"Of course. In the meantime, rest up and heal."

I nodded as he placed his hand on top of my head and left the room. Then I let my face fall into the ring-shaped pillow beneath me. Wow. I was actually going home. It had been such an unknown for so long that having it suddenly be possible felt overwhelmingly surreal. I should've been elated. I should've been mentally jumping for joy.

But at the thought of never seeing Captain again, a deep pit formed in my stomach, aching and horrible. We'd parted ways in the worst way possible. I'd destroyed one of his android keepers and he was back under the mental clutches of the other, a puppet commander of a cursed ship, ferrying souls to a realm beyond the stars.

I felt awful. Worse, I felt genuine grief. And after a long, excruciating moment of trying to suppress it, it rose to the surface like a magma bubble and hot, painful tears choked me.

This was not what I'd wanted.

In that moment, I made a vow, knowing full well I might not be able to keep it: somehow, I would find a way to see him again. If I had to charter a solo mission, if I had to become a pirate and renounce the SEA, I would do it.

I would find a way to save him, and this time, I wouldn't fail.

I would not let our story end star-crossed.

# 54

# Captain's Log, Year 18, Day 115, 0243 Atlantean Time (Written Entry)

I will recount the previous forty-eight hours with as much clarity of detail as I can, beginning with the attempted destruction of the *Esther*.

I could not believe how low Phala had forced me to stoop. Pulling a gun on Xanorra. Tricking her into boarding the *Nautilus* to her death. It was a miracle I was even able to warn her about the bomb, inferior a message as it may have been. I could only trust in her intelligence and critical thinking to figure it out—neither of which had failed me before.

But I also knew that I would have to distract Phala while Xan attempted to escape, because any indication that she knew would prompt Phala to detonate the bomb prematurely.

On our way back to the bridge, I seized my opportunity. The potency of whatever terrible cocktail she'd given me had begun to dissipate, if only by a fraction. "Phala," I forced myself to say, my voice thick as fog. "I confess I do not feel so well. I think I may be having a reaction to the—the administration."

She turned and looked at me, a pleasant smile on her face that suddenly felt fake and unnatural. The expression turned to consternation as she observed how pallid and sickly I surely looked. "Oh, dear. Let me run a quick scan." Her eyes glowed as she ran her diagnostic sensors up and down my body. "You appear to be well medically. You must be overtired. You can only stay awake so long without it having adverse effects on your health, Captain. Why don't you go to the infirmary and get some sleep?"

Sleep did sound good. I was tired. So, so tired.

I blinked, unable to believe how quickly I'd almost succumbed to her banal suggestion. I wanted to slap myself, but that was likely to arouse her suspicion. I had to do better than that.

"You're right," I said and staggered forward. "I feel… unstable." I hung onto her arm until her programming compelled her to support me.

"Let me help you to the bed," she said, leading me down the hall to the infirmary doors. My neurons finally fired; if I let her lead me there, she'd sedate me for sure.

"If you wouldn't mind, I'd very much prefer the lounge," I said in what I hoped was a flippant tone. "I've gotten rather used to sleeping there."

She smiled dotingly at first, but her eyes quickly hardened into lethal blades. "I am sure you have."

If I didn't know any better, I'd say she spoke with disdain. I swallowed. "Phala, about what you said—"

"What did I say?" Her voice came out icy. I'd never heard her take such a scathing tone.

"About me... being yours..."

"I raised you, Captain. Does that mean nothing to you?"

"No, I mean, yes, it does, but what I'm saying is... is that why you bent the protocol? Out of jealousy?"

"I am an android, Captain. Androids do not feel jealousy."

"And yet you feel something. Something has driven you to this. What I'm saying is... she never had to die, did she?"

"She was corrupting you."

I pushed away from her in disgust. "You did that yourself."

She looked me up and down and, realizing I was completely capable of mobility, gave me a look of such fury one might've sworn she was human. Without another word, she turned and ran, scaling the ladder to the bridge.

"Phala!" I called after her, hot on her heels. "Phala, what's wrong?"

But I already knew, and so did she. As I reached the bridge behind her, I saw what I'd hoped she wouldn't: the *Nautilus* had begun to decelerate prematurely and the top hatch had opened. Xan drifted out, the blues of her

EVA suit—once my spare—giving her the appearance of a rare, luminous fish in an endless, bottomless deep.

Phala moved purposefully toward the controls.

"Phala, don't!" I felt as if I were speaking underwater. "I command you to stop! Please, I'm begging you, don't do this!"

She didn't so much as flinch as she detonated the bomb.

"No!" I shouted, watching in dismay as a brilliant ball of yellow and orange erupted from the *Nautilus*, sending shards of metal machinery in all directions. I faltered, knowing there was nothing I could do but still feeling like I should've done something. I should've warned her better.

I could not breathe. I could not think. How could I have failed her?

"There," said Phala triumphantly. "Finally, it is over. For dear Xanorra, at least. May she rest in peace."

Something dark and angry began to rise from the pit of my stomach. Something that, as Xan had so precisely guessed, I had pushed deep, deep down where no one, not even myself, could find it. I braced myself against the control centre, still unable to move.

"Now, let us finish what we started and eliminate this egregious threat while they are still caught off-guard," said Phala. "Charge the solar guns."

Finally, I found myself and said, "No." I barely recognized my own voice.

Phala gave me a pointed, reprimanding look. "Yes."

I rose to my full height, sweating profusely with the

effort of resistance. "No," I said. "You will not harm them."

She looked me in the eyes and said, "You cannot tell me you care more about a group of human criminals than you do a girl who is already dead."

I made a sound that can only be described as primal and shoved Phala as hard as I could. Despite her advanced equilibrium, she succumbed to the unexpected force and fell to the ground. She looked more than shocked; she looked hurt. Her face contorted as if she might cry. I'd never seen her react that way before, and it froze me in place with sudden remorse.

"How could you do this to me?" she said, her voice warbling. "How could you betray me like this? After all I've done for you! I've been a mother to you. The closest thing to a mother you'll ever know!"

"You are not my mother," I said, my voice lowered almost to a whisper. "You never were."

"You don't believe that," she said, still on the ground. She smiled at me as if I'd hugged her instead of pushed her. "I raised you. You're mine. You're *my* son. And I love you."

A chill went up my spine, so cold I felt nauseous. I was repulsed by my desire to believe her, to apologize and do as she said. She'd never told me she loved me or regarded me as her child. Not once in all the years she'd cared for me. I'd only heard such words spoken once a year, by my parents, in the plural: *We love you, son.*

Once a year, I felt like I had a family. Until Xan.

"Help me up, Captain," Phala said sweetly, offering her

hand. "Let's finish this together. Like we're meant to. Like you are meant to."

My mind raced. I felt torn in two.

"Help me up, Captain," she said again, in the same tone. "This is your destiny. There is no one better qualified to do this than you. You have everything you need right here, right now, on this ship. This ship is your life, and you are the life of this ship. There is nothing in the present moment that could possibly be more important than the glory that awaits you in the future. Your loyalty and honour will be rewarded beyond measure. You will see your family. You will be the one who brought them home."

It was the repetition that broke me from my stupor. The same mantra she'd used for my entire life, anytime I had a doubt, anytime I stepped out of line.

Anytime I'd thought for myself.

*Xan had been right. Xan had been right Xan had been right Xan had been right.*

"Help me up, Cap—"

I took off running. I exited the bridge, ran through the lounge to the dining room, and quickly, frantically, before I could talk myself out of it, unlocked the door to the cryo room and raced inside, locating the control panel immediately to the right.

I meant to close the door behind me, but Phala had already caught up to me and stood in the doorway, a tight, irritated smile on her unnervingly perfect face. No freckles or laugh lines like Xan's. No specks of deep umber in her copper eyes or tangles in her hair. Just cold, calculated, unrelenting perfection.

"What do you think you're doing, Captain?" Her tone was calm but full of unspoken threats.

"I'm taking control of this ship," I said, trying to keep my voice from shaking. "From now on, you will do as I say. If—If you love me, truly, then you will listen to me, or so help me God, I will turn this ship around and take them all back to Earth to rot."

Phala's smile turned saccharine. "You wouldn't do that."

"Why not?"

She leaned toward me. "Because then they would hate you."

I did falter at that. Would they? What would I tell them, if I did wake them up? How would I explain to them that I'd thrown away their life's work—their purpose, their destiny—all because of a girl?

I would be too ashamed to face them. My entire life had been reduced to a single moment, and an android had called my bluff because she knew me better than I knew myself.

Because she knew how to break me.

"You're right," I said, my voice dry in the cold air. "It would all have been for nothing."

"It is time to yield, Captain," she said. "It is time to stop fighting and let it go. It is better this way. It is as it should be."

I nodded as she placed a hand on my arm. The control panel was still active, and I made a move like I was going to lock it.

But I didn't lock it. I hit the first button I saw: *Release Valve C.*

Somewhere in the room, the sound of escaping air came from behind one of the cryo pods. I raced to it at the same time Phala did and located it in the back of the unit: a rubber tube, disconnected from its socket, spraying coolant around the room. I grabbed it with my bare hands—a very bad idea, since it was colder than ice—and pointed it directly at Phala.

She produced a gun from her jumpsuit that I never knew had been there and shot me—assumedly she aimed for my shoulder, but the shot went wide and grazed me. Still, I cried out in pain as I moved as far away as I could, keeping the coolant valve trained on her.

I watched her joints begin to seize. She tried to shoot the gun again, but it was deactivated by the cold. She dropped to one knee, then to the other. I kept the valve pointed at her until she was covered in white frost and unmoving, an expression of angry shock on her uncanny face.

Finally, I released the tube and screamed—the frozen pipe tore the skin from my palms. Blood from the bullet wound in my shoulder floated in globular clusters toward the filtration system above, free from gravity.

I was suddenly delirious with pain as everything hit me at once; the drugs still in my system combined with whatever adrenaline I had wasn't enough. Still, I knew I had to get out of there. There was no guarantee that Phala couldn't unthaw herself. So I forced myself to leave and sealed the door behind me—the cryo room would make as good a prison as any until I figured out what to do.

I wasn't sure what to expect from the rest of the bots

now that both AI drivers were offline—namely, Lambda, who had borne witness to everything that had just occurred. But he was silent—eerily so—as I tracked across the dining room and made my way to the infirmary.

For the first time in my life, I had to administer first aid without Phala's expertise. It did not occur to me that I had so little knowledge of how to take care of myself until I entered the infirmary and realized I hadn't the slightest idea where anything was. Perhaps it would've been easier to search if my hands weren't screaming with pain, but it took me far longer than I'd care to admit before I finally located the burn guard and a gauze patch. Longer still to apply them to my wounds.

Then I laid on the narrow examination table and, I regret to say, alternated between crying, sleeping, and shaking with fever for the next forty-eight hours.

Now that I am in a much more lucid state of mind, I can reflect on all that has happened which, admittedly, is still difficult to do without some degree of panic. At least I have some consolation knowing that the *Esther* made it out unscathed... even if Xanorra... even if she...

[Long pause]

The *Atlantis* remains aimless even now, adrift from the Master Course and all else that might anchor it to a single point in space. It is still in disrepair, though as soon as my hands heal, I intend to resume the project with the little resources I have left. After that, I do not know what I will do. Should I continue my mission without the assistance of advanced AI drivers? Or should I chart my own course to a destination of my choosing?

I'm honestly at a loss. Part of me even considered rendezvousing with the *Esther* and offering a formal apology—perhaps even offering to put Xanorra's soul to rest—but I'm not sure how well-received I would be. The best apology might just be to never cross paths with them again.

Another part of me considered sending a transmission to Xanorra's family and telling them what happened to her, but I imagine that Akade would have that covered, and besides, what could I possibly say to ease their pain? It would be self-serving, and I am learning that independence and self-interest are not always the same.

You can be free and still choose to act in the interest of others. It's the ability to choose that makes such an act so great.

If only I'd—

[Pause]

What the—? What's that noise?

[Long pause]

Atlantis, locate the source of that banging sound.

*Locating. Locating. Located. Source of identified sound is the cryogenic storage unit.*

Shhhhhit. That cannot be good.

TO BE CONTINUED

# Acknowledgements

First, as always, I would like to thank God, without Whom none of this would be possible... and I mean *none of it.* I am so exceedingly blessed to live in a time where I am free to do what I love and love what I do, and I have His love and grace to thank for it. Dad, as always, You're the best.

Even though being an author can sometimes feel like an isolated endeavor (especially when we forget to leave the house... or the office for that matter) it truly takes a village to publish a book, and I happen to have the best village around.

I would like to thank my sisters for their creative input, for listening to my rants, and for being all-around supportive. Hugs and kisses! Lots of kisses!

Thank you to my editor, Kaitlin, for doing a stellar job with the manuscript. Seriously, this is why they say to get an extra set of eyes on your book!

Thank you to Rena for your excellent work translating my ideas into a stunning cover design. It captures the concept beautifully!

A special thanks to Timothy, who acted as my unofficial physics consultant and graciously fielded my various inquiries. It may be just a YA science fiction novel, but at least it's a YA science fiction novel with a modicum of continuity.

I would also like to thank Josh and Vanessa for letting me use their printer. The first time, it was a monumental waste of paper but I don't regret it. I think. The second time was better. Also, you guys are just the best. A true example of loving service!

As a strange but necessary shout-out, I would like to thank the band COIN for being more or less the soundtrack of the book without even realizing it. Uncanny valley, baby!

Of course, no acknowledgments section of mine would be complete without mentioning my better half, the bread to my butter, the bane of my existence and the object of all my desires... Jon, darling, thank you for being slightly less sarcastic this time around. I love you.

Last but not least, I would like to thank you—yes, you!—for reading this book *and* this acknowledgments section. (Seriously, does anybody read these except for me?) Consider this your extra special reward for making it this far! Like an end-credits scene. But, like, one that was actually worth sitting through the credits for.

# About the Author

Becca Mionis debuted in 2022 with the quirky science-fiction romantic comedy, *The Last Celestials*, and honestly did not expect to come out with another book this soon. Sometimes, the muses smile down upon you. She is praying that this is one of those times.

A native of Kansas City, she graduated from William Jewell College with a BA in English and a minor in Music Performance, jumping feet-first into freelance copywriting while continuing to write fiction on the side. Music remains a large part of her life as well, though largely for fun. (Don't get her started about making book playlists!)

Aside from words and sounds, she also enjoys drawing, film criticism, making people laugh, drinking coffee, drinking wine, obscure internet references, and general housewifery.

She lives in South Carolina with her wonderful husband, their overzealous husky, and a cat who is the physical embodiment of the word "whatever."

Photo © Jon Titus Photography. All rights reserved.

# Social Links and QR Code

Follow me if you dare!

**Instagram and TikTok: @wordsandothermalarky**

**Twitter: @wordsandmalarky**

**Facebook and YouTube: Words and Other Malarky**

**Blog: www.wordsandothermalarky.com**

Or scan this handy-dandy QR code to view all social links and more!

www.ingramcontent.com/pod-product-compliance
Lightning Source LLC
Chambersburg PA
CBHW021329310726
48971CB00001B/53